The

SHAMUS

WINNERS

The

SHAMUS

WINNERS

America's Best Private Eye Stories

Volume II: 1996-2009

Collected and Introduced

by Robert J. Randisi

Founder, Private Eye Writers of America

Perfect Crime Books

Baltimore

"And Pray Nobody Sees You" by Gar Anthony Haywood, copyright © 1995 by Gar Anthony Haywood, originally published in *Spooks, Spies & Private Eyes*. "Dead Drunk" by Lia Matera, copyright © 1996 Lia Matera, originally published in *Guilty As Charged*. "Love Me for My Yellow Hair Alone" by Carolyn Wheat, copyright © 1997 Carolyn Wheat, originally published in *Marilyn: Shades of Blonde*. "Another Day, Another Dollar" by Warren Murphy, copyright © 1998 Warren Murphy, originally published in *Murder on the Run*. "Akitada's First Case" by I. J. Parker, copyright © 1999 I. J. Parker, originally published in *Alfred Hitchcock's Mystery Magazine*. "The Road's End" by Brendan DuBois, copyright © 2000 Brendan DuBois, originally published in *Ellery Queen's Mystery Magazine*. "Rough Justice" by Ceri Jordan, copyright © 2001 Ceri Jordan, originally published in *Alfred Hitchcock's Mystery Magazine*. "The Second Coming" by Terence Faherty, copyright © 2002 Terence Faherty, originally published in *Ellery Queen's Mystery Magazine*. "Lady on Ice" by Loren D. Estleman, copyright © 2003 Loren D. Estleman, originally published in *A Hot and Sultry Night for Crime*. "Hasidic Noir" by Pearl Abraham, copyright © 2004 Pearl Abraham, originally published in *Brooklyn Noir*. "A Death in Ueno" by Michael Wiecek, copyright © 2005 Michael Wiecek, originally published in *Alfred Hitchcock's Mystery Magazine*. "The Heart Has Reasons" by O'Neil De Noux, copyright © 2006 O'Neil De Noux, originally published in *Alfred Hitchcock's Mystery Magazine*. "Hungry Enough" by Cornelia Read, copyright © 2007 Cornelia Read, originally published in *A Hell of a Woman*. "Family Values" by Mitch Alderman, copyright © 2008 Mitch Alderman, originally published in *Alfred Hitchcock's Mystery Magazine*. "Second Story Sunlight" by John Lutz, copyright © 2002 John Lutz, originally published in *Most Wanted*. "Aftermath" by Jeremiah Healy, copyright © 2002 Jeremiah Healy, originally published in *Most Wanted*.

Library of Congress Cataloging-in-Publication Data
The Shamus Winners. America's Best Private Eye Stories. Volume II, 1996-2009/
Robert J. Randisi, editor
1.   Detective and mystery stories, American   I. Randisi, Robert J.

ISBN: 978-0-9825157-6-1

Contents

Introduction

by Robert J. Randisi

JUDGING BY THE ALMOST THIRTY YEARS' worth of top-notch stories collected in the two Shamus Winners volumes, it's obvious that the private detective form is not only alive but fresh and thriving. That's no surprise. Writers from Hammett and Chandler to Macdonald, Paretsky and Parker have found the private eye an ideal observer of the changing American scene. So have the writers in these volumes. All reward the decision of the Private Eye Writers of America to launch the Shamus awards in 1982 as a way of recognizing outstanding work in the genre.

Gar Anthony Haywood was the second winner of the PWA/St. Martin's Press contest searching for "first" private eye novels. His book, *Fear of the Dark*, went on to win a Shamus after its publication. In 1996, Gar picked up another Shamus, this time for Best Short Story with "And Pray Nobody Sees You." Both wins came compliments of his character Aaron Gunner.

Lia Matera stepped up the following year with "Dead Drunk," from the legal anthology *Guilty As Charged*, edited by Scott Turow. Lia has also been nominated for the Edgar and Anthony awards. This story features one of her series characters, attorney Laura DiPalma.

The next year Carole Nelson Douglas edited an anthology of Marilyn Monroe stories called *Marilyn: Shades of Blonde*. Carolyn Wheat has written novels and short stories, edited anthologies and produced a popular book on writing called *How to Write Killer Fiction*. She took the Shamus for Best Short Story with her Marilyn story "Love Me for My Yellow Hair Alone."

Warren Murphy is the creator and author of the long-running

Destroyer series, featuring Remo Williams. He was nominated for a couple of Best Paperback Shamus awards in 1986 and '87, for books in his "Trace," series, and won in '85 with a stand alone called *Ceiling of Hell.* In 1999 he took the short story award with "Another Day, Another Dollar," from the Adams Round Table anthology *Murder on the Run.*

Akitada Sugawara, I. J. Parker's series character, investigates murders committed in Japan during the Heian period. She won her Shamus with the story "Akitada's First Case," and credited the win with helping her find a publisher for the fine series of Akitada books, of which there are now six.

Brendan DuBois, who had a story in Volume I, appears again with "The Road's End."

The first Shamus for a short story was won by a John Lutz tale that appeared in *Alfred Hitchcock's Mystery Magazine.* The magazine is a consistent publisher of solid crime fiction, and its pages have yielded eight Shamus winners. In 2002, it was Ceri Jordan's bleak story "Rough Justice."

The following year's winner, Terence Faherty's "The Second Coming," debuted in *AHMM*'s sister publication, *Ellery Queen's Mystery Magazine.* Faherty is one of a handful of authors who has won the Shamus for both a novel (*Come Back Dead*) and a shorter work. In both cases, the hero was private eye Scott Elliott, who works for a movie studio in World War II Hollywood. A new Elliott novel was scheduled for 2010, and a collection of Elliott short stories, *The Hollywood Op*, is due later in the year from Perfect Crime Books.

"Lady on Ice" earned yet another Shamus for Loren D. Estleman, who had two Amos Walker stories in Volume I. "Lady" appeared in an MWA anthology, *A Hot and Sultry Night for Crime*, edited by Jeffery Deaver.

Pearl Abraham, not generally known for writing mysteries, won a Shamus with her story "Hasidic Noir," which appeared in the anthology *Brooklyn Noir*, one of many "Noir" anthologies published by a small Brooklyn-based company called Akashic Books.

Michael Wiecek, after having been nominated once before with a Japan-based historical PI story, took the prize home in 2006 with "A Death in Ueno."

O'Neil De Noux is a writer of novels and short stories set in New Orleans. He has published several collections of short stories, including *New Orleans Confidential.* His Shamus-winning story is called "The

Heart Has Reasons." It appeared in *AHMM*. De Noux has had a long career in law enforcement, primarily in Louisiana, and in 1981 was named Homicide Detective of the Year.

Another writer not familiar in the private eye field, Cornelia Read nevertheless walked away with a Shamus for her story "Hungry Enough," which appeared in the anthology *A Hell of a Woman*, published by Busted Flush Press. Unable to attend the ceremony, she accepted the award via cell phone.

Mitch Alderman had been nominated three previous times before finally snagging the prize in 2009 with his story "Family Values." All his nominated stories appeared in *AHMM*, and all featured PI Bubba Simms.

We have two bonus stories in this volume, and they come from two writers who are almost regularly nominated for the awards—and indeed, either of these stories could have won in its respective year. John Lutz, with five short story nominations, gives us a Nudger tale, "Second Story Sunlight." And Jeremiah Healy, who has been nominated in this category *nine* times (he's the PWA's answer to Susan Lucci), writes in "Aftermath" not about his famous sleuth John Francis Cuddy but instead about a private eye named Rory Calhoun.

So here are crimes to solve, murders to prevent, justice (or revenge) to be served, and in the pages ahead you'll meet the private eyes who can handle all that and more—the Shamus winners.

Robert J. Randisi is founder of the Private Eye Writers of America. His recent books include two from Perfect Crime: The Guilt Edge *and* The Bottom of Every Bottle.

And Pray Nobody Sees You

by Gar Anthony Haywood

IT DOESN'T HAPPEN OFTEN, but every now and then a good story will buy you a free drink at the Deuce. Lilly has to be feeling charitable and business has to be slow, say, down to three lifeless regulars and maybe another new face, somebody who likes to treat a single shot of Myers's like a lover they're afraid to part with. Lilly will get tired of watching Howard Gaines slide dominoes across her bar, or listening to Eggy Jones whine about the latest indignity he's suffered at the hands of his wife Camille, and will demand that somebody tell her a story entertaining enough to hold her interest. Lilly calls herself asking but she's too big to ask for anything; everything she says sounds like a demand, whether it comes with a "please" or not.

She was in the mood for a story a couple of Tuesdays back and, as usual, looked to me first to do the honors. I don't always take the prize on these occasions, but I manage to get my share. Maybe it's the line of work I'm in.

This particular evening I answered Lilly's call with the following.

And watched the Wild Turkey flow afterward.

It started with a U-turn.

Brother driving a blue Chrysler did a one-eighty in the middle of Wilmington Avenue, two o'clock on a Thursday afternoon, in broad daylight. Mickey Moore, Weldon Foley, and me were standing outside Mickey's barbershop when we saw him go by on the eastbound side of the street, stop, then yank the Chrysler around like he'd just seen somebody who owed him money. We would have all ducked for cover, smelling the week's latest drive-by in the making, except that the driver looked too old to be a gangbanger and the three of us were the only people on the street. That left us nothing else to believe but that we'd just seen the act of a fool, nothing more and nothing less.

"You see that? That nigger's crazy," Mickey said.

"Sure is," Foley agreed, nodding his hairless head. I sometimes suspect Mickey keeps him around precisely for that purpose; he sure as hell never has to take his clippers to him.

"And look; not a goddamn cop in sight. Now, if that was *me*—"

"Or me," I said, thinking the same thing my landlord was thinking. I'd never gotten away with a U-turn in my life.

The Chrysler was now headed back in our direction on the westbound side of the street, cruising in the right lane the way cars do when the people driving them are looking for a parking space. It was an old '71 Barracuda, a clean and chromed-out borderline classic with a throaty exhaust and tires you could hide a small country in. It was grumbling like a California earthquake when it finally pulled to a stop at the curb, directly in front of us.

The driver got out of the car and approached us, his left arm folded up in a white sling. We let him come without saying a word.

"One of you Aaron Gunner?" he asked. He was a wiry twenty-something, six-one or six-two, with razor lines cut all along the sides and back of his head, something I imagined he'd had done in hopes of drawing attention from his face. It was sad to say, but the boy looked like a black Mr. Potato Head with bad skin.

"That's me," I told him, before Weldon or Mickey could point me out. "What can I do for you?"

He openly examined the front of Mickey's shop, as if he were looking for the fine print on the sign above the door, and said, "This is your office, right?"

"That's right. I've got a room in the back."

He glanced at my companions briefly. "All right if we go back there to talk?"

I shrugged. "Sure. Come on in."

Mickey was insulted by the slight of not being introduced, but he didn't say anything.

I led my homely visitor past Mickey's three empty barber chairs, through the beaded curtains in the open doorway beyond, and into the near-vacant space that has passed for my office for the last four years.

The lamp on my desk was already on, so all I had to do was sit down and wait for my friend to find the couch and do the same. He never did.

He just stood in front of my desk and said, "You're a private detective."

"Yes. Can't you tell?"

"I want to hire you."

"To do what?"

"I want you to find a car for me."

"A car?"

"Yeah." He nodded. "A '65 Ford Mustang, tangerine orange. Two-plus-two fastback, fully restored and cherried out."

"A '65?"

"Yeah. First year they were made. Probably ain't but fifty of 'em in the whole country still on the road."

"Two-eighty-nine, or six?"

"Come on. If it was the six, man, I'd let 'em have the damn car."

He had a point. A '65 Mustang two-plus-two without the V-eight under the hood might have been worth a few dollars to somebody, but any true collector would've considered it a stiff. Cherried out or no.

"It sounds nice," I told him.

"Man, fuck 'nice.' It's a classic. There ain't but fifty of 'em still in existence, like I said."

I nodded my head to show him I was finally paying attention. "And your name was . . . ?"

"Purdy. David Purdy. Look—"

"This car we're talking about, Mr. Purdy. I take it it belongs to you?"

"Does it belong to me? Hell, yes, it belongs to me. Why else would I be here talkin' to you?"

"I give up. Why *are* you here talking to me?"

"Because I got *jacked* last night, man. What else? Over on Imperial and Hoover, over by my girl's house. Little motherfucker shot me at the stoplight and took my goddamn car."

"You call the police?"

"The police? Of course. I told you, man, I got shot." He tried to gesture with his left arm, but just moving the sling an inch from his side seemed to bring tears to his eyes.

"So? What do you need with me?" I asked him.

Purdy answered the question with a crooked, toothy grin meant to convey incredulity. "Man, you're jokin', right? What do I need with *you*? I need you to get the goddamn car back for me. What do you think?"

3

He'd been looking for a foot in his ass since he'd stepped out of the Chrysler, and now he'd finally earned it. Still, I let the comment pass. I'd spent the retainers of rude jackasses before, and their money went just as far as anyone else's. Purdy's would be no different.

"You don't think the police can find the car," I said.

"Let's just say I'm not countin' on it," Purdy said. "Least, not until there ain't nothin' left of it but a goddamn frame."

"I take it you didn't have one of those electronic tracking devices on it. The kind the police can home in on?"

"No. I didn't."

"That's too bad."

"Yeah, it is. I fucked up. I put a lot of time and money in that car, then turned around and didn't protect it right. So it's gone. But that don't mean I gotta forget about it, like the cops said I should. Hell, no. I want that car back, Mr. Gunner, and I want it back now, 'fore some fuckin' chop shop can hack it all to pieces."

"If that's possible, you mean," I said.

"It's possible. It just ain't gonna be easy. I'd find the car myself if the shit was easy."

I fell silent, pretending to be mulling things over, when all I was really doing was deciding on a fee.

"Somebody said you were the man for the job, so I looked you up. But if you're not—"

"What do you figure the car's worth? Ten, fifteen grand?" I asked.

"Shit. Try twenty-five," Purdy said.

"Okay, twenty-five. Here's the deal. I locate the car within forty-eight hours, in its original condition, you owe me twenty-five hundred. Ten percent of its worth, cash on delivery. If I don't find it, or I do and it's already been chopped up, you only owe me for my time. Three hundred dollars a day, plus expenses, half of which you've got to pay me now, just to get me started."

"No problem," Purdy said. Nothing I'd said had made him so much as blink.

"No problem?"

"No, man, no problem. I told you: I want the car back, and you're supposed to be the man can get it for me." He was already peeling some bills off a wad of green he'd removed from his pocket.

"I'm gonna need a description of the carjacker and the license plate of the car. And a phone number where you can be reached at any time, day or night."

Purdy threw four hundred dollars on the desk in front of me and said, "You've got it."

I still had my reservations about the man, but now I was bought and paid for.

It was time to go to work.

The first thing I did was go see Mopar.

Mopar used to steal cars. Lots of them. It was what he did for fifteen years, from the time we were in high school together right up until his last bust, when a fight in the joint left him crippled for life and scared the thief right out of him, for good. His mother still called him Jerome, but he was Mopar to everyone else; back in high school, he could steal any car you cared to name, but he did all his racing in Chryslers.

Today, Mopar was in the body shop business.

He had his own place over on Florence Avenue, between Denker and La Salle. He'd started out working there, hammering dents out of Buicks and Oldsmobiles, then slowly bought into the business, buying bigger and bigger chunks as the years went by until finally, little over a year ago, he became the man holding all the paper. And all with only one good leg.

He was standing behind the counter in the office when I came in, just hanging up the phone. He was damn near as fat as Lilly these days, and only twice as jolly. The sight of my approach brought a broad grin to his face, same one he used to wear as a kid.

"Tail Gunner! What it be like?"

That was what he used to call me back in school, Tail Gunner. I can't tell you how glad I was that the nickname never caught on with anyone else.

"It's your world, Mopar," I said, burying my right hand deep in his. "I'm just livin' in it."

"Shit, you ain't livin' in *my* world. Otherwise, I'd see you more often 'round here."

I shrugged apologetically. "What can I say? I'm a busy man."

Mopar just laughed. "So what can I do you, man? This business or pleasure?"

"Afraid it's business. I'm looking for somebody I think you might be able to help me find."

"Yeah? Who's that?"

"A 'jacker. Boy about fifteen to eighteen years old, five-seven, five-eight, 130 pounds. Dark skin and dark eyes, with braces on his teeth. Likes to wear striped clothes and a San Antonio Spurs baseball cap turned sideways on his head, bill facing east. At least, that's how he was dressed last night."

"A 'jacker? Why you wanna ask me about a 'jacker?"

"Because you used to be one, Mopar. It hasn't been that long ago, man."

"Man, I wasn't never a 'jacker! I never pulled nobody out of a car in my life!"

"No, but—"

"These kids today, man, they're crazy! Shootin' people to steal a goddamn car. Man, I never even owned a gun 'til I got this place!"

"Okay, so you weren't a 'jacker. You're right, that was the wrong thing for me to say."

"Damn right it was."

"But your objective was still the same, right? To steal cars?"

Mopar didn't say anything.

"Look. I'm not saying you know the kid. I just thought you might, that's all. Because I know you've put a few of 'em to work for you in the past, tryin' to help 'em go straight like you did, and I thought, maybe this kid I'm lookin' for was one of 'em. Or maybe you've seen him hanging around somewhere, I don't know. It was just a thought."

Mopar just glared at me, his jovial mood a thing of the past. "You say this boy 'jacked a car last night?"

I nodded. "Orange '65 Mustang fastback, in primo condition. Owner says it happened over on Imperial and Hoover, a few minutes past midnight."

"A '65 fastback? You shittin' me?"

"Afraid not. Now you know why the man wants it found before somebody takes an air wrench to it."

"You mean the fool don't know they already did that eight hours ago?"

"I guess he's the optimistic type. I tried to tell him to save his money, but he's emotionally attached. So . . ."

I waited for the big man to make up his mind, but he seemed in no hurry to do so.

"Did I mention the fact that my client got shot? Clipped in the left wing, but it could've been worse. This kid who 'jacked him isn't just in it for the rides, Mopar. He likes to shoot people, too."

Still, Mopar offered me nothing but silence.

"Tell you what. Forget it," I said. "This was a bad idea, bothering you with this. Come by and see us at the Deuce sometime, huh?" I turned and started out of the room.

"You say the kid wears braces?" Mopar asked.

I turned back around. "That's right."

He hesitated a moment longer, then said, "I can't give you a name. But I can tell you where to look."

I told him that would be fine.

Mopar said the kid liked to hang out in front of a liquor store on Western and Eighty-first Street. Mopar remembered him because he'd had to chase him out of his shop once, when the kid had come around looking for one of Mopar's employees and had taken the news of the employee's recent dismissal badly. Every now and then since, Mopar'd see him at the liquor store, kicking it with his homies out on the sidewalk.

But he wasn't there Thursday night.

I know. I waited there six hours for him to show up. Three members of his crew were there—teenage boys dressed in oversized khaki pants and giant plaid jackets—but they were all the wrong size for the kid I was looking for, and none of them had braces on their teeth. I sat in my car across the street and thought about approaching them, but I knew all they'd do with my questions was tell me where I could stick them, so I decided to spare myself the aggravation and just stayed put.

When I'd inevitably given up watching the liquor store, I cruised the 'hood indiscriminately, hitting all the major intersections I could think of, but my results were the same. No kid with braces looking like a 'jacker on the prowl, no classic Mustangs in tangerine orange. I saw a howling parade of black-and-whites cut a swath through traffic on Normandie and Manchester, an old man roll off a bus bench into the gutter on Slauson and Vermont, and two hookers change a flat tire on a run-down convertible Pontiac on Prairie and 108th—but I didn't see any carjackers anywhere.

So I went home.

The next morning, I called Matthew Poole with the LAPD and asked him if he knew anybody in Auto. Poole doesn't owe me any favors, but the homicide man helps me out when he can all the same, I don't really know why. Maybe it's because he thinks we're friends.

7

The man Poole eventually put me in touch with was a cop named Link, first name Sam. Over the phone he sounded like one of those cops who came out of the womb flashing a badge and reading the obstetrician his rights; he was cordial enough, but you could tell he was of the opinion I was standing between him and his pension. I got right to the point and told him about Purdy, then asked him afterward if the story sounded familiar. The Mustang had been stolen only two nights before, I figured he ought to have heard something about the investigation, even if he himself hadn't been called out on it.

But Link said it was all news to him.

Nothing about the Mustang or Purdy struck him as familiar. And if a shooting had taken place during a 'jacking Wednesday night, he assured me he'd have known about it. In fact, he would have convinced me altogether that the whole of Purdy's story was a lie had my description of the kid I'd spent the previous night looking for not rung a bell with him.

"Striped clothes?" he asked me.

"Yeah."

"That could be Squealer. He's into stripes. You want to talk to him?"

He was offering to go pick him up for me.

"Yeah, but not formally. I need him conversant," I said, hoping he wouldn't be insulted by the insinuation the kid wouldn't talk downtown.

"You just want to know where to find him, then."

"If that wouldn't be too much trouble."

Link said it wouldn't be any trouble at all.

It took me all day to find him.

He wasn't at home and he wasn't at school. Link had given me a list of about a half-dozen places he liked to frequent, from the Baldwin Hills Crenshaw Plaza to the basketball courts at Jesse Owens Park, but he never appeared at any of them until a few minutes after 7 PM, when he showed up at a Baskin and Robbins ice cream parlor in a mini-mall on Budlong and Fifty-sixth Street, during my second visit to the site. His pants were black denim, no stripes, but his shirt was an oversized tee with alternating blue and green horizontal bands, and the cap turned sideways on his head was silver and black, the primary colors of the San Antonio Spurs. He had arrived on foot with two other kids who looked roughly the same age, a boy and a girl, and I had to watch the three of them eat ice cream and throw napkins at each other for well over an hour before he was ready to leave again.

I had hoped when the time came he'd leave alone, but I wasn't that lucky. He left the same way he came, with his two friends in tow. The trio walked northbound along Budlong and I trailed behind them in my car, keeping a good block, block and a half between us at all times. I was prepared to go on like this all night if I had to, but I wasn't looking forward to it. Of the forty-eight hours I'd given myself to find Purdy's Mustang, more than thirty were already gone, and the clock was still running. I had to get the kid alone, or he had to lead me to the car, one or the other. And fast.

Things were looking dark when Squealer and his homies led me to a house on Fiftieth Street between Harvard and Denker, then disappeared inside. There was light in only one window, and the place was as quiet as an empty grave. The thought occurred to me they might have crashed there for the night, and an hour later nothing had happened to rule that possibility out—until the porch light winked back on and Squealer emerged from the house again.

Alone.

I got out of my car on the passenger side and ducked low to hide behind it, waiting for the kid to saunter past on the opposite side of the street. I was going to make this quick. He'd already shot Purdy and I had no reason to think he wouldn't shoot me, given the chance, so getting the drop on him first seemed to be the wise thing to do. He was stepping off the curb to cross Harvard when I closed the distance between us and put him down, rapping the base of his skull with the butt of my Ruger P-85. He fell like a house of cards. I caught him on his way down, dragged him over to my car, and tossed him in.

Then we went somewhere to talk.

There was nobody on the beach.

It was too cold for romance, and too dark for sightseeing. The moon was heavily shielded behind a thick mask of cloud cover, and a mist hung over the water like a frozen gray curse. The kid and I would not be disturbed.

I had him trussed up like a calf at a rodeo. He was bound, gagged, and blindfolded, stretched out flat upon the wooden-plank walkway that ran beneath the Santa Monica Pier. His gun was in my back pocket, a small .22 I'd found shoved into the waistband of his pants. Down here, the sound of the crashing waves echoed between the pier's pylons like thunder in a bottle, thoroughly directionless, and you could taste the salt of the ocean spray with every intake of breath.

When I was certain he was awake, I knelt down beside the kid and said, "I want my car."

He took that as a cue to start thrashing around, but it didn't take him long to see the futility in it. He wasn't going anywhere.

"You haven't guessed by now, we're on the Santa Monica Pier," I said. "Down at the beach. Hear the waves down there? Care for a swim?"

I rolled him over a little.

He got the gist of my phony threat right away, and bought into it completely. I had to hold him down with both hands to keep him still.

"Okay. You get the picture. You don't tell me where my car is, I push you off this fucking pier and into the Pacific. Understand?"

He started to struggle again. I put my hand on his throat and asked him one more time: "Understand?"

Finally, he grew quiet and slowly nodded his head.

"Very good. Car I'm looking for is a '65 Ford Mustang. Orange. You shot me in the arm and stole it from me Wednesday night, out on the corner of Imperial and Hoover. Remember?"

Squealer made no move to answer, so I rolled him over again, one full revolution.

"You're runnin' out of pier, homeboy," I said. Then, after a while. I asked him again, "Do you remember the car?"

This time he nodded his head.

"Good. Now—I'm going to take your gag off, and you're going to tell me where I can find it. You're not going to scream, or cry, or call for your mama—you're just going to tell me where my car is. Otherwise . . ."

I let him think about that a moment, then peeled his gag away from his mouth.

"At the mall! At the mall, man!" he said, gasping to get the words out.

"What mall?"

"Fox Hills Mall, man! The Fox Hills Mall!"

"What, in the parking lot?"

"Yeah! In the parkin' lot! You know, the buildin'!"

"The building?" I had to think about that a moment. "You mean the parking structure?"

He nodded his head frantically. "Yeah, that's it! The parkin' structure!"

"What floor?"

"What floor? I don't know, man. Four, I think. Don't kill me, man, please!"

"Why'd you put it there?"

"Why? I don't . . ."

"Why didn't you take it in for chopping? Why'd you park it instead?"

"Shit, I wasn't gonna chop that ride, man! It was too sweet!"

"Too sweet?"

He nodded his head again.

"What were you going to do with it, you weren't going to chop it?" I asked him.

"I was gonna keep it. Just . . . let it chill at the mall for a while, then change it up. Get, new papers on it, an' shit, so's it could be my ride."

I should have guessed.

I put the gag back in his mouth and stood up. Where this kid had found the courage to shoot a man, I couldn't begin to guess. He was scared shitless and seemingly willing to do whatever was asked of him to stay alive.

Odd.

I was going to leave him as he was, anticipating the worst, bouncing about on the wooden walkway floor like a beached whale waiting to die . . . and then I thought of one more question to ask him.

Kneeling beside him again, I said, "Tell me something, June bug: What'd you shoot me for?"

And then he told me exactly what I'd thought he might. He said I'd made him do it.

The Mustang was on the third floor.

Parked in a distant corner all by itself and covered with a tarp. I peeled the tarp off to look it over carefully, but I knew it was the car I was after inside of ten seconds. Everything about it matched Purdy's description: model, color, license plate number. With one notable exception.

It was a '66.

The '65s had a crosshairs grill; this one had the eggcrate grill of a '66. Which made it a rarity, yes, but not a classic. A man who knew cars might conceivably spend a small fortune to recover a stolen '65, but a '66? I didn't think so. Any more than I thought a man would take a bullet fighting to hold on to a '66, as Squealer the 'jacker had claimed Purdy had done Wednesday night.

Obviously, there was more to this car than met the eye.

When I finally found out what it was, a little over ninety minutes later, I called Purdy to tell him the good news.

"It's over there," I said, pointing. "Across the street."

Purdy turned and saw the Mustang parked on the other side of La Brea Avenue, directly opposite the Pink's hot dog stand in Hollywood where we were sitting. I'd used the keys I'd taken off Squealer to come here, and had been well into my second chili dog when Purdy showed up.

"I don't believe it," he said now, eyeing the car.

"We were lucky," I said, feigning weary humility.

"Where did you find it?"

I shrugged. "Does it matter?"

"No. Not really. I just thought—"

"You have my money, Mr. Purdy?"

"Of course." He took an envelope from his coat pocket and opened it so I could see the bills inside, but didn't hand it over. "You mind if I look the car over first?" he asked.

"Not at all," I said, wiping chili from the sides of my mouth. "I'll just hold on to the keys."

That wasn't what he'd had in mind, but he could see the point was nonnegotiable. Without saying another word, he left to inspect the car, then returned a few minutes later.

"Twenty-five hundred dollars," he said, handing me the envelope he'd shown me earlier. He seemed infinitely relieved.

I told him thanks and gave him his keys.

He stood there for a moment, wanting to say more, then just turned and went back to the car. He got in, started the engine, and pulled away from the curb.

Halfway down the block, he made a U-turn.

And then his rearview mirror turned red.

Some people would say I set him up, but I don't look at it that way.

Purdy had hidden a two-pound bag of crack cocaine behind the Mustang's driver's side door panel, and when I found it out at the Fox Hills Mall parking lot that night, I knew I owed him. He'd played me for a sucker. Fed me some line about his classic car getting jacked, just so I could run down the small fortune in rock he'd stashed inside it.

And yet . . .

Technically, no harm had been done. The man had hired me to do a job, and I'd done it. I'd found his car, delivered it on time, and been paid the agreed-upon fee. So what if the whole thing was a lie? I'd still held up my end of the bargain, and Purdy had held up his.

I owed him, and yet I didn't owe him.

So I let him go. Sort of.

I put a little of his stash in his glove compartment with his registration, then put the rest back where I'd found it. I parked the car on the same street, in the same place where, only six weeks before, I'd gotten my last ticket for making a U-turn, on La Brea Avenue near Pink's. And finally, I parked his car on the northbound side of the street, facing away from the Gardena address printed on the business card Purdy had given me.

A setup? Not hardly.

All Purdy would have had to do to get off that night was not make that U-turn.

See? He screwed himself.

All I did was watch.

Later, at the Deuce, Lilly nearly busted a gut laughing. In the proper frame of mind, the giant barkeep's as appreciative of my cleverness as I am myself. Sometimes even more so.

"Tell me one thing, Gunner," she said.

"Shoot."

"You made any U-turns yourself since then? Or you out of the habit for good?"

I grinned at her, winked, and downed the last of my free drink, though all it was by now was ice water. "Naw," I said.

"Naw, what?"

"Naw, I'm not out of the habit. I just know how to do 'em right now, that's all."

"Do 'em *right*? And what way is *that*?"

"That's where you turn the wheel," I said, demonstrating, "and pray nobody sees you."

I pushed myself away from the bar and called it a night.

Dead Drunk

by Lia Matera

MY SECRETARY, JAN, ASKED if I'd seen the newspaper. Another homeless man had frozen to death. I frowned up at her from my desk. Her tone said, *And you think you've got problems?*

My secretary is a paragon. I would not have a law practice without her. I would have something resembling my apartment, which looks like a college crash pad. But I have to cut Jan a lot of slack. She's got a big personality

Not that she actually says anything. She doesn't have to, any more than earthquakes bother saying "shake shake."

"Froze?" I murmured. I shoved documents around the desk, knowing she wouldn't take the hint.

"Froze to death. This is the fourth one. They find them in the parks, frozen."

"It *has* been cold," I agreed.

"You really haven't been reading the papers." Her eyes went on high-beam. "They're wet, that's why they freeze."

She sounded mad at me. Line forms on the right, behind my creditors.

"Must be the tule fog?" I guessed. I've never been sure what tule fog is. I didn't know if actual tules were required.

"You've been in your own little world lately. They've all been passed out drunk. Someone pours water over them while they lie there. It's been so cold, they end up frozen. To death."

I wondered if I could get away with, *How terrible.* Not that I didn't think it was terrible. But Jan picks at what I say, looking for hidden sarcasm.

She leaned closer, as titillated as I'd ever seen her. "And here's the kicker. They went and analyzed the water on the clothes. It's got no chlorine in it—it's not tap water. It's bottled water. Perrier or Evian or something. Can you imagine? Somebody going out with expensive bottled water on purpose to pour it over passed-out homeless men." Her long hair fell over her shoulders. With her big glasses and serious expression, she looked like the bread-baking, natural foods mom that she was. "You know, it probably takes three or four bottles."

"What a murder weapon."

"It *is* murder." She sounded defensive. "Being wet drops the body temperature so low it kills them. In this cold, within hours."

"That's what I said."

"But you were . . . Anyway, it is murder."

"I wonder if it has to do with the ordinance?"

Our town had passed a no-camping ordinance that was supposed to chase the homeless out of town. If they couldn't sleep here, the theory went, they couldn't live here. But the city had too many parks to enforce the ban. What were cops supposed to do? Wake up everyone they encountered? Take them to jail and give them a warmer place to sleep?

"Of course it has to do with the ordinance. This is some asshole's way of saying, if you sleep here, you die here."

"Maybe it's a temperance thing. You know, don't drink."

"I know what temperance means." Jan could be touchy. She could be a lot of things, including a fast typist willing to work cheap. "I just don't believe the heartlessness of it, do you?"

I had to be careful—I did believe the heartlessness of it. "It's uncondonable," I agreed.

Still she stooped over my desk. There was something else.

"The guy last night," Jan said bitterly, "was laid off by Hinder. Years ago, but even so."

Hinder was the corporation Jan had been fired from before I hired her.

She straightened. "I'm going to go give money to the guys outside."

"Who's outside?" Not my creditors?

"You are so oblivious, Linda. Homeless people, right downstairs. Regulars."

She was looking at me like I should know their names. I tried to look apologetic.

Ten minutes later, she buzzed me to say there was someone in the reception area.

"He wants to know if you can fit him in."

That was our code for, *He looks legit.* We were not in the best neighborhood. We got our share of walk-ins with generalized grievances and a desire to vent at length and for free. For them, our code was, *I've told him you're busy.*

"Okay."

A moment later, a kid—well, maybe young man, maybe even twenty-five or so—walked in. He was good-looking, well-dressed but too trendy, which is why he'd looked so young. He had the latest hairstyle, razored in places and long in others. He had running shoes that looked like inflatable pools.

He said, "I think I need a good lawyer."

My glance strayed to my walls, where my diploma announced I'd gone to a night school. I had two years experience, some of it with no caseload. I resisted the urge to say, Let me refer you to one.

Instead, I asked, "What's the nature of your problem?"

He sat on my client chair, checking it first. I guess it was clean enough.

"I think I'm going to be arrested." He glanced at me a little sheepishly, a little boastfully. "I said something kind of stupid last night."

If that were grounds, they'd arrest me, too.

"I was at The Club," a fancy bar downtown. "I got a little tanked. A little loose." He waggled his shoulders.

I waited. He sat forward. "Okay, I've got issues." His face said, *Who wouldn't?* "I work my butt off."

I waited some more.

"Well, it burns me. I have to work for my money; I don't get welfare, I don't get free meals and free medicine and a free place to live." He shifted on the chair. "I'm not saying kill them. But it's unfair I have to pay for them."

"For who?"

"The trolls, the bums."

I was beginning to get it. "What did you say in the bar?"

"That I bought out Costco's Perrier." He flushed to the roots of his chi-chi hair. "That I wish I'd thought of using it."

"On the four men?"

"I was high, okay?" he continued in a rush. "But then this morning, the cops come over." Tears sprang to his eyes. "They scared my mom. She took them out to see the water in the garage."

"You really did buy a lot of Perrier?"

"Just to drink. The police said they got a tip on their hot-line. Someone at the bar told them about me. That's got to be it."

I nodded like I knew about the hot-line.

"Now"—his voice quavered—"they've started talking to people where I work. Watch me get fired."

Gee buddy, then you'll qualify for free medical. "What would you like me to do for you, Mr. . . . ?"

"Kyle Kelly." He didn't stick out his hand. "Are they going to arrest me or what? I think I need a lawyer."

My private investigator was pissed off at me. My last two clients hadn't paid me enough to cover his fees. It was my fault. I hadn't asked for enough in advance. Afterwards, they'd stiffed me.

Now the PI was taking a hard line. He wouldn't work on this case until he got paid for the last two.

So I made a deal. I'd get his retainer from Kelly up front. I'd pay him for the investigation but I'd do most of it myself. For every hour I investigated and he got paid, he'd knock an hour off what I owed him.

I wouldn't want the state bar to hear about the arrangement. But the parts that were on paper would look okay.

It meant I had a lot of legwork to do.

I started by driving to a park where two of the dead men were found. It was a chilly afternoon, with the wind whipping off the plains, blowing dead leaves over footpaths and lawns.

I wandered, looking for the spots described in police reports. The trouble was, every half-bare bush near lawn and benches looked the same. And many were decorated with detritus: paper bags, liquor bottles, discarded clothing.

As I was leaving the park, I spotted two paramedics squatting beside an addled-looking man. His clothes were stiff with dirt, his face covered in thick gray stubble. He didn't look wet. If anything, I was shivering more than him.

I watched the younger of the two paramedics shake his head, scowling, while the older talked at some length to the man. The man nodded, kept on nodding. The older medic showed him a piece of paper. The man nodded some more. The younger one strode to an ambulance parked on a nearby fire trail. It was red on white with "4-12" stenciled on the side.

I knew from police reports that paramedics had been called to pick up the frozen homeless men. Were they conducting an investigation of their own?

A minute later, the older medic joined his partner in the ambulance. It drove off.

The homeless man lay down, curling into a fetal position on the lawn, collar turned up against the wind.

I approached him cautiously.

"Hi, " I said. "Are you sick?"

"No." He sat up again. "What's every damn body want to know if I'm sick for? 'Man down.' So what? What's a man got to be up about?"

He looked bleary-eyed. He reeked of alcohol and urine and musk. He was so potent, I almost lost my breakfast.

"I saw medics here talking to you. I thought you might be sick."

"Hassle hassle." He waved me away. When I didn't leave, he rose. "Wake us up, make us sign papers."

"What kind of papers?"

"Don't want to go to the hospital." His teeth were in terrible condition. I tried not to smell his breath. "Like I want yelling from the nurses, too."

"What do they yell at you about?"

"Cost them money, I'm costing everybody money. Yeah, well, maybe they should have thought of that before they put my-Johnny-self in the helicopter. Maybe they should have left me with the rest of the platoon."

He lurched away from me. I could see that one leg was shorter than the other.

I went back to my car. I was driving past a nearby sandwich shop when I saw ambulance 4-12 parked there. I pulled into the space behind it.

I went into the shop. The medics were sitting at a small table, looking bored. They were hard to miss in their cop-blue uniforms and utility belts hung with flashlights, scissors, tape, stethoscopes.

I walked up to them. "Hi," I said. "Do you mind if I talk to you for a minute?"

The younger one looked through me: no one's ever accused me of being pretty. The older one said, "What about?"

"I'm representing a suspect in the . . . " I hated to call it what the papers were now calling it, but it was the best shorthand. "The Perrier murders. Of homeless men."

That got the younger man's attention. "We knew those guys," he said.

"My client didn't do it. But he could get arrested. Do you mind helping me out? Telling me a little about them?"

They glanced at each other. The younger man shrugged.

"We saw them all the time. Every time someone spotted them passed out and phoned in a 'man down' call, we'd code-three it out to the park or the tracks or wherever."

The older paramedic gestured for me to sit. "Hard times out there. We've got a lot more regulars than we used to."

I sat down. The men, I noticed, were lingering over coffee. "I just saw you in the park."

"Lucky for everybody, my-Johnny-self was sober enough to AMA." The younger man looked irritated. "'Against medical advice.' We get these calls all the time. Here we are a city's got gang wars going on, knifings, drive-bys, especially late at night; and we're diddling around with passed-out drunks who want to be left alone anyway."

The older man observed, "Ben's new, still a hot-dog, wants every call to be the real deal."

"Yeah, well what a waste of effort, Dirk," the younger man, Ben, shot back. "We get what? two, three, four man-down calls a day. We have to respond to every one. It could be a poor diabetic, right, or a guy's had a heart attack. But you get out there, and it's some alcoholic. If he's too out of it to tell us he's just drunk, we have to transport and work him up. Which he doesn't want—he wakes up pissed off at having to hoof it back to the park. Or worse, with the new ordinance, he gets arrested."

"Ridiculous ordinance," the older medic interjected.

"And it's what, maybe five or six hundred dollars the company's out of pocket?" his partner continued. "Not to mention that everybody's time gets totally wasted, and maybe somebody with a real emergency's out there waiting for us. Your grandmother could be dying of a heart attack while we play taxi. It's bullshit."

"It's all in a night's work, Ben." Dirk looked at me. "You start this job, you want every call to be for reals. But you do it a few years, you get to know your regulars. Clusters of them near the liquor stores. You could draw concentric circles around each store and chart the man-down calls, truly. But what are you going to do? Somebody sees a man lying in the street or in the park, they've got to call, right? And if the poor bastard's too drunk to tell us he's fine, we can't just leave him. It's our license if we're wrong."

"They should change the protocols," Ben insisted. "If we know who they are, if we've run them in three, four, even ten times, we should be able to leave them to sleep it off."

Dirk said, "You'd get law suits."

"So these guys either stiff the company or welfare picks up the tab, meaning you and me pay the five hundred bucks. It offends logic."

"So you knew the men who froze." I tried to get back on track. "Did you pick them up when they died?"

"I went on one of the calls," Ben said defensively. "Worked him up."

"Sometimes with hypothermia," Dirk added, "body functions slow down so you can't really tell if they're dead till they warm up. So we'll spend, oh God, an hour or more doing CPR. Till they're warm and dead."

"While people wait for an ambulance somewhere else," Ben repeated.

"You'll mellow out," Dirk promised. "For one thing, you see them year-in year-out, you stop being such a hard-ass. Another thing, you get older, you feel more sympathy for how hard the street's got to be on the poor bones."

Ben's beeper went off. He immediately lifted it out of his utility belt, pressing a button and filling the air with static. A voice cut through: "Unit four twelve, we have a possible shooting at Kins and Booten Streets."

The paramedics jumped up, saying "Bye," and "Gotta go," as they strode past me and out the door. Ben, I noticed, was smiling.

My next stop was just a few blocks away. It was a rundown stucco building that had recently been a garage, a factory, a cult church, a rehab center, a magic shop. Now it was one of the few homeless shelters in town. I thought the workers there might have known some of the dead men.

I was ushered in to see the director, a big woman with a bad complexion. When I handed her my card and told her my business, she looked annoyed.

"Pardon me, but your client sounds like a real shit."

"I don't know him well enough to judge," I admitted. "But he denies doing it, and I believe him. And if he didn't do it, he shouldn't get blamed. You'd agree with that?"

"Some days," she conceded. She motioned me to sit in a scarred chair opposite a folding-table desk. "Other days, tell the truth, I'd round up all the holier-than-thou jerks bitching about the cost of a place like this, and I'd shoot 'em. Christ, they act like we're running a luxury hotel here. Did you get a look around?"

I'd seen women and children and a few old men on folding chairs or duck-cloth cots. I hadn't seen any food.

"It's enough to get your goat," the director continued. "The smugness, the condemnation. And ironically, how many paychecks away from the street do you think most people are? One? Two?"

"Is that mostly who you see here? People who got laid off?"

She shrugged. "Maybe half. We get a lot of people who are frankly just too tweaked-out to work. What can you do? You can't take a screwdriver and fix them. No use blaming them for it."

"Did you know any of the men who got killed?"

She shook her head. "No, no. We don't take drinkers, we don't take anybody under the influence. We can't. Nobody would get any sleep, nobody would feel safe. Alcohol's a nasty drug, lowers inhibitions. You get too much attitude, too much noise. We can't deal with it here. We don't let in anybody we think's had a drink, and if we find alcohol, we kick the person out. It's that simple."

"What recourse do they have? Drinkers, I mean."

"Sleep outside. They want to sleep inside, they have to stay sober, no ifs, ands, or buts."

"The camping ban makes that illegal."

"Well," she said tartly, "it's not illegal to stay sober."

"You don't view it as an addiction?"

"There's AA meetings five times a night at three locations." She ran a hand through her already-disheveled hair. "I'm sorry, but it's a struggle scraping together money to take care of displaced families in this town. Then you've got to contend with people thinking you're running some kind of flophouse for drunks. Nobody's going to donate money for that."

I felt a twinge of pity. No room at the inn for alcoholics, and not much sympathy from paramedics. Now, someone—please God, not my client—was dousing them so they'd freeze to death.

With the director's permission, I wandered through the shelter.

A young woman lay on a cot with a blanket over her legs. She was reading a paperback.

"Hi," I said. "I'm a lawyer. I'm working on the case of the homeless men who died in the parks recently. Do you know about it?"

She sat up. She looked like she could use a shower and a make-over, but she looked more together than most of the folks in here. She wasn't mumbling to herself, and she didn't look upset or afraid.

"Yup—big news here. And major topic on the street."

"Did you know any of the men?"

"I'll tell you what I've heard." She leaned forward. "It's a turf war."

"A turf war?"

"Who gets to sleep where, that kind of thing. A lot of crazies on the street, they get paranoid. They gang up on each other. Alumni from the closed-down mental hospitals. You'd be surprised." She pushed up her sleeve and showed me a scar. "One of them cut me."

"Do you know who's fighting whom?"

"Yes." Her eyes glittered. "Us women are killing off the men. They say we're out on the street for their pleasure, and we say, death to you, bozo."

I took a backward step, alarmed by the look on her face.

She showed me her scar again. "I carve a line for every one I kill." She pulled a tin Saint Christopher out from under her shirt. "I used to be a Catholic. But Clint Eastwood is my god now."

I pulled into a parking lot with four ambulances parked in a row. A sign on a two-story brick building read Central Ambulance. I hoped they'd give me their records regarding the four men.

I smiled warmly at the front-office secretary. When I explained what I wanted, she handed me a records-request form.

"We'll contact you within five business days regarding the status of your request."

If my client got booked, I could subpoena the records. So I might, unfortunately, have them before anyone even read this form.

As I sat there filling it out, a thin boy in a paramedic uniform strolled in. He wore his medic's bill cap backwards. His utility belt was hung with twice the gadgets of the two men I'd talked to earlier. Something resembling a big rubber band dangled from his back pocket. I supposed it was a tourniquet, but on him it gave the impression of a slingshot.

He glanced at me curiously. He said, "Howdy, Mary," to the secretary.

She didn't look glad to see him. "What now?"

"Is Karl in?"

"No. What's so important?"

"I was thinking instead of just using the HEPA filters, if we could—"

"Save it. I'm busy."

I shot him a sympathetic look. I know how it feels to be bullied by a secretary.

I handed her my request, walking out behind the spurned paramedic.

I was surprised to see him climb into a cheap Geo car. He was in uniform. I'd assumed he was working.

All four men had been discovered in the morning. It had probably taken them most of the night to freeze to death; they'd been picked up by ambulance in the wee hours. Maybe this kid could tell me who'd worked those shifts.

I tapped at his passenger window. He didn't hesitate to lean across and open the door. He looked alert and happy, like a curious puppy.

"Hi," I said, "I was wondering if you could tell me about your shifts? I was going to ask the secretary, but she's not very . . . friendly."

He nodded as if her unfriendliness were a fact of life, nothing to take personally. "Come on in. What do you want to know?" Then, more suspiciously, "You're not a lawyer?"

I climbed in quickly. "Well, yes, but—"

"Oh, man. You know, we do the very best we can." He whipped off his cap, rubbing his crewcut in apparent annoyance. "We give a hundred and ten percent."

I suddenly placed his concern. "No, no, it's not about medical malpractice, I swear."

He continued scowling at me.

"I represent a young man who's been falsely accused of—"

"You're not here about malpractice?"

"No, I'm not."

"Because that's such a crock." He flushed. "We work our butts off. Twelve hour shifts, noon to midnight, and a lot of times we get force-manned onto a second shift. If someone calls in sick or has to go out of service because they got bled all over or punched out, someone's got to hold over. When hell's a'poppin' with the gangs, we've got guys working forty-eights or even seventy-twos." He shook his head. "It's just plain unfair to blame us for everything that goes wrong. Field medicine's like combat conditions. We don't have everything all clean and handy like they do at the hospital."

"I can imagine. So you work—"

"And it's not like we're doing it for the money! Starting pay's eight-fifty an hour; it takes years to work up to twelve. Your garbage collector earns more than we do."

I was a little off balance. "Your shifts—"

"Because half our calls, nobody pays the bill—Central Ambulance is probably the biggest pro bono business in town. So we get stuck at eight-fifty an hour. For risking AIDS, hepatitis, TB."

I didn't want to get pulled into his grievances. "You work twelve hour shifts? Set shifts?"

"Rotating. Sometimes you work the day half, sometimes the night half."

Rotating; I'd need schedules and rosters. "The guys who work midnight to noon, do they get most of the drunks?"

He shrugged. "Not necessarily. We've got 'em passing out all day long. It's never too early for an alcoholic to drink." He looked bitter. "I had one in the family;" he complained, "I should know."

"Do you know who picked up the four men who froze to death?"

His eyes grew steely. "I'm not going to talk about the other guys. You'll have to ask the company." He started the car.

I contemplated trying another question, but he was already shifting into gear. I thanked him, getting out. As I closed the door, I noticed a bag in back with a Garry's Liquors logo. Maybe the medic had something in common with the four dead men.

But it wasn't just drinking that got those men into trouble. It was not having a home to pass out in.

I stood at the spot where police had found the fourth body. It was a small neighborhood park.

Just after sunrise, an early jogger had phoned 911 from his cell phone. A man had been lying under a hedge. He'd looked dead. He'd looked wet.

The police had arrived first, then firemen, who'd taken a stab at resuscitating him. Then paramedics had arrived to work him up and transport him to the hospital, where he was pronounced dead. I knew that much from today's newspaper.

I found a squashed area of grass where I supposed the dead man had lain yesterday. I could see pocks and scuffs where workboots had tramped. I snooped around. Hanging from a bush was a rubber tourniquet. A paramedic must have squatted with his back against the shrubbery.

Flung deeper into the brush was a bottle of whiskey. Had the police missed it? Not considered it evidence? Or had it been discarded since?

I stared at it, wondering. If victim number four hadn't already been pass-out drunk, maybe someone helped him along.

I stopped by Parsifal MiniMart, the liquor store nearest the park. If anyone knew the dead man, it would be the proprietor.

He nodded. "Yup. I knew every one of those four. What kills me is the papers act like they were nobodies, like that's what 'alcoholic' means." He was a tall, red-faced man, given to karate-chop gestures. "Well, they were pretty good guys. Not mean, not full of shit, just regular guys. Buddy was a little"—he wiggled his hand—"not right in the head; heard voices and all that, but not violent that I ever saw. Mitch was a good guy. One of those jocks who's a hero as a kid, but then gets hooked on the booze. I'll tell ya, I wish I could have made every kid comes in here for beer spend the day with Mitch. Donnie and Bill were . . . how can I put this without sounding like a racist? You know, a lot of older black guys are hooked on something. Check out the neighborhood. You'll see groups of them talking jive and keeping the curbs warm."

Something had been troubling me. Perhaps this was the person to ask. "Why didn't they wake up when the cold water hit them?"

The proprietor laughed. "Those guys? If I had to guess, I'd say their blood alcohol was one point oh even when they weren't drinking, just naturally from living the life. Get enough Thunderbird in them and you're talking practically a coma." He shook his head. "They were just drunks, I know we're not talking about killing Mozart here. But the attitude behind what happened—man, it's cold. Perrier, too. That really tells you something."

"I heard there was no chlorine in the water. I don't think they've confirmed a particular brand of water."

"I just saw on the news they arrested some kid looks like a fruit, one of those hairstyles." The proprietor shrugged. "He had a bunch of Perrier. Cases of it from a discount place—I guess he didn't want to pay full price. Guess it wasn't even worth a buck a bottle to him to freeze a drunk."

Damn, they'd arrested Kyle Kelly. Already.

"You don't know anything about a turf war, do you?" It was worth a shot. "Among the homeless?"

"Sure," he grinned. "The drunk Sharks and the rummy Jets." He whistled the opening notes of *West Side Story*.

I got tied up in traffic. It was an hour later by the time I walked into the police station. My client was in an interrogation room by himself. When I walked in, he was crying.

"I told them I didn't do it." He wiped tears as if they were an embarrassing surprise. "But I was getting so tongue-tied. I told them I wanted to wait for you."

"I didn't think they'd arrest you, especially not so fast," I said. "You did exactly right, asking for me. I just wish I'd gotten here sooner. I wish I'd been in my office when you called."

He looked like he wished I had, too.

"All this over a bunch of bums," he marveled. "All the crime in this town, and they get hard-ons over winos."

I didn't remind him that his own drunken bragging had landed him here. But I hope it occurred to him later.

I was surrounded by reporters when I left the police station. They looked at me like my client had taken bites out of their children.

"Mr. Kelly is a very young person who regrets what alcohol made him say one evening. He bears no one any ill will, least of all the dead men, whom he never even met." I repeated some variation of this over and over as I battled my way to my car.

Meanwhile, their questions shed harsh light on my client's bragfest at The Club.

"Is it true he boasted about kicking homeless men and women?" "Is it true he said if homeless women didn't smell so bad at least they'd be usable?" "Did he say three bottles of Perrier is enough, but four's more certain?" "Does he admit saying he was going to keep doing it till he ran out of Perrier?" "Is it true he once set a homeless man on fire?"

Some of the questions were just questions: "Why Perrier? Is it a statement?" "Why did he buy it in bulk?" "Is this his first arrest? Does he have a sealed juvenile record?"

I could understand why police had jumped at the chance to make an arrest. Reporters must have been driving them crazy.

After flustering me and making me feel like a laryngitic parrot, they finally let me through. I locked myself into my car and drove gratefully away. Traffic was good. It only took me half an hour to get back to the office.

I found the paramedic with the Geo parked in front. He jumped out of his car. "I just saw you on TV."

"What brings you here?"

"Well, I semi-volunteered, for the company newsletter. I mean, we picked up those guys a few times. It'd be good to put something into an article." He looked like one of those black-and-white sitcom kids. Opie or Timmy or someone. "I didn't quite believe you, before, about the malpractice. I'm sorry I was rude."

"You weren't rude."

"I just wasn't sure you weren't after us. Everybody's always checking up on everything we do. The nurses, the docs, our supervisors, other medics. Every patient care report gets looked at by four people. Our radio calls get monitored. Everybody jumps in our shit for every little thing."

I didn't have time to be Studs Terkel. "I'm sorry, I can't discuss my case with you."

"But I heard you say on TV your guy's innocent. You're going to get him off, right?" He gazed at me with a confidence I couldn't understand.

"Is that what you came here to ask?"

"It's just we knew those guys. I thought for the newsletter, if I wrote something . . ." He flushed. "Do you need information? You know, general stuff from a medical point of view?"

I couldn't figure him out. Why this need to keep talking to me about it? It was his day off; didn't he have a life?

But I *had* been wondering: "Why exactly do you carry those tourniquets? What do you with them?"

He looked surprised. "We tie them around the arm to make a vein pop up. So we can start an intravenous line."

I glanced up at my office window, checking whether Jan had left. It was late, there were no more workers spilling out of buildings. A few derelicts lounged in doorways. I wondered if they felt safer tonight because someone had been arrested. With so many dangers on the street, I doubted it.

"Why would a tourniquet be in the bushes where the last man was picked up?" I hugged my briefcase. "I assumed a medic had dropped it, but you wouldn't start an intravenous line on a dead person, would you?"

"We don't do field pronouncements—pronounce them dead, I mean—in hypothermia cases. We leave that to the doc." He looked proud of himself, like he'd passed the pop quiz. "They're not dead till they're warm and dead."

"But why start an IV in this situation?"

"Get meds into them. If the protocols say to, we'll run a line even if we think they're deader than Elvis." He shrugged. "They warm up faster, too."

"What warms them up? What do you drip into them?"

"Epinephrine, atropine, normal saline. We put the saline bag on the dash to heat it as we drive—if we know we have a hypothermic patient."

"You have water in the units?"

"Of course."

"Special water?"

"Saline and distilled."

"Do you know a medic named Ben?"

He hesitated before nodding.

"Do you think he has a bad attitude about the homeless?"

"No more that you would," he protested. "We're the ones who have to smell them, have to handle them when they've been marinating in feces and urine and vomit. Plus they get combative at a certain stage. You do this disgusting waltz with them where they're trying to beat on you. And the smell is like, whoa. Plus if they scratch you, you can't help but be paranoid what they might infect you with."

"Ben said they cost your company money."

"They cost you and me money."

The look on his face scared me. Money's a big deal when you don't make enough of it.

I started past him.

He grabbed my arm. "Everything's breaking down." His tone was plaintive. "You realize that? Our whole society's breaking down. Everybody sees it—the homeless, the gangs, the diseases—but they don't have to deal with the physical results. They don't have to put their hands right on it, get all bloody and dirty with it, get infected by it."

"Let go." I imagined being helpless and disoriented, a drunk at the mercy of a fed-up medic.

"And we don't get any credit,"—he sounded angry now—"we just get checked up on." He gripped my arm tighter.

Again I searched my office window, hoping Jan was still working, that I wasn't alone. But the office was dark.

A voice behind me said, "What you doin' to the lady, man?"

I turned to see a stubble-chinned black man in layers of rancid clothes. He'd stepped out of a recessed doorway. Even from here, I could smell alcohol.

"You let that lady go. You hear me?" He moved closer.

The medic's grip loosened.

The black man might be drunk, but he was big. And he didn't look like he was kidding.

I jerked my arm free, backing toward him.

He said, "You're Jan's boss, aren't ya?"

"Yes." For the thousandth time, I thanked God for Jan. This must be one of the men she'd mother-henned this morning. "Thank you."

To the medic, I said, "The police won't be able to hold my client long. They've got to show motive and opportunity and no alibi on four different nights. I don't think they'll be able to do it. They were just feeling pressured to arrest someone. Just placating the media."

The paramedic stared behind me. I could smell the other man. I never thought I'd find the reek of liquor reassuring.

"Isn't that what your buddies sent you to find out? Whether they could rest easy, or if they'd screwed over an innocent person?"

The medic pulled his bill cap off, buffing his head with his wrist.

"Or maybe you decided on your own to come here. Your coworkers probably have sense enough to keep quiet and keep out of it. But you don't." He was young and enthusiastic, too much so, perhaps. "Well, you can tell Ben and the others not to worry about Kyle Kelly. His reputation's ruined for as long as people remember the name—which probably isn't long enough to teach him a lesson. But there's not enough evidence against him. He won't end up in jail because of you."

"Are you accusing *us*?" He looked more thrilled than shocked.

"Of dousing the men so you didn't have to keep picking them up? So you could respond to more important calls? Yes, I am."

"But who are you going to—? What are you going to do?"

"I don't have a shred of proof to offer the police," I realized. "And I'm sure you guys will close ranks, won't give each other away. I'm sure the others will make you stop 'helping,' make you keep your mouth shut."

I thought about the dead men. "Pretty good guys," according to the MiniMart proprietor. I thought about my-Johnny-self, the war veteran I'd spoken to this morning.

I wanted to slap this kid. Just to do *something*.

"You know what? You need to be confronted with your arrogance, just like Kyle Kelly was. You need to see what other people think of you. You need to see some of your older, wiser coworkers look at you with disgust on their faces. You need your boss to rake you over the coals. You need to read what the papers have to say about you."

I could imagine headlines that sounded like movie billboards. Dr. Death. Central Hearse.

He winced. He'd done the profession no favor.

"So you can bet I'll tell the police what I think," I promised. "You can bet I'll try to get you fired, you and Ben and whoever else was involved. Even if there isn't enough evidence to arrest you."

He took a cautious step toward his car. "I didn't admit anything." He pointed to the other man. "Did you hear me admit anything?"

"And I'm sure your lawyer will tell you not to." If he could find a half-way decent one on his salary. "Now if you'll excuse me, I have a lot of work to do."

I turned to the man behind me. "Would you mind walking me in to my office?" I had some cash inside. He needed it more than I did.

"Lead the way, little lady." His eyes were jaundiced yellow, but they were bright. I was glad he didn't look sick.

I prayed he wouldn't need an ambulance anytime soon.

Love Me for My Yellow Hair Alone

(33 Short Films about Marilyn Monroe)

by Carolyn Wheat

> *Only god, my dear*
> *could love you for yourself alone*
> *and not your yellow hair*
> —W. B. Yeats

1. The Watcher

THE HOTEL DEL CORONADO SQUATS on the silver strand of beach like a fat, aging duchess. Huge, sprawling, its rust-red roof like a giant mushroom cap, it dominates the Coronado oceanfront.

The woman sits on a beach chair, her face upturned to catch the rays of the sun she professes to hate. She is blond and pale; sun will dry and wrinkle her skin, she says often. Yet she inhales the sun's heat, she revels in the languorous feeling it spreads through her body. She undulates in her beach chair, shifting her perfect anatomy to expose more skin to the blinding light. She disdains the hat her companion proffers, waving it away with an impatient hand whose fingernails are meticulously manicured but unpainted. Not Hollywood hands, but the hands of a secretary or a bookkeeper.

The companion is a middle-aged woman with a soft, lived-in look. She wears a shapeless black dress; her feet are encased in support hose and orthopedic sandals. A Jewish housewife, thinks the man with the binoculars. He knows her husband is the high priest of Method acting, but he does not know that the Jewish housewife is herself an accomplished actress, a woman who is not permitted to work because of the blacklist. He thinks the high priest has sent his wife to baby-sit the temperamental star.

2. The Extra

And, boy, was she ever temperamental! She never, but absolutely never, got to the set on time. Once she showed up at noon for a nine o'clock call, and the minute she got there, Mr. Wilder picked up his megaphone and called "Lunch."

I was an extra on that movie, one of twenty Coronado kids who got to sit around on the beach and get our pitchers took, as my Okie grandfather said with a cackle when I told him about my summer job.

We were military brats, my pals and me. We grew up surfing before anybody in the rest of the country knew what a surfboard was. We bummed around on the beach and took jobs at the Del for pocket money, clearing tables or carrying suitcases and waiting for the day when we'd take the ferry to San Diego and start college and never come back to boring old Coronado where there was nothing to do.

Johnny Benson told me about the movie coming. You remember Johnny—his dad was Navy all the way and Johnny was supposed to go to Annapolis, only he didn't want to. His idea of heaven was MIT; kid was great at math and science. Only his dad thought scientists were pointy-headed weirdos who were either Jewish or faggots or both, and he was god-damned if any son of his was going to—

Well, you get the picture. So that was Johnny, and you wouldn't think a kid like that would care much about the movies or even about Marilyn Monroe, but you would be wrong because Johnny was seriously in love with Marilyn and the minute he heard that movie was coming, he decided he had to meet Marilyn. Really meet her, not just sit on the same beach as her, watching her through binoculars like all the other goofballs on Coronado.

3. The Private Eye

I was a Rita Hayworth man myself. That long, red hair, those full lips. Plus, she could dance. I'm not much of a dancer myself, but I love a woman who can dance. Marilyn, you could see she'd had to take a lot of lessons before she danced on screen, but Rita was a natural.

But a job is a job is a job, to quote that dyke writer in Paris. And besides, I always had a soft spot for Joltin' Joe. So he was divorced from her, that doesn't mean he can't take an interest? He can't hire a guy or two to keep an eye on her, he knows she's in some kind of trouble?

I wouldn't of taken the job if I hadn't believed I was working for DiMaggio. Honest. I would have turned that money down cold, even though making a living as a PI in San Diego was no picnic in those days. America's Finest City was fine, all right—too fine to need a lot of guys wearing gumshoes.

But I wouldn't have taken the money if I'd of known. Honest.

4. The Director's Assistant

Mr. Wilder was so patient with her. Like a father with a fractious child, he told her over and over again just what he wanted. He'd say the same thing twenty different ways, trying for the one phrase that would connect and bring out a performance. The other actors, Curtis and Lemmon and Raft, all they needed were one or two takes and they'd have it right. But Marilyn would shake her head and her lip would tremble and a tear would fall down the perfect face and then Makeup would have to come over and do her up again.

I'd stand there in the hot sun, holding an umbrella over Mr. Wilder's head so he wouldn't get heatstroke, and I'd watch her stumble over a line and stop, demanding another take.

Even when she got the lines right, she wasn't satisfied. "I need to do it again," she'd say in that baby voice. "It wasn't right."

Mr. Wilder would lean forward and whisper in her ear. I'd have to lean forward too, so the umbrella would shield him. She'd shake her head and wave him away. "I need to think," she'd say. "Don't talk to me, please. I'll forget how I want to play it."

As if she could know how to play the scene any better than Mr. Wilder did! As if she were some kind of genius and Mr. Wilder was nothing more than a ham-handed amateur who might screw her up.

The nerve of that little bitch, I thought, gripping the umbrella with white-knuckled hands.

Until I saw the rushes. Until I saw the tiny, subtle differences between the scene as Billy had instructed her to do it and the scene the way she felt it from within.

She was magic on the screen. Even Mr. Wilder said so. Later. Much later.

5. The Hotel Maid

He was always in the room. Whenever I came to clean, there he'd be, sitting on one of the wicker chairs on the balcony or writing at the desk by the window. He'd nod politely and tell me to go ahead even though I always told him I could come back when it was more convenient. That was what the management wanted us girls to say, so I said it. Some rooms the maids didn't get to clean until 5:00 in the PM on account of the movie people kept pretty strange hours.

"My wife's on the set," he'd say. I'd nod as if to say, where else would the star of the movie be?

But she wasn't on the set. Everybody knew Mr. Wilder and the other actors were going nuts because Marilyn didn't show until afternoon. Everybody knew except Mr. Miller. Except the husband.

The husband is always the last to know.

6. On the Beach

"She's just a pretend lady," the chubby little boy with the potbelly confided.

"I know," the little girl replied. She was an inch shorter than the boy and her hair was the exact same baby blond as the real lady's hair.

"She's a man dressed up like a lady," the boy went on. "For the movie."

"I know," the little girl said again. She walked toward the approaching waves; she stood on the hard sand and waited for the cool water to lick her toes. When the wave washed over her feet, she jumped and squealed, then ran back to the soft sand.

The lady who wasn't a lady walked funny. She wobbled and her heels buckled under her and the people crowding around laughed.

The little girl wasn't sure why the people laughed when the pretend lady walked. The real lady wobbled when she walked, too, only the people didn't laugh.

Once she wobbled so much she fell down on the stairs. If the pretend lady had done that, everyone would have laughed. But nobody laughed when the real lady did it.

7. The New York Journalist

"Hollywood," quips Bob Hope, "where every Tom, Dick, and Harry is Tab, Rock, and Rory." And where a white-trash

California girl named Norma Jeane Baker transformed herself into the most glamorous sex symbol of her time.

California is the edge of America. It's where you go to reinvent yourself, where you can leave behind the person you were and become someone new, shedding the past like a worn-out snakeskin. You expect the freeways to be littered with crackling, near-transparent carapaces of dead selves.

I gotta cut that last bit. Too goddamn literary for this rag. Maybe I can pull it out and reshape it for a piece in the *Times*. Yeah, the *Times*'ll eat that crap with a spoon. But for the *Mirror*, I need a little dirt.

She's late on the set. She's always late, they tell me, but this time it's different. This time she's not in Hollyweird; she's at this godforsaken hole near San Diego. So what the hell's she doing every morning instead of showing up for work?

She's not doing the horizontal mambo with her hubby, that's for sure. She leaves the room, but she doesn't go down to the set. Miller thinks she's with Wilder; Wilder thinks she's with Miller—and the whole thing smells to me like a nice big fishy story. A story I can clean up a little for the *Mirror* and spice up a little for *Hollywood Confidential*. In this business, there's nothing better than getting paid for the same story twice.

Three times, if I can toss in enough bullshit for the *Times*.

8. The Watcher

He trains his binoculars on the silver strand of beach. The prop men from the movie have strategically placed several wicker beach chairs that wrap around the sitter like a cocoon. In the movie, Tony Curtis, dressed like a twenties playboy, will sit in one of the chairs and Marilyn will mince past him and strike up an acquaintance.

He thinks it would be interesting if someone walked past the wicker cocoon and discovered that the person sitting inside, facing the ocean, had been dead for some time.

9. The Private Eye

This thing is a security nightmare. I can't believe Wilder lets everyone and his twin brother watch the shooting on the beach. They put up ropes to hold back the crowds, but any nut could pull out a gun and shoot Marilyn where she stands. Hell, someone with a good aim could pot her from a passing boat—and a lot of boats go by, people training binocs on the shore to get a glimpse of the stars.

Wilder's there in his white cloth cap, a cigarette dangling from yellowed fingers. He looks like a cabbie, not a famous director.

Lemmon's wearing a girl's bathing suit from the twenties. He's standing next to Marilyn, and they're both laughing. I can't hear what they're saying, but I have a good idea why Lemmon, at least, is enjoying himself.

He doesn't have to wear high heels on the beach.

10. The Drama Student

I saw him on Orange Avenue this afternoon. I don't know why, but I thought he was taller. And I definitely visualized him wearing a suit and tie. But he had on a pair of slacks and a striped T-shirt and a baseball cap. He looked like a father on his way to his son's Little League game.

The most famous American playwright of our time, and he was walking along Orange Avenue just like anybody else.

He walked faster than everyone else; he kept moving around other people. I guess they walk a lot in New York City.

He's here because of Her, of course. I don't imagine a man like him would even step foot in California if it weren't for being married to Her.

How can he write with all the distractions She brings into his life? How can a man of his genius be content to play second fiddle to a silly movie star? Why doesn't he realize that she can bring him nothing but pain, that he needs a woman of high intellectual attainment, a woman who will devote herself to nurturing his art, not pursue her own meaningless career?

11. The Actor

You do the work. Forget this self-indulgent bullshit about being ready or not ready. Forget this Method crap about getting in touch with your inner feelings. You show up, you hit the marks, you say the lines—hell, first you know the lines; you don't show up three hours late and ask for cue cards.

She was just off a movie with Larry Olivier. Can you feature that?

I've been in the business since I was younger than Marilyn and nobody ever let me get close to a movie with Olivier, and that no-talent blonde gets a movie with him and screws it up.

I'm a character actor; you could see this movie nine times and still not really notice my performance. Which is another way of saying it's a good performance, since I'm not supposed to be noticed.

Her husband, now, he understood what professional was. He was a writer, he knew how to produce. He knew that you have to put your keister in the chair and pound away on the typewriter every day whether or not you feel like it. He wanted Marilyn to act like a pro, to give a damn about the other people on the set. Every time she threw one of her tantrums or burst into tears, he died a little. You could see it; he'd grimace like a father whose kid is acting bratty at the officers' club.

12. The Acting Coach

I know what they call me on the set: the wicked witch of the East. They hate Easterners out here, which is amusing, really, because so many of them are from the East themselves. But they've gone Hollywood and I haven't.

The sun gives me terrible headaches, which is why I dress like a Bedouin, and yet I sit with Marilyn on the Ocean Terrace, going over lines and working on the scenes. I pass on bits of wisdom from my own acting days, spiced with little sayings from Lee, from the Studio.

"A scene is like a bottle," I tell her. "If you can't open it one way, try another."

She mumbles something I have to ask her to repeat.

"Maybe I should just throw the bottle away," she says in her wispy voice, which almost but not quite gets swept out to sea by the strong breeze.

13. The Cameraman

You know how they say in Hollywood that the camera loves somebody. It sounds kind of stupid when you say it; I mean, how can a camera love anyone? But it's true. You take Marilyn, now. All I do is point the camera at her and she lights up. Her face plays to the camera, tilting ever so slightly to catch an angle of light. Or she widens her eyes and the camera zooms right in on her baby blues.

She tosses her head and the camera records the swirl and fall of fine, golden hair.

We're shooting black-and-white, remember. And yet the camera catches, somehow, the precise shade of her blonde hair, the wide blue eyes. She is going to look wonderful on screen, lit from within like a Japanese lantern.

We're shooting black-and-white because of the boys. Wilder says if we were doing the movie in color, the drag bits wouldn't work; the makeup would be too garish.

He's right. The studio bitched at first, said nobody would ever pay good money to see a black-and-white picture again, color was here to stay. But for this movie, they'll pay. Curtis is great, Lemmon is greater, and then there's Marilyn.

The camera loves her, and I think I do too.

14. The Local Reporter

I can't believe this quote! Little old me from sleepy little San Diego with a quote that's going to make headlines around the world.

TONY CURTIS ON MARILYN: "KISSING HER LIKE KISSING HITLER."

Can you believe my luck in being actually in the room when Tony Curtis tells the world his glamorous costar is really more like the hated dictator?

Of course, I go on to explain in the article that what he really means is that in her relentless drive for perfection in every little thing she does, Marilyn sometimes drives her costars to distraction. But rest assured, I intend to tell the movie-going public, the results on screen will be worth it! They always are with La Monroe, aren't they?

15. The Studio Doc

You don't get rich in Hollywood by saying no to big stars. And Marilyn was one of the biggest. When she was in a picture, everyone on the set lived on Marilyn time. The stars, the extras, the director all sat around waiting for Her Highness to show up. On a good day, she made it before the lunch break. On a bad day, she didn't make it at all.

She lived on champagne, caviar, and Nembutal. Once, I tried to tell her she needed to taper off, not use the pills every night, especially if she was serious about wanting a baby. She looked at me with her beautiful, bleary eyes and said, "What night? My life is one long, goddamned horrible day that never ends."

I shut up and wrote another prescription.

16. The Continuity Girl

That last picture she made with Wilder, she didn't even have a name. Her character was called The Girl. That's all, just The Girl, as if any bubble-headed blonde in the world could have walked in and played the part.

That's what Wilder really wants from her. That she play The Girl, not a real person.

I'm forty-two years old. I've been in the picture business since I was nineteen. When I started, I was a girl, I guess. But now, it sounds pretty silly when people introduce me as "the continuity girl." Not bothering to find out my name, just calling me "the girl."

Just like Marilyn in *Seven Year Itch*.

I know where she goes in the mornings. I've seen her. I know I should tell Mr. Wilder. And I will—the first time he calls me by my name.

17. The Drama Student

He's writing a movie for Her. The greatest playwright of the twentieth century, and he's wasting his time writing a stupid movie.

I can't believe it. I can't believe he's that besotted.

If only I could talk to him. If only I could make him understand that he has a duty to his art. He needs to know there are people like me, who love him for what he's done. He needs to know he doesn't have to prostitute himself.

I have to talk to him.

18. The Psychiatrist

It was a classic case of Electra complex. Marrying an older man, a father figure. And of course, there was already a father figure in Lee Strasberg, not to mention her way of playing bad little daughter with her directors. She craved their approval, and she refused to earn it by behaving properly.

Classic.

Classic, and tragic. By the time she was making that movie, any competent therapist could have told her the marriage was coming apart at the seams. Anyone could have told her nothing would save it; certainly not a baby.

19. The Hairdresser

Sweetie, this movie is going to be a hoot. You haven't lived until you've seen macho Tony Curtis mincing around in high heels! The poor boy looks so uncomfortable. I'd just die if one of his butch friends like Kirk or Burt came on the set and saw his Cupid's bow lips. Honey, he's the spitting image of Clara Bow!

Oh, all right, I'll lay off the camp. Just for you, sweetcheeks.

Oh, don't be such a closet queen. I won't tell your Navy buddies who you like to kiss on weekends, so just relax, will you? What's she like?

The truth? She's like a poisoned bonbon, beautiful to look at, but, oh, Mary, don't —

All *right*.

She's like a child. A mean little child who'll do anything to get her own way.

God, what hets go through for a little taste of sex on the silver screen!

20. On the Beach

"Here comes the lady," the boy said. He squatted on the sand next to the sand castle he'd made with his pail and shovel. It was a simple castle; all he'd done was turn over a pailful of hard, wet sand and dig a little moat around it for the water to run in.

The little girl kicked at the shell and drew her foot back with a cry. "It hurts," she said. "It's too sharp." She picked up the offending object and threw it as hard as she could into the water. It landed with a plop about three feet away.

The lady came every morning. She walked along the beach in her bare feet, but she wore pants instead of a bathing suit. And she wore a scarf over her blonde curls. It was a funny way to dress for the beach, the little girl thought. Her mother wore a bathing suit and a white cap with a rubber flower on the side.

Maria turned the pages of her book. It was a book with pictures, and it was written in Spanish. She watched the approaching woman with an expression of indifference. She knew the blond lady was in the movie they were making at the big hotel, but it would never have occurred to her that the pasty gringa with the capri pants and the head scarf was *La Magnifica* herself.

The blonde scuffed her feet in the water, sending salt spray up in little fountains.

"Hi," she said as she got closer. "Catch any fish today?"

"How could we?" the boy replied with a crowing laugh. "We don't have any fishing poles."

"Oh, you don't need poles," the lady said with a shake of her head. "All you have to do is want the fish, and they'll swim right over and ask you to catch them."

"That's silly," the boy retorted.

"Would the fish die if we caught them?" the little girl wanted to know. "I wouldn't like it if they died."

"Oh, no," the lady answered. "That wouldn't be nice at all. The fish wouldn't die. They'd swim into your little moat here and you could scoop them up and take them home and put them in a glass bowl and watch them swim around."

"You still need poles," the little boy pronounced. He walked over to his sand castle and began to kick it with his tanned bare feet. "I saw the men fishing on the pier, and they all had poles."

"The fish I'm talking about are called grunions," the blond lady explained. Her forehead creased as she talked, like someone who really wanted them to understand. "They swim very close to shore, and you can really catch them in a bowl if you want to."

"Do you have any little girls?"

The lady stood very still. She looked toward the place where the sun would be if the fog weren't so thick. One hand touched her tummy very lightly and she said, "I hope I'm going to. Very soon."

She smiled, and the smile was like the sun breaking through the Southern California morning fog. "Very, very soon," she repeated.

21. The Extra

If Johnny had just kept his mouth shut, he might have gotten away with it. But then, if he had, nobody would have believed him, so what would have been the point?

The whole point was that he had to kiss Marilyn and all the guys on

Coronado had to know he kissed her. That way, his father couldn't get away with calling him a faggot on account of he wanted to go to MIT instead of Annapolis.

He started out just wanting to meet her, but all the guys razzed him when he talked about it, so he bet Carl Rasmussen that he wouldn't just meet Marilyn, he'd kiss her.

He'd kiss her right in front of the Del.

And Carl could watch, and then Carl could pay up, 'cause he, Johnny, was going to do it, and when he said he was going to do a thing, that thing was as good as done.

Which I could have told Carl was the truth because I was there that time in seventh grade, which Carl wasn't, being as his father was stationed in Hawaii that year. And I knew that if Johnny Benson said he was going to kiss Marilyn Monroe, then she was going to get kissed, come hell or high water.

What I didn't know was exactly how much hell there was going to be.

22. The Director's Assistant

"When Marilyn Monroe walks into a room, nobody's going to be watching Tony Curtis playing Joan Crawford."

That's an exact quote, I can assure you. I was in the room when she said it, right to Mr. Wilder's face. She made him reshoot the opening, said she wouldn't finish the picture unless he—

Yes, she said Joan Crawford—and isn't Miss Crawford just going to die when she sees that in print? I mean, I can't look at Tony in his costume any more without thinking of Joan.

Did I hear what Mr. Wilder said about doing another movie with Marilyn?

Well, yes, but I don't think I really ought to—

Well, since you already know, I guess it won't hurt to—

He said, "I've discussed the matter with my doctor and my accountant, and they tell me I am too old and too rich to go through this again."

Yes, that's what he said. But please don't quote me.

23. The Studio Doc

You've had two tube pregnancies, I reminded her. And then I had to explain for probably the fifteenth time exactly what that meant. You have two Fallopian tubes, Miss Monroe, I said. And what they're supposed to do is carry your eggs down to your womb so that if you get pregnant, the baby can grow in your womb like it's supposed to.

Understand?

I was using words I'd use to explain menstruation to a slow thirteen-year-old, and the look I'd get from her was as if I was trying to explain Einstein's theory. No comprehension.

Your trouble is that your eggs don't travel all the way to the womb. They stay in the tubes, so that when the sperm fertilizes the egg, it starts growing in the tube. This is called an ectopic pregnancy, and it won't work. The baby can't grow that way.

Your chances of having a normal pregnancy, Miss Monroe? Slim to none, I'd answer. With your history, slim to none.

24. The Private Eye

This job is pointless. I've got a film of Unguentine on my face so thick it traps gnats, that's how long I've been out in the sun watching Monroe. And so far, nobody's come close to her except a couple of toddlers, only it was her got close to them instead of the other way around.

If something doesn't happen by the end of the day, I'm off this job. Money or no money, DiMaggio or no DiMaggio.

25. The Drama Student

He wouldn't listen. He wrote me an autograph and said I should keep studying. He said he'd write me a recommendation to the Yale Drama School if I wanted him to, but he wouldn't listen.

I looked up into his face, all white and drawn with suffering, and I knew what I had to do.

I was wrong trying to talk to him. He's too noble and good to betray the woman he loves. The woman he thinks he loves. Next time I'll talk to Her.

Only I won't just talk.

26. The Extra

Johnny had it all planned. He needed a diversion, he said. Just like in the war. He needed somebody to help distract the people around Marilyn so he could step in and make his move.

He didn't mean any harm.

Honest.

He was just a kid who wanted to impress his buddies.

So we started by tossing a flying saucer back and forth on the beach. You know, those round disks you throw and somebody catches them? Anyway, Tug Murphy had one and we tossed it around, getting pretty close to where the grips were setting up the next shot. One of the grips yelled at us to move away, but we hollered and pretended not to hear. So the grip steps over to Tug and says something and Tug said something back, and pretty soon a lot of grips were walking over to straighten things out.

Marilyn was just standing there, in this funny bathing suit that didn't show nearly enough of her attributes, if you know what I mean. She was shivering on account of it was breezy out there by the shore. Nobody from the movie was standing near her. It was weird, like none of them wanted to be close to her. The funny old lady with the big black hat was sitting in one of the canvas chairs, watching like a hawk, but she was too far away to do anything.

Which was why Johnny made his move. He ran out of the crowd and made straight for Marilyn.

27. The Drama Student

I was watching in the crowd, waiting for my opportunity. I'd been there the day before, and the day before that, and there hadn't been an opportunity, but I was certain that today was the day my luck would change. And it did.

It was a boy, a stupid boy. He ran out of the crowd toward Her as if he was going to catch her in a flying tackle.

She screamed and her hand flew to her mouth and she jumped back. She jumped back toward me. Toward where I stood in the crowd with my knife at my side, waiting for my opportunity.

Waiting to liberate the greatest playwright in the English language from his stupid mistake.

28. The Private Eye

Like everybody else, I saw the kid. Like everybody else, I reacted—only, being a professional, I reacted a little faster. The trouble was, I was reacting to the wrong threat. I didn't see the girl until it was too late.

Until the little bitch raised the knife and screamed like a banshee in heat and lunged at Marilyn.

I had the kid in a wrestling hold I learned in high school, but I let him go and went after the girl.

But the kid was young and strong and I was getting beerbellied and slow. He got there first—and so did the knife.

By the time the cops came, I had her under control and the knife in my hand.

But the kid had been cut. Cut bad, too, judging from the amount of blood seeping into the white sand.

29. The Extra

Johnny saved her life. At least that was what she said.

All around her, people were yelling and screaming. Some of the women ran backwards, screeching as if they'd seen a hundred mice. The big guy grabbed the girl around her waist and took the knife away from her, but she wouldn't stop crying that she was going to kill Marilyn and nobody was going to stop her. Johnny and the big guy already had stopped her, but she didn't recognize that.

With all the yelling and running, you'd have thought Marilyn would take off for safety, run over to the old lady in the black hat or something. But she didn't. She just stood there while everyone else went crazy and then she knelt down in the sand and picked up Johnny's head and put it in her lap.

And when the guys with the stretcher came pushing through the crowd, she bent down and kissed him on the lips.

Which is when I turned to Carl Rasmussen and told him he'd better pay up or else. I didn't spell out what the or else was going to be because my voice was shaking so bad I thought I was going to cry.

Which was pretty weird on account of all that happened was that Johnny did what he said he was going to do.

30. The Cop

Sure, the movie people hushed it up. Can you blame them? The kid was okay—well, okay if you think thirty-eight stitches in the shoulder is okay, but you get my point. Nobody died or anything. They took the girl over to the state hospital, but this kind of publicity the movie didn't need, so they asked us all to keep it as quiet as possible.

And no, this isn't Hollywood, it's Coronado, but have you ever been anyplace where money doesn't talk?

Well, I haven't. So when the Chief said the whole thing never happened, I saluted smartly and said, What never happened, sir? You'll go far, boy, the old man replied. And he was right.

31. The Actor

Three words of dialogue; sixty-five takes. Sixty-fucking-five. That's the story of this picture in a nutshell. Wilder's going nuts, the actors are going nuts, the crew's loving the overtime, and this picture may sink into the ocean like a chunk of cliff in an earthquake.

32. The Letter

She sits at the little round table in her room. There's a piece of Hotel Del stationery in front of her, and a powder-blue typewriter in a plastic case.

She smiles at the paper, picks up a pencil, and draws on the hotel's logo at the top of the page. It shows the sprawling building, with its distinctive mushroom rooftop, beside the beach. She makes a quick stick-figure drawing of herself in the billowing waves and writes the word "help" next to it, as if the figure were drowning.

Then she slips the paper into the carriage return, smartly maneuvers it to a space below the logo, and types in the date: September 11, 1958.

The letter is to a friend in New York. She tells him that the boat she is on is sinking and refers to the Straits of Dire. She adds that she has nothing to worry about as she has no phallic symbol to lose.

She smiles wryly, then hits the carriage bar several times to leave room for the oversized signature she intends to write. Another thought strikes her, and she adds:

PS "Love me for my yellow hair alone"

33. The Local Doctor

"I asked for a doctor, not a nurse," the tall man with the dark-rimmed glasses said when he answered my knock.

I've heard this before; female doctors are not usual, even in the field of gynecology. "I am a doctor," I said, keeping my tone even. "May I see your wife, please?"

He stepped aside and let me in.

"She's in the bathroom," he said. There was an edge of disgust in his tone; he turned abruptly and made for the door. "Tell my wife I'm going down to the set to tell the director that she's too sick to film today." He was speaking loudly enough for the woman in the bathroom to hear, and he pronounced the word "sick" with quotation marks around it. I had the distinct feeling I had been summoned as a witness to the fact that Miss Monroe was feigning her illness.

I'd heard the rumors; I'd even read a movie magazine or two. I knew Marilyn's reputation as a difficult actress, and as a woman who ingested pills the way other people chewed gum.

So I stepped into the bathroom with a brisk, businesslike air, expecting to see a spoiled star with a barbiturate hangover.

She squatted on the toilet seat, her head between her knees. She groaned weakly and sobbed as I approached. Her arms hugged her stomach; on the floor next to the commode lay a silk slip soaked in blood.

POSTSCRIPT

Marilyn Monroe. who had all but completed shooting the new Billy Wilder comedy Some Like It Hot, *was hospitalized today in Southern California. Doctors announced she had suffered a miscarriage; Miss Monroe is married to Pulitzer prize-winning playwright Arthur Miller. Mr. Miller, emerging from his wife's bedside at an undisclosed hospital, declined to be interviewed.*

—New York *Mirror*

Another Day, Another Dollar

by Warren Murphy

STEPHANIE CROWDER WAS TOLD her brother was dead by the foreman who took her off the assembly line at the auto factory just outside Philadelphia. He told her he did not have the details but that the body had been found near Pittsburgh, and that someone in the personnel manager's office had the details.

"Okay. Look, let me finish my shift," Stephanie said.

"It's considered unsafe to let someone back on the line after a traumatic experience," said the foreman.

"I'm okay," said Stephanie.

She was installing doors in the new subcompacts and she had her rhythm for the shift and it would soon be over. There was a lot of noise, but there was always lots of noise on an assembly line. She could hum to herself. She could sing. She could even feel the rhythm of the line, and the shift was almost over anyway.

"You're supposed to be the next of kin. The only next of kin," said the foreman.

"Sure. I raised Nate. I'm sister, mother. He's the only person I've got. Can I get back to the line?"

"Did you hear me? Your brother is dead. There are some people up in the personnel manager's office who want to speak to you."

Stephanie Crowder shook her head.

"You didn't hear me?"

"He's not dead," said Stephanie. "He's not dead. Why are you saying that? Why are you saying those things? Because I'm a woman?"

She was crying, even though she had vowed, back when she began work on the line, that she would not cry in front of the men. She had come to the line fifteen years before, when women did not work the line. She had come out of the clean white office with the soft rugs and the gentle hum of the electric typewriters, where the loudest noise was a soft laugh from an executive, and if there was a spot on a desk, one called maintenance to remove it.

She had come down to this hellish din, fortified with warnings that women did not belong there. She had heard that she was too beautiful to be working down in the lines. There was always a lascivious wink with that, and she would ask:

"If I were white, would you say that?"

Stephanie Crowder was a beautiful woman with strong dark features and a sense of a majesty about her face. At first, almost everyone on the line had made a sexual advance, some even suggesting that she could make a fortune as a hooker, and even reaching into their pockets to prove it.

But Stephanie Crowder showed that she had what it took to do a day's work. She never complained and she never let anyone down.

Of course, for a while there she wouldn't lend anyone a dollar if he needed it for a blood transfusion. But they found out later it wasn't that she was cheap. It was just that she needed every penny for something. And when that had ended, more than a few years before, she became such a soft touch that her coworkers had to protect her.

She never dogged her work. She never buckled to either management or the union. She was, as everyone said, a standup guy. And soon, they called her "Steve."

For her part, Stephanie Crowder did not know what the fuss was all about. She had simply come to the line determined to show everyone there that she was as good as anyone else. In that, everyone agreed, she had failed. She was better than anyone else.

And Stephanie's first rule had been that she would not cry on the line, and now she was doing it.

"Why do you say things like that? Why do you say them?"

"Hey, Steve, I ain't making this shit up."

"Liar," she yelled. "Liar."

Two riveters seeing Steve Crowder yelling at the foreman knew something had to be wrong and it had to be the foreman. Steve Crowder wasn't a complainer, and that moron of a foreman had her crying and yelling. When the riveters quit, the other workers walked off the line too, because they thought there was a major grievance going on, and when they saw Steve Crowder crying and yelling, they were sure there was a major grievance going on.

The line stopped. Unfinished cars hung in mid-air. Riveting guns lay silent. Welding torches flickered out in a last dip of a blue-yellow flame as if the day were done.

"No," she cried. "No. No. No."

"Her brother died," the foreman explained sheepishly.

"Nate. God, no. Not Nate. Not my baby brother."

It took a while to get the line started up again. There were many women there now, unlike when Steve Crowder had come down there from the front office. There had been man jobs and woman jobs, just as generations ago there had been black jobs and white jobs. The auto industry led everything in America—from advancement to decline and then back to advancement.

And in this plant, they were all talking about Stephanie Crowder's brother. He had been killed in Pittsburgh along with his wife, and because he was black and his wife was white, some of them thought some racist did it. Whatever it was, he didn't deserve death, because if you knew Steve Crowder and you knew she had raised the boy, you knew he had to be a straight arrow.

Then one of Stephanie's close friends let everyone know why she had come down to the line in the first place. It had been that same baby brother, Nathaniel.

She had been a top secretary in the front office at twenty-one, some said the best typist, even among old-timers who had really learned well. Even way back then they were talking of sending her to school and making her an executive, or if not that, at least executive secretary to one of the vice presidents.

Then one day Stephanie Crowder came into her boss's office and said she wanted to work on the line. Her boss and the personnel manager and everyone else told her that was foolish, that she had a great future in the office.

"I need the money now," she had told them.

"You can get a loan."

"I need more money for a long time. And I don't want to owe anybody, thank you."

What she needed it for was her younger brother. Her parents had died and she was left to raise him.

"So that's why she wouldn't lend anybody money a long time ago?" asked one of the workers.

"Sure. She put him in a private school and then college and then graduate school. When she stopped paying for all that, she had money to spare," said the friend.

Stephanie Crowder did not hear her coworkers talking about her. She had followed someone to the personnel manager's office.

They were saying Nate was dead. They were wrong. They had to be wrong because Nate who was living very happily in Columbus, Ohio, was going on a vacation with Beatrice and the baby. He was an engineer now. He was doing very well. He knew how to save. She had taught him that. She had taught him the things he would need, all the things Dad would have taught if Dad had lived.

When Dad died, Nate was fourteen and beginning to hang around with a bad gang. There was dope. There were guns. And every time there was another shooting or drug incident, the schools would hold another sensitivity-training session for the white teachers to instruct them in what were supposed to be black values.

Well, the Crowders were black and they had values and those values weren't drugs and they weren't guns. Their main value was hard work and more hard work in a world that was not too kind to black people. It was saving. It was doing without. It was doing with less. It was living on secondhand everything because Dad refused to buy hot merchandise.

"Stealin' is stealin', Stephanie. Even if you don't see who was robbed. When you buy hot goods, child, you're stealin' from yourself."

There was pride in everything they owned because it was honestly come by. They didn't believe in big shiny cars. They didn't put all their money on their backs.

Dad and Mother were married in church and they didn't know each other physically until the night the reverend pronounced them man and wife.

They had a savings account. They had two children and they did not think philandering was cause for mirth and winking. In brief, they had very traditional black values and in their lifetimes, they lived by them.

Shortly after they died in an auto accident, Nate came home laughing about a "sensitivity outreach conference" where somebody had been stupid enough to pay him money to tell whites from the suburbs how their values were outmoded. Nate was always sharp and could talk a blue streak. He was fourteen. He had a pocketful of money. He talked jive. He was learning black English in school, busting verbs, slopping filth into his language, and laughing at it.

"Nate, Grandma talked that way because she didn't know better. But she wanted her children to know better. They didn't have schools for us when Grandma was young. But they do for you."

"You a jiveass nigger, turkey," said Nate. The first thing Stephanie did was to slap her younger brother silly. The next thing she did was enroll him at a private school outside Philadelphia. It was strict. It did not teach black English. In fact, it did not teach one course that was called relevant.

"That's what I want," she said. She didn't care what it cost. Nate was registered before she realized her secretary's salary wouldn't cover the tuition. It was then that she told the front office that she wanted an assembly-line job. She needed the money and she needed it right away. She did not tell them why. It was none of their business.

Later she would tell friends. Her values, her very black values, would not allow others to know of her troubles unless they were friends. She also did not want any favors because she was a woman. That was a black value too.

All she wanted was a job on the line.

She got it and when she first heard the din of the assembly line, she felt her head would break open in pain, but she told herself:

"Stephanie, don't you cry. Don't you dare cry here."

So she cried at night, when Nate couldn't hear her, and she cried for two years until, mercifully, her hearing started to go. And she didn't cry once on the line for fifteen years until the man came down to tell her Nate was dead.

Which couldn't be. Nate was such a fine young man. Nate couldn't be dead.

They had made a mistake. Lots of whites made mistakes when it came to identifying blacks. Maybe a black man had stolen Nate's wallet and was killed near Pittsburgh. Nate didn't want to worry her and he merely bought himself a new wallet. And the man who stole it, like many thieves, had gotten himself killed. Thieves were trash. They were killed all the time. And the people who found that thief's body just assumed that the black man was Nate.

That's what she was going to tell them in the personnel office.

They took her to a harshly lit cubicle behind frosted glass. Two men were there. They were Pittsburgh detectives. They told her that Nate and Beatrice were found strangled in some open land near the Pittsburgh airport.

"No, no. Nate's going skiing with his family," said Stephanie. She took off her grease-laden cap and shook out her wiry hair. She did not sit down, because she knew her pants would leave a stain on the furniture. "He must have lost his wallet," she said.

"Miss Crowder, we didn't identify him by his picture. We identified the body by fingerprints. Mr. Crowder was in a very sensitive technological job and his fingerprints were on file. So were his wife's."

"Nate," screamed Stephanie, feeling her legs go weak, not wanting to mess the chair up with her pants, not able to stand up. She leaned against the desk. "Nate. My baby brother. Nate."

"I'm sorry, ma'am," said one of the detectives.

Stephanie Crowder cried in the personnel office amid typewriters she had once been able to use better than anyone, in a very clean place that she was no longer used to working in. She did not know how long she cried, but when she finally looked up, there was a difference. The pain was still there, still to be felt, still to be suffered on so many nameless nights and mornings when little things would remind her of that fine young man now dead, and his beautiful wife, and their beautiful baby who would never have a chance to share her parents' love.

There was no more time for tears. There was a child to be looked after, a child to be raised right. Catrice was a black girl and she would need extra-special care because this was a world in which black girls were not safe from many things. There would be more time for crying perhaps when Catrice was grown up and strong, strong as her daddy had been.

"I will be seeing Catrice now. Where is she?"

"Who?"

"Catrice. Their baby. They went skiing with their baby."

"Was there a baby?" one detective asked the other.

"I don't know of any baby."

"Where is the baby? Where is the baby?" Stephanie Crowder was yelling again. The real horror was only beginning.

Because Stephanie Crowder did not blame all her troubles on whites did not mean she trusted them either. She knew too well how some whites thought that a black life was not quite a human life. She knew too well how a black child might not be as important in this world as a white one.

But what horrified her as she went from one office to another in Pittsburgh, and then to children's homes and juvenile courts and social services, was that the world was not safe for white children either.

When she gave her sketchy description of the missing Catrice, along with a half-dozen grainy snapshots her brother had sent her, a detective with compassion told her that the best thing she could do for herself was to forget the child.

"I'm not going to forget her. Do you know how dangerous it is out there for a little black girl? How easy it is for her to wind up with pervs? Or to be on dope? Nobody's going to care if she can even read or write. She's black and I've got to get her back."

"Lady," said the detective, "I'm not just talking about black children. Every year, maybe twenty-five thousand, maybe fifty thousand children disappear and are never seen again. That's like what we lost in Vietnam. And most of the kids are white. Do yourself a favor. Bury your niece in your heart."

"Sir, I am a Crowder. I do not give up."

"Then you're going to waste a life."

"I don't consider trying to save my kin a waste of my life. Failing to try would be a waste of my life. Good day, sir," said Stephanie Crowder. She walked out of the police station into the thick air of Pittsburgh, numb to the world and to the traffic. She did not know where to begin. It was a huge country.

She took a flight home because this one airline was even cheaper than the buses. It charged for the water. It probably charged to use the toilets, she told herself, so she didn't drink and she didn't relieve herself, and when she got back to her walkup flat in a dismal development in Philadelphia, she wrote down what she was up against and what she had going for her.

On the top of her list was that she would not give up. Somewhere in the middle was the fact that she had good looks. Somewhere else was the fact that she was a bit more intelligent than the average person. And then she threw it all away and wrote down one word.

"Crowder."

It was a slave name, taken from the whites who had owned her ancestors, but at no time had she ever believed that the whites who owned the name did it more honor than the blacks. In fact, if she were to be realistic about the whole thing, she had never met a white Crowder that she didn't feel a little bit sharper than, although of course she couldn't be sure. Daddy had told her that too: "Don't judge, Stephanie. Not until you know."

She was a Crowder and that was what she had going for her. She started on the list of things she had going against her. It began with the difficulties of identification, the size of America, the possibility that Catrice might not even be in the country. It included among other things that she was going to need a lot of money to support her rescue mission.

That problem was solved when she returned to the plant to ask for a leave of absence. The people in the plant had raised $19,625.83 for her.

"We didn't know what else to do. We all just wanted to help. We felt so damned helpless. So take a vacation, Steve. Do something good for yourself for a change."

"I'll do something good for myself."

The next day she started her leave of absence. She bought herself new clothes that cost a thousand dollars, even though she bargained for them in one of the low-priced outlets. She bought things that accentuated her fine full bosom, the sleek curve of her waist, with shoes that showed legs that were still stunning.

"Stephanie," she asked herself. "Are you going to use your body? Are you really going to use it?" And she answered herself. Absolutely. She was going to use her body because she didn't have an army.

It was not hard to pick up a cop in a Philadelphia bar. But what Stephanie wanted was a homicide detective. She found one, a man she thought was a little bit too sweet to be a policeman. He couldn't believe his good luck. Stephanie, in her new clothes and makeup highlighting her elegant features, turned heads in bars. The detective was also surprised at how interested she was in his work. She told him her name was Florence.

"Tell me," she said. "If a couple is murdered, how would you go about finding their killers?"

His name was Big Mo, he was middle-aged, smoked awful cigars, and said, "What do you mean?"

"Two people traveling are killed, found dead. How would you go about finding who killed them?"

"Traveling is bad. That's a bad one. Say they're found in their living room."

"I'd prefer traveling."

"You want to learn or you want to teach?"

Stephanie went to Big Mo's dirty apartment and listened to him describe examining the death scene, looking to see if there were any signs of robbery, and if there weren't, finding the last people who had seen the victims, talking to their friends. Especially talking to their friends.

"Why their friends?"

"Because ninety-five percent of all homicides are done by people who knew each other."

"So if there's a murder and you want to find the murderer, you talk to the friends."

"Unless, of course, they're traveling."

"Why does traveling make it different?"

"Because that means they probably don't know the people who killed them and if that's the case you're probably not going to collar the killers."

"Why not?"

"Because just about the only homicides we ever nail are the family ones. You know, boyfriend kills girlfriend, wife kills husband, like that."

"What about detective work? What about looking for clues?"

"We look. Of course we look."

"What for?"

"Clues."

"I know that, dammit. What kind?"

"Who their friends are."

Big Mo had a hand on her leg. She had already decided that she was going to let him proceed further. But she wanted more information first.

"Suppose they're strangled?"

"Ain't too many stranglings. I had one once't a year or so ago, some woman near the airport. I think maybe her husband did it 'cause he left her to go be a mountain man or something, but we never could find him to pin it on him. A strangling is something you remember. We get a lot of guns but mostly knives. If you really want to stop the big killing weapon in the country, end the kitchen knife. Outlaw the kitchen knife," said Big Mo, then thought of something that gave him a chuckle, something for a bumper sticker:

"If kitchens are outlawed, only outlaws will eat."

"So you had a strangling near the airport?"

"Yeah."

"That's a coincidence. I heard of another one like that near Pittsburgh," Stephanie said.

"And there was one up in Allentown six months ago. So what? Come on. We didn't come up here to talk business."

"There might be a gang doing all these killings," said Stephanie. She pushed away his hand.

"Nahhh, it's people see somebody does something and so they do it too."

"How do you know?"

"'Cause that's the way it always is," Big Mo said. "What do you want from me anyway?"

"I want to know who, what, when, where, and why."

"What are you, a reporter?"

"I just want to know."

She got no further answers that night, and Big Mo did not get lucky either. She went to police headquarters the next day to ask about the Philadelphia airport strangling, but was told it was none of her business. What was she, a reporter?

But the police did not know they were dealing with a Crowder. If Stephanie Crowder was to find her niece, she had to have information, and just plain citizens did not get information. They got public relations.

She flew back to Pittsburgh on the same cheap airline she had used the last time. In a suburb, she found a newspaper fighting a lawsuit claiming it discriminated against minorities. She went in and, using the name of Beverly, applied for a job as a cub reporter, pointing out that with a single hiring, the paper could fill two minority slots, a woman and a black. The interviewer didn't even ask if she could type.

She could type, but she couldn't write. Still, with her looks there were a half-dozen male reporters willing to show her. The one she accepted help from, though, was a gin-smelling overweight garbage can of a man who told her that her copy stank and that she shouldn't expect to learn how to write in a week or so, if ever. He resented the fact that she had gotten the job because of her sex and her color. He didn't hide that.

But this man knew how to write a story, and he showed her. Her copy came back from him with more red pencil than there was typing.

She knew then he was right. She wasn't going to learn how to write anytime soon.

"You don't have to learn how to write," he said. "Just keep on being a woman and being black. That may get you a Pulitzer Prize."

"I don't want a Pulitzer Prize."

"Then why'd you take the damned job?"

"Because I've got questions and I can't get answers unless I'm a reporter."

"What kind of questions?"

"It's private, but I'm trying to save somebody's life, somebody close to me."

"You type good, you think good. You ask good questions. Maybe I can get you by. But I've got to know what you're looking for."

"If I tell you, you'll turn it into a story and I don't want a story yet. I want somebody alive. I've got to be a reporter for that."

The reporter's name was Barney. He let her buy him a few beers. Then he let her buy him a few Scotches. They worked out a system where she gathered the facts—did the legwork, as he called it—and he wrote the story. She turned out to be a stunning legman.

A week later, the newspaper guild made her a member, and Stephanie immediately went to the city editor with a proposition.

When he heard the word "proposition," he said, "Any time," and winked.

It was a joke, of course, but Stephanie Crowder had not come up to the city desk to joke.

"I want to do a story on unsolved murders," she said.

"That's the police beat. You're on neighborhood news."

"I mean all over the country."

"What would we be doing a story about all over the country?" he said. "We're a dink paper in a dink town." The city editor was not a thirty-year employee on this small daily because he had much in the way of imagination or talent or skill. He became city editor the way most small dailies got their city editors, from the ranks of reporters who grew old without making major mistakes. His main job was to keep the paper safe. In a few more years, when he became even more cautious and less imaginative, he would be made managing editor. And if time and stomach problems did not take his life, sometime after that he might be made editor in chief, so he could speak at luncheons and dinners on the courage of the press.

"Are you against this story because some of the victims might be blacks?" Stephanie asked.

The city editor perceived a charge of racism looming over the horizon, threatening to obliterate his inevitable promotion to managing editor.

"How long would you want to work on this story?"

"A couple of months."

"Too long. You know how expensive it is to have a reporter cover a story. We can't have you go running around the country on one feature. It doesn't make sense. It's not racism. It's common sense. I happen to be very sensitive to racial issues."

"What if I take a leave of absence and you don't have to pay me?"

"Can't do that."

"Why not?"

"The guild. The union. They won't like it."

Stephanie had been around the newspaper long enough to know the reporters' union was not as strong as the United Auto Workers. On this newspaper, it was almost a social club.

"What if I get an okay from the union?"

"Well . . . I don't know."

But there was no okay from the reporters' union. The union saw this leave time as a device by management to get reporters to work for free. It saw a threat to the spirit of organized labor. It saw all kinds of dangers, but mainly it was composed of other reporters, who were afraid she might be on to a better story than any of them were doing.

Stephanie's friend, the sloppy drunk, had the answer.

"Just take off and do it," said Barney.

"Won't they fire me?"

"No. That would mean they have to do something. Somebody would have to make a decision. No reporter has ever gone off on a story by himself without pay before. If they don't pay you, you're not costing them anything. If they don't fire you, they can't be accused of racism."

"What about the union?"

"They'll be happy to see you leave town for whatever reason. You've already made them very nervous by suggesting such things."

"Thanks, Barney," she said and gave him a big kiss. But the stench of gin was so strong she had to back away immediately.

Stephanie Crowder, the descendant of Crowders and of people

whose African names had been torched from memories with whips and guns, was on the attack.

She could now ask who, what, when, where, and why. And what she found out right away was that not everybody else asked those questions.

Nate and Beatrice had been strangled in a field near the Pittsburgh airport, probably with wire, soon after getting off their Westworld flight. There were no signs of a baby or a stroller anywhere near the bodies. The money had apparently been stolen from Nate's wallet but not from Beatrice's purse. And some witness, whose name the police forgot to get, thought she remembered seeing the young couple talking to a young white couple who were carrying knapsacks and who dressed like hippies.

She went to Allentown and found out from the police that the woman killed near that airport had been robbed of exactly $48.65. She had been strangled. Her jewelry had not been touched. She had been traveling with her baby and the baby was missing.

A reporter now, with a valid up-to-date press card issued to a fake name, Stephanie Crowder went to Philadelphia and talked to airport officials and to the police and found out that the woman who had been murdered near that airport almost a year before had been traveling with a baby, who was not found. She was strangled too, and the killer took her watch but not her diamond wedding ring or her money.

A witness recalled seeing the woman talking to two young people. "I remember them because they looked like Sonny and Cher in the TV reruns,—you know, like dorky clothes and all that."

Stephanie Crowder rented a motel room, lay on the bed, and put her good no-nonsense mind to work trying to figure out these mysteries.

First of all, they weren't really robberies. Robbers wouldn't have left so much behind with the bodies. Whoever it was just took enough to make it look like a robbery.

Obviously, the real thing of value that had been taken was a baby, and she was very upset that none of the police had ever thought of trying to link up these separate incidents into a pattern of crime.

The murders were all by strangling and they were all committed against people who had flown Westworld American Air.

She had a hunch. She went to a travel agency and got all the brochures she could find on Westworld American Air, which billed itself as "the country's lowest-cost airline."

Back in her room, she found out that Westworld had its headquarters in Columbus, Ohio, and that it flew basically shuttle flights among a handful of eastern cities. There were Pittsburgh and Allentown and Philadelphia and four more cities, and after tireless phoning of those other four cities—"I'm a reporter and I need to know"—she found out that all of them had had people strangled and babies missing in the last eighteen months.

She closed the brochures and sat at the small writing table in her dingy room and rubbed her eyes, trying to contain her excitement.

Catrice was alive. Nobody committed murder to kidnap babies if they were just going to kill them. She was going to get her back. And then she was going to raise Catrice as she had raised Catrice's father. There would be horrors to overcome, but the Crowders were used to that. She would get the child back. She would go on.

She flew Westworld to Columbus, Ohio, and at four PM was hanging around in the hallways outside the Westworld offices. A group of young executive types came out, and she followed them to a nearby cocktail lounge where singles met. She listened to them talk and then selected the highest-ranking one who was married, and on the next day, she bought him a drink. His name was Keith. She told him her name was Clarissa.

Men always liked to talk about their work and Keith was no exception, and Stephanie Crowder had always been a very good listener. So it was that a few days later, Stephanie had the passenger lists for the seven flights which had ended with someone being killed and some baby being kidnapped.

She told Keith that she had to go away for a few days and went back to her hotel room to study the passenger lists. She had not really expected that she would find some couple whose names would turn up on all seven flights, and she didn't, so she wrote down all the names and addresses of people apparently traveling as husband and wife. There were forty-one couples on the seven flights. She started to weep when she saw the names of Nate and Beatrice on one of the passenger manifests, but she angrily brushed the tears away.

The next day she rented a car and bought a map of Columbus and began driving all around the city to the forty-one addresses.

Seven of the addresses did not exist.

She needed a cop again and she found one, a paper-thin, elegantly dressed black detective, whom she followed to an Alcoholics

Anonymous meeting. His name was Zach—she told him her name was Jasmine—and his hands shook nervously. She bought him coffee and told him she was a reporter working on a big story and the case would be his if he would just give her a little help.

He tried to find out what the story was, but Stephanie was not about to tell it to someone who had a drinking problem, even if he was recovering. She would have to know him a lot longer before she decided whether he could be trusted.

Besides, she meant to keep her promise. If there turned out to be a story here, she would give it to Zach, but only later. She told him exactly that, and Zach, with the hopeful fatalism that sustains the recovering alcoholic, simply nodded and took her list of names to headquarters, where he ran them through the department computers.

"We didn't have any of these seven couples in the computer," he said. Stephanie was so depressed she almost didn't hear him say, "But . . ."

"But what?"

"So I ran them through a different listing, and what do you know?" Zach was grinning. "Two of those names were used before as aliases by this couple of badasses."

"Who are they?"

"I pulled their sheets. Jack and Donna Kean. Theft, robbery, prostitution, con games. They're druggies. Man, they're young but they've been busy."

He showed her the long computer printout of Jack and Donna Kean's crimes. Looking at it, Stephanie Crowder said, "Why aren't they in jail if they're so bad?"

Zach took the paper back. "I looked that up too. They got a good lawyer, a guy named Fred Winslow."

"You know him?" she asked.

"Just by reputation. He's a rich guy out in the suburbs. He doesn't do much criminal law."

"Except for these two," Stephanie said.

"That's right."

"Odd, isn't it?"

"If you say it is."

When Stephanie went to the picturesque Ohio village where Fred Winslow lived and practiced law, she found out from page one of the local paper that he was being honored that night for "his trailblazing work in helping childless couples adopt unwanted children. He has enriched the lives of so many," the chairman of the testimonial dinner was quoted as saying.

While Winslow was delivering his speech at the local country club, Stephanie broke into his office, located his adoption files, and in one of them, found a photograph she recognized as her niece, little Catrice. She also found petty-cash receipts for air fares aboard Westworld American Air, on those seven days when people had been murdered and babies were stolen.

Catrice, listed as "abandoned, parents unknown," had been adopted by a family in Tenafly, New Jersey. They had paid the lawyer fifty thousand dollars in fees. Stephanie took the file folder with her and spent the whole night driving to Tenafly, a pretty, upscale town just across the Hudson River from Manhattan.

In the morning, she found the house where Catrice had been taken. She parked her car around the corner and walked by the house. It was Saturday morning, and she saw her little niece on a blanket on the manicured front lawn, being doted on by a young black couple. A plaque on the front lawn read:

FAMILY PHYSICIANS
DR. GERALD BATCHELOR
DR. ANNETTE BATCHELOR

Stephanie Crowder paused outside the house and looked over the white picket fence at the two doctors playing with their adopted daughter, who was smiling and cooing. When they looked up, Stephanie smiled and said, "Your daughter is beautiful."

"Thank you," the woman said.

"A gift from God," Stephanie said.

"We know."

And because she knew she was making them nervous by standing there, Stephanie Crowder choked back her tears, smiled, and walked away. Catrice was all right and she would be all right. She didn't need Aunt Stephanie to protect her from drugs and crime and poverty. Not now, anyway, and there would be time when she was all grown up to let her know that she had the blood of the Crowders in her veins and what that meant.

She walked to her car and started on the long drive back to Columbus, Ohio.

The next night, in what the local newspaper called "a tragic accident that has shattered the community," noted adoption attorney Fred Winslow was killed when his new Mercedes-Benz was forced off the road, apparently by a drunk driver who fled the scene.

A week later, Zach, the detective, received in the mail a badly written report documenting the murderous activities of Jack and Donna Kean, the baby stealers. The unsigned note that came with the report insisted that if the facts led to an arrest, Zach must be sure to personally call a small newspaper on the outskirts of Pittsburgh and let a reporter named Barney be the first to break the story.

The following Monday, Stephanie Crowder was back on the line in the auto plant outside Philadelphia. All day long, coworkers came up to ask if she was all right, and she gave them all the same answer: "I'm fine now."

Then the foreman asked her the same thing, and she said again, "I'm fine. Now let's let it drop. Did we come here to make cars or make conversation?"

Later in the day, Stephanie cut her hand on a piece of sheet metal. At the plant infirmary, the doctor closed up the wound with three stitches. Stephanie Crowder declined anesthetic and did not cry, even when the stitches were going in.

When the doctor commented on this, Stephanie Crowder said, "I'm a Crowder. We don't cry a lot. We just do what we've got to do. Now hurry up. I've got to get back to the line."

Akitada's First Case

by I. J. Parker

Heian Kyo (Kyoto): 11th century—sometime during the Poem-Composing Month (August).

The sun had only been up a few hours, but the archives of the ministry were already stifling in the summer heat. A murky, oppressive air hung about the shelves of document boxes and settled across the low desks. These were normally occupied by scribes and junior clerks, but at the moment they were empty.

Akitada, having celebrated his twentieth birthday with friends the night before—an occasion which involved emptying a cup of wine each time one failed to compose an acceptable poem—had overslept and crept in the back way. Now he knelt at his desk, feeling sick and staring blindly at a dossier he was supposed to be copying. He winced when two of his fellow clerks, Hirosawa and Sanekana walked in, chattering loudly.

"Sugawara!" Hirosawa stopped in surprise. "Where did you come from? The minister's been asking for you. I wouldn't give much for your chances of keeping your position this time."

Sanekana, a pimply fat fellow, sniggered. "You should have seen his face," he announced gleefully. "He was positively gloating at the thought of getting rid of you. Better go to him quick!"

Akitada blanched. He could not afford to lose his clerkship in the Ministry of Justice. It had been the only position offered to him when he graduated from the university. If only the minister had not formed such an instant dislike for him. Inexplicably, His Excellency, Soga Ietada, had found fault with everything Akitada had done until he had become too nervous to answer the simplest questions. As a result, the minister had banished him to the archives to do copy work alongside the scribes.

To make matters worse, his fellow clerks had recognized Akitada as a marked man and quickly disassociated themselves from him.

Akitada eyed Sanekana and Hirosawa dubiously. "I don't suppose you would cover for me?" he asked. "I might have stepped outside when you looked for me."

They burst into laughter.

With a sigh, Akitada rose.

His heart was beating wildly and his palms were sweating when he was shown into the great man's office with the painted screens of waterfowl, the lacquered document boxes, and the broad desk of polished cryptomeria wood. On the desk stood the porcelain planter with a perfect miniature maple tree, the bronze brazier with its enameled wine flask, and the ministerial seal carved from pale jade—all of them witnesses to Akitada's prior humiliations.

The minister was not alone. A thin elderly man in a neat, dark gray silk robe was kneeling on the cushion before the great man's table. "It is a matter of honor, Excellency, no, of life and death to me," he said, his voice uneven with suppressed emotion. "I have, as I explained, exhausted all other possibilities. Your Excellency is my last hope."

"Nonsense!" barked Soga Ietada. Being stout, he was sitting cross-legged at his ease, tapping impatient fingers on the polished surface of his desk. "You take it too seriously. Young women run away all the time. She'll show up one of these days, presenting you with a grandchild, no doubt."

The old man's back stiffened. He did not glance at Akitada, who hovered, greatly embarrassed, near the door. "You are mistaken," the man said. "My daughter left my home to enter the household of a nobleman. She would never engage in a fleeting, clandestine affair."

Soga raised his eyes to heaven, caught a glimpse of Akitada and glared, saying coldly to his guest, "As you say. I can only repeat that it is not in my power to assist you. I suggest you seek out this, er, nobleman. Now you must excuse me. My clerk is waiting to consult me on an urgent case."

Akitada's heart skipped a beat. Maybe it was not another reprimand after all. A case? Would he finally be given a case?

The older man bowed and rose. He left quickly, with only a passing glance at Akitada.

When the door closed, the minister's expression changed to one of cold fury. "And where were you this morning?" he barked.

Akitada fell to his knees and touched his forehead to the floor. "I . . . I was feeling ill," he stuttered. Well, that was the truth at least. His stomach was heaving and he swallowed hard, waiting for the storm to break over his head.

"No matter!" snapped the minister. "Your work has been unsatisfactory from the start. As you know, you came here on probation. Since you have proved inept at all but copying work and are now far behind in that, you cannot afford the luxury of ill health."

"Yes, Your Excellency. I shall make up the time."

"No."

Akitada looked up and caught a smirk of satisfaction on Soga's face. "I assure your Excellency . . . " he began earnestly.

"I said 'no'!" thundered the minister. "Your time has run out. You may get your property and leave the ministry this instant." He slapped a pudgy hand on the document before him. "I have already drawn up the papers of dismissal. They spell out your gross inadequacies in detail."

"But . . . " Akitada sought frantically for some promise, some explanation which might sway the minister's mind, at least postpone his dismissal. "Your Excellency," he pleaded, "you may recall that I earned my position by placing first in the university examinations. Perhaps if I had been given some legal work, I might have proved satis— . . . "

"How dare you criticize my decisions?" cried the minister. "It is a typical example of your poor judgment. I shall add a further adverse comment to my evaluation of your performance."

Akitada bowed wordlessly and left the room. He went straight to his desk, ignoring the curious eyes and whispers of Sanekana and Hirosawa, and gathered his things. These consisted of some writing implements and a few law books and were easily wrapped into a square of cloth, knotted, and tossed over one shoulder. Then he left the ministry.

Suffering under the humiliation of his dismissal, he did not pause to consider the full disaster—the fact that he would no longer draw the small salary which had kept rice in the family bowls and one servant in the house to look after his widowed mother and two younger sisters—until he had passed out of the gate of the Imperial City.

Then the thought of facing his mother with the news made his knees turn to water, and he stopped outside the gate. Lady Sugawara was forever reminding him of a son's duty to his family and complaining about his inadequate salary and low rank. What would she say now?

Before him Suzaku Avenue stretched into the distance. Long, wide, and willow-lined, it bisected the capital to become the great southern highway to Kyushu—and the world beyond.

He longed to keep walking, away from his present life, with his bundle of books and brushes. Somewhere someone must be in need of a young man filled with the knowledge of the law and a thirst for justice.

But he knew it was impossible. All appointments were in the hands of the central government, and besides he could not desert his family. A son's first duty was to his parents. He despaired of finding a clerkship in another bureau. If only there were someone, some man of rank, who would put in a good word for him, but Akitada was without helpful relatives or patrons of that sort.

He sat down on the steps of the gate, and put his head into his hands.

"Young man? Are you ill?"

Akitada glanced up. An elderly gentleman in a formal robe and hat regarded him with kindly interest. Belatedly recognition came. This was the man who had just been turned away by Soga, a fellow sufferer. Akitada rose and bowed.

"Are you not the young fellow who came in while I was with the minister?" the man asked.

"Yes." Akitada recalled the embarrassing subject under discussion and blushed. "I am very sorry, but I had been sent for."

"I know. But I thought you had an urgent case to talk over with the minister?"

Akitada blushed again. "I have been dismissed," he said.

"Oh."

A brief silence fell. Then the older man said sympathetically, "Well, it looks like we've both been dismissed. You look pretty low." He paused, studying Akitada thoughtfully, then added, "Maybe we can be of assistance to each other."

"How so?" Akitada asked dubiously.

The gentleman gestured for him to sit, then gathered the skirt of his gown and lowered himself to the step next to him. "I have lost a daughter and need someone to help me find her, someone who knows the law and can quote it to those who keep showing me the door. And you, I bet, could use the experience, not to mention a weekly salary and a generous reward?"

Akitada looked at the gentleman as the answer to a prayer. "I am completely at your service, sir," he said with fervent gratitude. "Sugawara Akitada is my name, by the way."

"Good. I am Okamoto Toson."

"Not the master of the imperial wrestling office?"

The modest man in the gray robe smiled ruefully. "The same. Let's go to my house."

Okamoto Toson lived in a small house which lay, surrounded by a garden, in a quiet residential street not far from the palace. He was a widower with two daughters. It was the younger who had disappeared so mysteriously.

Okamoto took him to a room which was, like the rest of the house, small, pleasant, and unpretentious. Yet Okamoto was known to be wealthy and he was well respected by nobility and commoners alike. He was a man of the people who had been drawn into the world of the great due to his knowledge of wrestling and his managerial ability.

The walls were covered with scrolls showing the rankings of wrestling champions, but one scroll was a painting of a court match with the nobles seated around the circle where two massive fighters in loincloths strove against one another. The emperor himself had attended and was enthroned under a special tent. Over toward one side of the picture, the artist had depicted the small figure of Okamoto himself.

Akitada wondered why the minister had dismissed such a man without giving him the slightest encouragement.

Okamoto's story was brief but strange. Recently widowed, he had been left with two young daughters. The older had taken over the running of the household, but the younger, Tomoe, was a dreamer who spent her time reading romantic tales and talking of noble suitors. Being apparently something of a beauty according to her father, whose face softened every time he spoke of her, she had attracted the eyes of a certain nobleman and permitted his secret visits—no doubt after the pattern of the novels she had read—and the man had convinced her to leave with him.

All this had taken place without the father's knowledge, and Okamoto was apologetic. Akitada gathered that the death of his wife had caused him to withdraw from all but court duties, and since his older daughter Otomi had run the household efficiently, he had seen no cause to worry.

It was, in fact, the older daughter who had reported her sister's elopement with a nameless nobleman.

At this point in the story, Okamoto excused himself to get his daughter Otomi. Akitada stared after him in dismay. Either the girl had been incredibly foolish or someone had played a very nasty trick on her. No member of the aristocracy would take a young woman as his official wife or concubine without her father's knowledge.

Okamoto returned with a pale, plain young woman in a house dress. He said, "This is my elder daughter, Otomi. Please ask her anything."

Akitada and the young woman bowed to each other. She went to kneel behind her father's cushion, her eyes downcast and her work-reddened hands folded modestly in her lap.

Akitada was unused to speaking to strange young women, but he tried. "Did you know that your sister had a . . . er . . . met someone?"

The young woman shook her head and said, "My sister did not confide in me. She is a foolish girl. She is always reading stories, and sometimes she makes them up. I did not think anything when she said she had fallen in love with a nobleman."

"You did not share a room?" Akitada asked, puzzled how a lover could have visited Tomoe without her sister's knowledge.

To his dismay, Otomi began to weep in harsh, racking sobs. Akitada shot a helpless look at Okamoto.

The older man smiled a little sadly. "Hush, Otomi!" he said, explaining, "The girls did not get along. Tomoe said her sister snored, and Otomi wanted her to stop reading by candlelight."

Otomi sniffled. "I think she just said those things because she wanted to be alone to receive this person. How could she go away with him like that in the middle of the night without a word to anyone! But my father has always allowed her to do whatever she wished."

Okamoto shook his head. "No, Otomi. You exaggerate." Turning to

Akitada, he said, "This is really not like Tomoe. No goodbye! Not so much as a letter! I am afraid the poor child has been abducted by a man who had no intention of treating her honorably. That is why we must find her." His short, stubby hands became fists. "This person of rank knew we are only ordinary people without learning and he thought it would be easy to fool us. You, being a young gentleman yourself, will understand much better than I the person who took my child. What do you think we should do? Please speak frankly. I shall not take offense. My child's life is precious to me."

Akitada hesitated. It crossed his mind that Tomoe had run off with some commoner, perhaps even a rich man's servant. He said awkwardly, "I do not want to worry you more, but I am wondering why the minister dismissed you. You are a highly respected man, and have had the honor of addressing His Majesty."

The older man looked uncomfortable. "I was a little surprised myself. Still, I am nobody. It is only my association with wrestling which brings me in contact with the 'good people.'"

Akitada turned back to the young woman. "I assume you never saw your sister's visitor. But perhaps she described him when she talked about him. Anything, the smallest detail, may help me to find him."

She nodded. "Tomoe said he looked exactly like Prince Genji. And that, like Prince Genji, he wore the most ethereal perfumes in his robes. Is there such a man among the great nobles?"

The question struck Akitada as incredibly naïve. He blurted out, "Prince Genji is a character in a novel."

"I thought so." Otomi's expression was almost triumphant. She reached into her sleeve and produced a crumpled bit of paper. "There," she said, extending it to Akitada. "She left this behind."

It was a poem, or rather a fragment: "By the pond the frogs sing in the branches of the fallen pine; / Let the two of us, like a pair of ducks, join their . . . " Either the author had been interrupted or had discarded a draft. But the brush strokes were elegant; both the calligraphy and style were those of a courtier. Apparently that much of Tomoe's story had been true.

Folding the paper, Akitada tucked it into his sleeve and said, "This may be some help." Okamoto's anxious eyes met his, and he felt great pity for the distraught father. "It is possible that the man was sincere in his feelings for your daughter," he said gently.

Okamoto regarded him fixedly. "He took Tomoe without my

permission." When Akitada nodded, he laughed bitterly. "The poem is just a bit of verse, that's all. The fine gentleman dashed it off at a moment's notice to turn a poor girl's head."

Akitada said helplessly, "Well, I'll make inquiries. Can you describe your daughter to me?"

Okamoto tried, but tears rose to his eyes, and Otomi spoke for him.

"Tomoe is in her sixteenth year," she said, "but well grown and tall for her age. She has an oval face, her skin is very white, and her eyes are large. Tomoe's hair reaches to her ankles and is very thick. I brush it for her every day." Otomi compressed her lips before continuing, "In front of her left ear she has a small brown mark which looks like a little bug. She hates it and always wears her hair loose so it covers her ears." She gave Akitada a fierce look. "My sister is very beautiful. She looks nothing like me at all."

Okamoto shivered and wiped the moistness from his eyes. Immediately Otomi rose to get another robe and draped it around his shoulders solicitously. "You are tired, Father," she said. "I shall fetch a brazier of hot coals and some wine."

Embarrassed, Akitada rose, saying, "I am very sorry for your trouble and shall try to help."

Okamoto rose also, leaning on his daughter's arm. "Allow me," he said and pulled a slender, neatly wrapped package from his sleeve. "This is a token of my gratitude for your interest and will defray any immediate expenses."

Akitada accepted with a bow and took his departure, wondering why the girl Otomi looked so complacent, almost happy, as she stood beside her father.

His first visit was to the headquarters of the municipal police to see if there had been an accident involving a young woman. He was shown to an office where a harassed-looking sergeant was bent over paperwork. Akitada sat down and waited.

"Of all the things to happen!" the sergeant muttered to himself. "And the coroner is sick! Heaven only knows if I got this right. No names, he says. How is a man to file a report without names, I ask you."

Akitada leaned forward. "A troublesome case?" he asked.

The sergeant looked up. "Oh. Sorry, sir. Didn't realize you were there." A puzzled frown, then a tentative smile. "Haven't I seen you in the Ministry of Justice?"

Akitada bowed slightly. "Sugawara Akitada," he introduced himself. "Junior clerk."

"Right! Yes, we've got a nameless suicide. And the report was brought in by a nameless citizen." He looked over his shoulder, then leaned forward to whisper, "It's all very hush-hush. Your boss talking to my boss. Actually it was the captain of the palace guard."

"Ah!" nodded Akitada. He asked in a whisper, "Masahira or Morikawa?" There was a right guard and a left guard of the palace.

"Masahira," mouthed the sergeant. He continued in a normal tone, "I've been told to file a report without names; just the 'unfortunate female victim' and the 'person who made the discovery.' On top of that we don't have a coroner's report. All I know is the girl was dead when we pulled her from the water."

A girl! Akitada became alert. "Perhaps," he offered, "I could be of assistance. I am not a coroner, but I learned a little forensic medicine when I was a student at the university."

The sergeant was relieved. "If you wouldn't mind taking a look," he said, getting to his feet. "Just a bit of the jargon and I can finish my report. We've got her in the back room."

The back room was a barren space, dim with the shutters closed, and contained nothing but a covered body on a mat. A faint smell of rotted vegetation hung in the air. The sergeant threw open the shutters, then pulled back the straw mat which covered the corpse.

Akitada held his breath. He saw the face first, and felt an almost physical pain that someone so young and beautiful should be forever lost to the world. Slender brows arched over eyes shaded by thick lashes, now wet against the pale cheeks. The small nose and softly rounded lips were almost childlike in their freshness and innocence. She looked asleep, and like a sleeping child, she touched a hidden desire to cherish and protect.

Too late! The long hair, matted with mud and rank vegetation, stuck to her skin, was tangled in the clammy folds of her fine silk clothes (lovely rose colors shading all the way to the palest blushing skin tone), and reached to her small, slender hands and feet. There was so much hair, so many layers of wet silk that she seemed to be wrapped in them as in a strange pink and black cocoon.

Akitada knelt beside her, feeling strangely reverent, his eyes on her face. He saw no marks on her except for a thin red line high on her neck beneath the jaw. It disappeared under her hair. He extended a hand, almost apologetically, and brushed aside a strand that covered her right ear.

There it was, a dainty dark brown mark, no bigger than an orange seed. According to her sister, it had worried her, but Akitada thought it most beautiful, this small imperfection in the otherwise perfect face of the girl Tomoe.

"Oh," he murmured, overcome with pity and regret. The puzzle had turned into something far more real that touched him deeply.

The thin red line widened and deepened just below the ear but did not continue around her neck. It was recent. Whatever had caused it had not been strangulation, though something might have been put around her neck and then jerked backward.

"What is it?" asked the sergeant. "Anything out of the ordinary?"

She was everything out of the ordinary to Akitada's mind, but he asked, "Did she have anything around her neck?"

"No. Well, was it suicide or what?"

"What makes you think it was suicide?"

"My boss told me it was. He said she left a letter or something before drowning herself."

Akitada sighed. It was too likely that Tomoe had written a tragic love letter. If Masahira was the lover, he was beyond her reach. He looked at the lovely silent face before him. A young romantic girl would have found the noble captain irresistible. Masahira was in his late thirties and one of the most handsome men at court. All the empress's ladies in waiting were said to be in love with him. For all that, Masahira had had an excellent reputation up to now. Married to a daughter of the chancellor, he had never been rumored to have affairs or even flirtations. If he was indeed the man, Tomoe must have seen him at one of the wrestling contests held in the palace. He would be in attendance, riding at the head of the imperial guard, resplendent in golden armor shining in the sunlight and seated on a prancing steed.

"Well?" urged the sergeant. "Shouldn't you take off her clothes?"

Akitada recoiled from the suggestion. Instead he gently opened her lips and felt inside. He pulled out a fragment of a water plant and some wet dirt. "She drowned," he told the sergeant. "The fact that she swallowed water mixed with vegetation and pond mud proves that she was alive when she fell in."

"Ah," nodded the sergeant. "I shall put it in my report."

Akitada turned her head and felt the skull, moving the wet hair aside from the skin. On her left temple he found a bruise, slightly swollen and discolored. Her hair had become glued to the scalp and as he pulled it loose the tips of his fingers came away red.

The sergeant peered. "Must've banged her head when she went in."

Akitada looked up. "Not if she committed suicide. She would have walked into the water. Unless she jumped from a high place and hit some obstruction. Where was she found?"

"She didn't jump. It was just a murky garden pond full of frogs."

Frogs! Akitada was momentarily distracted by the memory of the poem. He asked, "Was the water deep?"

"No. It only came to my hips."

Akitada looked at the sergeant. "Would you drown yourself in that? Where was this place?"

"Small villa in the western part. You know how things are over there. It's pretty much deserted. She was staying there by herself. Not even a servant. If you ask me, it was your typical love nest."

"Whose house?"

The sergeant cast up his eyes and grinned. "Ah! Your guess is as good as mine. The chief says it's immaterial. She committed suicide. Case closed."

"But what about her family?"

"We'll post a notice! If anybody missed her, they can claim the body." The sergeant looked worried suddenly. "It is suicide, isn't it? Or . . . an accident?"

"You mean, could she have run into something with her head and fallen in the water? I don't know. You will have to show me the place."

The sergeant frowned. "Aren't you first going to look at the rest of her?"

Reluctantly Akitada checked the small hands, the dainty feet in their white silk socks. Both were unmarked except by muddy water. Then he straightened her clothes gingerly. The dampness made the silk cling to her skin, outlining high, small breasts, a narrow waist, and delicately rounded hips and thighs. In spite of himself, Akitada felt the blood rise warmly to his face and looked away in self-disgust. Turning the body on its side, he found a long tear in the back of the outer gown. A sharp, thorny branch was caught in the hem, and the silk showed streaks of dirt and many small rips.

"Did you or the constables drag the body along the ground?" he asked the sergeant.

"No. Two of us scooped her out of the water and laid her on the mat she's on now. She weighed very little, even with all the water."

Akitada gently laid Tomoe on her back again, plucking at the layers of silk until she looked more decently covered. Then he rose.

"I am afraid, Sergeant, that this young person was murdered."

The sergeant turned first red than white. "No!" he said. "I can't put that in my report. I don't care what you think you saw, it can't be murder. The chief said *suicide.*"

Akitada shook his head. "It's murder," he said stubbornly. "She was knocked unconscious and then dragged to the water and drowned. Now let us go to this villa and see what we can find out."

The sergeant looked panic-stricken. "Are you mad? You shouldn't even be here. Come on." Taking Akitada's arm, he pulled him out of the room and locked the door after them.

"Now," he said as they were standing outside, "you'd better go home and forget all about this."

Akitada gave him a long look, then said, "As you wish," and walked away.

The sergeant stood and watched him turn the corner, wondering belatedly what Akitada's business had been.

Lord Masahira occupied his family mansion on the corner of Kitsuji and Nishidoin avenues. It was a large, generously staffed establishment, and Akitada had considerable difficulty being admitted. The man he was about to meet was a favorite with the emperor and related by marriage to the chancellor. That gave him the sort of power which would make even Soga grovel. No wonder the minister had dismissed Okamoto without the slightest encouragement. No wonder he had used his influence to keep Masahira's name out of the investigation. They were covering up a murder.

Akitada saw again the still face of the dead girl and the pain in her father's eyes, and a hot anger against Masahira filled his heart. He had known at the police station that he could not tell Okamoto of his daughter's murder without at least identifying her killer first. And Masahira was the most likely choice.

The handsome captain of the imperial guard was in a small garden enclosed by the walls of several buildings. He was sitting on the edge of the wooden veranda and had Akitada's visiting card in his hand. Glancing up, he said, "You are Sugawara from the Ministry of Justice?"

Akitada bowed deeply. He knew he was in the presence of one of the first nobles of the land but was much too angry to prostrate himself. Considering the collusion between this man and the minister, he also did not feel obligated to go into long explanations of his status.

When he raised his head, he saw to his surprise that the man before him had red-rimmed eyes and looked as if he had not slept. Beside him, on the polished boards, stood an untouched tray of food.

"Well? What does Soga want? " Masahira asked curtly.

If the minister found out about this visit, he would see to it that Akitada never worked again in any imperial office. On the other hand, Masahira's question proved that he had recently consulted Soga about Tomoe's murder. Righteous disgust gave Akitada the strength to continue.

"I am here on behalf of Okamoto Toson," he corrected Masahira. "He has asked for my unofficial assistance in locating his daughter Tomoe. Perhaps I should explain first that I have just come from police headquarters where I have seen the body of his unfortunate child."

A slight flush appeared on Masahira's pale face. "I see," he said tonelessly. "Well? I was under the impression that the matter was being handled by Soga. Is it money the old man wants? How much? Come on! Let's get it over with."

Akitada stiffened, remembering the grief and worry of Okamoto. "It is not a matter of money, and the young woman's father is not yet aware that she is dead," he said coldly.

"Oh?" Masahira waited.

Heavens, did the man think this was a blackmail attempt? Akitada flushed with fresh anger. "I shall, of course, report to him," he said quickly, "but I came to you first because I hoped that you might wish to see him yourself to explain what happened."

Masahira turned away. "No. You may tell Okamoto that I am responsible for what happened and that my life means nothing to me now. I am at his disposal if he desires to discuss the affair or avenge his honor."

Akitada was thunder-struck. He had expected fury, denial, bluster, but certainly not this quick admission of guilt. He looked at the man's back and wavered in his estimation. The broad shoulders sagged and his neck, bent, looked vulnerable for all its strong muscles and neatly brushed glossy black hair. But he could not afford to feel sympathy. Masahira was, at the very least, a sly seducer of innocent young women, at worst a heartless killer.

"I am afraid, it is not going to be that simple," he said, "not in a case of murder."

Masahira spun around. "What? Murder? She drowned herself. Because she thought I had deserted her."

"No. Someone knocked her unconscious, dragged her to the pond, and drowned her." Akitada outlined his observations of the evidence.

Masahira ran his hands through his hair. "It cannot be. Here! He fished a piece of paper from inside his robe. Read for yourself!"

The letter was still warm from lying next to Masahira's skin. Akitada unfolded it and read the childlike characters. "I cannot bear this lonely place any longer. I think you do not want me and will leave me to die alone. How could I ever have believed you? My sleeves are wet with tears. Soon they will be wetter still."

"Tomoe wrote this?" Akitada asked, returning it.

Masahira nodded. "I blame myself entirely. I should not have left her alone there. She told me she was frightened and begged me to stay. When I refused . . . " He turned away.

"You could have taken her back to her father," Akitada offered, his anger melting rapidly along with his suspicions.

"You don't understand." Masahira's voice broke. "I loved her." He put both hands over his face. "I could not bear to give her up."

"Then why did you not bring her here and legitimize the relationship," Akitada asked. "A man in your position is expected to have secondary wives."

Masahira turned and looked at him bleakly from moist eyes. "I meant to. In fact, I was preparing my household to receive her when it happened," he said stiffly.

Akitada digested this information and decided to accept it. "Regardless of the letter, which is ambiguous at best, someone killed her," he said at last.

Before Masahira could respond, the door opened and a tall, handsome woman entered. Her robes were costly, and her glossy black hair swept the floor behind her, but her features were thin and pinched. Lady Chujo, Masahira's wife and the chancellor's oldest daughter. When she saw Akitada, she gave him a sharp, appraising look before addressing her husband.

"I apologize if I am interrupting, husband," she said in the soft, nasal tones of the upper classes. "I wished to know if there is any news."

"My wife," introduced Masahira. "My dear, this is Sugawara Akitada. He has come from Okamoto Toson about Tomoe." To Akitada he said, "My wife is aware of the tragedy, but not, of course, of the fact that murder is suspected."

"Murder?" Lady Chujo's eyes flicked over Akitada without interest. "Impossible! My husband found the letter the unfortunate young woman wrote before walking into the pond. I suppose her father must be distraught. It is only natural. But you must convince him that he is wrong about this and that it is absolutely essential the unpleasantness be handled discreetly. Naturally you will also give him our condolences."

Akitada took an instant dislike to the woman. An unpleasantness, was it? To be resolved by a message of condolence? Aloud he said, "Madam, Tomoe's father is not yet aware of her death nor of her connection with your husband. I came here because explanations had better come from Lord Masahira."

The proud head came up and the lady stared Akitada in the eye. "Impossible," she said again. "A man in my husband's position cannot be expected to deal with such low-bred notions. The girl was a foolish child frightened by hobgoblins and fox spirits. I am certain the proper authorities will rule her death a suicide."

Masahira interrupted at this point. "Did you say Okamoto did not know she went with me? But Tomoe wrote him a letter before she left with me."

A letter? Here was another puzzle. Of course there was only her sister's word for the fact that Tomoe had left without notice. What if Otomi had known all along where Tomoe was?

Aloud he said, "He did not . . . does not know. He only suspects that Tomoe was lured away by a man of high rank. It was the sergeant at the police building who told me that you had reported her death."

Lady Chujo said irritably, "They should make certain such people can be trusted not to blab confidential matters to every curiosity seeker!" She glared at Akitada who was once again reminded of his own precarious position. A word from Lady Chujo to her father, and Akitada could find himself banished to the island of exiles in the far north.

He bowed and said apologetically, "Forgive me, but I was merely carrying out Mr. Okamoto's instructions." With brilliant inspiration, he added, "He is very distraught. No doubt the tragedy, when it becomes generally known, will win him much sympathy from his many friends and supporters."

Lady Chujo looked thoughtful, and her husband said quickly, "Yes, of course. I had better go and explain. Though I still don't understand how he could have been so completely in the dark. I made no secret of my intentions to Tomoe. It is unfortunate that the empty villa frightened her, but I thought that the young women would arrange for someone to stay with her. "

The young women? So Otomi had known!

"Indeed," cried Lady Chujo. "My husband was making even more generous arrangements for her, when she panicked. He was bringing her here. But, being a most superstitious person—one of those who are forever muttering spells and buying silly amulets against Heaven knows what—she simply went mad with fright." Lady Chujo was warming to her subject. "If she did not drown herself, then she ran into the water out of fear. It was an accident. It is really no one's fault, but the silly girl's."

Masahira said unhappily, "Don't! Tomoe was not silly. She was very sweet and very young. I should have looked after her better."

Lady Chujo bit her lip. She was clearly tired of the subject. Her eyes fell on the tray of food. "You have not eaten," she said. "Let me get some hot food. This dreadful incident will make you ill, and you know you are on duty tomorrow for the emperor's birthday."

"I am not hungry," Masahira said with a grimace, but she went to pick up the tray anyway. She left the room, scented robes and long hair trailing, without so much as a nod to Akitada.

"I do not wish to trouble you any longer, sir," Akitada said nervously, "but could you direct me to your villa?"

Masahira sighed and rose. "Come! I will take you myself. If you are right about its being murder, it would be a terrible thing, but at least I would not feel that Tomoe killed herself because of me."

Akitada had not expected the offer or the sentiment from such a powerful man and was surprised again.

They rode—Masahira had superb horses—and crossed the city quickly. In the western district, they entered an almost rural setting. There were few villas and some, now abandoned, had become overgrown with vegetation. Empty lots were covered with tall meadow grass which was alive with rabbits and deer. They passed a few small temples, their steep pagodas rising above the trees, but the streets were mere dirt tracks and the bridges, which crossed small rivers and canals, were dilapidated.

Yet here and there, in the midst of the desolation, a few secluded mansions and villas survived, their rustic fencing in good repair, and the thatched roofs mended. Masahira stopped at one of these, dismounted, and unlatched the gate.

At that moment, a curious figure detached itself from the shadows of the large willow tree at the street corner and walked toward them.

At first glance, the scrawny man appeared to be a monk. He was dressed in a stained and worn saffron robe, his head was shaven, and the wooden begging bowl, dangling from the hemp rope about his skinny middle, bounced with every shuffling step he took. When he reached them, he stopped and stared slack-jawed and with vacant eyes. Akitada saw that he wore several small wooden tablets with crude inscriptions around his neck.

"He's just a mendicant," said Masahira. "They live in small temples around here." He tossed a few copper coins to the man, while Akitada rode into the courtyard. Dismounting, he glanced over his shoulder at the beggar, who had not picked up the money, but was still standing, staring foolishly after them until Masahira closed the gate.

They were in a small courtyard of a charming house in the old style, all darkened wood and sweeping thatched roof.

Akitada looked curiously about him. A stone path led to the front door and then continued around the side of the house to what must be the garden. The cicadas were singing their high-pitched song in the trees.

Inside there was only one large room, but this had been furnished luxuriously with screens, thick mats, silk bedding, and lacquered clothes chests. There was also an assortment of amusements suitable for an aristocratic young lady. A zither lay next to a beautiful set of writing implements, games rested beside several novels and picture books, and a set of cosmetics and combs accompanied an elegant silver mirror. Three tall wooden racks were draped with gowns of silk and brocade in the most elegant shades and detailing, and Akitada counted no less than five fans scattered about. In the short time since she had left her father's house, Tomoe had been spoiled by her noble lover. He looked around for evidence of the sister's having been here, but found nothing.

Masahira wandered dazedly about the room, touching things. He brushed a hand over one of the gowns, then picked up a fan, looked at it, and let it drop again. "Well?" he asked.

"I understand that you could not spend much time with Tomoe," said Akitada, "but I have been wondering why she did not have at least a servant for companion?"

"There was a need for secrecy at first. I wished to keep the affair from my household. Tomoe herself insisted that she needed no one. But, as I said, I thought surely her sister . . . " He passed a hand over his face. "At any event, she became fearful. The foxes make strange sounds at night. She was not used to it. She developed a fear that I might meet with an accident and never return. She had dreadful dreams. One day I found her nearly incoherent. That was when I decided to bring her into my home." He sighed deeply. "Too late."

Akitada looked around the room distractedly. This had been the second reference Masahira had made to the sister. Had Otomi known of this place? If so, why had she lied? In his mind's eye, he saw again the complacent look on the plain girl's face as she stood beside her father and said, "My sister is very beautiful."

He became aware of the fact that Masahira was looking at him and asked, "May I see the pond now? And perhaps you could tell me how you came to find her body."

Masahira nodded. He led the way into the garden. They followed the stepping stones through dense shrubbery, but trees and weeds had grown up around the path and brushed and tore at their clothes. All around them the cicadas sang, pausing as they passed and resuming again a moment later.

"I had gone home to speak to my wife about Tomoe," said Masahira, holding a branch aside for Akitada. "To my surprise, she was immediately receptive to the idea. You must understand that I have no other women, and my wife is childless. She confessed that she looked forward to raising my children by Tomoe, and to having her companionship. Overjoyed, I returned the next day to tell Tomoe." He fell abruptly silent.

The stepping stones only went as far as a stone lantern. Here Masahira turned right. "The pond is this way," he said. His voice shook a little. In a distance, Akitada could hear frogs croaking. There was no sign of foxes, but the dense shrubbery rustled with animal life.

They emerged from the trees. The pond lay before them, basking in the hot sun.

"When I got to the house, it was empty, " Masahira said, staring at the still water with a shiver. "I was puzzled, for I knew Tomoe was afraid of the garden, but eventually I went to search for her there. I almost turned around when I got to the pond without seeing her."

The pond was shaped like a gourd, and they stood near its widest end. Up ahead, where it narrowed, a small bridge arched across a dense growth of water lilies and lotus. Clouds of small gnats hung low over the water, and dragonflies skimmed the surface. The sound of the cicadas was less strident here, but the atmosphere of the pond, stagnant in the summer heat and choked with vegetation, embraced them like a suffocating shroud.

Masahira pointed to a thorny shrub near the path. "I saw a small piece of silk there and knew she had come this way. That was when I went to look in the water." He walked forward to the muddy edge and stared down. "She was here."

Akitada joined him. The water was brown but not deep. He could see the muddy bottom, pitted here and there by the feet of the sergeant and his constable. A huge silver carp appeared, rose briefly to look at them and sank again. Other fish, fat, their colors dull gray and copper in the muddy water, shifted lazily across the mud, and a large frog, suddenly conscious of their presence, jumped in with a splash and swam away. In this neglected garden, human beings were the intruders.

Masahira said, "She could have slipped and fallen. But I cannot imagine what would have brought her out here."

Akitada glanced across to where a fallen pine projected over the water. "There are the foxes," he said.

Two young cubs had climbed up and looked at them curiously. Masahira cursed, clapping his hands sharply. The cubs yelped and ran. A moment later their mother appeared, a handsome vixen with a long bushy tail, her ears pointed and her sharp nose twitching to catch their scent.

Masahira clapped again, but the fox stood her ground. "They behave as if they owned this place," he complained. "I shall have workmen clean up this wilderness and drain the pond." He turned abruptly and walked back.

Akitada stayed another moment, looking at the fox. Then he also turned to go.

What had happened here? He no longer suspected Masahira. It was clear that he had loved the girl and had made arrangements to bring her into his family. Who then? The envious sister? A jealous lover? Or a stranger, some vagrant coming across the lonely girl? The image of the scarecrow monk flashed into his mind, and he hurried after Masahira.

He caught up with him in the house and asked, "That beggar outside the gate, do you know him?"

Masahira was surprised. "Yes. He is one of the monks in a small temple a short distance away. Why do you ask?"

Akitada, with the certainty of conviction, said, "He looked deranged. I think he got in and attacked Tomoe." Masahira shook his head, but Akitada added quickly, "Perhaps she caught him stealing. He could have picked up something and knocked her out." Looking around the room, he pounced on an iron candlestick, examined it and put it back disappointedly. Next he picked up the heavy silver mirror. "Yes," he cried. "I see a dent here and . . . " He dashed out into the sunlight with it, squinting at the rim. "There!" he shouted triumphantly. "Do you see it? That is a drop of blood and a long hair is stuck to it. This was used to knock her out. Now do you believe me?"

Masahira came to look and nodded. "Yes," he said sadly. "You must be right, but the man has always been quite gentle. He has never hurt a living thing. He is not very bright and sells talismans that the other monks inscribe with spells against demons."

"Of course," said Akitada. "Fox magic. He knocked at the door, and when Tomoe opened, he offered her one of his charms. I suppose they are those wooden tablets he had around his neck. Then he saw all these fine things and no one to watch them but a young, delicate lady. He helped himself and, when Tomoe protested, they struggled, and he hit her with the mirror. He thought she was dead and decided to hide the body in the pond."

Masahira frowned. "Could not someone else . . . ?"

"No, no. It all fits, " cried Akitada, rushing out. "Let us go back and tell the police."

When they reached the police building, the sergeant was talking to Okamoto Toson, who had finally come to report his daughter missing, and had ended up identifying Tomoe's body.

An uncomfortable scene ensued.

Okamoto's eyes went from Akitada to Lord Masahira. He recognized him instantly and prostrated himself. Masahira went to help him up, whispering something in his ear. Okamoto stiffened, then nodded.

Masahira turned back to Akitada, saying in a tight voice, "Perhaps it will be best if you leave things to me now. "

Akitada looked at Okamoto.

The old man was very pale, but he nodded. "Lord Masahira is right. You have done your part and quickly, too. If you will excuse me now and allow me some time to mourn and bury my child, I shall reward your efforts in a day or two."

Akitada flushed with embarrassment. He stammered that nothing was owed, that he was sorry to have brought no better news, and left as quickly as he could.

He slept poorly that night. Something kept nagging at him. When he finally fell asleep, he dreamt of foxes. At one point, the vixen appeared on the fallen pine. She raised herself on her hindlegs and paraded back and forth, dragging her tail behind like the skirts of a long robe, making a strange snickering noise. Then the fox's black eyes and pointed muzzle changed into the sharp features of Lady Chujo, who laughed, baring her fangs. He sat bolt upright, staring at the stripes made by the sunlight falling through the closed shutters of his room.

Stripes . . . lines . . . the thin, red line on Tomoe's neck . . . the monk selling amulets . . . charms against fox spirits. Of course. The frightened Tomoe had bought one and she had worn it before her death. Someone, the murderer, had torn it off her and had caused the red line on her neck.

Amulets! Lady Chujo had mentioned Tomoe's belief in amulets. How had she known?

Akitada threw on his clothes and ran to police headquarters. A yawning sergeant was just sitting down when Akitada burst into the office.

"That monk," cried Akitada. "Did you arrest him?"

The sergeant's mouth fell open again. He nodded.

"What did he say? Did he visit the girl?"

The sergeant nodded again.

"Well?"

The sergeant closed his mouth and sighed. "It's too early," he said reprovingly, "for so many questions, sir. However, the man absolutely denies killing the girl. He sold her a charm, that's all, he says. Of course, we can still beat him and get a confession that way, but Lord Masahira has asked us not to."

Thank God for Masahira, thought Akitada. He, Akitada, had made a terrible mistake. He asked, "Did he say when he sold her the charm?"

"Yes. The day before we found her." The sergeant shook his head. "It didn't do her much good."

"The monk is innocent. You must let him go."

The sergeant raised his brows. "On whose say-so?"

Akitada's spirits sank. He knew now who the killer was, but he would never prove it. No doubt the poor monk would be beaten into some form of confession and then condemned to forced labor at some distant frontier. And all of it was Akitada's fault. He had been wrong about the identity of the murderer three times. He had lost his job, failed Okamoto and Tomoe, and added the burden of guilt to his other miseries.

He went to see Lord Masahira.

Recalling too late that it was the emperor's birthday, Akitada fully expected to be turned away. Instead he was admitted instantly to face who knew what additional disaster.

He found the captain, dressed in the gray robe of mourning, standing on the veranda of his study. He held something in his hand and was staring at it fixedly.

The face he turned towards Akitada was drawn and white. Today Masahira looked old beyond his years, and Akitada was about to intrude into the man's grief with a dangerous knowledge. Reminding himself of the vacant-eyed monk in police custody, Akitada stammered, "Forgive the interruption, sir, but I have reconsidered the facts and I now know the monk is innocent. He merely sold one of his charms to Tomoe. It was the day before her body was found. I . . . believe someone else . . . " He broke off fearfully.

"Yes." Masahira's voice was flat, his eyes weary. "So you know what really happened?"

Hanging his head, Akitada murmured, "I believe so. Your lady . . . " He broke off. "I am very sorry, sir."

Masahira sighed heavily. "No sorrier than I. I am responsible, even though I did not kill Tomoe. It was my foolishness that caused the tragedy. A double tragedy. I thought my wife was too accommodating when I asked her if I could bring Tomoe here. I should have suspected."Masahira's voice was bitter. "I found this in my wife's writing box!"

Akitada glanced up. Masahira dangled a small wooden tablet with an inscription. The hemp string was broken.

The amulet.

"Lady Chujo must have gone to the villa after you told her," said Akitada. "She mentioned the amulet, but Tomoe had just bought it from the monk, and not even you could have known that."

Masahira said, "I did not." He added heavily, "My wife will not be arrested. But she has agreed to renounce the world and spend the rest of her life in a remote nunnery. The monk will be released, of course, but I must ask your discretion. I already have Okamoto's."

Akitada thought again of the dangerous ground he had trodden. Deeply grateful, he bowed. "Of course, my Lord. I only regret having brought such misfortune to you and your family."

Masahira waved this aside. "Okamoto is a most admirable character." He paused to look at Akitada. "I think," he said, "that, whatever your motives were originally, you acted from concern for him and pity for . . . " his voice shook, but he went on, "his daughter. You were quite right in your feelings about both." He broke off abruptly and turned away, weeping.

Akitada was backing from the room, when Masahira spoke again. His voice had regained the tone of authority. "About your position at the ministry. I have had a word with Soga. You are to return to work immediately."

The Road's End

by Brendan DuBois

T HE MEET TOOK PLACE at a small cafe next to the Hemingway House in Key West. It was a hot day for April and I sat outside on a small wooden deck at the cafe, sipping a frozen strawberry fruit drink. I had on a blue knit polo shirt, khaki pants and deck shoes. At my feet was a small knapsack that held bottled water, maps, and a 9mm Smith & Wesson semi-automatic pistol. A lot of the traffic going by on Whitehead Street were sunburnt tourists in bathing suits on motor scooters, hooting and hollering at each other. I thought for a moment about speeding traffic and what a spill on asphalt would do to all that exposed flesh, and decided that while messy, it could definitely improve the species' gene pool.

Across the way was a block of apartment buildings, painted a dull yellow. Chickens pecked slowly at the dead lawn, as laughing young men in shorts and lots of gold jewelry polished their motorcycles and BMW convertibles in the shade. Nice what crack cocaine sales can do to the local economy. There was movement to my left and she sat down, dropping a large Vuitton purse to the deck floor. She carried a Corona beer with a bit of lime floating in the liquid, and I didn't have the heart to tell her that particular drink wasn't in this year.

Her dark black hair was pulled back in a simple ponytail. She had on aviator's sunglasses and a round straw hat, and was wearing a light cotton sundress with lots of tiny blue flowers. I wasn't close enough to see what kind of flowers were there, but I was close enough to see how nicely she filled out the dress. She got right to the point. "He's here, isn't he?"

"Nice to see you, too," I said.

"I'm paying you for information and results," she said, quietly adjusting the folds of her sundress. "Not for idle chit-chat. So. He's here, isn't he."

"Yes, he is," I said. "Staying at a bed and breakfast a couple of streets over, on Simonton. Just got there yesterday."

"Do you think he knows I'm here as well?"

"Probably," I said. "Look, a lot depends on what you do. I still think—"

She turned and smiled at me, the smile without an ounce of compassion or humor. "Mister Foss, I pay you for a lot of things. Thinking isn't one of them. The time is still set for tonight, at Mallory Square. During the sunset."

"Lots of people there," I pointed out. "Tourists, street people, performers. Lots of witnesses."

She took a delicate sip of the beer. "That's all right. I like crowds."

"I don't"

"Too bad," she said, and then she left.

As he took his shower, he thought of being in Key West and he couldn't get over the flatness of it all. Monroe had grown up in the Green Mountains of Vermont and liked the lively nature of the landscape. The rolling hills and mountains. The dirt roads that led deep into the dark woods. The craggy notches in the steep hills, water streams coursing down the granite rock. But here . . . This whole place seemed like an amusement park for adults. Everything was too flat, too bright, too loud. The spindly plants and trees with odd leaves looked like they had been dropped as spores from outer space, there was not a high point to be seen, and the sun was too bright and too hot.

But he had to be here.

He shut off the shower and stepped out, toweling himself, feeling tired yet again. He knew he should take a nap—God, had he ever had a real good night's sleep these past months?—but he had work to do, if he was going to find her tonight. Lots of work. He looked at himself in the mirror, and as before, did not like what he saw.

In his mind's eye he knew what he should look like: the youngest detective ever in the Vermont State Police, lean body muscled and trim after hours of work in the gym and jogging on the narrow mountain roads, dark brown hair cut short, brown eyes sharp and inquisitive.

What he now saw was something different. His body had grown soft, after long hours on the road and lots of late-night fried meals and no time for exercise. His eyes were tired and often red-rimmed, and even his hair was different. It was now streaked with gray and it was longer, reaching his shoulder blades. He gingerly reached up and touched the shower-wet hair, at the right side of his head.

There. The ridge of scar tissue that snaked around the side of his skull, the fold of flesh that was a reminder, every second, every minute, every day, when he had been shot down in his unmarked cruiser, shot down and left for dead. Lucky for him the EMTs had been quick that day, for he had noted the crime scene photos later, while in the hospital, talking to his friends on the force. What he saw in those photos should have led to a gravesite. He recalled one photo— thankfully black and white—with him lying to one side, the seat belt still cinching him in. The side of his head was a mess, with blood, bone, hair and bits of brain tissue leaking out. His right arm was extended out, hand curled, like it was looking for some sort of ghost weapon to hold. He had looked at the photo a number of times and was always surprised at what he felt at seeing it, for he felt nothing. Not a thing. It was like he was looking at some life-sized and realistic mannequin of himself, made up and bloodied for a training program or something. Not real.

He touched the scar tissue on his head again. That was real. That and another photo.

Monroe went out to his room, got dressed in dark green shorts and a Hawaiian shirt that was black, with bright pink flamingos. He let the shirttails hang over the shorts. He put on a leather belt and fastened his weapons: Mace canister to immobilize, plastic handcuffs to prevent movement, and six-inch knife to wrap things up. It was too dangerous nowadays to try to move firearms across state borders, and during the last year, he had moved across many of them.

He sat down, went through some of his belongings on the nightstand, locating a torn sheet from a Key West guidebook. Mallory Square was circled, with the word "sunset" written next to it. The sheet had been placed into an envelope and slid under the door in his hotel room, up north last week and five hundred miles ago, as the long chase proceeded south. He also pulled out a blurry Polaroid photo. It showed a woman with dark black hair, pulled back in a ponytail. She was wearing a white turtleneck sweater and she was at a bar, talking to someone. A partner? A confederate? He put the photo down on the bed, touched his head again. Monroe wasn't sure.

But he was sure of two things. That woman in the photo, whom he had chased south to this place for many months, was the one responsible for the bullet in his head.

And if he was lucky, tonight he would pay her back.

On Simonton Street I leaned against a utility pole, a tourist's guide of Key West in my hands, my knapsack at my feet. The small two-story homes and buildings along the street were built an arms-width apart. Up the block was a place called the Sleepy Cat Inn, and when I saw him step out onto the sidewalk, wearing shorts and a shirt that looked it belonged on an island called Maui, I made my move. I went up to the inn, which consisted of a handful of reconditioned two-story bungalows, set around a swimming pool now empty of swimmers. I went up to Room 12 and after a quick moment or two with some unique tools that are against in the law in most counties, I was in. The room felt damp, like the man in here had just taken a shower. I made a quick toss of the room, saw the usual clothes, bundles of maps, guidebooks and a couple of paperback thriller novels. On the nightstand I saw an old photo, one I picked up and examined. My client. How nice to have everything confirmed. I put everything back in its place and within another minute or so, I was outside in the sunshine. In the pool a slim blonde was now treading water, wearing something skimpy and orange. She smiled and winked at me, and I smiled and winked back, and then walked away.

Sorry. This evening my heart belonged to another, one who was paying the bills.

Monroe planned for a quick meal at one of the dozens of restaurants that lined Duval Street, shoved in between T-shirt emporiums and stores that sold jewelry, painted conch shells and sand sculptures in glass bottles. He sat out back, near an exit door, and away from the throngs of people and the loud traffic that moved along Duval. The restaurant featured Italian food and thirty seconds after sitting down, he had forgotten the name of the place. That had been a recurring problem, ever since the shooting. Forgetting most things and at odd occasions, remembering certain, unimportant things. Like right now. He remembered smelling fresh chalk, wiping down a blackboard at recess time at the Catholic grammar school he went to, with Sister Mary Fatima working at her wooden desk, writing something with a big black fountain pen, the rest of the room empty. He closed his eyes for a moment, remembering everything about that day. Lunch was a bologna and cheese sandwich on white bread. Potato chips in a little plastic bag. Small chocolate bar for dessert. He had on gray slacks, white shirt and blue tie.

Quick, now. Last week. Where were we last week? One of the Carolinas. North or South? Couldn't remember. He clenched a fork in his hand. Could not remember.

Last year, then. The day we were shot. What was going on?

His eyes were still closed. He remembered odd snippets, like he was watching a network show during a wind storm, the television cable cutting in and out. He had been working a case, something involving smuggling across the Canadian border. Then, that day—it had been fall, that's right, fall, because the leaves were changing color—the woman in the photo. Somehow she came to the forefront. He was on his way to talk to her, to confront her. Then . . .

"Here you go," the waitress said, sliding a plate onto the table. "Enjoy your meal."

He opened his eyes, now remembering. A roadblock, on a small county road. A pickup truck. That had been it. And then . . .

A blow to the head. Darkness. Some lights, some weeks in the hospital. More darkness.

And then the chase began, the chase to find the woman, the one that had set him up.

Monroe picked up a fork, began eating his pasta dish.

Tonight, it would all happen tonight.

I munched on a couple of pizza slices out on the crowded sidewalk of Duval Street, waiting for him to leave the restaurant. This was my first time in Key West and I wish I had more time to poke around and enjoy it. I grew up in Boston, in one of the neighborhoods where you're identified by which church parish you attended, rather than by what street you lived on. It was an okay place, but it still had that old New England reserve and narrow focus. Feuds were passed down from generation to generation, like some awful heirloom—a horsehide couch, for example—that you hated but felt honor bound to accept. And there was a chilly way of dealing with neighbors that seemed to match the cold winds that came off Boston Harbor in January. My father, for example, knew our upstairs neighbor in our apartment building for more than thirty years, yet he still insisted on calling him Mr. Schwartz. I think he died without even knowing the man's first name.

Tourists and real conch residents strolled by me, heading to the free show at Mallory Square. Well, if there was one word to describe Key West, it sure wouldn't be reserved. There was a bright energy to everything, a sense of anticipation, that tomorrow would be an even better day than today. I looked past the ticky-tacky of the tourist shops and the bars with the loud music and signs advertising wet T-shirt contests, to the tiny homes with decorative wood scroll work around the windows, to the bars that seemed to attract the locals, people with leathery skin and wide smiles and a cheery attitude that said they were living in paradise, and if you were too dumb to know that, you were probably too dumb to keep on breathing.

I finished my pizza, wiped my hands on some paper napkins I had stuck in my pants pockets. My knapsack came off the sidewalk and went back over my shoulder. Keep focused, keep focused on the job and the client, I thought. A lot could go wrong in the next few hours, and I was being paid quite handsomely to ensure that it didn't.

Nice to know someone still had trust in my skills and abilities.

Monroe left the restaurant and joined the throngs of people going up Duval Street, heading to the general direction of Mallory Square. It felt like some great migratory movement and—

—he remembered a nature show, a television program on the old black and white TV set up in the corner of the living room, one Sunday night, eating freshly-made popcorn that Mom had made on the stove, watching a Disney program and a nature special, about caribous moving across the tundra, and that's what it was like, this movement of people.

He stopped for a moment, closed his eyes, and then opened them and kept on walking. Damn his memory. Damn it to hell.

But then he remembered, felt better. He knew some things for sure, and one was that the woman would be here tonight, in just an hour or so. Under his shirt he gently caressed the knife scabbard and kept on going up Duval Street.

I got to Mallory Square ahead of schedule and waited. My client was nearby, somewhere well hidden, I'm sure. I scanned the crowd and spotted the target with no problem, thanks to the Hawaiian shirt he was wearing. I sat on a stone park bench and tried to relax, taking a series of long, slow, deep breaths. I hoped this would wrap up quickly, and without too many problems. It had been a long haul and I was tired, but the money had been good, quite good.

I folded my arms, keeping an eye on the target. The money had been about the only good thing about this whole nutty affair. I had been reluctant to take the case, until my client eventually wore me down with her entreaties.

"It's dangerous, you know," I had said, back in my Boston office. "Lots of opportunity for things to go wrong."

"I don't care," she had said, hands clasped firmly around that same Vuitton handbag. "I hear you're the best at what you do."

"Who told you that?"

She shrugged. "Word gets around."

Sure does, I thought, opening my knapsack and taking out a bottle of water. After nearly a decade of patrol work, I had been a Boston detective for a few years and quickly realized that without kissing the right butt or supporting the right city council member, my career was eventually doomed. I cashed out, opened my own private investigation business, and quickly found an affinity for a certain type of work. I guess it has to do with my upbringing, being the oldest brother with four sisters. My younger sisters—though sometimes a torment and a tease—came to depend on me to help them out when asked. My sisters being who they are, they didn't ask often. But when they did ask for help, I jumped in with both feet and both fists.

My first client was a woman whom I had dated years ago while on the job, who went to law school at nights and got her degree. She and her small firm specialized in family cases, the ugly stuff that people whisper to each other in office hallways or household kitchens, of domestic abuse and custody rights and stalking cases. Very shortly I learned to enjoy resolving stalking cases the best, when an ex-boyfriend or ex-husband still refused to take no for an answer. My lawyer friend and client, who no longer dates men, doesn't ask me for too many details, which is fine. I just promise that the problem will be taken care of, and within a day or two, it usually is, after a lengthy and to-the-point visit. One or two times, though, the ex-boyfriend or ex-husband don't quite understand the intent of my message to leave their former girlfriend or wife alone, which has meant a repeat, more thorough, visit on my part.

On those few occasions, I hear that those ex-boyfriends and ex-husbands are now doing well, after months of physical therapy.

So what I was doing in Mallory Square was initially the same type of case I had handled dozens of times before.

But tonight, well, tonight was going to be something out of the ordinary.

I finished my water and waited.

Monroe looked around at the crowds of people, everyone pushing in to get as close to the edge of Mallory Square as possible, where there were docks and the wide expanse of water. He was initially dismayed at how many people were there. They were crowded in, almost shoulder to shoulder, watching the glow of the sun head to the western horizon, watching each other, or watching the performers and the tables and booths, selling everything from painted T-shirts to hot dogs and popcorn. The performers included a dog that walked on a tightrope, a man who would take a running start and dive through a plastic hoop, and a muscled, cursing man in black shorts and a tanktop who balanced a washing machine on his face.

How to find her, he thought desperately, how to find her in this circus?

He closed his eyes again, forced himself to relax. He would find her, he knew he would. And though he was by himself in this packed square, he knew he wasn't alone. All the way down south—from Interstate 91 in Vermont to I-95 in Connecticut and New York, along the old and narrow Route 1, all the way down the East Coast—he had gotten help here and there. A quick phone call in his motel room at night. A newspaper clipping on the front seat of his truck. And like last week, that guidebook page slipped into his room at night, a page that had brought him to Key West.

Monroe wasn't sure who was on his side, but he could guess. It had to be his old buddies on the force, ones who couldn't come out and say they were helping him. He remembered odd bits from the time after the shooting, from a medal award ceremony at his hospital bedside with the Governor of Vermont, to an uncomfortable meeting with doctors, lawyers and senior State Police officials, where he was officially put on medical leave for the rest of his life. No word about the woman, the woman who had set him up. No one would talk to him about it, which told him that she had to have been someone powerful, someone influential, someone who could squash a case like that.

So in Vermont he had started looking for her on his own, and after a month or two, the little tips came, the little hints, signals that he had not been forgotten, signals that he still mattered. Hints and signals that had sent him south on this long chase.

He turned and there she was.

Two young ladies in braided ponytails and wearing white shorts and white bikini tops, who were juggling flaming torches to the appreciative claps and shouts from the crowd, were threatening to break my concentration, and were doing a very good job of it.

So I tossed a dollar bill on the blanket before them and looked to the south, and there was my client, walking up from Front Street. She had on the same wide hat but was now wearing a white sundress, so white that it made her stand out. I swiveled my head and there he was, heading to her, his eyes focused like twin spotlights, heading right to her.

There, she was there, just like they had promised.

A brief touch under his shirt to his knife and he started walking, then walking very fast and then running, trying to get past all of the people in the square, all of the people here just to see a goddamn sunset and they were in the way, all of them

He brushed past them, bumping and jostling, and there she was, still there at the edge of the square, and he saw that she had now noted him. There was a look there, of recognition, of . . . something else, and then fear.

She turned and started running as well.

He tried to move faster, tried to get to his knife, as the people behind him started clapping and cheering as the sun began to set.

For a guy who had been living out of motels for the past year, he sure moved fast. He plowed through the crowd like an icebreaker going through a frozen lake, and I got up and moved with him, flanking him from the right. I took a series of deep breaths, getting focused, keeping an eye on my client—who had now turned and had walked quickly around a brick building—and then on the target—who had broken out in a fast trot. I started running as well, unzipping the knapsack while on the move, reaching in with my free hand. Then the target moved around the building corner and I tried to catch up with him, the two of us now on Front Street.

Monroe lost sight of her for a second, and then there she was, the white dress making her stand out, as she moved along the street. He could feel himself getting closer, getting so close that he could make out the way she moved, the dress flapping against her legs, as she moved towards a parked car, a black limousine, about twenty yards ahead.

So close!

He willed himself to move faster, make those out-of-shape legs pump and race and force himself to catch up, to get within range.

He pulled out the Mace canister, ran through his mind of what he was going to do next, because he knew he was going to make it, he was so close, just another yard or two and he'd grab her and Mace her face, and then—well, there were a few quiet alleys around here, so many people where out on the square, watching the sunset—then, he'd get to work.

A few more seconds, that's it.

Yes!

He reached out to grab her shoulder and—

He was back in the front seat of the police cruiser, closing in, and his head exploded.

In my years on the Boston police force I've done a few things I've not been proud of, from not saying anything as a rookie and watching some of the older cops trade "favors" with the working women in the Combat Zone, to when I was a new detective and looking the other way as seized drug money mysteriously shrunk from ten thousand dollars at the bust site to five thousand dollars when it was inventoried at the station.

But that was nothing compared to how I felt when I caught up with the target and pulled out my 9mm, and smartly rapped him on the side of the skull, where I knew he was weakest.

He fell like a sack of lead shot and as I put the pistol back into my knapsack, I said out loud, for the benefit of whatever witnesses were sober enough to see what was going on, "Jack, I told you not to drink so much. Here, let me help you."

Which is what I did, I guess. I half-dragged, half-carried him over to a park bench. I propped him up and checked his breathing, which was steady. He started murmuring, moving around, and I looked up and saw my client staring at me, hate in her face, and then she got into her limousine and disappeared down the street.

I checked the target's breathing one more time, and then left, feeling like I was going to throw up.

The things I do for a paycheck.

Monroe walked slowly for long minutes, hand touching again and again the raised bump on the side of his head. So close, damn, he had been so close and then—

What had happened?

He touched his head again. Ambushed, that's what. Ambushed just as he was within a few yards of settling this thing, once and for all. Damn that woman.

He wandered for a few minutes, trying to let the pain in his head ease away, as the other pain inside him grew in dismay at what had happened. Damn it, so close, so close, and would he ever have a chance, ever again?

Before him there was a knot of tourists, laughing, and there were flares of light as pictures were taken around an object, a large object that looked an ocean buoy, marooned on land. Monroe came closer, to see what all the attention was about, and then he saw it was a marker of some sort. Painted red, black and yellow, it said SOUTHERNMOST POINT, and the sense of failure grew inside of him, and then he remembered something else, when he was in fifth grade, trudging home from the school bus stop, report card now soggy in his sweaty fist, because it had two D's listed inside, a D in English and a D in math, and how was he going to tell Mom and Dad that he had failed like that, how was he going to do it?

He stared at the monument, at the laughing tourists, the taste of failure strong in his mouth. The road's end. He had chased her here all the way south, and for what?

And would he ever have the chance again?

I made a quick stop to the motel room, and then met up with her at a marina on the other side of the island, not part of Old Town, and not particularly attractive. There was a lot of chain motels and chain stores and chain fast-food restaurants, and lots of bright neon. I wished I was back in Old Town.

We were upstairs in a private bar and she looked up at me, the attractive face still soured some by the look of hatred I had seen a half hour ago, the look of hatred that had been directed at me and not the target. There was an empty glass by her elbow, and I saw she was working on at least her second drink of the evening.

"And?" she said, her voice sharp.

I sat down and looked for a bartender, but the room was empty. No drinks for you, I thought, as I said, "As well as could be expected. I kept him under view after you left, and he got up and started walking."

"So he wasn't seriously injured?"

"Not that I could tell."

"And you think that's as well as could be expected?"

I stared at her, forgetting for the moment how much she was paying me. "Yes, I do. And considering what he had planned for you, I'd think a bit more appreciation on your part would be expected."

She took another stiff swallow, grimaced. "You do, do you."

"Yes, I do."

Then she sighed and her brittle exterior seemed to melt away, and she looked away from me for a moment and her eyes filled. "Damn," she said, sighing. "You're right. It's just that . . . damn . . . It's a hell of a thing, isn't it, when you have to worry about being killed by someone you love, isn't it?"

"It is," I said, remembering our first meet, back in my Boston office. "It certainly is."

"It's because of that shooting," she said, defiantly.

"Yes."

Then, she re-told me the story, as if making up for whatever guilt she was feeling, I guess. "Late last year, a selectman in our town, he snapped after he lost an election. Took his collection of guns and started hunting his enemies in the town. I was the editor of the town paper and probably right on the top of his hit list. Monroe . . . he was in the area, heard on the scanner what was happening, went up to my house and was ambushed . . . shot right in the head."

Lord, I needed a drink. She kept on looking away from me.

"He suffered some brain damage, including memory problems. And the other thing."

"I know," I said. "For some reason, whenever he thought of you, he remembered the shooting. And he thought the two were connected, that you were behind it."

She nodded, took another sip of the drink. "That's right. At first he was kept in a secure hospital but he . . . he kept on trying to escape, trying to set himself free, trying to get after the woman he thought had injured him. He was like a caged animal in there, getting worse and worse, and finally, I signed him out, in my own care. It took a lot of work and some affidavits, but I let him loose. I had to. You have sisters, don't you, Mr. Foss?"

"I do."

"Then if you're close to them, you know what it's like. You'd do anything for them, anything at all. And since I had come into some money earlier . . . Well, I had the means to take care of him."

"By letting him chase you across the United States?" I asked, repeating again the same question I had asked her earlier in Boston.

"Yes," she said, now looking at me, tears streaming down her cheeks. "Because he's my brother."

Monroe stepped into his motel room, saw the plain brown envelope on the floor. His heart started racing. Could it be? Could it? He picked it up, his hands shaking, and opened it up.

Inside was a picture of an old fort, something from the Southwest. It was a postcard, of the . . .

Damn, the Alamo, that's it.

San Antonio. He flipped the postcard and on the back was scribbled a date, a date just a month away.

He smiled. The chase was still on.

She asked me, "Will you continue your work for me, in San Antonio?"

"No," I said. "I can't keep on doing this. It's . . . it's too difficult, I'm sorry. I'm more used to black and white cases. This one's too gray for my tastes."

"I understand," she said.

I said to her, "And there's nothing else you can do? No other doctors, therapy, medicines?"

She shook her head no. "My brother is a cop, Mr. Foss. That's all he knows. He thinks he's doing something important, something that keeps him going. I can't stand the thought of him being locked up somewhere as a vegetable. At least this way, he's alive, he thinks he's performing a vital service."

I looked at her one more time. "Do you intend to keep on doing this, year after year?"

"I do," she said.

"He might find out," I said.

She stayed silent for what seemed a very long time. She cleared her throat.

"He might not," she said. "And that's all I can do for him."

Rough Justice

by Ceri Jordan

IT WASN'T A GOOD MORNING for looking at corpses.

For a start, there was last night's vodka, which had congealed into a glutinous lining in Nick's stomach and begun ejecting anything else it found down there. Then there was the small matter of being woken at six, a bare three hours since he'd fallen fully clothed into his bunk. And then there was the snow.

After ten years in Inverness, Nick had thought he knew about snow. It was gray, it was wet. It clogged the fields in the countryside, and in the city, the drains. He hadn't come over here expecting Tahiti, but for God's sake, they could have warned him about the snow.

Kosovar snow was white and brittle and so cold that when a flake landed on exposed skin, you felt like someone had taken a knife to your face. It didn't drift, or melt, or turn to slush, not even in the cities. It just landed, and froze. And it only came by the ton.

They'd abandoned the military jeep at the foot of the hill. The driver, a red-faced boy who looked too young and too fat to be in the army, had claimed it was all-terrain and it would climb that hill, easy, mate, but Nick wasn't in the mood for bravado. He'd got out before the boy had time to finish his spiel. Jaroslav had followed, and the boy had turned the engine off and settled down to sulk.

Half a dozen paratroopers were standing around the body as if guarding it from some unseen enemy. They'd stuck sticks in the ground and strung some tape between them, fencing off the immediate area. It was only as Nick struggled over the final rise into the slight hollow where the body lay that he realized the tape said DANGER MINES in three or four languages.

The nearest para grinned weakly. "Don't worry, sir. We just didn't have any POLICE tape."

"Oh God," Jaroslav sighed, massaging his temples through the fur-lined hood of his jacket. "Why can't someone invent a way of killing people without making such a mess?" The para opened his mouth to protest, closed it again, unsure of whom he was dealing with and all too aware of the complexities of politics and power structures in a country torn between administrations.

Nick nodded across the hill to the few strands of barbed wire dividing one frozen field from the next. A group of children were clustered in the shelter of a single wind-blasted tree, pointing and gawking. "Jaro, why don't you go ask the locals if they saw anything?"

Jaroslav waved one gloved hand as if this were all beneath him but nodded and stalked away feeling in his voluminous pockets for bribes. The para lifted the tape, and Nick ducked beneath it and approached the body.

He'd been called to a shotgun suicide once—a farmer, one of those bloody nutters who shouldn't be given shotgun licenses—and it had looked pretty much like this. No skull, no face. Just bits and pieces.

The body was intact T-shirt, uniform trousers—mental note, search for his outer layers, no one goes out overnight in this weather in a T-shirt. Unlaced boots. Crouching, he checked the soles. Grit and ice. Could have come from anywhere.

"Do you know who he is?"

"Sergeant Jim Rowley," the para said stiffly. "Royal Engineers. Part of a five-man mine-disposal team stationed in the village here. Left his barracks last night after dropping hints he was, ah, visiting a woman and never came back."

"Was that allowed? I mean, don't you need permission to leave—"

"Disposal teams," the officer spat "Think they're entitled to behave like James Bond."

Nick stood up. His feet were numb already, and he was beginning to long for the warm classroom he'd found so claustrophobic for the last two months. "And you're sure it's actually him? I mean, there's not much . . . "

The para ducked under the barrier, lifted the T-shirt in a brief mechanical motion. As if he were handling meat.

Jim Rowley's chest was a mass of tattoos. A dragon, Nick thought; one of those huge coiled things that you have to get done in several sessions or the shock would kill you. Reptilian wings blended cleverly with Rowley's lower ribs, claws hooked around his navel. The faded lines of the creature's head protruded above the neck of his T-shirt, disguised by a frosting of snow.

Nick bent closer. "Did you know him?"

"Knew of him. Why?"

"Did he get into fights a lot?"

The para looked quickly at his companions and shrugged.

"Because he's covered with bruises. Some of them fresh, but a lot—" Nick ran a finger across the purple swelling above Rowley's kidney, the one that might almost have been part of the tattoo if you weren't looking too closely. "He's taken a beating several times, and recently And I wouldn't mind betting that's connected to why someone decided to blow his head off."

"I don't want to do this," Nick announced the moment the secretary had closed the door behind him.

General Almain just sighed and gestured for him to sit down.

United Nations headquarters in Viskava had once been the local technical college, and it still had a drab and clinical air. Under the untidy heaps of paperwork, the general's desk was scarred by years of over-enthusiastic chemistry experiments, rings and runaways charred into the cheap pine.

"I suppose," Almain mused with barely concealed regret, "I can't actually order you to assist us. But as I understand it, all police instructors volunteering for duty over here are in line for the honors list. Pity for you to lose your CBE over one little case."

Nick shook his head in disbelief. "I'm not here for that. And I'm certainly not here to act as your scapegoat when this Rowley's family start clamoring for answers. I was under the impression that you had these people called military police. Let them do it."

Almain almost choked on his coffee. "There are two MPs within a hundred mile radius of this base, and frankly, I wouldn't trust either of them to detect the fact that their pants were on fire. They won't notice I've gone over their heads until it's too late, and there's nothing they can do about it if they do."

Apart from make his life a misery until the day he left. Wouldn't that be fun?

"Okay. The local police. Surely it's their jurisdiction—particularly if we suspect the assailant was a local."

"Ah, the local police." Almain smiled dryly. "Would that be the Serbian police, most of whom are awaiting trial for war crimes, or the Kosovar Albanian police, whom you haven't finished training yet? Neither sounds terribly suitable. You, on the other hand, are a twice-commended retired detective writing a thesis in, what was it?"

" 'Field Forensics and the Murder Squad Detective.' A title that my supervisor hates, but not half as much as he hates the content, my schedule, and the fact that I've taken three months out to hide from my academic failings in a country willed into existence to salve the West's guilt."

"Very impressive. Now, given the choice, whom would you choose to handle the case?"

Nick closed his eyes and made a mental note to refuse all future party invitations from anyone who made their own vodka.

Jaroslav was waiting outside, rolling a lit cigarette between his gloved fingers and watching the half dozen men rebuilding the house on the opposite corner. It had lost most of its frontage in a near-miss that had left a forty foot crater in the road outside, and they were busy shoring up the internal ceilings with scaffolding poles. Despite the wind several had stripped to the waist, leaving a trail of abandoned garments on the jagged walls and window ledges.

"So," Jaroslav smiled, casting the cigarette aside. "We are to play Sherlock Holmes. Or rather, you are, with your trusty companion at your side. What was his name, Watson?'

"Yes," Nick conceded, wrestling with the door of Jaroslav's ancient monstrosity of a car. "Dr. Watson. Very funny. Come on, let's get back to this godforsaken village. I want this over with as quickly as possible."

Climbing into the driver's seat, Jaroslav said soothingly, "It won't take long. Obviously the sergeant was intimate with someone's daughter or wife, and they took their revenge. An open and closed case, don't you think?"

Nick, who didn't know what he thought, settled for, "Did you find out anything from those children?"

"Why—oh yes, the children." The engine coughed into action, all but drowning his reply. "They said they heard shouting in the village, three or four in the morning. But that could have been anything. Anything at all."

Ten minutes out of town, they were waved down at a roadblock. A remarkably blond soldier blinked at the official permit pasted to the inside of the windscreen, addressed them in quiet and oddly American-sounding English. "I'm sorry, we will need to search the vehicle. Purely routine."

Jaroslav was already handing him the keys to the boot.

A blue-bereted soldier poked uncertainly around the wheel arches while his companions opened the boot, peered in at the empty back seat. None of them seemed quite sure what they were looking for. Finally the blond man returned the keys, saluted briskly. Unsure how to respond, Nick spared him a weak smile.

"Waste of time," Jaroslav growled, gunning the engine. His car had an aversion to stop-start journeys, and something had begun to rattle ominously behind the dashboard.

"It's routine," the soldier repeated a little stiffly "A fugitive could have hidden himself in your trunk while you were not looking."

"You've searched the whole area a dozen times," Jaroslav reminded him with a hint of malice. "Whoever you're searching for, they are not here."

"Perhaps," the soldier murmured, stepping back as the wheels threw up a hail of mud. "But if not—where are they?"

If they have any sense, Nick thought dourly, winding the window closed, they'll be somewhere warm and sunny and a million miles from here. And I'm beginning to wish I were with them.

They took the main road this time into Krajac itself, only to find it exactly the same as all the other villages Nick had passed through since his arrival. A few decayed looking farms on the outskirts giving way to a couple of intersecting streets of uneven houses painted in icing-sugar pinks and browns. Cars peeked out from under tarpaulins, uncertain electric light flickered in narrow windows. Once they passed a woman feeding chickens in her barren front yard. She turned to watch them as they passed, but there was no curiosity in her eyes, only a flat, dead acceptance. The chickens pecked her feet to return her to reality.

They skirted one bomb crater on the way in, half-full of dirty ice, but there was no other sign of damage. No burned houses, no shallow roadside graves. Perhaps the conflict had miraculously failed to ignite here, smothered by good neighborliness and an abnormal degree of common sense.

More likely the place had been fully Serb to begin with, and they'd stood smugly by while other villages drove out their unwanted neighbors, congratulating themselves on having come up with the idea first.

Jaroslav parked outside the largest surviving building, a salmon-pink house in the Bohemian style, and turned the engine off. "I see no reason for a translator to attend the autopsy. The corpse will not be saying anything of interest."

"And I thought you were getting a taste for police work."

"Personally, I prefer my soldiers alive—and a good deal more attractive than Sergeant Jim. It says very little for the available entertainment in Krajac if some poor woman had nothing better to do than spend her nights with him."

"Supposition," Nick reminded him. "We still don't know whom he was meeting, or why."

"Ah, Dr. Holmes, very true. Very true."

Nick opened the passenger door. The cold hit him like a hammer, dived through buttonholes and sleeves and the layers of his scarf to assault his inadequate thermal vest. "Watson," he said, "was a doctor. Holmes wasn't, I think."

Jaroslav rolled his eyes heavenward and set off for the building on the opposite corner. It had the broad, angular windows of a department store, but the clustered cafe tables and the lopsided Coca-Cola sign outside marked out its new function well enough.

Feeling a sudden twinge of envy—or perhaps simply thirst—Nick climbed the steps to the Royal Engineers HQ to interrogate a corpse.

"All pretty straightforward," Captain Wilder said for at least the eighth time as they headed through the house to the newly designated morgue. "Shotgun blast to the head obvious cause of death. Some bruising and skin scrapes, probably some sort of struggle. The local doctor took some samples, but frankly, I can't see there being drugs or anything involved. Where on earth would he have got them?"

"There's always someone," Nick observed, to keep his mind off the gilt-icing decor. "Even out here."

"Can't even get a decent cup of tea, I fail to see how . . ." Turning left into a short windowless spur of corridor, he opened the final door. "Here we are. We'll want to ship the poor chap out later today, so anything you want to know, you'd best look for now."

A cupboard or wardrobe lay face-down in the center of the empty room with a long bundle of white sheets arranged on top. Flakes of fresh snow swirled in through the open windows.

"Bit nippy, I know. But with no refrigeration facilities . . . "

Noise from the street leaked in, echoed strangely from the bare walls. Children's shouts and laughter, brittle and distant. Nick wondered if they were the same kids who'd found the body; whether they were traumatized, or boasting, or whether murder had become meaningless, after so many discoveries, so many shots in the night.

Unwrapping the body, he lifted Jim Rowley's bloodied knuckles to the light.

Boxer's knuckles, rough and slack-skinned. Blood under a fingernail; perhaps his killer's, perhaps his own, but out here, miles from a lab or even a reliable power supply, there was no way to tell.

Oh yes, there'd been a fight. But not the kind the captain was thinking. Not a quick, desperate scuffle, unexpected and one-sided. A fist-fight A bare-knuckle match. A contest.

"He was a Forces boxing champion," Wilder observed, following his train of thought. "Shelf full of trophies, back home. Not the sort of thing they teach in the police, I suppose."

"I learned before I joined the force. I'll bet Sergeant Rowley did, too. An after-school club, a gym. On the streets."

Wilder frowned as if some treasured assumption had been unexpectedly shattered.

"Got a few trophies myself;" Nick conceded. "Gave it up, though."

"Lack of time, I suppose."

"No. There was an accident. Almost killed someone."

The captain took a step back, into the shadows of the unlit room."Is that what you think happened here?"

Nick folded the broad hand back into the sheets, keeping his gaze averted from what little was left above the neck. "Doesn't look accidental to me."

"I suppose not."

"I heard Sergeant Rowley had been visiting someone in the village regularly. A woman."

Captain Wilder raised an eyebrow. "I find that unlikely. My men do a very dangerous job. They need their wits about them at all times, and lack of sleep could easily prove fatal."

Certainly did in this case, Nick thought, covering the body again.

"As for a woman—well, these things are discouraged, but they do happen. He must have kept the secret extremely well, but . . ."

Nodding thanks, Nick turned away.

Someone knew.

Someone always knows. A friend, an enemy, the town gossip, the quiet girl in the corner who seems to know no one and see nothing. An old woman connected to the world only by the twitch of her curtains. A child. Someone.

All I have to do is find them.

Jaroslav wasn't in the cafe.

Nick ordered coffee, and the dark skinny girl nodded and bustled back to the counter. A group of wizened men in thick coats and grubby embroidered caps regarded him impassively for a moment, then returned to studying the draughts board laid out on the table before them.

As far as he could tell, no one was actually playing. The counters were scattered, mid-game, but either the old men had lost interest or the game wasn't theirs in the first place. Perhaps the board just sat there day after day, each successive occupant of the table either ignoring it or shifting counters at random, no one ever ending the game.

The girl returned with a tiny cup of black coffee, leaving a trail of steam in the air behind her. The cafe didn't seem to be heated, and she was wearing a pullover beneath her faded overall.

The coffee was too hot to drink, and he had nothing better to do so he called after her, "Do you know Jim Rowley?"

Just a frown, a slight lifting of the shoulders. "No English," she said without irony and began scrubbing at the counter with a dirty rag.

"Ah, classic detective work in action," Jaroslav smiled.

A bell pinged as the door closed behind him. Stripping off his gloves, he sat down opposite, ruffled frost from his hair. The girl began pouring him coffee without any discernable signal.

"Where have you been?"

"Exploiting contacts. I think I might have a clue for you." He met Nick's gaze, held it. Enjoying the moment. "The name of the woman Sergeant Rowley met last night."

The conversation at the old men's table stilled just for a second; running the moment back in his head, Nick matched the disturbance to the words "Sergeant Rowley."

"Really?" He sipped the coffee, suddenly aware of the stillness, the blank candor of Jaroslav's gaze.

"Country people love to gossip. When a woman is upset, in trouble, it doesn't stay secret for long."

"Even from strangers?"

Jaroslav looked vaguely offended. "My grandmother lived her whole life in this village. I am not a stranger to them."

Nick nodded. The girl brought another coffee. Jaroslav blew on it for a moment, set it down untouched.

"So. You found this woman, and she said—"

"Please. You are the detective, not me. I told her you would be discreet, and she agreed to talk to you."

It was a brief drive consisting mostly of a rough dirt track leading from the lower end of the village. They passed the UN barracks, an uneasy mixture of prefabs and commandeered cowsheds, and drew tense stares from the soldiers on duty at the gate. Half a mile farther and Jaroslav turned left, onto a spur of tarmac beside a large whitewashed house. Frost-blacked pears rotted on the trees lining the driveway, turned to pulp under Nick's shoes as he picked his way to the door.

Jaroslav had already knocked twice and produced no response. As Nick joined him in the shelter of the crumbling porch, he lifted the latch and nudged the door open, calling something that sounded like a name.

The kitchen was thick with dust. Jaroslav moved through into the next room, but Nick remained. examining the dirty plates heaped on the tin draining board, the few rusted tins at the back of the larder surrounded by rat's droppings.

"She's gone," his companion called from somewhere upstairs accompanied by the creaking of long-unused floorboards.

Nick turned and walked back out into the snowy afternoon light.

An old woman was standing in the road staring daggers at Jaroslav's car. Seeing Nick, she tensed and waved her walking stack at him as if to ward off attack, yelling excitably.

"She says," Jaroslav murmured, suddenly close, "that Mrs. Duban was picked up by her husband twenty minutes ago. If we leave quickly, we may still catch them."

Nick, who had definitely heard the word "Serb" in that last sentence, shook his head. Spreading his hands in surrender, he took a couple of steps forward, trying out what he hoped was a reassuring smile.

The old woman's shoulders hunched, but she didn't run. She didn't look like she was capable of it.

"She's terrified, Nick. Duban had a reputation for violence. It's no accident that he survived the Serbs when so many—"

Smiling until his jaw ached, Nick asked the woman, *"Sprechen Sie Deutsch?"*

Her eyes narrowed to slits, and she replied in quiet, accented German, "They are gone. Long ago."

"I need to find out what happened to a UN soldier. Sergeant Rowley."

Her mouth twisted in disapproval. "Dead."

"Yes. I know that. But who killed him?"

"Ask the men in the cafe."

"The cafe? In the village?"

"Go challenge them to a game. Then you'll find out." A final, defiant glance past him to Jaroslav and she turned away. "If your friend won't tell you."

Gripped by the conviction that as long as he didn't move, didn'tgive any unseen enemy the excuse, she would be safe, Nick stood and watched her walk away.

"I see that your need for a translator was greatly exaggerated."

Suddenly aware that he had no idea whether Jaroslav spoke any German, Nick turned back to the car. His companion was sitting in the driver's seat, door still open, hands clasped on the wheel as if in prayer.

"Well," Nick announced, keeping his tone cheery, casual, "this woman isn't here. Back to the village, I think."

The car engine turned over. "For some of us," Jaroslav agreed and slammed the door.

Nick started forward, but he was ten steps too far out, and neither brave nor stupid enough to throw himself in front of the vehicle. Tires skidded on the wet leaves, metal scraped the gatepost, and suddenly the car leapt past him in a rush of warm air and roared away down the lane, scattering gravel in its wake.

Jaroslav didn't even look back.

Nick stood there for a moment weighing his options and finding them nonexistent. Walk. Stand here. Go back inside and look for clues—what clues? The woman had been gone for months. She'd never met Sergeant Rowley, never played any part in this mess.

Jaroslav had lied to him.

Jaroslav knew what was going on.

Well, at least someone did.

Buttoning the collar of his coat, Nick turned and began following the tire tracks back into town.

It could have been worse. He met a supply truck coming out of the UN barracks and, flashing his passport and papers, bagged a lift back into Krajac. Even empty, the truck had difficulty maintaining forty miles an hour, and any kind of incline reduced it to walking speed. The lanky Scotsman at the wheel gunned the accelerator and mumbled a steady stream of obscenities, trying to browbeat it into submission.

During the journey Nick had plenty of time to sort the evidence, and still none of it made any sense. What was the connection? Why the bruises? Why Jaroslav? Why set up this stupid story with the nonexistent woman? To close down the investigation?

If Jaroslav thought that was an adequate coverup, the Serb police had obviously been very bad at their jobs.

Impact with another pothole started him back to full wakefulness. They were lurching into Krajac's main street, an empty vista transformed by the slanting light of dusk. The builders had given up for the day, and as the truck jerked to a halt outside the cafe, Nick realized it was deserted.

So much for that lead.

"There you go, mate."

Nick opened the door, recoiled from the wind. "Thanks."

"Next time tell your driver to pick you up on time."

"Yeah. I'll do that."

The truck pulled away. Nick walked up the steps, rattled the cafe door. No sign of life. Suddenly too tired to continue, he sat down on the dusty concrete and watched lamps flicker into life in nearby windows.

Another cold dark night in a cold dark place; useless television aerials swaying in the wind, useless telephone wires draped among the trees, nothing left for modern man to do but huddle like his ancestors had done and dream of better days.

He needed a drink.

"American?" the old man asked.

Nick jerked upright, feeling sweat prickle across his shoulder blades. The man must have crossed yards of empty street to get here, but he hadn't seen a thing And now, hunched inside an overcoat the color of dung, the faded squares of a chessboard tucked under his arm, he was standing at the foot of the steps, grinning with broken teeth and correcting himself. "English, yes?"

"Yes. Look, I don't have any money—"

"Jaroslav said you would come."

Nick just stared at him.

"Said not to talk. But I think, anyone who comes, why not? All of us, the same enemy."

"What?"

"Here, tonight. Ten. We show you."

"Show me what?" Nick yelled at the man's back. "Hey!"

The man just kept walking.

Coming to his feet, Nick felt bones creak, stiffened by the cold. He was two steps from the road, psyching himself up to run, when he realized that the patterned wood under the old man's arm wasn't a chessboard at all.

Draughts. The unplayed game the old men had lingered over in the cafe. The German-speaking woman's suggestion to "challenge them to a game." His only clue, his only thread of a sanity in a case turned mind-game.

Sinking back on the frosted concrete, Nick watched the old man hobble into a side street and disappear.

He was back on the steps at nine forty-five, pacing and shivering and still unsure that he was doing the right thing. Fragments of ancient thrillers collided in his head, weaving possible futures for him. Cars racing out of the night to whisk him away; a femme fatale swaying out of the shadows; Jaroslav smiling, stepping from a doorway like Orson Welles.

As far as he could tell, the most likely outcome would be a trip to join Sergeant Rowley in the UN's pathetic morgue, and it would serve him right for coming over here in the first—

There was a vehicle approaching.

Stepping back into the doorway of the makeshift cafe, Nick folded his arms in what he hoped was a defiant manner and watched the shabby farm truck rattle up the street towards him.

Half a dozen men were huddled in the back, shoulders hunched, heads low; like soldiers behind fragile cover. As the truck braked, he scanned the bundles at their feet. Warm clothing, bottles of cola, plastic containers that just had to contain sandwiches. What was this, the Sunday school picnic?

One of them looked up, his face unreadable, and jerked a thumb at the only space left.

Get in.

Hoping to God no one in UNHQ was working late, or at least that they had better things to do than look out of the window, Nick hauled himself clumsily over the tailgate and sat down on a empty sack.

The truck lurched forward. None of the other passengers had even looked at him.

"Nice night for it," he offered, less an icebreaker than a retaliation for their silence.

The man who'd signaled for him to join them spared him a withering glance and returned to chewing on something that was staining his teeth a peculiar frothy red.

The truck turned east, passing through the most densely populated area of the town and out into the suburbs. Lit houses became darkened houses, and then, evolving in reverse, only bare bones: blackened rafters reflected in lakes of shattered glass, an urban graveyard.

Seven or eight ruins from the abrupt edge of town, the truck turned right, bumping across what had once been someone's lawn towards a tin-roofed barn. Knotholes and cracked shutters bled a warm yellow light and the buzz of a crowd fierce with anticipation.

The chewing man kicked the tailgate down and jumped clear. Suddenly aware of the stares of his companions, Nick lowered himself carefully from the truck. Frozen mud crunched beneath his shoes.

Somewhere inside the barn, someone was screaming for mercy.

"So," Jaroslav observed, blowing smoke into the lamplight, "I see you found your way here after all."

There were other lights, other sounds—above all the crazy dance of shadows on the whitewashed walls beyond, enacting his worst nightmares—but there would be time for them. Right now there was just Jaroslav standing over the lamp and the table and the wooden vat of cloudy homemade beer, and saying, "I panicked, of course. I should have known you would not accept that there was a woman, a woman who'd changed her mind, and run. But I suppose this was inevitable. Rowley found us, so eventually someone else—"

"Is that why you killed him?"

Jaroslav looked at him for a moment. Then he dropped his cigarette, crushed it underfoot, and stepped back to give Nick a clear view of the game.

They'd marked the arena with a circle on the ground. Like a Black Mass, he thought stupidly as the white arc light faltered and returned, flattening the men in the ring to paper silhouettes. One, a big redheaded man, was stripped to the waist, jeans and bare feet below, kicking up white sand as he circled. His opponent was a boy who hardly looked old enough to merit the filthy army fatigues he wore. There was blood crusted at the corner of his mouth, and he flinched every time his opponent moved.

"What is this?"

"He—" the redhead, flexing his muscles now, playing to the cheers of the crowd "—is a farmer from Mivar. The boy was a member of a paramilitary group that attacked the village in the early days of the conflict. He—the boy, himself—is known to have killed three unarmed men and raped a girl of fourteen. What the others did does not bear recounting."

The muscles of Nick's stomach cramped in anticipation. "And now he pays."

"Oh yes."

"And Rowley?"

"Came to fight. There is frustration on all sides: the guilty go free, disappear across borders; politics interferes with justice . . ." Jaroslav smiled. "Rowley cared nothing for justice. He just enjoyed a fight."

The redhaired man feinted fast, a right hook pulled barely before impact. The boy staggered, fell backwards, landing across the daubed circle. The nearest observer, a stocky man with a shotgun cradled in his arms, kicked him in the back, and he struggled back over the line.

The crowd stirred uneasily, yells subsiding to murmurs. The boy was making no attempt to stand up.

Nick closed his eyes, hoping the scene would change, the yells become the grunts of harmless farm animals and the barn restfully dark. Jaroslav's voice intruded, calm and urbane against the sounds of gathering bloodlust. "Of course Rowley had to prove how much better he was than some mere Kosovar. He had to take on two men at once. The stronger they were, the better. Last night he took an unlucky punch. His skull fractured, that much was obvious. There was internal bleeding, pressing on the brain . . . he died, And of course some fool decided he couldn't be found with a fractured skull, that was too great a clue, we had to use a shotgun on him, obliterate the evidence . . . "

The crowd was booing.

The farmer was circling the boy, kicking listlessly at his huddled form. Eyes closed, arms folded about his bloodied head, the boy remained curled into a ball. The crowd's displeasure drowned any sound he might have been making, but Nick couldn't shake the feeling he was praying.

"Move," he murmured, shouldering past Jaroslav. Jarring the beer table in passing, he forced a path between the murmuring onlookers. The crowd fell away before him, and he could feel the heat of the arc lights as be stepped superstitiously over the circle of red paint and seized the boy by the collar, trying to haul him to his feet.

Silence.

So sudden, so total that, schooled by months of blunders, he looked automatically at Jaroslav for explanation.

Trailing to the edge of the circle, his translator smiled lazily and said, "That was foolish."

"Just tell me what—"

"Think of it as a game of tag. You've just become 'it.' That is, you've just offered to fight him to the death."

The redhaired man looked at Nick for a moment, anger and disgust mingled in his eyes, then turned and stamped away. Someone came forward with a towel; others held his shirt, pressed a beer into his hand, as solicitous as ringside trainers pampering their champion.

The boy wouldn't stand. Releasing his grip, Nick let him fall to the ground. Sand fanned out from the impact, settled on his shoes. "I can't fight—"

For the first time real concern showed in Jaroslav's face. "Then I suggest you learn. Because if you try to take him out of here alive, Nick, they will kill you, and I am unarmed and have neither the way nor the will to stop them."

They gave him a moment to prepare. Gestured for him to remove his shoes; would have taken his shirt, too, but there was a sting in the air and he needed to be ready for a quick exit.

The boy was no longer responding either to insults or to violence. Someone threw a glass of beer in his face amid what Nick took for protests about the waste of good alcohol, and two hulking bystanders repositioned him directly across the arena from Nick

"Jaroslav?"

"If this is some kind of getaway plan—"

"I want you to tell them I'm taking his body. He's wanted, right? I'm going to take him in. Get a promotion. Killed him in self-defense, you see. That's my price for keeping quiet about this."

Jaroslav exhaled heavily, turned aside to speak to several of the shotgun-wielding men guarding the ring. The onlookers were refilling their glasses, jostling for access to the beer like playful partygoers, their banter loud but strangely tense. It reminded him of a racetrack, or the regulars' corner at a bookie's. Talking to hold the tension at bay, fill the time until the big event.

The boy was crying.

Fighting nausea, Nick looked down at his clenched fists, finding them suddenly small and frail.

He'd done it once. Scared himself into a lifetime of retreat, of negotiating and swallowed anger and unrealized dreams. He'd done it once, he could do it again.

"He's yours," Jaroslav conceded, stepping back into the gloom as a sudden scramble for places resolved into a row of blankly expectant faces. "Whatever it is you really want him for . . . "

Stepping into the circle, Nick looked down at the boy.

This wasn't going to work. Unless . . .

With a scream like a frightened child, the boy sprang up and rushed him.

Great. The farmer he won't touch, but me, he'll fight. Because he thinks he can take me.

He probably can, too.

Nick sidestepped, but the boy's fist caught him in the lower ribs, spinning him. The crowd managed a ragged noise that could have been approval or display. Even with the other contender a wanted war criminal, they didn't seem that eager to support him.

Their ingratitude stung, somewhere deeper than he'd expected, and he turned his anger on the softest target. Channeling his momentum into his fist, he punched the boy in the lower back, sending him sprawling. This time the cheer was a little more convincing.

No time to play games. No time to consider what might happen if this didn't work, if the power just wasn't there any more—

The boy was coming at him again. Ducking a flailing blow, Nick stepped inside his opponent's reach and drove a fist into his chest.

Full strength, no hesitation. Hard enough to break ribs but hoping that wouldn't happen. Hard enough to rupture the lung, but that wasn't the goal either—

The boy's eyes rolled back in his head, and one by one his joints buckled, depositing him in a heap across Nick's bare feet.

No cheers. He would have hated them, hated their implication, but their absence disturbed him all the same. No satisfaction, even. Just an uneasy murmuring, eyes downcast, hiding behind their beers and their hands.

The stocky man rolled the boy's body over, pressed two fingers to his throat, grunted. The crowd's murmurs diminished, and one by one they turned away.

"Too easy," the official said. "Go, then."

Kicking his shoes back on, Nick scooped the boy's dead body into his arms and began to drag him from the ring.

It had been sixty seconds, at least. Longer. He was moving too slowly. And none of these vehicles had keys in them, what was he supposed to do for God's sake, he was a police officer, not a car thief—

The truck he'd arrived in. Keys still in the ignition.

Dumping the boy on his back in the frozen mud, Nick bent down, pressed both hands to the boy's still heart, and pumped.

A breath, more pumping; natural, automatic. He'd done all this before. Saved lives. Little old ladies keeled over in suburban streets, bluefaced babies in shopping centers. Had his photo in the paper once.

Think of that. Think of the successes, the good times, not the failures and the disillusionment that drove you out here in the first place. Not the boy whose heart you stopped with a lucky punch that got you thrown out of the boxing club, that got you labeled Killer Nick in the first place . . .

Pump, pump. Breathe. And—

Wait.

A fluttering eyelid, a hint of a pulse at the boy's throat. A rattling inhalation, all his own work.

Shaky, but it was going to have to do.

Lifting the boy into the front seat, Nick scrambled in beside him and turned the key. The engine jolted to life; the boy coughed and fell forward against the seatbelt.

Turning the truck up a slight incline, letting gravity settle the boy back into his seat, Nick rubbed sand from his eyes and tried to remember the route to the UN barracks.

It was after the third sharp turn that he really became aware of pursuit. He must have seen the headlights almost at once, miles back, but they'd been part of the illusion, part of the nightmare of looming forest and gritty, tractionless roads edging rivers and fields and sheer unfathomable drops into the dark.

They'd been biding their time. Waiting for him to skirt the edge of town. Waiting for the perfect ambush ground. And there was nothing he could do but drive faster, take more risks, and try not to look back.

Light flared in the wing-mirror, a tiny reflected spark. A match, he thought, seizing on a poor clue to prove the obvious; then the rear tire blew, louder than the unheard gunshot, and he was trying to pull the rickety truck out of a sixty mph spin, darkness looming to his right and to the left the outline of a low stone wall, slewing in fast—

Pain exploded in his chest. So it was true, you never heard the bullet that killed you . . .

No. Wait. Not a bullet. The seat-belt, cutting hard into his ribs. Bone ground as he drew breath.

Gripping the steering wheel with both hands, he pushed himself back into the seat. The pain cleared his head, and he blinked into the darkness, trying to rationalize the silhouettes. Trees, branches shivering. Someone moving, circling the lopsided truck at a distance as if it contained some wild animal on the point of escape.

"For God's sake, Jaroslav . . . " The name made him cough, and he was glad of the interruption. He had no bribes now, no excuses, and he didn't have the strength to beg.

Gloved hands wrenched the passenger door open, reached for the seatbelt clasp. Locking both arms around the boy's waist, Jaroslav hauled him out into the snow.

"You'll have to leave, of course," he said, his voice blurred by the wind as he retreated a few steps, bent over to deposit his unresisting burden on the ground.

"Before or after I report you and your—"

"They won't be there tomorrow night There are other places, other fugitives."

"Like him?" Nick fumbled free of the seatbelt, struggled to move himself across the seat to the open door. "He's a child, Jaroslav, whatever he did—"

The shot reverberated among the trees, a flat, hollow noise like half-heard thunder. Jaroslav pulled the magazine from his pistol and let the gun fall.

"You said you were unarmed."

"We're all liars here," Jaroslav observed pleasantly, and walked away.

Nick closed his eyes. There were sirens somewhere out in the night. Shots didn't pass unnoticed, not this chose to the barracks. Someone had beard. Someone would come.

All he had to do was decide what to say when they did.

The Second Coming

by Terence Faherty

1

I WAS SITTING IN THE MAIN CONCOURSE of Union Station when I spotted her. I was supposed to be meeting a train, but it was running late, as trains tended to do in 1964, so I'd granted myself ten minutes to smoke a pipe in the station's cool and cavernous waiting room. It was one of my favorite places in Los Angeles because it reminded me of the identically named station in my hometown of Indianapolis. Not that the architecture was the same. The LA station's was Spanish mission meets the Hollywood Bowl, while Indy's was strictly Victorian robber baron chic. It was the scale of the space that jogged the memories. And the variety of people inside that space. No place in the world for watching people like a train station. Which brings me back to her.

She was my age—the flip side of forty-five—but better preserved. Very well preserved, everywhere but her face, which was worn in a way I found all too familiar. Being an old married guy, I would have noted the Marie Wilson figure and the shoulder-length auburn hair and moved on to the next subject, if it hadn't been for the way this subject was dressed. She wore a tight pink cashmere sweater above a gray A-line skirt too long and too wide at the hem for the space age. Even more dated was her footwear: saddle shoes and socks that stopped just north of her slender ankles. Bobby socks, in other words, those symbols of a whole generation of young women, the bobby-soxers, the makers of Frank Sinatra's career, the breakers of innumerable GI hearts, the dusters of soda fountain stools from Bakersfield to Bangor.

That generation had long since gone the way of Sinatra's curls, gone into motherhood most of them, producing a whole new crop of handfuls. But here was one of the original specimens in front of me. Briefly in front of me, as she was nervously moving up and down the concourse, never lighting anywhere for long, her gaze returning again and again to the station clock, which was moving way too slowly to rate that much attention.

I tapped out my pipe, got to my feet, and wandered her way. She'd paused by a magazine stand, though she already carried an example in one pale hand. Like her outfit, her magazine was out-of-date. I recognized the red masthead and the black-and-white photography of *Life*'s 1940s design. When I drew closer, I made out the subject of the cover story, actress Geraldine Fitzgerald, and the date of the issue, August 7, 1944, and the hairs on the back of my neck did a little samba.

Then she looked up, and our eyes met. Hers were a watery brown. And frightened, but she might have been passing the same judgment on my steely blue ones just then. Before I could tip my hat and offer my name, Scott Elliott, she turned and hurried off toward the end of the grand hall that led down to the platforms.

I watched her until she'd disappeared down the stairs. Then I caught another pair of eyes, also brown, not frightened. They belonged to a porter who was leaning against the green-and-gold tile wainscoting of the wall to my left. He didn't look away, so I crossed to him, resisting the urge to shake my head with every step.

"Morning," I said.

"Morning," he said back.

"Notice the brunette in the pink sweater?"

"Been noticing her. She's been flitting around here better part of an hour."

"Seen her before?"

"Maybe I've seen her before. Twenty years before. We had all kinds of little girlies like that around here then. Meeting their soldier boys or telling them goodbye. Never liked the goodbyes much."

"I meant, have you seen her around here recently?"

"Does she stop by regular? Nope. Couldn't call once every twenty years regular."

2

I stood there wondering for a time after the porter had moved off in search of a lonesome bag. His memories of wartime goodbyes and reunions had put flesh on the idea I'd gotten when I'd spotted the bobby-soxer's magazine. It was that this sad-eyed woman was reenacting a day from twenty years ago. The day she'd said goodbye to her sweetheart maybe. Or the day his train showed up without him. That one jibed better with the look she'd been giving the station clock, the look of someone meeting a train she been waiting for forever.

What my little fantasy wouldn't jibe with was my own experience of the service. No soldier going overseas knew for certain he'd be back at all, never mind the day and hour. The only ones who could even hazard a guess were the survivors who'd made it stateside and been handed their discharges at some middle-of-nowhere processing center. Of course, something could have happened to her soldier between the time he'd called or wired her from Seattle or Albuquerque and the scheduled arrival of his train. The shock of that irony—a man survives the fighting and dies or disappears within hours of home—might still be echoing twenty years later.

I looked at the big wall clock that had so fascinated the woman in question and found that it was time to meet my own overdue train. Not that I found my current assignment half as interesting as a certain overage sweater girl. But she'd headed down to the tracks herself, so for once my duty and my curiosity were tugging on the same end of the rope.

Unfortunately, duty, in the form of a studio executive named Larry Nesbitt, found me first. Nesbitt was a bench warmer at United Artists, but still young enough to dream of making the starting nine. Hollywood had been lousy with Nesbitts back before the war, toothy, wavy-haired yes-men with very vague job descriptions. Their ranks had been thinned considerably by the ongoing studio shakeout, but I still knew more than my share, working as I did for a private security firm so discreet its operatives had no job descriptions whatsoever. Nesbitt had been a satisfied customer of Hollywood Security's some months back. Now he'd hired us for what my boss, Paddy Maguire, termed a "standard hand-holding job."

Nesbitt didn't see things quite that way. "Elliott, where the hell did you get off to? The train was due in five minutes ten minutes ago. We're not meeting my Aunt Sophie, you know."

We weren't meeting Lady Bird Johnson either, but you couldn't tell that from the state of Nesbitt's nerves. As it happened, we weren't meeting anybody. We were there—my client and I and two studio flunkies with a hand truck—to accept delivery of a motion picture, *The Story of the King*. Not United Artists' wide-screen Technicolor version. That was currently in post production, with release scheduled for sometime in '65. We were awaiting the return of the original, the 1919 silent produced and directed by Thomas Ince, probably the most famous of Hollywood's lost films.

It was also one of Hollywood's most famous flops, a life of Christ that had inflamed the Bible belt and been condemned from pulpits of every denomination. The problem had been timing. In 1919, Cecil B. DeMille had yet to make Sunday-school movie making respectable. Worse, Ince's Messiah, an actor named Victor Lawrence, had been arrested in Chicago on a morals charge just as the film had hit theaters. According to legend, Lawrence's fall from grace had been the source of the long-standing superstition that it was unlucky to show Christ's face on the screen.

It had certainly been unlucky for Ince and his backers. Those prints that hadn't been destroyed by angry churchgoers had ended up in the studio's own furnace. When museums of modern art had begun collecting silent masterpieces in the forties, no print or negative of *The Story of the King* could be found.

But now, on the eve of the big-budget remake's release, a print had turned up. In atheist Russia, of all places. Nesbitt had heard of it from a friend at the New York museum that had haggled over it with the Soviets. He'd talked his United Artists bosses into underwriting the purchase—to the tune of a hundred grand, more than the film's original budget—in exchange for the right to use the rediscovery to promote the upcoming epic.

Nesbitt had then personally arranged for Hollywood Security to see the film safely from the train station to the studio vault. Silent movie thieves being a rare breed, I figured I was there as window dressing, an extra in a carefully orchestrated photo opportunity. Only there were no photographers in sight. And no newshounds. I asked Nesbitt where he was hiding them.

"I'm not," he said, looking up the empty tracks for about the fiftieth time. "I didn't call anyone. I'm not calling anyone until the studio gates are locked behind us. I'm not kidding, Elliott. I haven't slept the last three nights worrying about today. My neck's sticking out a mile; I can feel it. Those museum people had to jump the gun and issue that press release about how much we'd paid for this thing. That story was picked up by every paper in every tank town this train's been through."

"Why didn't you fly it out?"

"Planes crash."

I was familiar with this argument against air travel, Paddy having used it since Will Rogers's last landing, so I returned to the publicity angle. "I thought free ink was the whole idea."

Nesbitt gave me a look I often got from Hollywood insiders, the look that always made me feel like an outsider. "Without that film, there'll be no free ink."

I tapped my suit coat at the spot that would have been hiding my gun if I'd thought this was the kind of job that required wearing one. "Then we'll just have to see it makes it home."

3

Not long afterward, a bored voice came over the public address system to announce the arrival of the missing streamliner. Then the anticipatory rumble—the one you first feel through the soles of your shoes—began. It built and built, becoming a sound as sinister and elemental as any Bernard Hermann score. By the time the red and silver diesel had reached the end of the platform, I could barely hear Nesbitt yelling in my ear: "The baggage cars will stop down there."

He trotted off after his two assistants. I would have followed him—not trotting—if I hadn't caught sight of her, the Spirit of 1944.

She'd certainly come out of nowhere like a ghost. I'd scanned the crowd for her without success throughout Nesbitt's lament. But suddenly there she was, moving away from my post at the baggage cars, just as the application of the train's many brakes made calling out to her impossible. A second later, the general confusion on the platform would have made posing a casual question like "What year do you think it is?" equally difficult, so I reluctantly followed my real client in the opposite direction.

I found Nesbitt throwing what weight he had around. He'd already arranged to accept delivery right there on the platform, instead of the more civilized setting of the baggage office. Now he was insisting that the film canisters be unloaded before anything else. If by some chance they'd actually made it to California safely, he wasn't going to risk their being smuggled off the train in some innocent-looking crate or trunk.

The freight agent was an ex-NCO with the air of a man who had heard everything twice and hadn't been impressed the first time. Nevertheless, he humored Nesbitt, disappearing into the baggage car, chewing a pencil as he went.

I used this intermission to check the passenger end of the platform. The bobby-soxer was there, standing out now that the train's modest human-being load was scattering. She was doing little dancer's darts toward the few unescorted men still exiting the train: two steps toward each figure and a quick one back. Despite the distance between us, I could see she was panicking, that those brown eyes of hers were as wide as a doll's.

I took a step or two of my own down the hot concrete. Then Nesbitt called, "Hey, Elliott! Get back here!"

The agent had placed two octagonal cases near the sliding door of the car. He was holding some paperwork under Nesbitt's nose, distracting him with it. My calculation of the likely length of that distraction was interrupted by a scream.

I caught a glimpse of the time traveler as she ran into the station proper. By that time I was running myself. Nesbitt was yelling again, but I was more conscious of the startled people I was dodging than his angry words. I caught a glimpse of the old copy of *Life*, crumpled on the ground. It helped me select the right doorway from the series of identical doorways leading off the platform. Beyond the tiled opening were stairs, which I took two at a time. I paused on a landing where all the parallel staircases from the track level merged into two big ones that led up into the concourse. There was no sign of her, but I kept climbing.

At the top of the stairs, I ran into my friend the nostalgic porter, almost knocking both of us down.

"Who you chasing?" he asked as we steadied one another.

"The woman in the pink sweater."

He shook his head. "No, sir. She hasn't come up here. I'd have noticed her, bag or no bag."

She might have doubled back to the platform on one of the other stairways. Or she might have taken a tunnel to one of the other platforms. Neither move made much sense, so I decided to go back the way I'd come. Nesbitt would be down there, awaiting my explanation.

Or so I thought. There was no sign of him or his helpers on the blazing platform. No sign of the NCO freight agent, either, though his troops were busy unloading the baggage cars. I was about to ask one of them where everyone had gotten off to, when I heard my name. One of Nesbitt's two sidekicks came out of an arched tunnel, waving to me and yelling for help.

I followed him into the passage, a smooth-floored ramp used to roll baggage carts up into the station. Ten steps inside, Nesbitt was seated on the floor, holding a bloody handkerchief to his head. The second flunky was there too, standing next to his empty hand truck.

"They went up," Nesbitt said. "Two of them, with guns. Hurry."

I sprinted up the passage, alone, without a gun. I stayed alone until I hit daylight again on the loading dock apron. Then I had the indifferent traffic on Alameda Street for company.

4

"I'm not blaming you, Scotty," Nesbitt said. He'd said it so often over the past few hours that the words had twisted themselves inside out, becoming an accusation instead of an absolution. Or so it seemed to my guilty ear.

We were seated in the office of Paddy Maguire, titular head of Hollywood Security. I use the titular wiggle advisedly. Paddy, a sixty-plus guy who could pass for Pat O'Brien's meatier brother, had developed a profound disinterest in things, including the business he'd founded almost twenty-five years earlier. The malaise had come on him late the previous fall, after his anger over John Kennedy's murder had boiled itself away. But he was listening to Nesbitt politely enough.

The studio exec was also polite, though his anger had yet to boil off. He'd changed from his train-meeting suit to sports clothes, and a small white bandage nestled in his wavy hair. "I might have tried to help this woman myself, if I'd noticed her," he was saying. "Though it's obvious now that she was only there to distract you. Obvious to me."

Paddy left off lighting a corona long enough to say, "To us too."

"So I'm not interested in damaging the reputation of your firm. Even if I were free to speak frankly to the newspapers."

"Which you're not," Paddy said between attempts to blow out his match.

"Which I'm not. In fact, I'd like to give you a chance for a comeback. I'd like Scotty to be the one who delivers the ransom money." He touched his bandage lightly. "I've had my fill of dealing with those two gentlemen."

I didn't think much of the idea, beyond wondering if this new scheme explained Nesbitt's sudden affection for my first name. Paddy said, "You're sure there's going to be a ransom?"

"The film's worthless to anyone but us and a museum. And no museum will touch it now. And remember, the guy who did the talking said, 'You'll hear from us tomorrow.'"

"And, 'No cops,'" Paddy added with a shadow of his old smile, the sentiment being dear to his heart. "That's all he said?"

"That's all."

"And the studio will pay?"

"They'll have to. The newspapers may not have the whole story, but they have enough."

I'd done my best to smuggle Nesbitt and his bloody head out of the station, but there'd been too many witnesses, though none of them had seen anything useful, like the make and license number of the getaway car.

"I wouldn't worry about much play from the papers," Paddy said. "They've got to figure it's all a publicity stunt."

Nesbitt was still in a forgiving mood. "I don't blame them for that," he said as he stood. "In fact, the whole farce will be great for publicity, if we get the film back. I'm counting on you two for that. I'll call you the minute I hear something."

Paddy walked Nesbitt out, perhaps to distract him from the threadbare stretches of the entryway carpet. I sat where I was, filling my pipe. When that project was over and my boss still hadn't returned, I got up and went in search of him.

I found Paddy on our front walk, presumably in the very spot where he'd said his goodbyes to Nesbitt. He was rocking on his heels and looking up at a passing cloud.

I bummed a match from him and said, "So we're certain that woman was in on the heist?"

"You're not? A little hot for pink sweaters in August, wouldn't you say?"

"She was wearing the clothes she'd worn twenty years ago."

"Twenty years ago in August, according to that billboard-size clue, the magazine she flashed at you. I don't remember the Augusts back then being any cooler. But that sweater of hers was just the kind of detail you'd think of if you were dreaming up a bobby-soxer costume. Especially if you were trying to catch a man's eye. And here's another little thing. You guessed she was your age."

"So?"

"So you were a trifle old for a corporal twenty years ago, so she would have been very old for a bobby-soxer. No woman of twenty-five would have dressed that way in '44. Dressing like your kid sister is a more recent fashion trend."

He sounded so much like the Paddy of old that I barely minded the points he was scoring at my expense. "Sorry I didn't spot her as a ringer."

"You can't be blamed for a suit fitting you when it's made to measure. And she was certainly custom made for you, an ex-GI given to dwelling on the past when he's not actually dwelling in it. Who knows you that well, I wonder?"

"Half the lowlifes in this town, given my post-army career."

"At least half," Paddy agreed. "I still smell a publicity stunt. How sure are you that it was really Nesbitt's own blood he was waving around on that handkerchief?"

"I watched them sew up his scalp."

"No playacting then. Ah, well. I guess we'll just have to wait to see what tomorrow brings."

5

I decided I couldn't sit around waiting for tomorrow to ambush me. So after I left Paddy I drove over to Vine Street just north of Melrose. Commercial properties were crowding out the little bungalows that once had prospered in that neighborhood. Those residences that were left had commercial sidelines, often as not. The one I parked my Thunderbird next to was a combination private home and casting agency, the Hanks Agency. It was run by a former screenwriter named Florence Hanks, whom I'd met in 1947 when she'd been scribbling away for Warner Bros.

I was figuring it like this. If my damsel in distress really was a fake, she was probably an actress. Her performance on the platform had suggested some aptitude in that department. I was further figuring her to be a down-on-her-luck actress for the following reasons. One, the deal she'd gotten involved in was shady. Two, I hadn't recognized her and I would have if she'd had even half a career. And three, failed actresses were commoner than palm trees around Hollywood.

And there was one reason more. I had some experience of the acting profession, having spent some time in it myself before the war. That was the past Paddy and others accused me of dwelling in, not my army days. So I knew what the acting dream was like and I knew what waking from that dream was like. And I was wondering if the familiar wear and tear I'd seen on the face of my mystery woman might not be the telltale leavings of a dream that had flickered out.

All of which led me to the Hanks Agency. It was the kind of institution a desperate actress would pass through, sooner or later. And Florence had a memory for the transient faces of extras and also-rans that was second to none.

She kept her beer cold too. She opened us a couple and lit herself a cigarette as we settled down in her living room with her books of mug shots. That's what she called them. Actually, they were albums of publicity stills. Enough photos of eager young hope to break a heart, if we'd had one between us.

"The way you describe her," Florence said, "I'm thinking it was someone dewy-eyed in the forties, grimly determined in the fifties, and now just grim." She held her cigarette in the backhanded way Betty Davis had taught women to hold them, though it might have been the way Florence had taught Davis. "These are women I had on file in the fifties, so they're our best bet."

She looked pretty much the way she had when I'd first met her. She'd hennaed her hair back then and worn enough face powder to make her teeth look ochre, and she still did. Timeless elegance, she might have called it.

"Have you considered hookers?" she asked.

"Not recently."

"I mean, have you considered the idea that this decoy dame might be a hooker? That'd be a good title, by the way: 'The Decoy Dame.' Very Earl Stanley Gardener. I'm writing again, did I tell you? Mystery stories. *Ellery Queen Magazine.*"

"Remind me to subscribe."

"She'd be old for a hooker though. Old for a stripper too. Most dreamers her age have given up and headed home. That's what I really should have gone into after Warners. And don't ask if I mean stripping."

The thought hadn't entered my mind, but I smiled politely.

"What I'm saying is, instead of trying to place young hopefuls in the movies, I should have started a relocation service for the ones who'd given up. Gotten them jobs in Boise or Muncie or. . ."

"Poughkeepsie?" I suggested.

"Perfect," she said, clinking her beer glass against my bottle. "Probably would have made a decent living at that. Not to mention all the good I could have done, all the wasted lives I could have rehabilitated."

I might have taken offense at that, as a potential customer of Hanks's hypothetical rescue service, if I hadn't turned a page just then and found my ghost. The face was less lined—unlined, in fact—and she was smiling an open, trusting smile that seemed as out of place, given my experience of her, as a goatee. The big brown eyes—not frightened then—had been her best feature. They were heavily lashed, and the photographer had managed to suggest unfathomable depths. That detail fit.

"Got her?" Florence asked. "What do you know? Slip her out of there. Her name and address should be on the back."

They were. The name was Joy Keedy. The address was an apartment not far away on Mariposa.

"That address was current in 1952," Florence said, squinting at her notations on the photo's back. "So I wouldn't count on it. But at least you have a name." She repeated that name a time or two. "I'm sure I remember her. She did some photo layouts, some television. Maybe a movie even. Last I heard, she was marrying some gaffer at RKO. It should have been a happily-ever-after. I wonder what happened."

"I'll let you know," I said, handing her my empty.

"Do that, Scotty. I may need it for 'The Decoy Dame.' They pay by the word, you know."

6

Florence was right about the Mariposa address being stale. No one there remembered a Joy Keedy. She might have left a forwarding address, but the place had changed hands since '52, and none of the records had survived the putsch. I couldn't go by RKO to ask around for a gaffer who may or may not have married a buxom brunette, since that studio was only a happy memory. So I went home.

There my loving wife and my two loving children listened to the story of my day while trying to suppress their loving smiles. Later the kids went off to see the latest Beach Party movie. Ella and I opted for an evening of dancing, our private code word for sex. Ella asked me if I wanted her to model a tight pink sweater as a warm-up, but we did fine without it.

The call from Nesbitt came in early the next morning. He'd received the filmnappers' demands: ten thousand dollars, delivery details to be phoned in after five.

"They're not greedy," Paddy observed after hanging up. "Whatever else you can say about their manners."

I spent the day trying to get a line on Joy Keedy, without success. She wasn't paying dues to any of the unions or guilds in town. She didn't have a telephone or a police record or even a library card. If she was driving a car, she was doing it under another name.

Ella tied up our line around four just long enough to tell me to be careful and to stress that it was just her standard concern, that she hadn't felt any special tingles or received any omens. The phone didn't ring again until after seven. It was Nesbitt, too keyed-up to say any more than he'd be right over.

He arrived carrying a little leather satchel that might as well have had "ransom money" printed on each side. "The place they picked is Fanita Canyon. It's a little cul-de-sac about a mile south of where Topanga Canyon Boulevard crosses Mulholland Drive."

That area was a ways out and lonely. "The far side of the moon wasn't available?" I asked.

Nesbitt ignored the crack. "At the top of the street there's a house for sale. It's empty, only tonight at nine there'll be a man there with the film. His partner will be watching for cops from somewhere nearby, so there can't be any cops. You give the guy in the house the money and he gives you the film. Two cases, six reels in each case. I've spoken to my friend at the museum in New York. He said each can has a paper label with the name of the original production company, Excelsior, typed on it. We need all twelve, remember."

"One for each finger and ear," I said.

Paddy had been busy checking the money over. "All in order," he said. "Pour yourself a drink, Mr. Nesbitt. I'll just see Scotty to his car."

Paddy carried the satchel, swinging it like a lunch pail. When I paused at the Thunderbird's door, he reached out and tapped the front of my coat at the very same spot I'd tapped when I'd reassured Nesbitt back at Union Station. Tonight there really was a gun under the gabardine.

"Good," Paddy said. "Never liked a money drop on a dead-end street. Keep your wits about you."

7

Calling Fanita Canyon a street was giving it all the breaks. It was actually a dirt track scarring a denser corner of the wooded hills just north of the point where Topanga Canyon Boulevard tops the Santa Monica Mountains and begins its plunge into the San Fernando Valley. I took my time climbing Fanita itself, keeping the Ford in low gear and scanning the woods for the lights of neighboring homes. I didn't see so much as the blue-gray glow of a television.

Then my headlights picked up a for sale sign rising out of the weedy verge at a cockeyed angle. I parked the Thunderbird, shut it down, and waited for my eyes to adjust to the darkness. My dome light didn't undo this precaution when I finally got around to opening my door, as I'd removed its bulb some years before at Paddy's insistence.

The night was clear but moonless. I could just make out the outline of a flat-roofed ranch thirty yards from the road atop a stony outcrop well clear of the trees. There was a light in one front window, a weak yellow light. A lantern maybe, which would make sense if the electricity was shut off. Nearer to hand was a path bordered by boulders that might have been displaced when they leveled the lot for the house.

I put the doctor's bag in my left hand, unbuttoned my suit coat, and started up. It occurred to me, belatedly, that I'd have both hands full on the trip back and no way to use my gun. I told myself I wouldn't need one by then, probably didn't need one at all. Then the first shot rang out.

That's telling it wrong. I saw the muzzle flash before I heard the shot. It lit the part of the house I'd been studying, the part farthest from the yellow window. I saw a man framed in an open doorway. Then I was lying facedown in the dirt, trying to flatten myself and draw my gun at the same time.

Even with all that going on, I had time to wonder who the hell the man was shooting at. Had Nesbitt called in a police backup he hadn't mentioned to Paddy and me? The second shot settled the issue. I didn't see this one, but I heard it clearly, heard it leave the barrel, heard it ricochet against a boulder to my left and then chip one to my right. I was the target.

It made no sense for him to be shooting at his paymaster, but there it was. I crawled to the downrange side of one of the larger rocks and prepared to do some nonsensical shooting of my own.

I never got the chance. I heard the sound of furniture falling over with an accompanying crash of breaking glass. The yellow window went black for half a second. When the flickering light came back, it did it in a big way.

The house had to be built of kindling, the fire took over so fast. I crouched there waiting for the shooter to come out, but he never did. By the time I decided to go in after him, it was too late. Flames blocked every opening. Whoever or whatever was in there was in for keeps.

8

The little house went out almost as quickly as it had gone up. The fire department had a hand in that—I'd heard their sirens before I'd given up the idea of getting inside—but mostly it was fuel exhaustion. Still, the firemen kept the blaze from spreading to the surrounding forest, so they more than earned their pay.

The speed of their arrival was explained to me by a fireman named Barney. "There's a fire tower just up the ridge. They probably could smell this thing, it was so close. Our station's down at the Mulholland intersection. That's why it didn't take us any time to get here."

He was a young man, by my standards, but he sported an old man's soup-strainer moustache. "Not that we could have done much good if we'd been next door when it started," he continued, "not as fast as that fire spread. There must have been some kind of accelerant, something like gasoline tossed around to jump start things. The kerosene from one little lamp couldn't get the whole house going that fast. You say there might have been someone inside?"

"Might have been. Might have been some reels of movie film too. Could they have come through okay?"

"How old a movie?" Barney asked, very interested.

"Old. Nineteen nineteen."

"How many reels?"

"A dozen."

The fireman whistled. "There's your accelerant right there. They used nitrate stock back then. Very unstable stuff. Burns like old Chicago."

Hope died hard for me. "They were in metal cans."

"Those just act like the casing on a grenade. Sorry, Mr. Elliott. That movie's gone. Was it valuable?"

The price ranged from ten thousand to the stars, depending on your point of view. But I didn't discuss that issue with Barney. It came up later, when I was chatting with a police lieutenant named Grove. It was nearly dawn by then, and one well-protected fireman had begun poking around in the still-warm ashes of the house while the rest of us looked on. There'd been a police presence almost from the start in the form of a single cruiser. I'd used its radio to send a brief account of the evening to Paddy and Ella via a friendly dispatcher.

That same radio call had brought Grove my way. He was too important a man to bother with a little house fire, but he'd taken an interest in Hollywood Security years before. Specifically, he'd expressed a desire to be on hand when Paddy and I finally got what was coming to us, or words to that effect. He saw promise in the current situation.

"Let me get this straight," the lieutenant said. He was an oily guy physically. Personality wise, he was totally without lubrication. "You're hired to get a hundred grand worth of film back, film that was previously snatched from under your nose. Instead, you panic and shoot the guy who did the snatching. He knocks over a lamp and burns down a house, movie and all. Sounds like one of your more efficient operations."

"I never fired a shot," I said.

"The neighbors say it sounded like a battle up here."

"What neighbors? The coyotes?" I unholstered my forty-five and handed it to him.

He examined it briefly and handed it back. "Fellow named Seitz phoned it in. You passed his driveway a hundred yards down the hill."

Barney joined us then. "No sign of a body," he said to Grove.

As disappointing as that was to the policeman, he let it pass without comment. He was distracted, as I was, by two blackened objects Barney carried in gloved hands. One of them was a film reel coated in something that looked like gritty tar. The other was half of a film canister. There was no sign of a paper label on it, or even the residue from one.

"Sorry, Mr. Elliott," Barney said for the second time that morning.

Grove was grinning. "Tell me you guys will have to cover the whole hundred thousand. That should swallow up everything but the gold fillings in your crooked boss's crooked teeth."

"Those too," I said, but I said it to myself.

9

Grove left shortly after that, to catch some sleep he predicted would be the best he'd had in years. He wished the same for me, but not sincerely.

I gave him a healthy head start. Then I untangled my Ford from the fire trucks and started down the hill. Right away I spotted what I hadn't been able to spot the previous evening: a neighbor's house. I even spotted the neighbor, an older gentleman in pajama bottoms and a sweatshirt, rubbernecking at the head of his drive. Seitz, I thought, the guy who phoned the cops.

The idea of a phone that close reminded me that I owed Paddy a follow-up. Next thing I knew, I was stopping and leaning out my window. "Any chance I could use your phone?" I called to Seitz.

"Do you know what went on up there last night?" he called back.

"About half of it."

Half was enough for Seitz. He waved me into the drive and then led me down it, walking tender footed in his carpet slippers. He wanted his story first, but I told him he was welcome to eavesdrop and I'd fill in the gaps later.

Paddy was still at his desk. I repeated the little I'd passed to him via the police department—the exchange hadn't happened, a fire had, and I was okay—and then explained it in some detail. I ended with Lieutenant Grove's fond hope that Hollywood Security would be picking up the tab.

"The devil we will," Paddy said. "We're a security firm, not Lloyds of London. It may come to the same thing in the end though. Nesbitt was mad as hell over the possibility that something had happened to the film. He'll be worse when he hears it's a certainty. He was threatening a press conference for later today. To blame us for everything that's happened, I gather. I'd rather lose the cash than what's left of our reputation. To think it could end over this after all we've been though. A hand-holding job."

After a little sighing time, he added, "I'll let Ella know you're on your way," and hung up.

Though puffy-eyed from no sleep and doughy in general, Seitz was a quick study. "You were ransoming a movie? No kidding? Why would anyone pick poor Hector's house for that?"

It was a legitimate question. "Because it was empty probably. And lonely. How long's it been for sale?"

"A long time. Hector's been struggling to hang on ever since RKO went under. It's been one bad job after another for him ever since."

"I knew a Hector who worked for RKO," I said, playing it casual. "He was a gaffer."

"Different guy," Seitz said. "This Hector was an electrician."

A gaffer was an electrician, but I didn't point that out. Nothing like pedantry for spoiling a budding friendship. And I was feeling very friendly toward Seitz. Especially after he'd told me Hector's last name—Olenik—and the address of the apartment in Santa Monica where he and his wife Joy were staying.

<h2 style="text-align:center">10</h2>

I was hoping Joy would answer the door, disguised as a USO hostess perhaps, but Hector did. He was a one-eyebrow type dressed in an undershirt and black trousers. Someone had punched him in the left eye recently. A day or so earlier, judging by the color of the shiner, which was purple with yellow undertones.

I didn't expect him to place me, but he did. He might have spotted me back at Union Station. Or maybe he recognized the scent I was wearing, burning ranch house. He tried to shut the door, but I was on my way in by then. I showed him my gun and asked to see his.

"I don't have one," he said, with what sounded like sincere regret.

"You had one last night," I pointed out.

Then Joy was with us, moving with the same nervous grace she'd displayed at the station. She was more fashionably dressed today, in Capri pants and a white top. Like her husband's undershirt, her blouse was sleeveless, but it had a straight neckline, more's the pity.

"He's telling the truth," she said, stepping between Hector and my gun. "He threw his in the bay last night."

"Sit down then," I said. "Hands on your knees."

They chose a dingy sofa against one dingy wall. When they sat, their shoulders came together, either from affectionate habit or worn cushions.

"I'd like to know why you shot at me," I said. "But save that till the end. Start with what this was all about."

"Like we know," Hector said. He was sullen and getting worse by the minute.

Joy said, "We really don't know. Not anymore. Honest, mister. He wouldn't explain about the fire."

"Who wouldn't?"

"Don't tell him," Hector said.

She looked like she might honor and obey that, so I said, "It was Larry Nesbitt, right?"

"How did you know?"

I'd guessed it because the setup at the station had to be the work of someone who knew me, and neither of the Olenik twins did. That suggested Nesbitt, a guy I'd worked with some months earlier. Plus, like Paddy, I was still smelling a play for free newsprint. So had Joy, once.

"We thought it was all for publicity. That's what he told us when the deal first came up. Hector met him a few weeks ago when he got a little fill-in work at United Artists. Nesbitt knew we wanted to get out, Hector and me, that we'd had enough of this town. He called a couple days ago to say he had a way for us to make a little traveling money. He had this old movie coming in, *The Story of the King*. We were supposed to steal it and ransom it. There'd be a lot of free publicity for the remake, and we could keep the ransom money. That's how we'd get home."

She had a little girl's voice, which might have been the reason she hadn't made it in pictures, those voices going badly with brunettes standing five eight. The voice was almost certainly the reason I asked, "Where's home?"

"Michigan," she said. "Grand Rapids. That's home for me. That's where we're going. Where we thought we were going."

Until I showed up. "All three of you going east? Hector here had an accomplice at the station. And a lookout last night."

"That was a good friend of ours," Joy said. "He helped Hector at the station as a favor. But he wasn't there last night. It was Mr. Nesbitt's idea to say he was. We can't tell you his name."

I let it go for the moment. "So Nesbitt planned everything, even told you what to wear to distract me."

"Yes," Joy said. "He said you wouldn't be able to resist trying to help me." She leaned a little heavily on the last two words, but I forgave her for it.

"And he told you where to show up to snatch the film."

That one was for Hector, who reluctantly said, "Yes." As he said it, he reached up and touched his purple eye.

Joy explained. "He punched Hector for hitting him too hard."

"Like I know how to pistol whip people," Hector muttered.

"When was this?"

"The night of the robbery," Joy said. "Nesbitt came by here to say the plan had changed. We were supposed to burn the film."

"In a ranch house you couldn't unload, which was mortgaged to the rafters but insured the same way?" I asked. "How much did Nesbitt know about you two? Or how much am I supposed to believe he knew?"

"Burning the house was my idea," Hector admitted in his grudging way. "Nesbitt wanted us to burn a stolen car, but what do I know about stealing cars? This way we got rid of the house and got the ransom money. Nesbitt promised he'd pass it over later. I wasn't worried about the fire. I knew the fire tower on the ridge would call it in before it could spread."

"Whose idea was it to shoot at me?"

"Nesbitt's. He said I should throw a couple of shots your way, light the fire, and run."

"Why did he want the movie burned?"

Joy took over again. "That's the part he wouldn't explain. He said he didn't have to explain, that we were in too deep to ask any questions."

I wasn't, so I'd just have to ask the man myself. That left the problem of what to do with Hector and Joy. I was still kicking it around when Joy said, "Do you want it?"

I begged her pardon.

"The movie. *The Story of the King*. Do you want it?"

"I just saw what's left of *The Story of the King*," I said. "I clean better looking stuff out of my pipe."

Hector shook his head. "What you saw at the house were cans of old newsreels. I picked them up at a second-hand store in Pasadena."

Joy was nodding. "The movie's in there." She pointed to a beat-up cabinet I'd pegged as their television set. "We never even opened the cases."

I investigated and found the two octagonal carrying cases I'd briefly glimpsed thought the door of the baggage car. I pulled one out and told Hector to open it. While he was at it, I addressed his wife.

"Figuring on an extra payday?"

"What?" she asked. Then she blushed. "No. Nothing like that. We just couldn't bring ourselves to burn it. I couldn't."

I believed her, and not just because she sounded like early Peggy Ann Garner. I thought I'd guessed her true motivation. "You couldn't burn it because it's a life of Christ."

"No," she said again. "I've never been very religious." She gave me an up-from-under look and asked, "Have you ever seen a movie called *Night Storm*?"

I said I'd missed that one.

"It was a Richard Conte picture. Nineteen fifty-two. I'm in it. In one scene of it. Mr. Conte tries to pick me up in a bar. It's my only movie."

"So?"

"So I'd hate like hell for every print of *Night Storm* to be lost. There'd be no record then that I'd ever been out here. No record that I'd ever been on earth."

She pointed to the silver can Hector had extracted from the case. "That's the last print of *The Story of the King*. Mr. Nesbitt said so. It might be the only picture some girl from 1919 ever got to be in, the only record she was ever here. I couldn't let it be burned. We were going to take it with us, arrange for it to be 'discovered' in a few years. Now you can take it."

Her husband was holding the can out to me. From where I stood, I could read "Excelsior Productions" on its paper label. "Open it," I said.

It took some prying, but Hector got it done. The room immediately filled with a chemical smell that reminded me a little of some of the explosives I'd encountered in the field artillery. The can contained a film reel, but the reel was swimming in a rusty brown goo. Unstable,

Barney had called the old nitrate stock, and he hadn't exaggerated. Joy's lost starlet of 1919 was out of luck. That goo was all that remained of *The Story of the King*.

Right away I saw how it had all come to pass. The Russians had slipped the New York museum and United Artists a worthless print. Nesbitt's museum buddy had discovered the truth and informed Nesbitt, who had worked out a scheme to destroy the film and save both their jobs. That's why he hadn't had any press at the station. He hadn't wanted anyone to examine those cans. Now he'd get more free publicity than he would have if the film had been intact. All at the expense of Hollywood Security.

"Close it up," I said. "Carefully. And put it back in the case. Then both cases and us three go down to my car."

I'd intended Joy to do half the lugging, but Hector gallantly carried the whole load. I unlocked my trunk for him, slipping out the leather satchel I'd stashed there the night before, the one containing the ransom money. I'd put my gun away, so as not to attract the attention of passers-by, but what I did next attracted plenty, which was to knock Hector down. Being a nice guy, I hit him in his right eye, the good one. "That's for the ricochet," I said.

Then I dumped half the satchel's contents, five thousand dollars, next to him on the sidewalk. I knew Paddy would hide me for it, but I did it anyway.

"You'll have to make Grand Rapids on that," I told Joy. "Good luck. I'll watch the late show listings for *Night Storm*."

12

Nesbitt's little press conference was underway when Paddy and I arrived, which was just how we'd timed it. The event had drawn representatives from the local dailies and even a television film crew, which cheered Paddy somewhat. My boss had been displeased, as I'd predicted, when I'd handed him only five thousand tax free dollars to lock away in his office safe.

Nesbitt's mood seemed to be extreme grief, which was impressive, grief being a hard one to pull off with wavy hair. He must have finished listing Hollywood Security's many failings, because the words that caught in his throat as we marched in were part of a lament for Thomas Ince's lost masterpiece.

"Good news," Paddy boomed, ostensibly addressing Nesbitt but actually playing to the camera and its attendant microphone. "Hollywood Security, Incorporated, managed to carry out the exchange only slightly behind schedule. Here it is, *The Story of the King*, all twelve reels of it, just as it was purchased from our friends the Russians with no less than one hundred thousand dollars of the studio's money. I took the liberty of phoning ahead so a vintage projector could be set up in one of your screening rooms. I'm sure you won't begrudge these ladies and gentlemen of the press a brief glimpse of this work of art."

There was a smattering of applause, started by the studio employees there to lend Nesbitt moral support. They'd be supporting him literally before long, if his bloodless face was anything to go by.

Paddy acknowledged the hand, turned to leave, and then turned back. At the same time, he slipped an envelope from his breast pocket and winged it toward the podium. "Our bill," he said and winked a wink I hadn't seen in months.

Lady on Ice

by Loren D. Estleman

OUTSIDE, IT WAS eighty-nine degrees at ten PM, with percentage of humidity to match, and I was experiencing the early stages of frostbite.

I was sitting on a bench otherwise occupied by semiprofessional hockey players, each of whose pads, jerseys, and weapons-grade adrenaline were more effective insulation against the proximity of the ice than my street clothes. The arena had been conjured up out of an old Michigan Company stove warehouse on the Detroit River, with the Renaissance Center undergoing a public-friendly renovation on the one side and twenty toxic acres being parceled out to gullible buyers wanting riverfront condos on the other. Veteran Detroiters were aware that asbestos and car batteries had been leaking poisons into the earth there since Henry Ford, and so the athletes on the ice outnumbered the fans in the bleachers.

I wasn't playing, and I was only half paying attention to the game. When I want to see apes brawl, I can always tune in to the Discovery Channel. I was providing security for a Detroit Lifters guard named Grigori Ivanov who, at the moment I realized I could no longer feel my face, was busy pummeling a French-Canadian center skating for the Philadelphia North Churches. Ivanov didn't seem to need my help with that.

The team owner, a Fordson High School dropout who'd made a couple of hundred million selling pet grooming products over the Internet, had gambled most of his capital on the notion that a summer hockey league would go over as big as Sergeant Spaniel's Tickbuster Spray. Now he was finishing out the team's second season under a court order forcing him to play his team or pay off the remaining time on the players' contracts.

In the midst of all this, Ivanov had started receiving letters from an anonymous party threatening to throw acid in his face if he didn't remand his salary over to a fund to save the Michigan massassauga rattlesnake from extinction. Since most people, particularly those with small children, aged relatives, and beloved pets, would just as soon see the region's only venomous viper go the way of the passenger pigeon, and since hockey stars in general looked as if someone had already thrown acid in their faces, no one was taking the threats seriously.

No one, that is, except the owner's attorneys, who warned him of the legal consequences on the off chance Mr. Anonymous wasn't just blowing smoke. But Ivanov was a reclusive type, with relatives in the Ukraine awaiting money from him to make the journey to America and no wish for any undesirable publicity that might move the State Department to deny them entry visas. That ruled out the police. I'd come recommended on the basis of an old personal-security assignment that had wound up with no one dead or injured (three cracked ribs didn't count, since they were mine), and since I was on my sixth week without a client and considering trading a kidney for the office rent, here I was on the night of the hottest day of summer, rubbing circulation into my face while visions of hot toddies danced in my head.

The score was lopsided in Philadelphia's favor. By the final buzzer, the only audience left was either too drunk on watered-down beer to move or sweeping up Bazooka Joe wrappers in the aisles. I pried my stiff muscles off the bench and moved in close to Ivanov as the Lifters started down the tunnel toward the showers.

The kid had on a bright green T-shirt, or I might not have spotted him bobbing upriver through the red-and-yellow jerseys. The concrete walls were less than ten feet apart, and the players averaged six feet wide. It was a tight crowd, and I had to wedge myself in sideways to keep from being squeezed to the back, which is no place for a body-guard. As it was, I couldn't get to my gun and had to body-check Ivanov out of the way when the kid's arm swept up and yellow liquid sprayed out of the open vial in his hand.

I hadn't time to see where the liquid went. I hurled myself between two padded shoulders, grabbed a fistful of green cotton, and pulled hard. A seam tore, but the kid's forward momentum started him toward the floor, and I came down on top of him and grasped the wrist of his throwing arm and twisted it up behind his back. The empty vial rolled out of his hand and broke into bits on the concrete floor.

I placed a knee in the small of his back and ran a hand over him for weapons. He hadn't any. By this time, the players had backed off to give us room. I got to my feet, pulling the kid up with me by his twisted arm, and slammed him into the wall, pinning him there while I looked at Ivanov.

"He get you?" I asked.

He'd put a hand against the wall to catch himself when I'd shoved him aside. He pushed himself away from it and touched his face, a reflexive gesture; the lawyers weren't the only ones who'd suspected something was behind the letters besides a crank. "No. I am OK."

The kid was shouting something. I took hold of his hair and pulled his face away from the wall to hear it.

"I didn't want to hurt anybody!" he was saying. "I just wanted to scare him. It was just colored water."

I looked at the wall farther up the tunnel. It had been painted green until a moment before. Now there was a large runny patch with smoke tearing away from its bubbling surface. A patch about the size of a man's face.

"Your name's Amos Walker?"

I'd seen the speaker once or twice at police headquarters, but we'd never exchanged a word except maybe to ask for a button to be pushed on the elevator. He was a big Mexican in his forties who bought his sport coats a size too large to leave room for his underarm rig and wore matching shirt-and-tie sets to save himself time dressing. His graying hair was thick enough to be a rug but wasn't, and he had a red, raw face that looked as if he exfoliated with emery paper. The name on the ID clipped to his lapel was Testaverde. He was a detective sergeant with Special Investigations.

I said my name was Amos Walker. He was holding my ID folder, so there didn't seem any point in denying it. We were standing in a hall at headquarters by the two-way glass looking into the interview room where the kid with the stretched-out T-shirt was answering a detective's questions in front of a camcorder. The air conditioner wasn't working any better than it did in any other government building, which was all right with me. My nose was still running from the chill in the arena.

Testaverde returned the folder. "That was quick thinking. Baby-sitting your specialty?"

"I almost never do it. Hours of sitting around on your hip pockets, seasoned by ten seconds of pure terror. But a job's a job."

"One might say *our* job. Why, do people pay taxes if they're going to hire the competition?"

"If they refused, you'd arrest them. Anyway, this one had a muffler on it. It's the only edge I've got. You've got all the people and whirlygigs."

"Well, the rabbit's out of the hutch now. Let's have a listen." He flipped the switch on an intercom panel next to the window. The kid's shallow voice wobbled out of the speaker.

" . . . vegetable dye, I don't remember what kind. All I know is there wasn't any kind of acid."

The detective, a well-dressed black man named Clary, read from his notebook. " 'High concentration of sulfuric and hydrochloric acid.' That's what Forensics scraped off the wall. It scarred the concrete, Michael. Think what it would have done to Ivanov's face."

"I filled the tube from the tap and put in the coloring, I wouldn't even know where to lay hands on that other stuff."

"Hydrochloric you can get in any hardware store. People soak their faucet filters in it to remove rust. Sulfuric you can drain out of an ordinary car battery. I want to believe your story, Michael, but you're not helping much. Who could have switched the tubes?"

"I don't know." His mouth clamped shut on the end.

Clary scratched his chin with a corner of the notebook. "Let's go back to those letters you wrote. You said you were jealous of Ivanov's success."

Testaverde switched off the speaker. "Robin Williams is funnier. But he has to make sense. This punk's got serious problems if he's jealous of a third-rate stickman on a crummy semipro hockey team."

"Red Wings players are harder to get close to."

I was barely listening to myself. Michael Nash was seventeen but could pass for two years younger: an undernourished towhead in an old T-shirt without lettering, faded carpenter's jeans, appropriately baggy, and pretend combat boots. He was only an exotic dye job and a couple of piercings away from the common run of self-esteem-challenged youths you saw taking up space at the mall. Nothing about his story made sense unless you fitted in the one piece he was leaving out. After that, it came together like a Greek farce. I didn't bother suggesting this to Sergeant Testaverde; he'd already have thought of it. Cops aren't stupid, just overworked.

Grigori Ivanov got away from the Criminal Intelligence Division after recording his statement and autographing a hockey puck for an officer whose kid followed the Lifters. I waited and rode down with Ivanov in the elevator. I asked him who wrote the letters.

He gave me that eyebrowless look you saw a lot of on Eastern European faces before the Iron Curtain rusted through; the one they showed KGB agents and officials of the U.S. State Department. "The boy," he said. "Michael Nash?"

"You wouldn't show me the letters before. Can I see them now?"

"What is point? It is over. Send bill."

"You said they weren't typewritten. I'd like to see the handwriting."

He smiled. It would take a good dentist to decide which teeth hadn't grown in his mouth. "You wish to determine personality?"

"No, and I don't read head bumps either. But I can usually tell a man's writing from a woman's."

"What woman?"

"The kid's protecting someone. When you're a seventeen-year-old boy, the someone is usually female. But then, you'd understand that. You're protecting the same person."

The elevator touched down on the ground floor. He gathered himself to leave. I mashed my thumb against the Door Close button. He grew eyebrows then. I'd seen that same look when he was trying to pry off the Philadelphia center's head with his stick.

"It's a theory, anyway," I said. "The cops will buy it; they don't care as long as the case closes. If there's another reason and I have to go out and find it, I might take the long way back, past Immigration."

The fight went out of him then. In a sport coat and silk shirt, he looked smaller than he did in pads, and now he was almost human scale. "We go somewhere?"

The cop shop is just off Greektown, which is always open, thanks to the casino. The street was speckled with zombified strollers whose air-conditioning had broken down at home. There was a scorched-metal smell in the air, peculiar to that city of wall-to-wall automobiles on a heated summer night. We ordered coffee in a corner booth in a place that reeked of hot grease and burnt cheese. Ivanov hunkered over his cup, looking like a nervous goalie. "She is—was—underage."

"What's her name, and how far did it go?"

His story started in the old country. Trinka Svetlana, a Ukrainian figure skater with Olympic hopes, had met Ivanov when he was skating for a team in Kiev. He was twenty-three; she was sixteen. When Detroit bought his contract and started unwinding red tape to import him, the pair had been living together secretly for six months. He promised to send for her the moment he had the cash. That was three years ago. In the meantime, she'd made her way over with an aunt's help and was living with her in Rochester Hills. Trinka surprised Ivanov one night, waiting for him outside the arena. She'd expected a joyful reunion, but the look on his face when he recognized her ended that. He'd been married to the daughter of the owner of the Lifters for a year.

She fled when he broke the news. Two weeks later, the first of the letters came, threatening to throw acid in Ivanov's face if he didn't agree to leave his wife and return to her.

"What about the Massassauga Relief Fund?" I asked.

"I read about some such thing in the newspaper. Everyone in America supports a cause, no? I thought it would, how you say, throw off the suspicion." His eyebrows disappeared again. "This thing, it is like that movie. *Fatal Extraction?*"

I didn't correct him. His dumb hunkie act had worn through. "She hasn't assimilated," I said. "The thing to do in America is to bring charges against you for statutory rape and contributing to the delinquency of a minor, not to mention encouraging the hopes of innocent rattlesnakes under false pretenses. That means deportation. No wonder you wanted private protection instead of going to the cops."

"Well, she is scared off now. What is your interest?"

"There's a kid in Holding because he thought he was throwing a pie in your face, and it turned out to have a rock in it. I'm curious to meet the person who put it there."

"What pie? What rock?"

I got up and put down money for the coffee. He seized my wrist in an athlete's grip.

"You won't tell Immigration?"

I broke the grip with a maneuver I hadn't used since Cambodia. "Too busy. I need to get an estimate on putting the Berlin Wall back up." I went out into the scorched-metal air.

There was a V. Svetlana listed in Rochester Hills. I tried the number from a booth, and a husky female voice confirmed the number and told me to leave a message. I disobeyed.

I opened the window in the car, mostly to let out the stale air. My congestion was clearing, and I had just begun to feel the heat. Coming up on one AM, and the stoops of apartment buildings and single-family houses were occupied by men in damp undershirts and women in shorts and tank tops, smoking and drinking from cans beaded with moisture. Some of them looked as if they'd been hit over the head with something, but most were smiling and laughing. Winter had been long and cold and not so far back.

It was one of the homes in the older section of Rochester Hills, which means it didn't look as if it came with a heliport. The roof was in good shape, it had been painted recently, and the lawn would pass inspection, free of miniature windmills and lighthouses.

"Mrs. Svetlana?" I asked the creature who answered the doorbell.

She looked at me with slightly sloping Tartar eyes in a face that had given up its first wrinkle—a vertical crease above the bridge of the nose—and probably got something well worth having in the trade. Her hair was an unassisted auburn, cut short at the neck but teased into bangs to lighten the severity. The nose was slightly aquiline, the cheekbones high. Stradivari had made a pass at her lips and taken the rest of the week off. She had on a blue satin dressing gown and flat-heeled sandals and looked me square in the eye at six feet and change.

"Miss," she corrected. "It's late for visitors."

"Not many women would open the door this late." I showed her my ID. "Are you Trinka Svetlana's aunt?"

"You woke me up to ask me that?"

I liked her accent: Garbo out of *Ninotchka* by way of Nadia Komanich. "Trinka's boyfriend is in jail. I want to ask her a couple of questions about how he got there."

A light glimmered in the Oriental eyes. "Grigori?"

"Michael."

Her face shut down. It had never been fully open. "She's a beautiful girl. I can't keep track of her young men." She started to push the door shut. I leaned against it.

"I'm betting she can. Girls are organized about that kind of thing."

"She isn't here." She pushed harder. She had plenty of push, but I had thirty pounds on her, and it was too hot to move. She gave up then. "She's at the rink downtown, practicing her routine." She rolled the *r*.

"Routine?"

"Her figure skating act. Everything today is a show. To skate expertly is no longer enough. She wants to go to the Olympics."

"She wanted that in the Ukraine. She wanted Grigori, too. Does she still want Grigori?"

"Grigori is a pig." Spittle flecked my cheek.

"No argument from the U.S. Which rink?"

"There is only one."

I straightened, and she pushed the door shut. By that time it was redundant. With women like V. Svetlana around, it was a wonder there weren't still missiles in Cuba.

The Iceland Skating Rink's quarter-page ad in the Yellow Pages said it closed at midnight. There was a light on in the city block of yellow brick building when I parked in a lot containing only a two-year-old Geo and a Dodge Ram pickup with a toolbox built onto the bed. When no one came to the front door, I walked around to the side and kicked at a steel fire door until it opened wide enough to show me a large, black, angry-looking face and a police .38.

"What part of Closed you need me to explain to you?" It was a deep, well-shaped voice. Motown had a lot to answer for when it moved to LA.

"You left a light on. I'm with Detroit Edison." He looked at my ID. "That ain't what it says."

"One of us is lying. I need a minute with Trinka."

"Don't know no Trinka."

"Yeah. I'm just the scrub team. The first string won't like that answer any more than I do. It's a long drive from Thirteen Hundred and a hot night. They'll be sore."

Thirteen Hundred is the address of Detroit Police Headquarters. He opened the door the rest of the way and put away the .38. His uniform was soaked through. The air-conditioning budget at Iceland went into keeping the rink from turning into a swimming pool.

I followed him down an unfinished corridor to a glass door. "See if you can get her to go home," he said. "I like her, but I need this job." He left me.

Inside, a trim figure in a royal blue leotard glided around on the ice. It was just her and me and Sarah Vaughan singing "Dancing in the Dark" on a portable CD player propped up on the railing that surrounded the rink. I leaned next to it and violated another rule by lighting up a Winston.

Trinka Svetlana was as tall as her aunt and could have been her daughter. Her hair was longer and a lighter shade of red, but disregard fifteen years and the laws of physics, and I might have been looking at the same woman. She had an athletic build and muscular legs, more shapely than the broken Popsicle sticks they use to sell hose on television. Her white skates cut wide, nearly silent loops on the ice.

I found the volume on the CD player and turned it down. I didn't want to startle her by switching it off. She noticed the change and slowed down, looking at me. She didn't stop.

"Nice form," I said. "I give it a ten, but my favorite's the luge."

"Who are you?" Her accent was heavier than her aunt's, but she didn't sound any more rattled.

"Not important. Michael's in jail."

Even that didn't stop her. She drew a wide circle around the edge of the rink. "Michael?"

"Nash. N as in nice-to-a-fault. A as in adolescent. S as in stupid. H as in hell. Or Holding. Same definition. He threw a bottle of acid at Grigori. Grigori Ivanov? I as in infidelity—"

"I know who he is." It was the first emotion she'd shown. "Michael's a nice boy. Why would he want to do that?"

"He believed your letters. Don't say, 'Letters?' No more spelling bees." My face was stiffening all over again. That night in summer was the coldest winter I'd ever spent. "He thought it was colored water in the vial. Any thoughts on where he got that idea?"

She skated in silence. Sarah had stopped singing. I switched off the player.

"He said he filled it himself from the tap," I said, "but I figure he lied about that, too. Whoever filled it used hydrochloric and sulfuric acid in concentrate. Very hard on the complexion."

She stumbled and almost fell. She caught her balance and skated up to the rail. Her eyes were larger than her aunt's, but they hadn't been so large a moment before. "Who sent you?"

I told her.

"Aunt Vadya?" She was breathing heavily, and her face glowed with moisture. It had collected in beads along the top of her collarbone. On TV you never saw how much they were sweating.

"She didn't rat you out. In the Ukraine she grew up in, she learned how much truth to tell when. What I want to know is, why didn't you do the job yourself? Your aim probably would've been more accurate."

"It was water. I filled it and put in the coloring. Are you the police? Why did you arrest Michael? He's just a boy."

This sounded like truth. It didn't have the ring of conviction that went with a lie. But then she was a performer.

I put cop in my voice. "We arrest them whether it's nitro or Kool-Aid. If it's Kool-Aid, we don't hold them. When it's something else, we try them as adults."

She believed me then. I wouldn't have bet money on it a minute earlier. "Grigori. Did—?"

"Did his face melt? Six inches this way or that, and it would've. It sure made a mess out of a painted concrete wall. Not that he'd have had to look at himself in a mirror. He'd have had to skate for a team for the blind."

"That's impossible! I never—it—"

She stopped, not because I'd interrupted her. Something had clicked for both of us.

"Was that vial ever out of your sight after you filled it?" I asked.

She started shivering.

I told her she could pick up her car later. I drove her to 1300, got Sergeant Testaverde out of his office, and introduced him to her. He locked himself up with her for twenty minutes. At the end of it, he sent a car to Rochester Hills.

The four of us waited in the office. Michael Nash and Trinka sat on the vinyl-upholstered sofa—close, but not touching, and without speaking. She'd put on a sweatsuit over her leotard and changed from her skates into a pair of pink running shoes. Dressed like that and with her hair twisted into a ponytail, she looked younger than nineteen, closer to Michael's age. She stared at the linoleum, he looked at a CPR chart on the wall and chewed his lower lip. The sergeant, seated behind his desk, mopped at his face and neck with a hand towel and glowered at me sipping hot coffee from a Styrofoam cup in the scoop chair.

"Do you have to guzzle that in front of me?" he snarled. "It just makes me hotter."

"That's your problem. I think I'm coming down with a cold."

"You can stay home and nurse it after Lansing jerks your license. Impersonating an officer."

"I did an impression of one. There's a difference."

"I'd sure as hell like to know what it is."

"It wouldn't do you any good. You have to shut off half your brain, and half s all you got."

"That a Mexican joke?"

"I don't know any Mexican jokes. They haven't been up here long enough. It's a cop joke. Force of habit. You'd have got around to Trinka after you finished sweating Beaver Cleaver."

"Thanks for the vote of confidence." He reached back and twisted the knob on the window fan, looking for a speed faster than High. Maintenance turned off the air conditioner at midnight.

A uniform poked his head in and said the suspect was in Interview Room 3. Testaverde stood and pulled his shirt away from his back. "Keep these two company." He stabbed a finger at me. "Let's find out what half your brain turned up."

Detective Clary was still at his post, but he wasn't asking many questions. Vadya Svetlana, having changed into a simple but by no means unfashionable green dress, but otherwise looking much as she had standing on her own doorstep, sat at the table Michael Nash had occupied, speaking directly to the video camera.

"You Americans talk of family until it means nothing," she said. "You couple it with other words—family values, family workplace, extended family—as if it needed the help. I will tell you about family. When the Nazis shelled Leningrad, my grandmother was visiting friends outside the city. She tried to sneak back in, carrying her baby—my uncle—and holding her firstborn's hand—my mother's hand—and almost stumbled into an SS patrol. She took cover in a doorway. When the baby began to cry, she smothered it with her hand so the soldiers wouldn't hear and slaughter them all. She killed her son to save her family."

After a moment, Clary cleared his throat. "Let's move closer to the present. Why did you replace the colored water in the vial with acid?"

"Because my niece is a fool." The camera whirred, wanting more.

"Most kids are," prompted the detective. "Most guardians don't turn it into a reason for mayhem."

"Most guardians don't have Cossack blood. When someone dishonors you, the name of your family, you don't just scare him. You say, 'Boo!' What is that? No, you say it with a knife in the belly."

"If you feel that way, why didn't you do it yourself?"

"The boy wanted to do it. He said it was too dangerous for a girl. When a boy wishes to play at soldiers, it is not a woman's place to interfere."

"Except in the business of the vial."

"You frighten a pig, he runs away squealing. The fright goes away, the pig comes back. What you expect, he will stop being a pig? If you want a pig to stop being a pig, for the honor of your family, you must kill him."

"But you didn't try to kill him."

She shrugged. It was an entirely Slavic gesture, not to be imitated. "It is America. You make the adjustment."

Officer Clary was silent. We were silent. She lifted her eyebrows and looked directly at us. The glass was a blank mirror on her side.

"What did I say?" she asked. "It is my English?" Testaverde switched off the intercom. I thought he shuddered a little. It could have been the cold.

Hasidic Noir

by Pearl Abraham

Williamsburg

IT WAS A DAY NO DIFFERENT from other days, a not unusual day in which I was doing not unusual things in my own slow way, what my wife who is quick in everything refers to, not always appreciatively, as my meditative manner. I've tried to explain that slowness is my method, the way I work, that this is how I solve my cases and earn a living.

Yes, she says, that's all right while you're working, but a meditative mind doesn't serve such tasks as feeding a child or stopping for a quart of milk on the way home.

She doesn't know that she's asking for the impossible. At the end of the day when I close and lock the door to my office, she wants me to turn the lock on my thinking mind, along with my desk and files, and arrive home free and clear, prepared to give her and the children my full attention. And probably she has a right to such a husband, but the habit of brooding can't be turned on and off at will.

On this not unusual day, doing my not unusual things, stopping before morning service at the *mikvah* for the immersion that all Hasidic men take once a day, twice on Fridays in honor of the Sabbath, the word my brooding mind picked out of the male rumble was MURDER.

Murdered in cold blood, I overheard a man say.

The delayed response—the speaker was probably under water—when it came, was a Talmudic citation, not unexpected in a world in which the Talmud makes up a large part of every young man's curriculum. More was said, there were details, some of which I'd previously heard and dismissed as talk, and names—the victim's, the victim's rival, and also for some reason the victim's brother-in-law —and I was all ears.

I waited my turn for immersion with murder on my mind. After all, such violence isn't a daily occurrence in our world. And the victim, a man belonging to Hasidic aristocracy—a nephew of the Grand Rabbi Joel Teitelbaum—known as the Dobrover rebbe, one of two relatives in line to inherit the Grand Rabbinic throne, wasn't just anyone. The rivalry between Dobrov and Szebed had been part of the Hasidic scene for as long as I could remember, dating back to the old rebbe's first stroke. For years there'd been volley after volley of insults and injuries between the two congregations, and the tales of these insults grew long beards. Along with others in the community, I'd grown a thick skin and generally remained unruffled by even the tallest of such tales. But murder! That was unheard of. And where did the Dobrover's brother-in-law, Reb Shloimele, administrator of Szebed's boys' school, enter into this story?

I spent the rest of the morning at my desk, closing the files of the usual, petty white-collar crimes, my regular paying cases, but my mind was preoccupied with this murder, which had arrived without a client, no one to pay for time or expenses. After so many years of hoping for the opportunity to stand the detective's real test, praying even, God protect us from evil, for a case replete with gun, body, widow, the complete grim pattern, here it appeared, a Hasidic murder, a rarity in this community, and I couldn't pass it up.

I'd had a modicum of experience working homicide, on the fringes really, assisting the New York Police Department on several cases in the nearby Italian and Spanish neighborhoods. The police chief still calls occasionally with questions about this part of the city that an insider could answer easily. And now, after so many years, it was as an insider that I'd come across this murder, and it was also as an insider that I knew to judge it a politically motivated crime with perpetrators from the top brass. With the Dobrover rebbe out of the way, Szebed could take the Grand Rabbinic throne without a struggle. If I seem to be jumping to conclusions, note that I grew up in this community and continue to live here; I am one of them.

Anywhere else, murder, even when it occurs with some frequency, is front-page news; in the Hasidic world, it's kept out of the papers—another sign that this was an inside job. Our insular world, may it long survive, transported from Eastern Europe and rebuilt in Williamsburg, New York, an American shtetl, has made a point of knowing and keeping politicians, judges, and members of the press in our pockets. I knew too well how this worked.

I also knew that asking questions was not an option. One question in the wrong place, one word even, could alert those who didn't want talk. When the highest value in a community is loyalty to the greater cause, meaning the continuity of the status quo, all means to this end are imbued with religious significance, and are thereby justified. It was quickly becoming clear to me that this murder had been handed me for a reason, that it was for this case that I, a Hasidic detective, the first one in the history of Hasidism, had been bestowed upon a community that usually eschewed new things. I owed it to the higher powers that created me to pursue the murderers, but I would have to watch my step.

At noon, I walked the ten blocks to Landau's on Lee, my regular lunch counter, selected not necessarily for its excellence in food but for its distance from my office, because my wife insisted on some daily exercise, though I was partial to their sweet and sour pickles and their warm sauerkraut, having grown up on them, and would have walked twenty blocks for a Landau frankfurter with all the trimmings. On this day, I hoped to overhear something useful. It was late November, a cool stimulating day. I buttoned my black coat, pulled my black hat forward, and wrapped the ivory silk muffler twice around my neck, a gift from my wife when we were bride and groom.

The windows of Landau's were already steamy with cooking. I took the three steps down, entered, was greeted by the elderly Reb Motl Landau, who has known me, as he likes to say, ever since I was this high, indicating a place above his own head. I'm tall, 5'11", which is considered especially tall in these parts, populated as it is by mostly small-boned Jews of Hungarian descent, *modyeros*, the Romanian Jews like to call them, intending a bit of harmless deprecation since the word is also the name of a particular nut eaten there.

Without waiting for my order, Reb Motl set a loaded tray down in front of me, as if he'd seen me leave the office ten minutes earlier. My lunch: a frankfurter as starter, beefburger as entree, along with two sour pickles, a glass of water, and an ice-cream soda, nondairy of course.

I took my first bite, a third of the dog, noted the three-person huddle at the far end of the lunch counter, and raised an eyebrow in question.

Reb Motl nodded, drew five fingers of one hand together, meaning patience please, and went to serve another customer. He never played dumb and deaf with me. And we didn't waste words.

When Reb Motl returned, he picked up my crumpled wrappers as if this is what he had returned for, and grumbled, What don't you already know?

The word on the street? I asked.

You mean word at the *mikvah*, he corrected.

I nodded.

Guilty, he said.

I raised my eyebrows in question, meaning, Guilty of what?

Read the book, Reb Motl said.

What book? I asked, using only my shoulders and eyebrows.

Published to make the sins of Dobrov known, Reb Motl said, and moved on. This was a busy lunch counter and he couldn't afford to pause long enough to forfeit the momentum that kept him efficient.

I stopped at the bookstore on my way back to the office, wended my way past the leaning towers of yarmulkes at the entrance, the piles of ritual fringes, stacks of *aleph-bet* primers. As always, Reb Yidel was behind the counter, and when I asked for the book, which turned out to be a pamphlet, really, he pointed to a stack beside the register. I looked at the title page to see who had undersigned this bit of slander, and found no name, no individual taking responsibility for it. The printer, however, was a company known as the printing house for Szebed, and I said to myself, of course it would be Szebed, who else, but I was also disappointed. The motivation behind Szebed's publication of such a pamphlet was too obvious, too facile to be interesting, and I wished for a more complicated community with more difficult cases, more obscure motivations, a case that required mental agility, intricacies I could take pride in unraveling. It was use of the mind that had attracted me to detective work in the first place.

Reb Yidel rang up my copy but remained unusually silent. Know what this is all about? I asked casually, as if my interest were entirely benign.

He shrugged, a careful man with a business and family to protect, and an example to me, who was also a business and family man, who could also benefit from caution. But it was precisely such caution that the perpetrators counted on to help them get away with their crime. They knew that few, if any, among us would risk antagonizing a powerful congregation with fat fingers that reached everywhere.

Any truths? I pressed on.

Who knows? he shrugged. I was pretty sure he knew, and waited.

There's a kernel of truth in every lie, he quoted.

And who is credited with writing the pamphlet? I asked as harmlessly as I could manage.

It is believed to be the work of Reb Shloimele, Szebed's school administrator, Reb Yidel answered neutrally.

The same Reb Shloimele who is also brother-in-law to the Dobrover? I asked, knowing the answer.

Reb Yidel nodded, but declined to say more. I slapped a five-dollar bill down on the counter and left without waiting for the change. Here finally was a detail to ponder, a motivation to unravel.

At my desk I thumbed through the cheaply printed pamphlet. There were accusations of corruption in the Dobrover kosher seal. Discrepancies were cited. A box of nonkosher gelatin, pure pig treife, was discovered in the kitchen at Reismann's bakery. The egg powder used in Horowitz-Margareten matzohs came in unmarked industrial-size boxes. And the pizza-falafel stores in Borough Park, also known to be under the Dobrover seal, were inspected no more than once a month. How much could go wrong in the twenty-nine days between inspections? the writer asked rhetorically, then concluded that for a kosher seal, Dobrov's stamp stank of non-kosher.

I turned to the next chapter. So far, this was the kind of gossip you hear and dismiss regularly. What wouldn't Szebed do to annex Dobrov's lucrative kosher-seal business?

The next chapter attacked the Dobrover's intimate way with his disciples, their secretive, late-night gatherings and celebrations, accused him of messianic aspirations, and ended with the warning that the dangerous makings of the next false messiah were right here in our midst. This too I'd heard previously and considered hearsay. Besides, the days of messianic upheaval and dangers, dependent as they were on seventeenth-century superstitions and ignorance, were long past. We were living in a world in which every yekel and shmekel could read the news, had Internet access. The information super-highway, to use the words of a smart but foolish president, has arrived in our little community in Williamsburg too.

These allegations were followed by an interview with a former disciple in which a discerning reader would quickly recognize that the words had been placed in the mouth of the unwary young man. There were incriminating quotes from a Dobrover son and daughter, who, the pamphleteer pointed out as further evidence of criminality, had turned against their own father. The final chapter featured the court arguments that led to excommunication. From this, a facile argument for divorce followed, since the wife of an excommunicated man would suffer unnecessarily from her husband's exclusion.

I closed the book in wonder. In the standard course, such a series of events—going from initial suspicions to allegations to accusations to excommunication by the court—would span a lifetime. For all of it to have gone off in a couple of years and without much of a hitch, a well-planned program must have been in place. But who had planned so well, who had known the ins and outs of Dobrov, and who had so much private access to family members? I needed to find the children, talk to the sons, the eldest daughter too. Did they understand that they'd been used—abused, rather?

At five, when Hasidim gather in the synagogues for the afternoon service, I turned the lock on my office door and walked to the Szebed synagogue, congregation of the murdered man's cousin and rival for the Grand Rabbinic throne. Inside I noted the recent interior renovations to the brownstone. Exterior work was still in progress. And was it jubilation I sensed in certain members of the congregation, jubilation at the Dobrover's death?

I took a place at the back of the room, where I would have a good view of all who came and went. During the service, I noticed an earnest young man dressed in the style of a Litvak, an outsider, his face thin and pale, an unhappy face. What was he doing here mid-week? It happened now and then that someone's Litvak relative visited for a Sabbath and attended services in a Hasidic *shtibel*, but this was mid-week, when young men were at yeshiva; furthermore, this wasn't any *shtibel*, it was Szebed.

After the service, a birth was announced, the name proclaimed: Udel, daughter of Sarah. Wine, plum brandy, egg kichel, and herring were brought in, and I watched as the cup of wine was passed from relative to relative. The young man appeared to be one of them, because he too received the cup. I eyed him as he went through the motion of sipping and passed it on. Not an outsider. Definitely related. Probably a brother to the young wife, though why would a Szebeder marry into a Litvak family? I wondered.

I went up to the table, poured myself a thimble of brandy in friendly gesture, and casually asked another family man beside me, And who is the young man?

Why, Dobrov's youngest son, brother-in-law of the new father, the man said.

Oh, I said, I didn't recognize him now that he's grown up—the usual nonsense adults speak, mere filler. Beneath the filler, I was beside myself A Dobrov son dressed in the short coat and hat of a Litvak, *peyos* tucked behind his ears. His father and grandfathers must be churning in their graves. And where were the signs of mourning, the ripped lapel on the jacket, the loose flap on the shirt under it? There was none of that. And during the service no prayer for the soul of the deceased had been recited either. Clearly, the son wasn't mourning the father, not openly anyway.

I mingled among the men, made my way up to the young man as smoothly as I could manage, put my hand out to wish him a *mazel tov*. He extended a limp, unwilling hand, responded with the merest nod. His eyes, however, scanned my face, didn't seem to find what they wanted, and moved on. An unhappy soul, I thought, a very disturbed young man. I attempted to squeeze some reassurance into the pale thin hand, clapped it with my other hand before letting go, then taking a roundabout path made my way to the door, slipped out unnoticed, I hoped, and walked up and down the block, with an eye on the comings and goings at this house, a brownstone whose upper floors served as the Szebeder residence. The new mother, I guessed, was staying here with her newborn, and I wanted to see and know what might be going on among the women.

It was over half an hour before my stakeout was rewarded. The door opened, the Dobrover widow came to the door buttoned up in her long black fur and carrying her purse. Attending the widow to the door was her daughter, the young mother, and behind her, the Szebeder rebbetzin. Without warning, the daughter threw her arms around her mother and sobbed noisily. I'm quite certain there were wet trails on the mother's cheeks too. They remained this way, the daughter clinging to her mother, for some moments, then the mother disentangled herself and walked down the wide brownstone stairs.

Here finally were signs of mourning. I was quite certain this is what the tears were for, since giving birth is not normally, that is if the child emerges healthy, an occasion for tears.

Not knowing what else to do, I followed the older woman at a distance. As widow of the Dobrover, she should be mourning, sitting out the seven days of *shiva*. Instead, here she was, walking in the streets, leading me to an address I didn't know, not the residence of Dobrov, and it was then I remembered the divorce. Having divorced the Dobrover she couldn't mourn him. Imagine her feelings. I wondered at the torment every member of this family must be experiencing. The death of a husband and father one had disowned in life on what were surely false accusations; this was a tragedy.

It was a deep blue evening with a moon and stars brighter than the street lights, and the shadows of men on their way home grew long and lean. I wrapped my silk muffler tight against the wind, At home it would be past the children's dinner hour, they would be in bed by now, and I turned in that direction, up Ross toward Marcy Avenue, to tuck them in for the night, reflecting on the vulnerability of a wife and chil-dren, the ease with which an entire family can be destroyed.

I was in time to read several pages about the current favorite, the miracle-performing BeSHT and his disciples, and remained bedside long enough to see willpower lose out to fatigue. One by one, from the youngest to my eldest, who to prove her superiority to her younger siblings made a valiant effort every night to be the last one to fall asleep, their eyes closed.

In the kitchen my wife was washing up, putting things away. I joined her at the sink with a dishtowel, and told her about following the rebbetzin to a strange address.

Don't you know anything? my fine rebbetzin asked rhetorically. The poor woman remarried about a year ago, to a widower about fifteen years older than her. People say she was led by the nose for a long walk, to the end of the block and back again. By a scheming brother-in-law who convinced the world, the wife, and the children of the Dobrover's sins.

And what happened to the younger children? I asked.

Taken in by the brother-in-law, Reb Shloimele. The younger daughter, barely seventeen, was palmed off to her first cousin, Reb Shloimele's son, a bum, rumor has it, who would have had difficulty finding a father willing to hand over his daughter. The younger son, still a *cheder* boy at the time, was raised in Reb Shloimele's home, and at the age of thirteen, sent off to a Litvak yeshiva, with the intention, it was said, to further hurt the father.

That explained the strangeness of a Dobrov son in Litvak garb. And again Reb Shloimele made himself felt in this sordid story. I shook my head. So much evil under the noses of the most pious men, and in their names. I felt an obligation to bring this murder to light, to clear the innocent and accuse the guilty, but how to go about it? And whom to name? This brother-in-law was a mover and shaker, a *makher* in Yiddish, but he couldn't have acted alone. There were powerful men behind him but I couldn't accuse all of Szebed. And who would risk the congregation's ire, help point the finger, and haul the shameless sinners into Jewish court? None of the rabbis appointed to our house of judgment would risk political suicide. Since I couldn't expect assistance on the inside, I would have to go outside.

I attended my evening study session, then started walking toward home, but found myself instead on Keap Street again, in front of the Szebed residence, looking for something, I wasn't sure what. The door opened, I stepped into a nearby doorway and watched the young Dobrover son in his short coat and hat emerge alone, hurry down the stairs, and turn right on Lee. I followed at a distance, curious, wondering where he would go. He led me to 446 Ross, to the Dobrover home, dark and shuttered, and stood at the foot of the stairs looking up. Would he go up the stairs and enter his old home, which the angel of death had invaded? He didn't. After long minutes, he turned away and walked back. What struck me as exceptionally cruel was his inability to mourn publicly, a ritual intended as an aid to grief and recovery. Standing in the way of mourning were the laws of excommunication. An excommunicated man, considered dead, was denied living mourners; there would be no one to say *kaddish* for the Dobrover's soul. His enemies had succeeded in cutting him off both in life and in death.

It was my turn to walk the streets and think.

The perpetrators had used public opinion to help make their case to the judges. I too would have to take my case to the public. And since I couldn't afford print—even the cheapest pamphlet costs a goodly sum—I would have to use the poor man's version: the Internet.

At my desk the next morning I found a chat room with organized religion as its topic, soon steered the conversation to religious politics, and posted my story as an example of corruption, proclaiming the Dobrover's innocence. I didn't have to wait long for the important questions to come up, the who and why of every whodunit, and I pointed my finger to the brother-in-law as prime perp, offered as explanation the oldest motivation, envy, the reason Cain raised his hand against his brother Abel. I was convinced and was able to convince others that without the green worm of jealousy, the Dobrover rebbe and his family would have remained untouched.

Consider this brother-in-law: a promising yeshiva boy who in maturity proved to be a minor scholar with an impatient mind incapable of complex argument. Marrying the sister of the Dobrover rebbetzin, herself a woman of fine rabbinical stock, was his undoing. He would have sat at the table, listened to the deeply scholarly talk, and squirmed in ignorance. The first years of his marriage, he sat pressing the yeshiva bench unwillingly, because the husband of the Dobrover's rebbetzin's sister had to be a scholar, then seized the first opportunity that came his way and became the director of the newly founded Szebeder boys' school. The position fulfilled his need to move about and accomplish things, but at the Sabbath table the sense of his own inferiority would have deepened. And without scholarship to occupy his mind, he became a plotting busybody. The rivalry between the two congregations presented him with an opportunity. Knowing he would never be a significant player in Dobrov, he determined to curry favor at Szebed. Indeed, his reward for interfering in the life and marriage of Dobrov was proof enough of his motivation: He had recently been appointed administrative overseer of the entire Szebed congregation, not a scholarly position, but respectable enough to protect him from his detractors. In taking him on, in other words, I was taking on the whole of Szebed. The anonymity of the Internet, I hoped—I hadn't used my name—would protect me.

And that's where I miscalculated. I didn't count on the Internet's long and wide reach, nor its speed. Religious corruption, whether among priests or rabbis, has a captive audience in America. Well-meaning, sympathy-riddled letters came pouring in, as if I was the one who had suffered the heavy hand of the court. The chat room conversations went on for hours and days, and when I was too exhausted, continued without me, spilled over into new chat rooms. I spent hours online, returned to my office after services and dinner, and remained until midnight typing.

Who were the people chatting? A mixed group—the word *crowd* would be more correct—it turned out. There were both knowing and unknowing participants, meaning Hasidic and not. Also a good number who asked questions that revealed they knew nothing at all about Judaism. Within days, a reporter from the *Village Voice* asked for an interview, then a staff writer writing for the *New Yorker*'s "Talk of the Town." I agreed to give the interviews as long as I remained anonymous. I didn't meet them in person.

Is it necessary to say that I wasn't making my wife happy? She argued that I would remain anonymous only to outsiders. Anyone on the inside who wanted to know who was behind this would soon figure it out. Once known, my name would be mud, and our lives would be shattered. And of course she had a point. Good women are often prescient.

First an anonymous threat to cease and desist or suffer consequences was posted in what I was by now thinking of as my chat room, named *Hasidic Noir* by a participant, a wise-guy. I was accused of lying. Where were the mourners? this faceless voice asked. No one had performed *keria* (the ripping of the lapels), no one was sitting *shiva* (seven days of mourning), and no one had recited the mourner's *kaddish* (the prayer for the soul of the dead). He concluded with a declaration that there was no Dobrover rebbe or Dobrover congregation, that I was a careerist who had fabricated a murder for the sake of publicity.

Clearly this was coming from an insider with knowledge of the vocabulary and customs, someone who knew that excommunication rendered a man nonexistent to the community, hence his argument that there was no Dobrover rebbe.

The chat room became a divisive hive, with people taking sides, demanding to know what the words meant, who was the liar in this story, how to find out. One cynical participant raised the irrelevant question of my, not the murderer's, motivation. If the brother-in-law is jealous Cain, he asked, who is this snitch, and what's he going for? The next morning the *Village Voice* published the interview, and late that evening, when my wife and I were already in bed, there was a knock at the door.

I drew on my flannel dressing gown, removed the Glock I keep in the locked drawer of our night table, and instructed my wife to remain in bed. I opened the door, loaded gun in hand, pointing. These men should know what there is to know. Three Szebeder bums stood red-faced, mouths open, breathing hard. They must have used the stairs. If you didn't know better, you'd think they'd been imbibing. But I knew that if there'd been any excess, it had been verbal not alcoholic. To achieve a tough's appearance they'd had to talk themselves into a frenzy.

The barrel end of the gun quickly quieted them, as it often does those who want to live. The middle one in the group produced a letter. I opened it in front of them, keeping the gun aimed, keeping them fearful and rooted in place. At a glance, the letter appeared to be a court summons. The Jewish court, made up of the same rabbis who'd helped bury the Dobrover, was now calling me in.

I congratulated myself on achieving something of a goal. Two weeks ago these men wouldn't have given me the time of day. Now they were all ears. But if I didn't want to lose all that was precious to me—my wife, my children, and my livelihood—I would have to plan well. I would tell my story, but I would tell it publicly.

I looked at the quivering men at my door and felt sorry for them, mere messengers. We were told to bring you in, one mumbled.

Tell the court I'll see them tomorrow, at 9 AM sharp, in the revealing light of day. There will be no nighttime shenanigans. Good evening.

I shut the door and waited for the sounds of their steps, first shuffling, then sprinting to get away. I bolted the door, inserted the police lock, looked in on the children who had slept through it all, assured my wife that everything was under control, and got to work on the small laptop I keep at home.

When I finally returned to bed at three in the morning, my wife hugged me silently and did her best to remind me that I am only a man, of flesh and blood, not iron. I knew that even though she was against what I was doing—for reasons of safety rather than principle—she couldn't help but be proud of the way I was handling it.

I slept well, and in the morning dressed as usual, in my charcoal gray suit, white shirt, black overcoat, and silk muffler. I pocketed the Glock as protection against the court's manhandling, their method of intimidation. This was a non-jurisdictional court, therefore without metal detectors, and without the routine of body searches, both unnecessary. A handful of appointed rabbis, intrinsically honest, would act as judges, but they owed their livelihoods to their patrons, the men who nominated, appointed, and paid for their services. There would be some younger scholars available to act as mediators. Also present would be the man who was bringing the case against me. Who would it be? I expected to see the man I'd fingered, the jealous brother-in-law, or if he didn't want to show his face, a representative.

I followed my regular routine, stopped first at the *mikvah*, which was buzzing. It was a perfect setting for murder, an underground hell, where locker room odors envelop you on entrance through the unassuming side door. Hurrying down the stone stairs and long tiled hallways, the curl and drip of the waterlogged vapors take over and then the low rumble of bass and tenor voices. At the entrance to the lockers, the bath attendant hands you your towel, one per person, and you move along toward your designated locker and the bench in front of it. You undo your shoes, remove your socks, left foot first, then the left leg of your pants, and so on, in the order in which you were taught to undress. Dressing, you reversed it, right foot first, insuring against the possibility of getting the day off on the wrong foot. And still the act of undressing provokes other indiscretions. While your hands arts at work, your ears don't remain idle. They tune into the nearest conversation in the aisle, then onto the next nearest, and so on, staying with each one long enough to hear whether it's of interest. And of course there always is something of interest, a bit of information, gossip someone heard at home the night before, husbands picking up at the *mikvah* where their house-bound, child-bound, telephone-addicted wives left off the night before.

I didn't have to wait long to hear my own name, and then the name of the man I'd fingered, Reb Shloimele, the chief administrator of Szebed, though to hear the talk, not for much longer. A well-respected man of the community the day before, today his name was mud. With the generous helping of hyperbole typical of *mikvah* gossip, someone equated Reb Shloimele's crime with that of the biblical Amelek's,

Israel's oldest enemy. In other words, Reb Shloimele was a sentenced man.

This time I expected the crowds, and the journalists with cameras. And I knew how much Szebed would hate it. The rabbis wouldn't approve, No one would like it, but the publicity would serve to protect me. I pulled the brim of my hat down to conceal my face and made my way through the throng. Questions, microphones, and cameras were pressed on me. I walked straight through, succumbing to none. The Internet had done the work, the chat rooms had been devilishly successful; it was enough. I had no reason to add fuel to the fire and further enrage the sitting judges.

Inside, without much of a greeting and none of the usual friendly handshakes, two men attempted to lead me, strong-arm style, to my place at the table, completely unnecessary since on my own I'd shown up at the courtroom. I shook them off and walked alone, pulled out the chair, sat. The judges frowned, but said nothing. They were pretending at busyness, each taking a turn at thumbing through a pile of continuous-feed paper in front of them, the tabs and holes that fit a dot matrix printer's sprockets still attached. Someone had provided them with a complete printout of the chat room conversations, a fat manuscript titled *Hasidic Noir*. I suppressed a smile.

Throat-clearing and short grunts indicated the start of proceedings. One judge asked whether the defendant knew what he was accused of.

No, I said. As everyone here knows, I am a God-fearing, law-abiding Hasid whose livelihood is detective work. I solve petty crimes, attempt to bring to justice those who break the law, my small effort at world repair.

There was a long pause. Read this then, the judge said, and handed me a sheet of paper.

The complaint against me: libel, for attempting to besmirch a man's name, to ruin a reputation.

The rabbi sitting directly across the table waited for me to finish reading, then said, You know as well as we do that a man guilty of libel must be judged, according to Jewish law, as a murderer. Destroying a man's reputation is a serious crime.

I nodded and said, I'm well aware of that law because it is precisely what I believe Reb Shloimele guilty of.

I made a long show of extracting the cheap pamphlet from my briefcase, pushed it across the table, and announced, as if this were a courtroom complete with stenographers, Let the record show that this slanderous pamphlet was submitted by the defendant as evidence of Reb Shloimele's guilt. Murder via slander, false slander, moreover, since not one of the accusations have been proven true without doubt.

I paused, looked from face to face, then continued slowly: And this court is guilty of acting as an accomplice to this murder. Even if Reb Shloimele managed to gather enough signatures to support the excommunication, and all the signatories were surely his Szebeder friends, by what right, I ask on behalf of Dobrov, did it grant the Dobrover rebbetzin a divorce and break up an entire family. Since you're citing Jewish law, you also know that breaking up a marriage unnecessarily is equal to taking life.

The rabbi's fist came down on the table with a thump. Enough, he said. Neither Reb Shloimele nor this court are on trial. Our sins are beside the point right now. You, however, have a lot to answer for. If you thought or knew that someone had been wronged, you ought to have come directly to us, and quietly. Instead, you took the story to the public, and not just the Jewish public. You are guilty of besmirching not only the name of a respectable man among us, but also the name of God, and worse, in front of the eyes of other nations. Retribution for befouling the name of God, as you well know, arrives directly from heaven, but this court will also do its part. You will be as a limb cut away from a body. Your wife and children will share your fate.

I took stock of the situation, decided that I was willing to take my chances with God, and since in the eyes of these men I was already judged guilty, I couldn't make my case worse. I took a deep breath and went all the way.

Which of you here would have been willing to listen to my story? Which of you here isn't paid, one way or another. by the Szebeder congregation. According to the law of this nation in which we live, you qualify as collaborators, and therefore ought to recuse yourself from this case. I exhaled and stood. And if, as further proof of your guilt, you require a body, here it is.

I took long strides to the door, opened it. As planned, an EMS technician wheeled into the room the Dobrover rebbe himself, frail and wraithlike, a man of fifty-three years with an early heart condition, attended by his young son in the Litvak frock.

The Dobrover appeared before us all as the Job-like figure that sooner or later every mortal becomes, but in his case the suffering had come at the hand of man rather than God, and that made all the difference.

The room remained silent for long minutes. An excommunicated man shows himself in the courtroom for only one purpose: to have the excommunication nullified, to be reborn to the community. This court had difficult days, weeks, probably, of work ahead.

I'd done my part for Dobrov. Now it remained to be seen what Dobrov would do for me. In the meantime, no one took notice when I snapped my briefcase closed loudly, adjusted the brim of my hat, and left. I had become a dead man, unseen and unheard.

A Death in Ueno

by Mike Wiecek

T HE TINY RESTAURANT OPENED directly onto Tokyo's central fish market, a low step the only barrier to the slurry of icemelt, blood and waste spilling across the concrete. Two hours before dawn Tsukiji was in full cry, crowded by hundreds of men in cheap rubber boots pushing hand trucks, hauling crates, arguing over prices. Earlier the restaurant's dozen seats had been filled by workers gulping ramen before the boats began to arrive; later it would be beer and grilled fish from the day's catch. Now, with the market at its busiest, the restaurant was almost deserted, as Sakonju had expected.

The only other diner was a muscular man in twill who stood as Sakonju ducked under the restaurant's low entrance.

"Hattori," the man introduced himself. "Obliged."

Sakonju nodded and sat, signaling for tea from the matron, who brought over a cup and disappeared back into the rear.

"Sorry about the time," said Hattori. "I've gotten up at midnight for twenty-one years. I forget that other people don't."

"I'm nearby," Sakonju said. He looked at the deep lines in Hattori's weather-beaten face. "You probably haven't been sleeping much at all lately."

After a moment Hattori nodded. "Yes. Ever since the call came, last Thursday." He shook his head abruptly. "I mean, since I heard. I was on the boat, out for a two-week trip north, and the radio wasn't working, so they couldn't reach me for almost ten days. By the time I got back, they'd already cremated him."

"You go out alone?"

"Yes." Hattori's hands were nicked and scarred, heavily

callused. "My brother came a few times, long ago, but that didn't last."

"Were you close?"

"No." Pain etched Hattori's voice, and he looked away. "No, and now I regret that more than anything. He got caught up in gambling when we were young, and then it was drugs, and alcohol, and after he didn't have any place to live we lost touch completely. I mean, now and then he'd call, and sometimes I'd be home to answer. Once a year or so I tried to help, but he always refused."

"And how did he die?"

"He was beaten," said Hattori. "With a concrete brick, the police said." He was silent a moment. "They found him at a construction site." He pulled a thin, crumpled tearsheet from his pocket and flattened it neatly. "This is all I have: a receipt from the city crematorium. They couldn't reach me, and he was a pauper, so they just . . . finished up."

Sakonju sipped his cooling tea and waited a while, listening to the cacophony echoing through the market outside. A forklift barreled past, leaving diesel stench in its wake.

"What do you want from me?" he asked.

"The police don't seem to care who killed him. Just another homeless guy, good riddance."

"Did they give you anything else, any other information at all?"

"They said they had a name–Jinguji, someone my brother apparently knew, but that was it, they couldn't find him. Like I said, they didn't seem to be trying hard."

He looked at the wooden chopsticks in his hand, and suddenly clenched his fist, snapping them in two and dropping the pieces to the floor. "I asked around. You're an investigator, you can help me find the murderer. People say you're good."

"Maybe." Sakonju considered Hattori's set face. "I'm not sure I understand, though. You said you weren't close to your brother. . . . " He let the question hang, and Hattori didn't answer for a time.

"Our mother died the day after I was born," he said eventually. "Our father's sister looked after us while he was on the boat, weeks at a time. We'd see him two or three times a month. It was hard . . . he disappeared in a typhoon when I was sixteen. A Maritime Agency cutter found the boat, they figured he'd been washed overboard."

Sakonju waited. After a moment Hattori continued.

"My brother was older, but I inherited the boat. He'd already been getting into trouble, my father must have thought he couldn't handle it." He broke off. "Over the years, the more he drifted away, the more I blamed myself."

"How can I say this?" Sakonju was still watching Hattori's face. "Nothing you do will bring him back. It's over for him."

"Of course." He hesitated, tried to explain. "I have to know that at the end, I finally did the right thing."

"Why?"

"I owe it to him–and myself." He was staring at the table. "This is for me."

"All right. " Sakonju nodded, like he'd come to a decision.

Hattori looked up. "So you can help me find the killer?"

"Thirty thousand yen per day," said Sakonju. "But I usually work alone."

"Fine." Hattori refolded the receipt and placed it carefully back into his pocket, buttoning down the flap. "I've spent most of my life on the ocean, by myself," he said. "I know how to wait."

Dusk found Sakonju in Ueno, Tokyo's northeast commuter hub, a rambling station surrounded by dilapidated office blocks and soft-porn houses. Heavy traffic crawled along the wet, neon-lit streets. He started in Ueno Park, notorious for the hundreds of homeless men usually huddled on its benches and walks, but the cold November drizzle had driven most of them elsewhere.

"The police found him at Ueno last year," Hattori had said that morning. "Picked him up on a sweep, then they called me. But he was released before I saw him." His body had been found in a half-finished new building not far away.

Soaked through, Sakonju decided that further searching outside was pointless. He returned to the station and shook off the damp amid a rushing flow of suits and umbrellas.

A maze of tunnels, connecting at odd angles and ramping up and down, led to the various subway lines. Along the periphery, traffic thinned out, and the city's destitute appeared, sleeping in corridor alcoves, seated with their plastic bags, muttering to the walls or staring into space. Eventually he found the permanent encampments, neat rows of cardboard shelters along a wide corridor near the Asakusa

Line. Under the stuttering fluorescents people had lashed together old boxes and plastic fiber to create a subterranean shantytown, low walls for privacy and a bit of protection.

Behind a large concrete pillar he came across several older men seated on the floor. Small bottles of vending machine sake and *shochu* liquor stood half-empty between them. They were arguing about baseball–the same discussion that could be heard among countless groups of salarymen in their bars, between workers off-shift, across the counters of ramen stalls.

"Hattori? The fellow who was killed, sure, we knew him, he was around sometimes." They were drunk, unsurprised at Sakonju's questions. "Nice guy."

"Where did he stay?"

Shrugs. One drank off his jar. "Try Tatsu–I used to see him and Hattori together."

"Down there," said another, gesturing vaguely. "Doesn't come this way much lately." He snickered through missing teeth. "Too good for us, I guess."

"How about someone called Jinguji?"

The man stopped smiling and looked away. He mumbled a negative while the others shook their heads, their boisterousness evaporating.

"Jinguji?" Sakonju asked again.

"Nothing to do with us," said one finally, his face closed.

Sakonju knew the conversation was over. He gave them a few thousand-yen notes and walked on.

He found Tatsu thirty minutes and several inquiries later, curled up behind three walls about a meter high and built from waxed cardboard crates which, from the smell, had contained onions and burdock. He was wrapped in a green blanket, watching a handheld TV, small earphones connected by a looping sound cord. Several plastic and nylon bags held his possessions. He jumped when Sakonju prodded his side.

"Yes, yes, I'm sorry . . . " he hurriedly pulled off the earphones and hid the TV away, patting at several bags and then focusing. "Not police, are you?"

"Hardly." Sakonju squatted beside him. "A friend of yours was killed a couple weeks back, barely a kilometer from here."

"Hattori?" Tatsu pushed himself to a seated position. "Terrible. But not really my friend."

"Know him well?"

"He was . . . you know." He tapped the inside of his left forearm with his right thumb.

"Drugs." Sakonju said it flatly.

"Maybe." His breath smelled of shochu. "You can't trust a guy like that."

"When did you see him last?"

Tatsu looked at him blankly. "A few weeks ago?"

Sakonju said nothing for a moment. "How about Jinguji?"

A look of fear crossed Tatsu's face. "Jinguji . . . " His voice trailed off.

"Who is he?"

Tatsu swallowed hard. "Big guy, mean-looking, started showing up at the callouts a few months ago. Hattori and him got together, seemed like."

"What do you mean, got together?"

"You'd see them talking, Hattori would do him errands, like. Carry packages, maybe."

"Where can I find him?"

Tatsu opened one hand and pushed away the question. "I don't know. Around. Don't ask me."

Sakonju returned at five the next morning, walking in the damp false dawn through deserted streets on the far side of Ueno Park. The callout took place at the head of an alley off Kototoi Avenue. Two dozen men milled in the cold, a few smoking, most raggedly dressed–old canvas jackets, worn split-toe boots. Some had come from the hostels, others from the station or other kips in backstreets and empty buildings. They talked to pass the time, waiting with a quiet dignity that had surprised Sakonju when he first encountered it.

The crowd looked him over then kept their distance, regarding him warily, conversation dying away. After a few minutes Sakonju recognized a man with his lunch in a neatly tied *furoshiki* and a laborer's towel wrapped around his neck, a passing acquaintance from previous work that had taken him through this particular strata of Japan's collapsing economy.

The man nodded back. "They think you're with the company," he said.

"Like what, an accountant?"

The man smiled. "Not exactly."

A pair of trucks pulled up, flatbeds with open rails and canvas tops, their headlights fuzzy in the pre-dawn mist. Four men in buzzcuts and leather jackets swung down from the cabs and looked over the laborers, who were assembling themselves into a more organized pair of lines.

"Demolition," said one of the drivers, clearly the leader. He was wearing mirrored sunglasses despite the near-dark. "In Saitama. But we only need ten of you." He began to sort and bully the men into the truckbeds.

As Sakonju stepped forward two of the toughs glanced over, then moved to intercept him.

"Looking for work, friend?" asked one.

Sakonju examined him. "No," he said. "I wonder if you've seen Jinguji-*san* lately?"

Overhearing, Sakonju's acquaintance looked back in surprise, considered the situation, then abruptly turned and faded away. Activity and conversation ceased as the buzzcuts turned their attention to Sakonju, who flexed his hands once then stood waiting, relaxed.

"No, " said the leader. "Haven't run into him lately."

"When was the last time?"

His sunglasses were perfectly still. "You with him?"

"Does it matter?"

"Let me explain," he said softly. "We're a company in the construction business. Legitimate. We pay our taxes, on time, just like any downtown *kacho*. We treat everyone fairly–do an honest day's work, you get an honest day's pay. Jinguji . . . Jinguji doesn't seem to understand that. He wants to disrupt our harmony."

"I appreciate harmony," said Sakonju.

"Who are you, then?"

Sakonju glanced around and decided he'd learned enough. "No one who wants to haul rocks all day," he said.

"Then perhaps you'd best be on your way." As the tension eased he jerked his head, and warily the toughs began to chivvy the laborers into the trucks again.

Around the corner Sakonju's acquaintance drifted out of the shadows.

"You know Jinguji?" he said.

"No."

"He began showing up a couple months ago. Hard worker–but then he began to talk more, once people were willing to listen."

Sakonju nodded. "He's organizing, isn't he?"

"No, not really. Or maybe, not yet. Just talking, explaining. Lots of these guys, they don't really know how they ended up here, breaking their backs and barely getting by. Jinguji has a way of making it all clear."

"What do you think?"

"I enjoy his company." Around the block they could hear the trucks start up, and the man paused, listening until they'd driven away. He turned back to Sakonju and smiled thinly. "You want to know where he lives?"

The boarding house was a ramshackle wooden building that had been thrown up right after the war, temporary housing in use about six decades longer than planned. Rusty buckets under the gutter drains spilled water onto cracked paving blocks around the entryway. Stooping, Sakonju pulled off his boots and slid open the inner door, referring to the scrawled slip his acquaintance had provided. It was still early, even darker now that the sullen rain had begun again, and snoring and hacking could be heard along the narrow corridor.

He knocked at Jinguji's door, waited a few minutes, and then forced the lock. A cheap latchbolt, it gave easily, and he quickly slid the door shut behind him.

The room was tiny, only three and a half mats–perhaps two meters square–and his search took barely ten minutes. A cardboard mailing box held a few changes of clothing: faded workshirts and black pants, some thin socks. A futon was rolled neatly in the corner, with three blankets folded on top. Some newspapers and *manga* were piled by the door, and a small appointment book lay nearby with some pens. The entries were brief, seeming to relate to various construction jobs.

Behind the clothing box, plugged into the wall, Sakonju found a small power adapter, but it wasn't connected to anything. He frowned at the electrical cord, then sat back and studied the room again, mentally quartering the space and eyeing each section in turn. After a few minutes, he nodded to himself and reached under the low *kotatsu* table, which was just high enough to accommodate the legs of someone seated on the tatami. He quickly found the slim box clipped to its underside, and a moment later he'd freed the laptop and opened it on the table.

"So what was in it?" Hattori asked, ignoring his bowl of soba.

"Don't know. It was passworded, and the few simple tricks I have weren't good enough." Sakonju showed him a floppy disk. "A client taught me how to get some crack routines off the Internet, but I don't really know what I'm doing."

"Then you didn't learn anything."

"No," said Sakonju. "The fact that he had the computer was enough. He's definitely not a simple laborer, and I doubt he's selling drugs."

"Why are others afraid of him?"

"They're not afraid of *him*, they're afraid of what he might bring." Sakonju finished off his curry rice. "The *yakuza* run most of the day labor. Now that times are hard, the jobs are more scarce, and if you want to work you can't afford to annoy them. Someone like Jinguji is a huge annoyance . . . they'd come down on him hard."

"Who is he working for?"

"No one. Or everyone, he'd probably say. I imagine he's connected with one of the radical unions, but how closely–it's hard to say."

"If my brother took up with Jinguji–"

Sakonju cut him off. "We don't know. Nothing but speculation until we find him."

Hattori made an impatient sound, then finally turned his attention to his noodles.

"Was your brother an addict?" Sakonju asked.

"Drugs? No, I don't think so. Used them for a while, but drinking seemed to be the real problem."

"Did the police mention it? Needles in his pockets, like that?"

"No."

They ate in silence for a while. Hattori finished his bowl, drank off the broth, and pushed it aside.

"I want to go with you," he said abruptly.

"What?"

"When you called you said we had to meet before eleven. You haven't mentioned any other leads." Hattori's gaze was intense. "I figure you saw something in Jinguji's pocket calendar, something scheduled later today, and you want to get there at the same time."

They studied each other for a long moment.

"We're just going to talk to him," said Sakonju finally.

Hattori nodded. "Of course."

Outside the rain had receded to a midday drizzle, and they walked quickly between two- and three-story concrete buildings crowding the dreary streets. Having spent most of the day outside Sakonju was wet through, the sharp wind painfully cold. Hattori wore only a thin nylon jacket but he strode along impervious, unaffected by the weather.

The demolition site was an oblong block fenced with blue plastic and bamboo scaffolding. The building that had previously occupied the lot was now a heap of broken concrete and rebar. Some of the laborers Sakonju had seen at the callout were scavenging plumbing and metal fixtures; most were slowly transferring the rubble to a battered dump truck backed halfway in.

They didn't approach, but waited down the street in a narrow bar whose sliding glass doors allowed them to watch the site from dry seats.

"He'd better show soon," said Hattori, who'd managed to nurse a single beer for two hours.

Sakonju shrugged. "The address of this job was listed in his calendar. It's the kind of place you'd expect him to show up–small job, guys to talk to, not so many enforcers around to run him off."

"I hope you're right."

It was late afternoon when Jinguji finally appeared, but he came from the other direction and the first they noticed was the laborers standing in a circle, at a cautious distance from the dump truck. As Sakonju and Hattori approached an argument became audible, then peaked in yells abruptly cut off.

They rounded the dump truck to see three men closing on a fourth, throwing him against the truck's side as one picked a meter-long piece of pipe from the scavenged pile. Jinguji ducked the first swing, which clattered against the truck and smashed a running light. Two of his opponents grabbed at his arms and tried to hold him still.

"No damage," said Sakonju as they hopped the fence and he knew Hattori understood. Sakonju struck the first man with the sharp edge of his hand, just above the elbow. The *yakuza* dropped the pipe, crying in surprise, and as he turned Sakonju kicked him behind the knee, driving him to the ground. At the same time Hattori grabbed the second tough from behind, one hand on each arm, with a strength from years hauling nets on the open seas. He wrenched the man off Jinguji and tossed him aside like he weighed nothing.

"That's enough!"

Jinguji's shout cut through the melee with a power Sakonju hadn't expected. As the assailants paused, Jinguji shoved aside the third *yakuza* and moved quickly forward. In the space of a couple seconds, he pushed Sakonju and Hattori back out onto the sidewalk, and they backed away. The *yakuza* watched them go but did not pursue.

They stopped under the shelter of an expressway overpass some distance away, the rain now falling in sheets between the bridge and the buildings around it.

"Thanks," said Jinguji. He was tall and wiry, with a sharp jaw and a piercing gaze he held on them unblinking. "How did you find me?"

"Who said we were looking?" asked Hattori, but Sakonju just ghosted a smile.

"Broke into your room this morning," he said. "We're not with another gang, if that's what you're wondering."

"Oh, I knew that. Rival thugs, you would have waited until they finished with me, *then* moved in." He wiped his wet hair backward. "You certainly look the part, though."

"What were you trying to do?"

Jinguji made a gesture of indifference. "Talking only takes you so far. If they see you stand up to the *yakuza* in person, now and then, it helps them understand what they could do together."

"There can't be many of you out here."

"Eleven in our organizing committee, across Tokyo. But the general membership is growing fast."

"Still," said Sakonju. "You must need more help . . . pay your volunteers anything?" Jinguji looked at him quizzically, but said nothing. "Let me be particular: Hattori-*san*."

"Ah." Jinguji sighed. "Now I understand." He looked more closely at them. "Family? I might see a resemblance."

"Yes," said Hattori shortly. "You hired him?"

"He was interested, and he had started to work with us, yes. I advanced him some money." He looked down. "I'm very sorry for your loss."

"He was killed because of you," said Hattori with a cold anger.

"No," said Sakonju, placing a hand lightly on Hattori's arm. "Not exactly."

Jinguji nodded agreement. "They would never kill one of us," he said. "Even the beatings I've gotten have been minor. Just a little discouragement, you might say. Think about it–if they murder someone to send a message, the police are going to get it just as clearly, and we're nowhere near worth that kind of trouble."

"He's right," said Sakonju. "Anyway, the last place they'd commit such a crime would be one of their own sites–it shuts the job down, on top of everything else. The company employing them would never stand for that."

"But–I don't understand." Hattori subsided in puzzlement.

"How much did you pay him?" Sakonju asked Jinguji.

"Forty thousand yen." His sharp face was gaunt in the rainy twilight. "My mistake was to hand it over all at once."

Sakonju nodded. "Yes, it was too much." He turned to Hattori. "I think I know where we have to go next."

They arrived well after nightfall, the tunnel floors dirty from the rain-soaked shoes of commuters thronging homeward. Sakonju led the way and they found Tatsu still in his cardboard kip, the blanket now folded beneath him as a seating pad, a Styrofoam container of yakisoba and a bottle of Asahi Super-Dry for his evening meal.

"No, don't get up," said Sakonju.

Tatsu had stopped eating and squinted at them suspiciously. "What do you want now?"

"You lied about the drugs," said Sakonju. "He wasn't an addict."

Tatsu shrugged. "So I was wrong."

"That little LCD TV–twenty, thirty thousand yen, maybe? When did you buy it?"

Tatsu frowned and a few moments passed.

"He wasn't your friend, really," Sakonju said. "But he had to tell someone when he got all that money. Probably bought something decent to drink, wanted to share it around."

"No."

"Or if he didn't say anything, you figured it out anyway–maybe he bought himself a night in a clean hotel, or you just noticed him being unusually cagey. Doesn't matter."

Tatsu hunched into himself but said nothing, still staring at them. Hattori stood carved of stone.

"You probably met him at the construction site after work one day–it's close enough, maybe it was a convenient place to get out of the rain. Then it was just a question of waiting until he was alone, and taking advantage of what was at hand."

"No . . . I don't know what you're talking about."

Sakonju shook his head and pulled out his cell phone. He dialed the local police number and then they waited, no one saying anything, while businessmen in wet raincoats hurried incuriously past.

The Heart Has Reasons

by O'Neil De Noux

FOR TWO DAYS SHE CAME AND SAT under the WPA shelter in Cabrini Playground with her baby, sometimes rocking the infant, sometimes walking between the oaks and magnolias, back and forth. Sometimes she would sing. She came around nine AM and around lunchtime she'd reach into the paper bag she'd brought and nibble on a sandwich. After, she would cover her shoulder with a small pink blanket and nurse her baby beneath the blanket. Around five PM, she would walk away, up Dauphine Street.

On the third morning the rain swept in, one of those all-day New Orleans rainstorms that started suddenly then built into monsoon proportions. The newspaper said to expect showers brought in by an atypical autumn cool front from Canada, which would finally break the heat wave that has lingered through the sizzling summer of 1948. I grabbed two umbrellas and found her huddled under the shelter.

"Come on," I told her, "come get out of the rain." I held out an umbrella. When she didn't take it immediately, I stood it against the wall and stepped away to give her some room. She looked younger up close, nineteen, maybe eighteen and stood about five-two, a thin girl with short, dark brown hair and darker brown eyes, all saucered-wide and blinking at me with genuine fear.

I took another step away from her, not wanting to tower over her with my six foot frame, and smiled as warmly as I could. "Please. Come take your baby out of the rain." I opened the second umbrella and handed it to her.

Slowly, a shaky white hand extended for the umbrella, those big eyes still staring at me. I took a step toward the edge of the shelter.

A loud thunderclap caused us both to jump and the baby started crying.

I led the way back across the small playground, the umbrellas pretty useless in the deluge, and hurried through the brick and wrought iron fence to narrow Barracks Street, having to pause a moment to let a yellow cab pass. She moved carefully behind me and I held the door to my building open for her.

I closed the umbrellas and started up the stairs for my apartment. "I'll bring towels down," I called back to her, then took the stairs two at a time.

Moving quickly, I grabbed two large towels from my bathroom, lighting the gas heater while I was in there and pulled the big terry-cloth robe I never wore from the closet, draping it over the bathroom door before leaving my apartment door open on the way out. She stood next to the smoky glass door of my office, rocking her baby, who had stopped crying. She still gave me that frightened look when I came down and extended the towels to her.

"Top of the stairs, take a left. My apartment door's open." I reached into my suit coat pocket and pulled out a business card. "That's my office behind you. The number's on the card. Go upstairs. The heater's on in the bathroom and take your time. Lock yourself in. Call me if you need anything."

I shoved the towels at her and she took them with her free hand. I pressed the business card between her fingers as she moved away from my office door. She took a hesitant step for the stairs, stopped and watched me with hooded eyes now.

Stepping to my office door, I told her, "I'm Lucien Caye," and nodded at my name stenciled on the smoky glass door. "I'm a detective."

Her lower lip quivered, so I tried my warmest smile again. "Go on upstairs. You'll be safe up there. Lock yourself in."

The baby began to whine. She took in a deep breath and backed toward the bottom step. Glancing up the stairs, she said, "First door on the left?"

"It's open," I said as stepped into my office. "I'll start up some eggs and bacon. I have a stove in here." I left the door open and returned to the row of windows along Barracks Street where I'd been watching her. A louder thunder clap shook the old building before two flashes of lightning danced over the rooftops of the French Quarter. The street was a mini-canal already, the storm washing the dust from old my gray, pre-war 1940 DeSoto coach parked against the curb.

"Bacon and eggs," I said aloud and turned back to the small kitchen area at the rear of my office. I had six eggs left in the small refrigerator, a half-slab of bacon and milk for the coffee. I sniffed the milk and it smelled OK.

I called my apartment before going up. She answered after the sixth ring with a hesitant, "Yes?"

"It's Lucien. Downstairs. I'm bringing up some bacon, eggs and coffee, OK?"

I heard her breathing.

"I'm the guy who got you outta the rain. Remember? Dark hair. Six feet tall. I brought an umbrella."

"The door's not locked," she said.

"OK. I'll be right up." When she didn't hang up immediately, I told her, "You can hang up now."

"All right." She did and I brought a heaping plate of breakfast and a mug of café au lait. I'd left my coat downstairs, along with my .38 revolver. Didn't want to spook her anymore than she was already spooked.

She was sitting on the sofa, her baby sleeping next to her. In the terry-cloth robe, a towel wrapped around her wet hair like a swami, she looked like a kid, not a mother. The baby lay on its belly, wrapped in a towel. I went to my Formica kitchen table and put the food down, flipping on the light and telling her I'd be downstairs if she needed anything else.

"Is that a holster?" she asked, staring at my right hip.

"I told you I'm a detective." I kept moving toward the door, giving her a wide berth, hoping the fear in her eyes would subside.

"Thank you," she said, standing up, arms folded across her chest now.

I pointed down the hall beyond my bathroom. "There's a washer back there for your clothes and a clothesline out back, if it ever stops raining."

She nodded and said, "I'm Kaye Bishop." She looked down at her baby. "This is Donna."

I stopped just inside the door. "Nice to meet you Kaye. If you need to call anyone, you know where the phone is."

I hesitated in case she wanted to keep talking and she surprised me with, "You're not how I would picture a detective."

"How's that?"

Her eyes, like chocolate agates, stared back at me. "You seem polite. Maybe too polite."

"You've been out there for three days. You all right?"

"We'll be fine when Charley comes for us."

"Charley?"

"Charley Rudabaugh. Donna's father. We're not married, yet. That's why I'm staying with the Ursulines."

Nuns. The Ursuline convent on Chartres Street. Oldest building in the Quarter. Only building which didn't burn in the two fires that engulfed the city in the Eighteenth Century, or so the story goes. For an instant I saw Kaye Bishop in a colonial costume, as a casket girl, labeled because they'd arrived in New Orleans with all their belongings in a single case that looked like a casket. Imported wives from France, daughters of impoverished families sent to the new world to marry the French settlers. The Ursulines took them under wing to make sure they were properly married before taken off by the early, rough settlers. Looks like they're still taking care of young girls.

"The church took us in." Her eyes were wet now. "We're waiting until Charley can get us a place."

Donna let out a little cry and Kaye scooped up her baby and moved to my mother's old rocking chair next to the French doors that opened to the wrought iron balcony wrapping around my building, along the second floor. As she rocked her baby, she reached up and unwrapped the towel on her head, shook out her hair and rubbed the towel through her hair.

The baby giggled and she giggled back. "You like that?" She shook her hair out again and the baby laughed. Turning to me, she said, "Can you get my purse? It's in the bathroom."

I brought it to her and she took out a brush and brushed out her short brown hair. Donna peeked up and me, hands swinging in small circles, legs kicking.

"She's a beautiful baby," I said backing away, not wanting to crowd them.

Kaye smiled at her daughter as she brushed her hair, the rocker moving now. I was about to ask if the eggs and bacon were OK when she started humming, then singing in a low voice, a song in French, a song that sat me down on my sofa.

My mother sang that song to me. I recognized the refrain . . . *"le coeur a ses raisons que la raison ne connait point."* Still don't know what it means. I wanted to ask Kaye but didn't want to interrupt her as she hummed part of the song and sang part.

I closed my eyes and listened. It was hard because I could hear my heart beating in my ears. When the singing stopped and I opened my eyes, Kaye was staring at me and I could see she wasn't afraid of me anymore.

Two hours later, I was about to call upstairs to suggest I go over and pick up Charley, bring him here when she called and said, "Could you get a message to Charley for me?"

"Sure."

"He's working at the Gulf station, Canal and Claiborne. He's a mechanic," she said with pride.

Slipping my blue suit coat back on, I looked out at the rain still falling on my DeSoto. It wasn't coming down as hard now but I took the umbrella anyway after I went back and slid my .38 back into its holster. I started to grab my tan fedora but left it on the coat rack. Hats just mess up my hair.

It took a good half hour to reach the station on a drive that normally took fifteen minutes. Every car in front of me drove so slowly, it was as if these people had never seen rain before in one of the wettest city in the country. I resisted leaning on my horn for an old man wearing a hat two sizes too large for his pin head, wondering why he couldn't get his Cadillac out of first gear.

Forked lightning danced in the sky, right over the tan bricks of Charity Hospital towering a few blocks behind the Gulf station as I pulled in. The station stood out bright-white in the rain, illuminated by its lights normally on only at night. I parked outside the middle bay with the word "tires" above the doorway. The other bays, marked "lubrication" and "batteries" were filled with jacked-up vehicles.

Leaving the umbrella in my DeSoto, I jogged into the open bay and came face up with a hulking man holding a tire iron.

"Hi, I'm looking for Charley Rudabaugh."

He lifted the tire iron and took a menacing step toward me. I stumbled back, turning to my right as I reached under my coat for my revolver.

"Sam!" a voice boomed behind the man and he stopped but kept leering at me with angry eyes.

I kept the .38 against my leg as I took another step back to the edge of the open bay doors so he'd have to take two steps to get to me. I'd have to run or shoot him. Neither choice was a good one. A second hulking man, even bigger, came around the man with the tire iron. Both wore dark green coveralls with the orange Gulf Oil logos over their hearts.

The bigger man growled, "Who the hell are you?"

"Kaye Bishop sent me with a message for Charley."

"Kaye? Where is she?" He took a step toward me and I showed him my Smith & Wesson, but didn't point it at him.

"I'm a private detective. You wanna tell me what's goin' on?"

"You got an ID?"

Don't remember ever seeing Bogart, as Sam Spade or Philip Marlowe, showing his ID to anyone, but I had to do it–a lot. I reached into my coat pocket with my left hand and opened my credentials pouch for him and asked, "Where's Charley?"

The bigger man looked hard at my ID. "I'm Malone," he said. "Charley works for me. Where's Kaye?"

"At my office." I slipped my creds back into my coat pocket.

Malone turned his face to the side and spoke to his buddy with the tire iron. "He's too skinny to work for Joe. And his nose ain't been broke. Yet."

The man with the tire iron backed away, leaning against the fender of a Ford with its rear jacked up.

"I told you where Kaye is. Where's Charley?" I re-holstered my revolver but kept my distance.

"Don't trust the bastard," said the man with the tire iron.

I could see, in both sets of eyes, there was no way they were telling me anything. Maybe they'd tell Kaye. I suggested we get her on the phone. I stayed in the garage as Malone called my apartment from the office area. When he signaled for me to come in and get the phone, the first hulk finally put the tire iron down.

"Kaye?"

"Charley's in the hospital," she said excitedly. "Can you bring me to him?"

"I'll be right there." I hung up and looked at Malone. "You wanna tell me what happened now?"

Charley Rudabaugh was a good kid, a hard worker, but he borrowed money from the wrong man. Malone learned that tidbit that very morning when a goon came by with a sawed-off baseball bat and broke Charley's right arm.

"I was under a Buick and couldn't get out before the goon got away."

"Was it this Joe you thought I was working for?"

"No. A goon works for Joe Grosetto."

Malone explained Grosetto was a local loan shark. I asked where I could locate this shark but neither knew for sure. Charley would.

Kaye and Donna were waiting for me in the foyer of my building. I brought them out to the DeSoto under the umbrella and drove straight to Charity Hospital, parking at an empty meter outside the emergency room.

Charley Rudabaugh was about five-ten, thin build with curly light brown hair and green eyes. He smiled at Kaye and kissed Donna and finally noticed me standing in behind them. His right arm in a fresh cast, Charley blinked and said, "Who are you?"

I let Kaye explain as she held his left hand, bouncing a gurgling Donna cradled in her free arm. He looked at me suspiciously, sizing me up, giving me that look a male gives another when he just showed up with his woman. When Kaye finished, more nervous now, she asked Charley what happened to him.

He turned to her and his eyes softened. He took in a deep breath and said, "Haney." She became pale and I pulled a chair over for her to sit, then went back to the doorway.

"He didn't ask where I was?" asked Kaye.

Charley shook his head. "He just wanted the money."

Kaye's eyes teared up and she pressed her face against his left arm and cried. Charley's eyes filled too and he closed them but the tears leaked out, down his lean face. Donna's arms swung around in circles as she lay cradled and I waited until one of the adults looked at me.

It was Charley and I asked, "How much money are we talking about?"

"This doesn't concern you."

Kaye stopped crying now and wiped her face on the sheet before sitting up.

I tried a different tack. "What school didya' go to?" The old New Orleans handshake. This was no public school kid. He told me he went to Jesuit. I told him I went to Holy Cross. Two Catholic school boys who'd gone to rival schools.

"Your parents can't help?" Jesuit was expensive.

"They don't live here anymore. And don't even ask about Kaye's parents. This is our problem."

"Everyone needs help, sometimes."

"That's what you do? Some kinda guardian angel?"

I shook my head, thought about it a second and said, "Actually, it's what I do most of the time. Help people figure things out."

"We can't afford a private eye."

I tried still another tack. "How do I find this Grosetto? This Haney?"

Charley shook his head. Kaye wouldn't meet my eyes so I left them alone, went out in to the waiting area. Ten minutes later a blond-headed doctor went in, then a nurse. I caught the doctor on the way out. It was a simple fracture of both bones, the radius and ulna between wrist and elbow.

"It was a blunt instrument, officer," the doctor said. "Says he fell but something struck that arm."

I thanked the doc without correcting him that I wasn't a cop. The nurse was obviously finishing up, telling them how Charley had to move on soon as the cast was hard. Kaye turned her red eyes to me and I took in a deep breath. "I'll take you to the Ursulines, OK?"

Her shoulders sank. I turned to Charley. "So where have you been staying?"

"He's been sleeping at the Gulf station," Kaye said.

He shot her a worried look.

"They don't know," Kaye added. "He stays late to lock up and sleeps inside, opens in the morning."

I put my proposition to them to use my apartment and stepped out for them to discuss it, gave them another ten minutes before walking back in. Kaye shot me a nervous smile, holding Donna up now, the baby smiling too as her mother jiggled her.

I looked at Charley who asked, "I just wanna know why you're doing this."

"How old are you, Charley?"

"Twenty. And Kaye's eighteen. We're both adults now."

I nodded slowly and said, "I watched a young mother and her baby spend three days in that playground, avoiding the kids when they came, keeping to themselves until the rain blew in. I've got two apartments, one converted into an office downstairs with a sofa bed, kitchen and bath. I've sleep down there before. You got a better offer?"

Charley and Kaye wouldn't volunteer any information about Grosetto and Haney and there was no way Malone and his tire-iron friend were going to be much help. But I knew who would. He was in too, sitting behind his worn government-issue gray metal desk, in a government-issue gray desk chair in a small office with gray walls lined with mug shots, wanted posters and an electric clock that surprisingly had the correct time.

Detective Eddie Sullivan had lost more of his red hair, making up for it with an old-fashioned handle-bar moustache. Grinning at me as I stepped up to his desk, he said, "I was about to get a bite."

"Me too."

So I bought him lunch around the corner from the First Precinct house on South Saratoga Street at Jilly's Grill. Hamburgers, French fries, coffee and a wedge of apple pie for my large friend. Sullivan was my height exactly but out-weighed me by a hundred pounds, mostly flab.

Eddie Sullivan was the Bunco Squad for the First Precinct, since his partner retired, without a replacement in sight. He handled con artists, forgers, loan sharks and the pawn shop detail, checking lists of pawned items against the master list of stolen articles reported to police. I waited until he'd wolfed down his burger and fries and was starting in on his slab of pie before bringing up Grosetto and Haney. He nodded and told me he knew both.

"Grosetto's a typical Guinea, short, olive-skinned, pencil thin moustache, weighs about a hundred pounds soaking wet. Haney is black Irish, big, goofy-looking. Typical bully." He stuffed another chunk of pie into his mouth.

"Grosetto? He mobbed up?"

Sullivan shook his head. "He wishes but he ain't Sicilian. I think he's Napolitano or just some ordinary Wop. You got someone willin' to file charges against these bums?

"Maybe. I need to know where they hang out."

"Easy. Rooms above the Blue Gym. Canal and Galvez."

I knew the place and hurried to finish my meal as Sullivan ordered a second wedge of pie. He managed to say, between mouthfuls, "I'd go with you but I gotta be in court a one o'clock. Drop me by the court house?"

As he climbed out of my DeSoto in front of the hulking, gray Criminal Courts Building, Tulane and Broad Avenues, he thanked me for lunch, adding, "See if you can talk your friend into pressing charges. I could use a good collar."

"I'll try."

The Blue Gym was hard to miss, sitting on the downtown side of Canal and Galvez Streets. Painted bright blue, it stood three stories high, the bottom two stories an open gym with six boxing rings inside, smelling of sweat, blood and cigar smoke. I weaved my way through a haze of smoke to a back stairs and went up to a narrow hall that smelled like cooked fish. A thin man in boxing shorts came rushing out of a door and almost bumped into me.

"Oh, 'scuse me," he said.

"I'm looking for Grosetto."

He pointed to the door he'd just exited and rushed off. I reached back and unsnapped the trigger guard on the holster of my Smith & Wesson before stepping through the open door to spot a smallish man behind a beat-up wooden desk. The man glared at me with hard brown eyes, trying to look tough, hard to do when he stood up and topped off at maybe five-three and skinny as a stick-man. He wore a shark-skin lime green suit.

"Who the hell are you?" he snarled from the right side of his tiny mouth.

I stepped up, keeping an eye on his hands in case he tried something stupid and said, "How much does Charley Rudabaugh owe you?"

"Huh?"

"How much?" I kept my voice even, without a hint of emotion.

The beady eyes examined me, up and down, then he sat and said, "You ain't Italian. What are you? Some kinda Mexican?"

I wasn't about to tell this jerk I'm half French, half Spanish, so I told him, "I'm the man with the money. You want your money, tell me how much Charley owes you."

"Three hundred and fifty. Tomorrow it's gonna be four hundred."

"I'll be right back." And I didn't look back as I strolled out, making it to the nearest branch of the Whitney Bank before it closed. My bank accounts, I have a saving account now, were both in good shape after the Duponceau Case. As I stood in the teller line, I remembered the salient facts that brought such money into my possession—

It was a probate matter. When it got slow, I'd go over to civil court, pick up an inheritance case. This one was a search for any descendants of a recently deceased uptown matron. Flat fee for my work. If I found someone, they got the inheritance, if not, the state got it. I'd worked a dozen before and never found anyone until I found Peter Duponceau, a fellow WWII vet, in a VA Hospital in Providence, Rhode Island.

Not long after I caught a bullet from a Nazi sniper at Monte Cassino, he collected a chest full of shrapnel from a Japanese bombardment on a small island called Saipan. Peter was the grandson of the recently deceased uptown matron. His mother was also deceased. When I met him to confirm his inheritance, he was back in the hospital for yet another operation. At least the last months of his life were lived in luxury in a mansion overlooking Audubon Park. He left most of his estate to several local VFW chapters and ten percent to Lucien Caye, Esquire. When the certified check arrived, I contemplated getting an armored car to drive me to the bank. I couldn't make that much money in five years, unless I robbed a bank or two.

Grosetto was back behind his desk but there was an addition to the room, a hulking man standing six-four, outweighing me by a good hundred pounds of what looked like grizzle, with a thick mane of unruly black hair and a ruddy complexion. He wore a rumpled brown suit as he stared at me with dull, brown eyes, Mississippi River water brown. My Irish friend Sullivan described Haney as black Irish, probably descended from the Spanish of the Great Armada, the ones who weren't drowned by the English. The ones who took the prevailing winds, beaching their ships along the Irish coast to be taken in by fellow Catholics to later breed with the locals. I would have given Haney only a cursory look, except I didn't expect he'd be so young, early twenties maybe.

Stepping up to the desk, I dropped the bank envelope in front of

Grosetto. "Rudabaugh sign anything? Promissory note? IOU?" I knew better but asked anyway.

Grosetto picked up the envelope and counted the money, nodding when he was finished. I turned to Haney. "You still have that baseball bat?"

He looked at Grosetto for an answer and then looked back and I could see he wasn't all there.

"Try that stunt again and I'll put two in your head. And I'll get away with it."

"Alls I want is the girl," Haney said.

"What?"

He looked down at his feet, all shy-like and said, "I seen her," looking up now with those dull eyes, "*Real* pretty." He followed with a childlike chuckle.

I turned back to Grosetto, "Better let him in on the real world."

Grosetto was smiling now, or trying to with that crooked mouth. "He usually gets what he wants."

"Not this time," I said.

No use arguing with idiots. When I got back to my office, I located my black jack, a chunk of lead attached to a thick spring, covered with black leather, brand named the Bighorn because it allegedly could cold-cock a charging bighorn ram. I only used it twice back when I was a patrolman and it worked well enough to incapacitate bigger, combative men. Then I put away my .38 and brought my army issue Colt .45 caliber automatic and loaded it, switching holsters now. I needed something with stopping power.

I called upstairs and Kaye answered, telling me the baby and Charley were asleep.

"I need to get a couple things, OK?"

She let me in and I quickly packed a suitcase with essentials, grabbed a couple suits and fresh shirts. Before stepping out, I waved her over and we whispered in the hall. I told her they owed Grosetto nothing. How? I told her someone had given me a lot of money and now I was giving them some.

"Charley won't stand for it. We'll pay you back."

I shrugged, then watched her eyes as I told her I'd met Haney. She blanched, so I followed it with, "Back at Charity, why did you ask Charley if Haney asked where you were?"

She took a step back, crossed her arms and said, "He's my half-brother."

Sitting at my desk in my dark office, I watched the rain finally taper off.

"What about your parents?" I'd asked Kaye up in the hall. She told me her father was dead and her mother had abandoned her when she was five and wouldn't say anything else about the matter, not even who'd raised her.

I was thinking—at least they were safe for now—just as I spotted Haney standing next to the playground fence across the street. Didn't take him long to find us. He stood there for a good ten minutes before coming across the street.

I expected the baseball bat, not the revolver stuck in the waistband of his suit pants as he stepped in the foyer of my building. I'd moved into the shadows next to the stairs, black jack in my left hand. Slowly, I eased my right hand back to my .45 as he saw me and said softly, "Where is she?"

The sound of squealing tires behind him made him look over his shoulder. When he looked back I had my .45 pointed at his face and said, "That'll be the cavalry."

Two uniforms alighted from the black prowl car and came into the building with their guns out. It was Williams and Jeanfreau, both rookies when I was at the Third Precinct.

I lowered my weapon. "He's got a gun in his waistband."

Williams snatched Haney's revolver and Jeanfreau cuffed him and dragged him out.

"Aggravated assault, right?" Williams checked with me for the charge.

"Yeah. Hopefully he's a convicted felon." A felon with a firearm would hold Haney for quite a while.

"Thanks," I called out to my old compadres. Williams called back, "Your call broke up the sergeant's poker game. But only for a while."

Charley sat shirtless at my kitchen table holding Donna with his good arm, Kaye in my terry-cloth robe again, getting us coffee, them looking like a family now and I had to tell them about Haney.

Kaye blanched at the news; Charley just nodded while Donna gurgled.

"How close are you?" I asked.

"I'm not even sure he's my half-brother," Kaye answered. "He claims to be. Claims my dad was his father. I never met him until he showed up at the hospital when Donna was born."

She didn't volunteer any more and I didn't want to cross-examine her, sitting at my table, all three adults sipping coffee which wasn't bad and I'm picky about my coffee.

I turned to Charley and said, "We need to press charges against Grosetto. I'll back you and we'll put the slime-ball away. My buddy Detective Sullivan is chomping at the bit to nail him."

Charley shook his head and told me, in careful, low tones how he wanted Grosetto and Haney and all of it behind him, how he was going to pay me back whatever it cost me. I tried for the next half hour, but there was no changing his mind. He said he didn't want to be looking over his shoulder for the rest of his life. God, he was so young.

The coffee kept me up a little while, but the rain came back that night, slapping against my office windows as I lay on my sofa-bed. Why was I lying there? Why wasn't I out on the town, dancing with a long tall blonde in a slinky dress? Maybe bringing her here or going to her place and helping her slip into something more comfortable, like my arms.

I knew the answer. It was upstairs with those kids, so I lay waiting for trouble to return, knowing it would.

Arriving at the Criminal Courts Building early, I searched the docket for Haney's name, wanting to get a word in with the judge before his arraignment. When I couldn't find his name, the acid in my stomach churned. I snatched up a pay phone in the lobby and called parish prison, speaking to the shift lieutenant who took his time, but looked up the name for me.

"Haney. Yeah. Bonded out four-thirty AM."

I asked more questions and got the obvious answers, a friendly judge and a friendlier bail bondsman had Haney out before sunrise. The only surprise was that Haney had only two previous arrests, both misdemeanors, no convictions.

I should have gotten a speeding ticket on the way home, but no one was paying attention. Catching my breath when I reached the top of the stairs, I tapped lightly on the door. Even a bachelor knows better than to ring a doorbell with a baby inside. Kaye answered and I let out a relieved sigh, which disappeared immediately when she told me Charley wasn't there.

"Where'd he go?"

"To work. Malone picked him up." Her eyebrows furrowed when she saw the worried look in my eyes. I pointed to the phone and she opened the door wider, telling me, "Malone said a one-armed Charley was better than any of his other mechanics."

She knew the number by heart and I dialed. Malone answered after the fifth ring and I warned him about Haney being out of jail.

"Didn't know he was in jail."

"Well, he had a gun last night, so be on the lookout."

Then I called Sullivan to make sure the patrol boys did a drive-by at the Gulf Station before I went to see Grosetto.

He was behind the desk wearing the same lime green suit, sporting that same crooked slimy grin when I walked in on him, the place reeking of fish again.

"Where's Haney?"

Grosetto tried growling, which only made him look like a randy terrier, instead of a gangster. His hands dropped below the desk top and I turned my left shoulder to him, pulling out my .45, letting him get a look at it.

"Put your hands back on your desk and they better be empty."

"Who da' heller you commin' in here, tellin' me what to do?"

"Where's Haney?"

He tried smiling but it looked more like a grimace. "I'm glad you come by. You needa tell Charley he owes another fifty. I, how you put it, miscalculated the amount." This time it was a smile, sickly, showing off yellowed-teeth.

I shot his telephone, watched it bounce high, slam against the back wall, the loud report of my .45 echoing in my ears. Pointing it at his face now, I said. "Put your hands back on your desk."

He did, his eyes bulging now. I backed up and locked the door behind me and came back to the desk as I holstered my weapon, slammed both hands against the desk, shoving it across the linoleum floor with him and his chair behind, pinning him against the wall.

"Tell Haney I'm looking for him."

Three boxers and two trainers were in the narrow hall. I opened my coat and showed them the .45 and they backed away cautiously, none of them saying anything until I started through the gym. A couple brave ones cursed me behind my back, but kept their distance.

I figured Haney was loony enough to come by but it was Grosetto, just before midnight. He wore a gray dress shirt and black pants, hands high as he stepped into my building's foyer. I was sitting in darkness, half-way up the stairs, sitting in my shirt and pants with my .45 in my right hand.

"That you?" he called out when I told him to freeze. I'd unscrewed the hall light.

"What do you want?"

"I come to tell you somethin'."

I went and patted him down, closed and locked the building door then shoved him into my office, leaving the door open. He smelled like cigarette smoke and stale beer. I made him stand still as I moved to my desk and leaned against it.

"All right, what is it?"

"I made a mistake. Charley don't owe me nothin'."

"Good."

He tried smiling again, but it still didn't work. "I checked on you. You got some rep. You know. War hero. Ex-cop. Bad when you gotta be bad." He looked around my office for a second. "You check up on me?"

"In the dictionary. Under scum bag."

"You funny. You owe me a phone, you know."

Maybe it was the twitch in his eye or the way he sucked in a breath when I heard it, a thump upstairs. Grosetto should never play poker. It was in his eyes and I was on him in three long strides, slamming the .45 against his pointed head, tumbling him out of my way.

I took the stairs three at a time, reaching the top of the stairs as a gunshot rang out. My apartment door was open and a woman's screaming voice echoed as I ran in, scene registering as I swung my .45 to the right toward the figure standing with a gun in hand. The gun turned toward me and I fired twice, Haney bouncing on his toes as the rounds punched his chest. The gun dropped and he fell straight back, head ricocheting off an end table.

Kaye, with Donna in her arms, moved for Charley as he lay on the kitchen floor, a circle of bright red blood under him. Holstering my weapon, I leaped toward them as Kaye cradled his head in her arms.

He was conscious, a neat hole in his lower abdomen, blood oozing through his white undershirt. I jumped back to the phone and called for an ambulance. When I turned back, Charley was trying to sit up.

"Don't!" I jumped into the kitchen, snatched an ice tray from the freezer, broke up the ice, wrapped it in a dishcloth and got Kaye out of the way with Donna screeching now. I pressed the ice against the wound and told Charley to keep calm, the ambulance would be right there. Then I remembered I'd locked the foyer door and had to go down for it.

Charley was still conscious when they rolled him out with Kaye and Donna in tow. Williams and Jeanfreau had accompanied the ambulance and used my phone to call the detectives.

"What'd you shoot him with?" Williams asked, pointing to the two large holes around Haney's heart. I pointed to my .45 which I'd put on the kitchen counter before they came in.

It was then I remembered Grosetto and brought Williams down to my office. The little greaseball was just coming around and Williams slapped his cuffs on him and brought him up to have a look at Haney. The dead man looked younger in death in a yellow shirt and dungarees, his eyes even duller now, his face flaccid. To me he looked like an eighth grader trying to pass himself off at a high school. His shoes were tied in double knots as if his mom had made sure they wouldn't come undone.

It took the detectives forty minutes to get there. I made coffee for all and was on my second cup when Lieutenant Frenchy Capdeville strolled in, trailing cigarette smoke, a rookie dick at his heels. Frenchy needed a haircut badly, his black hair in loose curls over the collar of his brown suit.

His rookie partner had tried a pencil-thin moustache, like Frenchy's but his was lopsided. "Joe Sparks," Frenchy introduced him to me. Sparks, also in a brown suit, was sharp enough to keep quiet and let Frenchy run the show, which he did, quickly and efficiently.

After the coroner's men took Haney away, they took me and Grosetto to the Detective Bureau, Frenchy calling in Eddie Sullivan. While they booked Grosetto, I gave a formal statement about the first man I'd shot since the war. Self-defense, defined in Louisiana's Napoleonic Code Law was—justifiable homicide.

It didn't take a detective to discover how Haney had come in the back way, through the broken fence of the building next door, across the back courtyard and up the rear fire escape to break the hallway window.

"How'd he get in the apartment?" I asked Kaye as we sat in the hall at Charity Hospital the following morning, while Charley slept in the recovery ward. Dark circles around her eyes, she looked pale as she rocked Donna slowly. Thankfully the baby was asleep.

"I heard scratching against the door and thought it was the cat, the black one that's always around."

"Did he say anything?"

"No. He just shoved past me and shot Charley. Then he stood there looking at me."

A nurse came out of Charley's room and said, "He's awake now."

I didn't go in. I went back home to look up my landlord.

Charley Rudabaugh spent six days in the hospital. When I brought him home and walked him past my apartment door to the rear apartment, he balked until Kaye opened the door and smiled at him.

"What's going on?"

Kaye pulled him in and I stood in the doorway, amazed at what she'd done with the place in a few days. It came furnished but she'd brightened the place, replaced the dark curtains with yellow ones, the place looking spotless. Donna, lying on her back in a playpen in the center of the living room was trying to play with a rubber duck, slapping at it and gurgling.

It took Charley a good minute to take in the scene as Kaye eased up and hugged him.

"Here's the deal," I told them over coffee at their kitchen table. "The landlord gave us a break on the place. I'm fronting y'all the money. You don't have to pay me back, but if you insist, you can, but get on your feet first." I'd just put any money they gave me in a bank account for Donna's education.

Then I explained about how it really wasn't my money. It had been a gift and I was sharing it. "Everyone needs help sometimes. And you two have had a bad time recently."

I could see Charley was still confused, but not Kaye, beaming at him, paying little if any attention to me. I thanked her for the coffee and stood up to leave. Charley's eyes narrowed as he asked, "I understand what you say, but it's just hard to figure you ain't got some kinda motive. Everybody does."

I started for the door, turned and said, "Sometimes things are exactly as they appear to be."

Kaye moved to her daughter and began humming that same song, repeating the line in French again, "*le coeur a . . .*"

"What is that?" I had to ask.

"It's the reason you're doing all this." She smiled at me, looking like a school kid in her white shirt and jeans. "An old French saying that goes, 'The heart has reasons of which reason knows nothing.'" She smiled down at her baby.

It wasn't until later, as I sat in my mother's rocker looking out the open French doors of my apartment, out at the dark roofs of the Quarter with the moon beaming overhead, that I heard my mother's voice back when she was young, a voice I haven't heard for so long, as she sang, "*le coeur a . . .*"

Then it hit me.

The heart has reasons of which reason knows nothing. Kaye hadn't meant just me. It cut both ways. She'd also meant Haney, and I felt the hair on the back of my neck standing up.

Hungry Enough

by Cornelia Read

"I ABSOLUTELY ADORE driving drunk," said Kay. "It's so damn *easy*." The top was down on her little two-seater Mercedes—one of those burnished days, after a week of rain.

She surprised me by careening right onto Hollywood Boulevard, off Cherokee.

"Darling girl," I protested, "the Cahuenga Building went that-a-way. I'm an hour late as it is."

The wind was ruining our hair.

She plucked a strand of platinum from her lipstick. "One tiny stop, Julia. I have a few things for you at the house."

Kay'd offered me birthday lunch at Chasen's, her treat. I held out for Musso and Frank's so I had the option of walking back to work.

"You gave me your solemn oath," I said. "Only reason I agreed to that fifth martini."

"Wouldn't you rather arrive sober than punctual?"

"I need this job, Kay."

"You need a husband, Julia," she said. "You're twenty-five years old."

"I seem to recall having already suffered through this lecture. Somewhere between cocktails three and four."

"Honey," she said, "it's practically 1960 and you're dying on the goddamn vine."

"I happen to like the vine. Marvelous view. Fee fi fo fum, et cetera, et cetera . . . "

"Three years in Los Angeles, and what do you have to show for it?"

I had one ingénue turn on *Perry Mason* and a succession of glossy headshots to show for it, as Kay knew perfectly well. She, meanwhile, had a rich producer husband.

"Another Greyhound bus pulls into this town every five minutes," she continued, "packed to the gills with fresh-faced little mantraps—"

"—I cannot believe you're willing to be seen driving this tacky thing," I said. "Powder blue with white upholstery?"

"Says she who takes dictation from the man in a powder blue suit," said Kay. "Promise me you're not sleeping with him. He wears socks with clocks on them, for chrissakes."

"Promise *me* this color scheme wasn't your idea."

"Of course not. I found it in the driveway last week, complete with jaunty bow over the hood. Another little kiss-and-make-up incentive from Kenneth."

Kenneth, her rich producer husband, snared last year at a Sunday brunch swim party in Bel-Air. He'd been sunning himself on a raft in the water's shallow end. Kay sauntered up in bathing suit and heels, crooked one finger, and said, "Hey you, out of the pool."

Tuesday morning, his third wife chartered a plane to Reno.

I caught her eye in the rear-view mirror. "Darling, this car practically shouts *divorcée*—"

"—A girl can dream, can't she?"

"For chrissake, Kay-Kay," I said, "If you're that unhappy, why not leave him?"

"Because I finally have some leverage, Julia, now that I've seen what that plate glass is for."

This was an inch-thick slab suspended above their bed on golden cables. Kay had recently discovered her husband lying beneath the transparent platform while baby-oiled young blond men wrestled one another atop it. Defecation earned them bigger tips at the end of the night.

"Did I tell you," she said, "that he actually thought I'd go down on him while those appalling creatures moiled around in their own filth?"

"Whereupon you told *him* he was out of his ever-loving mind and stalked out of the room," I replied, leaving out the part about how she showed up at my place that night with a bottle of Seconal, already half-consumed.

She turned to flash me a grin, then held up her wrist to flash something blue-white, flawless, and far more enduring. "Look what arrived with my breakfast tray, just this morning."

"Harry Winston?"

"Cartier," she said. "He's learning."

She hauled the wheel left again, shooting us down a palm-tree-lined boulevard.

I shrugged. "So you'll put up with it. You're one of the wives now."

"This year," she said.

I rolled my eyes. "And whose job it is to swab down the sheet of glass, afterwards?"

"Search me," she said, "but I hope to hell it's that little shit Carstairs."

Carstairs was Kenneth's secretary—a snippy little man who was still quite blond, possibly British, and ten years past earning his keep unclothed. He and Kay loathed one another. Trying to get him fired was her primary form of entertainment, after shopping.

We pulled up to a stoplight. The man in the Cadillac next to us wrenched his neck, getting an eyeful of Kay.

She ignored him with intent, one sly finger twisting the pearls at her neck. "I'm not ever going to be goddamn famous, now, am I?"

"'Course you won't," I said. "Fame is reserved for those fresh-faced little mantraps who can't go home on the Greyhound."

"I'm better looking."

"Fairest one of all," I said. "But you aren't hungry enough. You never were."

"And you're too goddamn smart."

"Have to be," I said. "I'm a goddamn brunette."

"Mere lack of will. Doesn't mean a life sentence."

"I prefer that collar and cuffs match, thanks ever so."

She stomped on the brakes and swerved right, bringing the car's powder-blue nose to a halt six inches shy of her driveway's cast-iron gates.

A uniformed flunky sprinted forth to swing them wide.

Kay checked her makeup in the side mirror, ignoring the man's salute.

She punched the gas before he was quite out of the way, spraying his shins with gravel.

I looked back and waved, mouthing a belated "thank you."

"I'm serious about your future," said Kay. "Had we but known at Barnard you'd end up mooning over some cut-rate detective—"

"—or that you'd end up playing beard for the man you married?"

She laughed at that, rich golden peals that trailed behind till the end of her curving drive.

"What a monstrous pile it is," Kay said, cutting her eyes at the Deco-Moorish facade she lived behind.

She walked away from the Mercedes without bothering to close her door.

Someone would take care of it. Someone always did.

"I've got to call my service," she said, as we walked inside, our heels clicking against marble and echoing back from the domed entry ceiling.

"Why the hell do you have a service?"

"Because Carstairs manages to lose every message intended for me."

She peeled off her white gloves, tossing them in the general direction of a gilt-slathered side table. I kept mine on.

"I can't stay all afternoon, Kay."

"Go upstairs to my dressing room," she said. "I've laid out some things for you to try on."

"I don't need your clothes."

"I spent the morning with that little woman at Bullock's, picking out a few 'delightful frocks' for delivery here in your size. Allow me that one small pleasure."

"And if I should happen to come upon Kenneth, ogling something untoward above your marital bed?"

"Tiptoe past without making a fuss. I'll throw in a fur."

"For chrissake, Kay."

"And solemnly swear you won't have to kiss my ass for a week."

"Make it two."

"Greedy guts," she said, as I started up the stairs.

As it turned out, her husband couldn't have ogled anything at all.

There wasn't much left of his face, after the slab of glass had swung down to catch him under the chin.

The pair of golden cables at its footboard-end had given out. The closer one lay curled along the carpet at my feet. Three of its four strands had been neatly sliced, the last left to fray until it snapped.

Kenneth wouldn't have seen it coming, nor would his pack of wrestling boys. There were four sockets in the ceiling, little brass-lined portholes cut into the plaster. Two were now empty. The cables had been severed up in the attic, out of sight.

I lifted the phone on Kay's side of the bed, pressed the second line's unlit button, and dialed GLenview 7537.

There was a click before my employer picked up on the third ring, grumbling.

"Philip?" I said. "I know I should have been back hours ago—"

"—This is why I never wanted a secretary," he cut in. "Too much damn trouble."

"It gets worse. I'd like to take you up on your offer of a birthday gift, after all."

"A bit late to have something engraved."

"I'm with Kay. We need your help with a bit of a situation."

He took down her address when I explained what that situation was.

"Twenty minutes," he said. "Promise me you won't touch anything."

"I'm wearing gloves," I said.

"That's my girl."

Philip rang of but I kept the receiver to my ear.

"Don't hang up just yet, Carstairs," I said. "Have Kay wait for me on the terrace. Fix her a drink so she'll stay put."

He exhaled.

I knew he hadn't yet called the police. The scent of ammonia was still too heavy in the room.

"After that," I said, "Come back up here with fresh rags. You missed a spot on the glass."

Philip walked into the library an hour later. I'd sent him upstairs alone.

"Happy birthday," he said, "though I'll hold off on wishing you any returns of the day."

The room was all Gothic walnut, excised whole from some down-at-heel peer's estate—the dozen muddy portraits of faithful dogs and dead grouse included.

Carstairs made sure there was always a fire in the grate, air conditioning calibrated to offset its heat as needed.

"Nasty little scene to stumble across, upstairs," said Philip.

"Horrible," I said.

"Has it hit you yet?" he asked.

I shook my head.

He took my hand in both of his. Pressed it a bit too hard. "It will," he said, "and I want you sitting down when it does."

He glanced over at Kay, stretched out asleep on a leather sofa. "Your friend seems to be bearing up rather well."

"I made her take a Seconal."

"Only one?"

"We had gin for lunch."

I let him pull me toward the fireplace.

"You're shaking." He put an arm around my waist, lowered me gently into a wing chair, then sat in its mate a few feet away. "The boys are gone?" I asked.

"Carstairs handled it. He's had some practice."

"And you're sure they won't say anything?

"Would you, Julia?"

I looked at the fire. "Of course not."

He nodded. "I've told him to phone Kay's doctor. Then the police. Then her lawyer."

My hands got jittery in my lap. "Philip, she didn't do this."

"I'm happy to believe that," he said. "You may have a bit more trouble convincing the detectives."

My gloves felt wet.

He looked at his watch. "Tell them that the pair of you came by the office before she brought you here. That was a little after two. I gave you the rest of the afternoon off."

"A little after two," I said. "'What time did we get here?"

"You don't know. You called me the moment you found him, of course. I told you to let me handle it from there."

"Kenneth keeps some decent Scotch in that desk, if you'd like."

He shook his head. "Tell me how long you've known about the state of Kay's marriage."

"A month. Something like that."

"And how long had *she* known, before confiding in you?"

"Less than an hour. She drove straight to my apartment that night."

He thought about that. "Four weeks ago, Sunday?"

"I suppose it was."

"You called in sick the next day."

"I apologize for that, Philip."

"No need," he said.

"We were up all night." I looked to make sure Kay was still asleep. "She had a miscarriage."

"How far along?"

"Not very. She hadn't told Kenneth yet."

"Did she want the baby?"

"Even after she walked in on him," I said. "Maybe *more*."

"She thought it would help?"

"Women so often do, don't they?"

"I'm happy to report I have no personal experience in that arena."

"Lucky you," I said.

He rose from his chair and walked behind it. "What do you *really* think—was it Kay, or was it Carstairs?"

"I've already told you what I really think."

"So you have," he said.

"For God's sake, Philip, can you imagine Kay with a hacksaw?"

"I can't imagine Kay filing her own nails."

"And she's been with me since morning."

"I doubt it was done today," he said. "Could have been any time over the last month."

"All the more reason it had to be Carstairs, then."

"Not sure I'm following your logic."

"Philip, Kay *sleeps* in that bed

"—Still? You're sure about that?"

"I am," I said. "Yes."

"Any proof other than your say-so that she *hadn't* set up camp down the hall?" he asked. "Under the circumstances, one might presume she'd have wanted to ix-nay the arbor of connubial bliss with a stout ten-foot pole. Can't imagine they're short of alternate quarters, given the size of this place."

"Kay takes breakfast in bed every morning. Dry toast, black coffee, and half a grapefruit—broiled. I'm sure someone on stall could verify finding her there."

"Even so," he said, "those last strands looked strong enough to hold, as long as nobody put extra weight on the glass."

"But what if they *hadn't* been strong enough, despite appearances to the contrary? Philip, there's no way she could have been certain. The glass might've just as easily killed Kay and Kennel both, while they slept."

"I suppose so."

He crossed his arms and leaned on the top of his chair, looking at the fire.

"Kay would have done it this morning, if at all," I said. "You know I'm right."

"And you'll tell the police she's been with you since breakfast? Helping out at the office?"

"She was at Bullock's," I said, "choosing dresses for me."

"Which left Kenneth free to pursue outside interests for several hours. Safe to say he had Carstairs make the arrangements, without help from the rest of staff. Boys delivered quietly at the service entrance, shuttled upstairs with none the wiser?"

"Carstairs must have brought the things from Bullock's upstairs himself," I said. "He wouldn't have let anyone else through to Kay's dressing room."

"Ducks in a row for Kay, then," said Philip. "Unless this was an elaborate suicide, Carstairs takes the rap."

It all hit me then—the bulldozed pulp of Kenneth's face and everything else, straight through to that moment.

I thought I would be sick, right there on the rug.

Philip wandered over to Kay, still asleep on the sofa.

"We'll make sure the police get a good look at her hands," he said. "Not a mark on them, and severing that cable must have been a bear."

He turned back toward me.

I peeled off my gloves and raised both hands, turning them slowly for his inspection, front to back.

Philip tried not to look relieved.

"I'll bring Carstairs in here," he said. "Make sure he's trussed up and ready to go."

He was wrong, of course. The cables had been a cinch to cut, four weeks ago Monday.

I'd chipped the polish on one fingernail, but the second fresh coat of red had been dry a good hour before Kay woke up, back in my apartment.

She'd have done the same to keep me from harm: without question, without hesitation, and without my knowledge. Kay is my oldest friend, as I am hers. We take care not to burden each other with the onus of gratitude.

Conscience now clear in that regard, I turned from the fire to watch her sleep—my hands still, my nausea at bay.

Philip paused in the doorway, one foot across the threshold. We both heard the siren in the distance.

"Wouldn't hurt the appearance of things if you cried a little," he said, not looking back. "Plenty of time before they get all the way up the drive."

Family Values

by Mitch Alderman

B UBBA WAS DRIVING HIS BRONCO on Cypress Gardens Boulevard with the windows down enjoying the perfect April afternoon in central Florida when the car phone rang. He let it ring. This was too nice a day to ruin by talking to anyone. The traffic was thin since most of the personal buses belonging to the tourists had headed their way north at the end of spring baseball season. Retirees, who had probably never ridden in a bus in their lives, now had a compulsion to drive one cross country. He had just mailed a bill to Arnie at State Insurance for a week's surveillance and there was money in his wallet. What me work? was his thought. The phone stopped ringing. He smiled and the ringing began again. He quit smiling and answered the phone, "What?"

"It's Gilroy. Want to make a hundred for an hour's work?" It was Tommy Gilroy, partner with his brother of the biggest bailbond business in Polk County.

"I have no need for money today."

"So you already ate lunch, big deal, you'll be hungry tomorrow. I need a quick favor. Have you got your phony sign stuff and can you be at Combee Road and 92 in thirty minutes or less?"

"What's happening?"

"My brother's having a root canal. None of my helpers are in town and I have a bond getting ready to run. I need you to draw them to the front door so he stays in the house until I can slip in the back and cuff him. A hundred bucks, an hour. No fuss, I promise."

"Okay, I'm on my way." It might be fun to do something physical after a week of watching a warehouse to catch the swing shift foreman loading his own truck.

Bubba increased the speed of the Bronco and changed lanes to catch the light at Highway 17 to take the back way across Winter Haven and Auburndale. He caught the light at Recker Highway and 92. In twenty-three minutes Bubba was in the edge of Lakeland proper and stopped beside Gilroy's Lexus in the shopping center parking lot. Tommy Gilroy stood by his front door as the Bronco rocked to a halt. He wore a black leather jacket and had a pump shotgun propped on the passenger seat.

"Follow me. The trailer's off Old Combee," Tommy said as he climbed in his white Lexus. They headed north for ten minutes until Tommy turned left onto a two-lane blacktopped road. About fifty yards later, he stopped and got out of his car, walking back to the Bronco.

"He's lives at his mother's trailer just beyond the curve in the road. The trailer's white with blue awnings. Big oak tree. He's driving a green Taurus."

"Why are you revoking his bond?"

"I heard they're ready to arrest him again. For that carjacking that went bad Friday night. I've bonded him before, but it was for grand theft auto. He sells the occasional car to the chop shops in Tampa. But this is the big time. If he hears they want him for murder, he'll be gone instead of in court tomorrow. And I'm stuck with a twenty-five-thousand-dollar bond."

"You didn't get any security?"

"My stupid brother took his mother's trailer as security. If he was here, I'd kick his butt. That's the last thing I need is a widow's trailer. So you drive past the said trailer and see if the Taurus is there. There is a road, turns just past the trailer. I'll park down it and come up to the back door. You go to the front door and attract their attention. If he sees me, he'll be off like Benny the Bunny."

"I'll be the propane guy."

"Fine. Whatever. Just get going before he heads to Iowa or somewhere else I can't find him."

Bubba opened the rear hatch of the white Bronco and rummaged through his stuff. He had an assortment of color-coded magnetic signs that purported to be identifiers for the official suppliers of utilities for the county. He especially liked the orange and blue ones for Polk Propane Gas, which actually said, Polk Propain in the Gas. He put one on each of the doors. Bubba had learned long ago that at six foot five and 300 pounds he was never going to be invisible, so he settled for being dismissible. He put on an orange fluorescent vest and a white hard hat. He'd carry a clipboard when he went to the door. He'd set an orange cone by the rear of the Bronco when he stopped at the trailer. The people inside would never notice Gilroy sneaking across the back yard. Unless they had a big dog, then Gilroy had a problem.

"I'm set."

"Give me five minutes. Then drive up. Don't let him run out the front."

"Not a problem."

Bubba sat in the Bronco and thought about how much fun the theater of the absurd was. Police work, bail bonds, investigating insurance fraud; all the world's a stage. Today was the magical misdirection tour.

When the time came, Bubba screeched to a halt in front of the trailer, got out and placed the orange cone by the rear of the Bronco. Clipboard in hand, dark glasses in place, he headed up the walk. He'd seen curtains flutter when he arrived. They would all be watching him. He knocked on the door. There was a murmur of voices and the door opened. An old woman asked what he wanted. When she spoke Bubba realized that she couldn't be more than forty-five or so. But sun and cigarettes and beer had taken their toll on her skin.

"Our records show that you have a propane tank."

"Yes, do our cooking and water heating with it. Is there a problem?"

"Just that it might be an older C-132 model with the reciprocating bivalve." The woman nodded like she had even more idea of what that was than Bubba did. Through the open door, he could see a young woman and a man sitting on the couch in the living room. A toddler staggered across the carpet after a ball. "There has been a recall order from the supplier and I've been assigned to check this area." Bubba tapped his finger on the clipboard to make the pronouncement official. The woman looked up at him and nodded again. Come on, Gilroy, he thought.

"If I could just check your tank," he said. Now Gilroy was easing in the back door. He nodded toward Bubba.

"Sure. I guess so," the woman answered.

"Sir, could you show it to me?" Bubba asked the man sitting on the couch. He looked at Bubba in surprise and started to rise. When he put his hand on the arm of the couch, Gilroy popped the edge of the handcuff on his wrist. The clickety-clack of the ratchet was audible across the room. When the man stood, Gilroy spun him and fastened the other cuff. Jerking the cuffs upward, he frog-marched the now-yelling man out the front door, past Bubba. The cold, practiced efficiency was impressive. Bubba tipped his hat at the women who were starting to yell questions. He grabbed the orange cone, tossing it on the passenger seat as he cranked the Bronco and U-turned back toward Bartow. The last view he had was of the young woman holding the child on her hip and walking across the yard after them.

They pulled back into the shopping center parking lot. While Bubba removed the signs and the vest, Gilroy came over with a C-note showing in his hand.

"That went fine. You ought to consider going to work for us fulltime. We could open a branch office."

"And what would I do with all that money?"

"Buy a new SUV before this one is declared a historical treasure. Anyway, here's your money. I appreciate this. Let me get this mope back to the jail and clear my paperwork. Drop by some time and we'll have a beer. Tell lies."

They shook hands. Gilroy was already driving south on New Combee Road headed for Bartow by the time Bubba entered traffic. Bubba smiled; it had been a fun afternoon. Now time for a good supper. Where to go out? Better yet. A big porterhouse steak from his favorite butcher grilling on the back porch. Elvis would enjoy the bone de jour.

The next morning Bubba was feeling complaisant sitting behind his desk in the office. He'd done forty minutes on the treadmill at Big Al's Iron Works, then cooled down with the routine of stretching exercises that were supposed to restore the flexibility in his lower back and return the youthful ease he'd once possessed while doing heavy squats. Bubba wasn't sure about that but at least he could still reach the laces on his New Balance crosstrainers. He'd showered, shaved, then breakfasted at the Haven Cafe with the usual gang of citrus people, business owners, A/C repairmen, politicians, and tourists: the people who ran Winter Haven. It was a quarter till nine; the brew was dripping in the Mr. Coffee; his feet were on the corner of the desk. All was right with Simms Investigations.

Footsteps came down the hall. Since there were no other offices besides his on this floor, Bubba knew someone was looking for him. Work. He took his feet off the desk and tried to look pleasant, while occupied with business. But he couldn't stifle the yawn as the door opened and a young woman with a child on her hip walked in.

"Did I wake you?" she asked with a small smile as she stopped in front of his desk. Bubba recognized her from the day before.

"Just boredom. I'm sorry about yesterday. Nothing personal, you understand, just legal work."

"I understand." Her makeup didn't cover the bruise under her left eye, a couple of days old. The child balanced easily in her hip. She was slim with straight blond hair down past her shoulders, wearing jeans and a Busch Gardens T-shirt with a giraffe's face above the logo.

"Please sit down. Want coffee? It's fresh."

"That would be nice." She moved lightly even with the boy on her hip. She sat on the couch and stood the child on the carpet. Her blue eyes contrasted with green-yellow of the bruise.

"Cream, sugar?"

"Two of each. Hot, sweet, and pale. Just like me. That's what Robert says." She blushed and dropped her head to fuss with the child who had decided that this office was worthy of exploration. He had his eye on Elvis's chew rope, but his mother had the waistband of his shorts in hand. The little boy was clean, hair cut short and brushed back. His shirt had a blue druid, or something, on it.

"So Robert Carter is your husband?" Bubba asked as he fixed the coffee. Carter's mug shot had been the front page attraction on the morning paper. Charged with carjacking and the murder of a young woman named Charlene Bridges in Lakeland. The victim was the socially prominent second-wife of a land developer and builder in Lakeland. The efficiency of the police had been recognized several times in the lead article. Gilroy and Bubba had not been mentioned at all.

"We've been together for seven years now. Stevie is his son. I'm Jennifer Mangram." She accepted the coffee and took a sip without relaxing her grip on the waistband. "Good. Thanks."

"How did you find me?" Bubba asked after he sat down behind the desk. He didn't think he'd left one of his business cards behind. And Gilroy never told anybody anything he didn't have to.

"The phone book."

"Under Fake Propane Guy?"

"No. When you came to the door I thought you looked familiar, then when you tipped your hat, I recognized you. You did the same thing the other time I saw you."

"When was that?"

"Fifteen years ago when I was seven. You came to our house to tell us my daddy was dead in a car wreck. A semi bumped his pickup into the side of freight train on Highway 60 east of Lake Wales."

"God, yes, I remember that. I'd just taken over as the sergeant for that area. So, he was your daddy. Now, I helped put your baby's father in jail. I'm surprised you came here."

"You were so nice to my mama that night and you were just doing legal stuff yesterday. Over the years, I've seen your name in the paper, like when you when you found out who killed Little John Dupree. But now I want your help. Robert didn't kill that poor woman."

"How do you know?"

"He was home with me and his mother. We watched TV all night."

"Did you tell the Sheriff's department, the detectives?"

"Yes. They said thank you and hung up. So I came to see you." Bubba could see the muscles in her forearm as she squeezed the coffee mug. Stevie was leaning at a forty-five degree angle in his attempt to escape.

"Who is Robert's lawyer? Tell him."

"Bill Johnson. He's legal aid. I called him yesterday. He said I'd be useful at the trial." She sat the coffee cup on the carpet and picked Stevie up.

"The police tend to ignore alibis from wives and mothers."

"But Robert didn't kill that woman. He's even worked for Mr. Bridges before. Doing landscaping. He wouldn't stab anyone. I want you to find out who did it. If he goes to trial, he'll get convicted sure as the world is flat."

"I think the world's round."

"Not if you've never left Polk. County. Looks mighty flat to me." Stevie was squirming around and starting to take what looked like a deep breath for yelling.

"Put him down. He can't hurt anything."

"But he'll chew that rope thing and unless you have really bad habits, I think it belongs to a dog." She sat the baby down, walked over and put the chew rope out of reach. A multi-color sunrise showed above the belt line of her jeans.

"Elvis is at home today. Why do you think they'll convict him if he didn't do it?"

"He's got a record. Grand theft auto. Assault. He gets into fights."

"Was he on meth when he hit you?"

"He doesn't . . . No, he was upset because he'd just found out his mother had had to put up her trailer as security for his bond, in addition to the twenty-five hundred we paid. I was just in the way." The baby climbed into Bubba's recliner and perched there regally.

"He hit you often?"

"Not often. And he has never even spanked Stevie. He really is a good man. He keeps on getting better and better. If he can stay out of jail, in a few more years, he'll be a fine man. There's still a lot of boy in him."

"Jennifer, the Sheriff's department is good at what they do. If they think he did it, he most likely did."

"He didn't. I know it."

"Because he was home with you?"

"Because I know him. He might steal a car when times get tight. He might get his ass kicked when he's high. But he would never kill a woman like that one was."

"I charge two hundred fifty dollars a day."

"Here's two days worth. I'll get you whatever you need." Bubba raised his eyebrows at the sight of the bills she brought from her back pocket.

"It's legal. I'm a cocktail waitress at the Peacock Club up on 192 by Disney. Started working there when Robert got laid off in February. I've been off the last week waiting for the eye to clear. I look good when I dress up. I can work every night if I have to to get Robert out of jail."

"Two days and no more if I decide I can't help. I'll call his lawyer and let him know I'm working on the case."

She nodded. Bubba wrote her a receipt. Then he pulled out his yellow note pad and started to ask her questions: phone numbers, addresses, lawyer's number and so forth. Two pages were full when he finished. She even had a Carter family group picture at Busch Gardens that showed him clearly enough among the other skinny, sunburned crackers for identification. Stevie spent the time chewing on the arm of the recliner.

When they finished, she attached Stevie to her hip and headed for the door. She stopped in the doorway and said, "I'll call you tomorrow morning about ten." Bubba nodded and then Jennifer flashed him a smile that remained after she left. I can understand why he keeps her, but why in the world is she keeping him?

Bubba opened his briefcase and pulled out this notebook. He found Polk County Sheriff's Detective Lieutenant Ray Bisse's phone number and punched it in. Bisse answered it on the first ring.

"Good morning Ray. Congratulations on nailing the carjacker," Bubba said.

"Thanks. I was feeling good before I heard your voice. Don't tell me the Colonel has taken this slimeball's case? That's all we need is his lawyer tricks getting this guy off."

"Not the Colonel this time. The wife. She says he's innocent."

"Of course she does."

"Says he was home that night."

"Did they go to church or just have a prayer meeting at home?"

"Such a cynic. Why are you so sure it's him?"

"Why should I tell you anything?" Bubba could picture the big jaw muscle clenched as he asked the question. They'd been friends for almost twenty years. As his sergeant, Bubba had trained Ray when he a patrolman; but since Bubba's retirement he was, while not the enemy, no longer an equal.

"Because if you don't, someone else will. It's all part of discovery. And this way we continue our long friendship and professional relationship. Besides I'll buy you lunch at John's."

"I'm dieting this week, but maybe you'll leave me and the department alone if you know we have the right guy."

"Maybe. Why are you so sure?"

"The vic's husband saw him leaving the convenience store with a six-pack as he walked in."

"I saw this guy two days ago and I can't remember what he looks like, except like every other peckerwood who grew up in Polk County. Skinny, wearing his Billy Ray Cyrus hairdo."

"And the same Lion Country Safari T-shirt that Gilroy brought him into the jail with. By the way, good work on that."

"He came out of the store. That's it?"

"His fingerprints on the outside of the BMW. Surveillance of him getting into the BMW."

"I thought it was a carjacking."

"The vic's husband left the car running while he went in for some cigarettes. The wife was curled up sleeping in the passenger seat. Your mope must not have seen her through the tinted windows until it was too late. The tape shows the car screeching out after he gets into it. We found the car a couple of miles away. Dead woman in it. Stab wounds to the chest. This time your client's going to sit on Ol' Sparky's lap. Murder One for this."

"Ray, I trust your judgment. Are you sure this is the guy?"

"Come look at his sheet. Grand theft auto. Twice. Assault three times. Domestic battery. DUI. This guy's a walking time bomb and we got him off the streets."

"I agree he sounds like a dirtbag, but did he kill this woman?"

"Her husband said he did. The tape shows his skinny, mullet-headed ass walking past the BMW. Thirty seconds later, he runs back to it, climbs in and it's gone. He did it."

"Clear face getting into it."

There was a pause. "No. His back. Face going out of the store. His skinny, mullet-headed, white T-shirt back getting in the car thirty-two seconds later."

"What's Carter say?"

"SODDI. But just who that some other dude that did it was, he doesn't know. He touches lots of cars he says. Compulsion. Then the lawyer tells him to be quiet. And I think I am going to take the lawyer's advice. I'm shutting up."

"Ray, I told his wife that I'd stay with this until I was sure one way or the other. You say you have the right guy. But I know that if he isn't the guy then you want whoever used the knife, not just a conviction. If you leave a copy of the tapes at the front desk, I'll have a messenger pick it up."

"Bubba, you're swimming in a cesspool this time. Don't sink." Bisse hung up.

Bubba felt the urge to move. The office was too small now. He hated it when clients lied to him, even though he expected it. As he walked down the stairs and out to the parking lot, he wondered why Jennifer had lied about her husband being home with her. She had to know he'd find out. After all he was advertised as a private detective. Maybe that was his first test. If he couldn't see a lie that big, then how could he dissolve an open and shut case of murder. As he opened the Bronco, he decided to take a look at the convenience store where the abduction took place. Driving always relaxed him. He'd take Elvis along. Elvis would enjoy the ride with his head out the window even if he didn't find any clues.

The convenience store was only two blocks off US 92 North in one of the unincorporated areas still waiting for Lakeland to annex it. US 92 was a bustling six-lane ribbon of furniture stores, chain restaurants, fastfood joints, motels, and anything else that would be of interest to the people driving to the North Lakeland Mall. Bubba had never worked this area when he was a sergeant. He'd stayed mostly to the easterly, more rural side of the county. But he recognized the ambience around the convenience store. The Chamber of Commerce would never put this block on their brochure. It was another free-trade zone. The good citizens of Lakeland could drive a couple of blocks past the advertised specials of US 92 and barter for what they needed. Four young facilitators stood in the shade of an oak tree at the corner of a vacant lot beside the convenience store. They pointedly ignored Bubba as he parked at the front of the store. Neither he nor the Bronco had lost their former official demeanor. Elvis howled as Bubba went inside the store.

The clerk was willing, even happy, to talk about the carjacking even if he had not been there that night. Bubba bought a 44-ounce diet soda in a cup and a Slim Jim for Elvis. As he walked out the door, he could see the surveillance cameras mounted high on light poles. Prominent signs requested you to smile for the cameras. The clerk had told Bubba that they hadn't been robbed since the lights and cameras had been installed. Robert Carter must have some serious impulse control issues to take a car from here. The Mall was only two miles away and the pickings were always easy there.

Bubba climbed into the Bronco and peeled the wrapper back on the Slim Jim. This was the dog's test. If he couldn't find artificially scented food in the front seat of a Bronco, how could he find a raccoon at night? The smoky aroma brought Elvis to attention. He passed the test.

Bubba cranked up the A/C and left the windows down. Then he drove onto the vacant lot and stopped beside the four young men who were casually watching the traffic flow past.

"Good afternoon, gentlemen. I was looking for Joker Marchant stadium, where the Tigers train."

"You're the joker. Beat it. Your exhaust is bad for my allergy," the tallest of the four said. Then he stepped to the other side of the shade. One of the others, short but stocky, stepped up to the truck window and reached his hand out to Elvis.

"What is this? Undercover K-9?"

"Elvis is a bluetick hound from Tennessee. He tracks miscreants."

"Smells more like a Slim Jim to me."

"You are correct. Since you seem to be an alert young man, you might be able to help me."

"Why would I want to help a cop? Even an old cop?"

"I'm a private detective now." Bubba reached across the seat and handed him a card. "I am investigating the carjacking from the convenience store."

"What a load of crap that was. We had to move two blocks away all weekend while the cops and news trucks were all over the place. Bogus deal, man, bogus."

"Do you recognize the guy holding the baby?" Bubba held the picture out with a twenty folded between his fingers.

"For fifty I might put on my reading glasses."

Bubba nodded and reached into his shirt pocket. He held the money in his other hand.

The young man took the picture and held it close to his face. "Yep, I recognize him. He stops by occasionally."

"Was he here the night of the carjacking?"

"Who knows? We don't exactly take reservations or schedule appointments. Besides I wasn't working that night."

"What's he stop by for?"

"He's a peckerwood. What do you think he stops by for?"

"Meth?"

"You are a detective. He and his brother crank it up once in a while."

"His brother?"

"Yeah, the guy with the tiger shirt in the picture. Don't you know anything?"

"Sometimes I wonder."

Cars started slowing down and speeding off. "Conversation is over, Private Detective Simms. Business calls. My fifty please."

Bubba handed him the fifty. He took it and gently shook Elvis's head making his ears flap. Bubba backed out onto the street and drove away; Elvis howled back at them. A car stopped at the curb and the tallest man was there when the window went down.

The Carters' trailer was only about five miles away, fifteen minutes at most. In person seemed to be the most civilized way to return the money Jennifer had given him, less the fifty. He'd promised to stay with the case until he was satisfied. He wasn't all that satisfied by the day's results, but he certainly felt sure. He parked in the same shady place he'd used before. He ran the windows up enough that Elvis wouldn't squeeze out. The middle-aged woman was sitting on the porch in an aluminum chair, smoking. A metal ash tray stood next to the chair. Bubba stopped at the steps.

"Mrs. Carter, I'm Bubba Simms."

"I know. You helped take Robert away."

"Is Jennifer here?"

"Getting ready for work. The shower just stopped. She'll be out in a minute."

Bubba nodded and leaned against the pole at the bottom of the steps. She had pointedly ignored offering him the other aluminum chair. Either she was angry about him taking Robert away or thought he'd flatten the chair.

"She hired you, didn't she?"

"Yes."

"Find out anything?"

"Yes."

"What?"

"I'll tell her."

"I bet you will. She'll jump you through the hoops just like she does Robert. She looks so sweet and innocent, but she looked that way when Robert got tired of paying and brought her home to live. Now she leads him around like a puppy dog. But then Robert's weak, not like Taylor, his older brother. Taylor wouldn't let no woman lead him around, no way."

Bubba continued to lean against the pole, glad for the ten feet of separation from the woman. The screen door to the trailer opened and Jennifer stood there in a short robe and long legs with a towel wrapped around her hair.

"Mr. Simms. Did you find out something already?"

"That you lied to me. I'm returning your retainer."

"What? No, you can't. . . . Stevie's crying. Wait right there. I'll be right back." The door slammed shut. Bubba could hear the boy crying.

"So she lied to you too. I'm not surprised. But I still see how you looked at her, knowing she was a liar and all. Men. All alike. And I've seen my share having to raise those two boys all alone. Men." The woman had a smile of satisfaction as she stubbed the cigarette out in the sand.

Bubba began to see how she'd had to raise those two boys all alone. He felt like nailing the money to the porch support and driving away.

"You going to get my Robert off?"

Bubba pointedly ignored her.

"If you find out who did it, you going to tell the Sheriff or just keep it to yourself, thinking you can sneak back and get next to Miss Jennifer?"

"Shut up, Myrtle," Jennifer said as she opened the door. She was barefooted, with jeans and T-shirt, Stevie perched on her hip. Her blond hair was a tangled mess pushed back off her face. She stepped toward Bubba. "What's going on?"

He reached into his pocket and held out the bills. "I'm returning your retainer. You lied to me about Robert being with you."

She glanced over her shoulder at Myrtle. "Walk over to your truck where we can talk." Bubba followed her. She patted Elvis's nose poking through the window crack. She turned to face Bubba. "Of course, I lied. If I had told you he was out somewhere and wouldn't tell me where, would you have taken the case? Hell no."

"The police have him on video tape at the scene, his fingerprints are on the victim's car. He buys crank from dealers in that area. I'm satisfied he did it. It wasn't merely your lies." He held out the money. She slapped his hand away. The bills fluttered to the grass.

"Robert didn't kill that woman. I know it. In here, I know it." She tapped her chest with her free hand. Bubba tried not to watch the hand too closely. The shirt was damp from her shower.

Bubba tapped his head. "In here, I know he was there and he did it."

"He didn't. I ain't going to allow my son to grow up without his father. I grew up without mine and I know who I became. Robert and Taylor grew up with her alone and I see who they are. Stevie will have a father. No matter what I have to do." Her blue eyes were cold but direct with meaning. "Find out who did it. I'll pay you whatever you charge."

Bubba broke contact with her eyes. He could smell apple shampoo. "If he didn't do it, then what was he doing that night?"

"Probably buying meth, after promising me and Stevie he wouldn't. Probably him and Taylor getting high."

"Why didn't he tell the detectives?"

"Taylor's on probation for possession. He tests positive, he goes back to prison. Robert wouldn't let that happen."

"Taylor will let him face first degree murder to avoid violating his probation?"

"Sure. Taylor's mean, but Robert admires him. Wants his big brother to respect him. Besides what good would it do for Taylor to talk? Who's going to believe a crank head that his brother didn't steal a car, kill some woman?"

Bubba nodded. She was right. A meth addict brother wouldn't be much of an alibi. Stevie was rubbing his nose on Elvis's. Elvis licked Stevie's face without Jennifer noticing it. She was still staring at Bubba.

"So Robert's just a victim of circumstance. Wrong place, wrong time."

"It happens. We both know that. Besides Robert and Taylor like Mr. Bridges. Taylor ran one of his maintenance crews until a couple of months ago when the building market got tight. Robert worked on the crew too. They were both just waiting for Bridges to open back up and put them to work. They liked him. Didn't treat them like a couple of burnouts."

"So Robert's real alibi sucks too. We can't just prove he didn't do it. We have to prove someone else did it."

"I know he didn't do it. Will you look into who did do it? For me, please. For Stevie?" She reached out and touched Bubba's forearm. He could hear Myrtle's cackle from the porch. He nodded.

She smiled and rearranged Stevie on her hip. "I have to get to work now. Take the money back. If you need more, let me know." Her blue eyes were alive. Bubba felt their intensity. Then she turned and walked across the yard. He bent and retrieved the money. The stretching exercises seemed to be working. She waved as she entered the trailer. Myrtle gave him the finger.

Bubba was not relaxed by the time he reached home despite the half hour drive, but the messenger had left his package against the front door. Bubba opened it and removed the two tapes. After watching each of them four times, he knew there was something there, but he wasn't sure what it was. Turning off the TV, he went to the back porch to sit in his rocker and throw the tennis ball through the open door. The ball would roll down the slope and Elvis would track it down and return it. By the time the ball was soggy and Elvis panting, Bubba felt ready to go to work. Who-done-it time.

When the wife is killed, look at the husband. Page one of detective manual. It was only a quarter after five; Arnie should still be in his office.

"Hey, Arnie, how's the world of unpaid claims," Bubba said when Arnie answered on the speaker phone. Bubba could hear Arnie fade and grow louder as he walked laps around his office trying to lose weight.

"Growing bigger by the minute. What can I do for you?"

"Does State have any interest in the Bridges murder?"

"Thank god no. The Rock gets all of that. I was talking to Homer

225

over there about that this morning. They have a key man of a million on her."

"Key man? She worked for the construction company?"

"Not hardly. Did you ever see her? I met her once and wow. But for some tax reason or other, she was a partner in Bridges, Ltd. The things middle-aged developers will do for trophy wives. So she was in the same group policy for all the real players. Homer is moaning in his beer. Soon as they convict that guy, The Rock has to write a check. Bridges is pushing them now, wants his money. Better them than us."

"Interesting."

"Is there something I ought to know?"

"I was just wondering if you needed me to look into the murder."

"Bubba, what's going on? You don't call for work, ever. You know something."

"Not really."

"Here's Homer's number. Make yourself a buck or two if you can. Just remember who brought you to the dance."

"Thanks, Arnie."

Bubba hung up and fixed himself a glass of iced tea. Elvis was asleep on the porch. After watching the tapes again, Bubba opened his address book and called Gilroy. Tommy would be at his office until nine or so. Lots of work in the evenings and early mornings. The receptionist put Bubba on hold. Gilroy said, "What's shaking?"

"I need some info that I can't get this late in the day. I thought you might be able to."

"What is it?"

"Do you know Taylor Carter?"

"Of course. The one you helped with's older brother. The real bastard of the family. What do you want to know?"

"You ever bond him?"

"Of course."

"How about pulling a TRW on him for me? See what's shaking with him?" There was a short silence.

"What are you working on?"

"Robert's wife hired me to look into the murder. Says he didn't do it. Says he was off with his brother."

"What an alibi that is. Hang on a second. I'll punch him up. Okay, here we go. Ninety days late, ninety days late. Electric, phone, truck payment. All past ninety until Monday. How about that. He got righteous on Monday. Must have robbed someone over the weekend."

"Thanks, Tommy."

"No problem. Now you owe me one."

Bubba made a few more calls that resulted in a few more calls and conversations that lasted until after eleven. All that resulted in an appointment at the Polk County jail for ten the next morning.

Bubba was dressed up in his khaki slacks and a dark blue Polo shirt when he arrived at the Sheriff's Office in Bartow at a quarter to ten. He stopped and talked to the desk sergeant and two of the secretaries before Lieutenant Bisse came out to escort him back to Interrogation Room 3.

"I brought donuts from Roy's," Bubba said as he held the white sack aloft.

"I hope you brought more than that, though the best donuts in the county are always appreciated," Bisse said, then took possession of the sack.

"Everyone here."

"Still waiting on Carter's legal aid. He's on his way."

They arrived at the room. It was a twelve by fifteen room in bureaucratic green. There was a wooden table bolted to the floor. Six metal chairs were distributed around the table. A TV on a roller stand with a tape player attached sat in the corner. A well-dressed woman with curly brown hair sat at the far end of the table. She had a cup of coffee in front of her; an open briefcase to the side. She smiled.

"Roy's. I knew we could count on you, Bubba," she said. Linda Brill was the assistant state's attorney handling Carter's prosecution. She and Bubba had worked together on a number of cases while he was a sergeant in the Sheriff's Department. Bubba had found her to be intelligent, clever, focused and a joy to work with when he remembered not to stare at her chest. "I hope the rest of your ideas are as helpful."

The three of them were enjoying a glazed donut when the door opened and a young man, skinny with glasses and premature male pattern baldness, entered carrying a briefcase. He smiled. "Donuts. I didn't have breakfast yet." He turned to each person and stuck out his hand. "Bill Johnson." Everyone introduced themselves. "Are we all set?" he asked. They nodded. "Are we ready for my client?"

Bisse nodded and left the room. He returned with a cup of coffee in a disposable cup for the legal aid attorney. They could hear the clank of a deputy coming down the hall. A prisoner in handcuffs and wearing the standard orange jumpsuit entered in front of a huge deputy who grinned at Bubba. "Hi Sarge." He unfastened one cuff, ran the end through the D-ring at the end of the table and refastened it to the left wrist, then left the room.

Robert Carter looked much like he had sitting on the couch when Bubba had first met him, except for the color of the clothes. His hair was wet, combed back, curling at his shoulders. His brown eyes darted around the room. "Why am I here? Can I have a donut?" Biss placed a paper towel in front of Carter and sat a donut on it.

"You are here, Mr. Carter," Linda Brill said, "because Mr. Simms here, working for your wife and your lawyer, convinced us to talk to you again and review the evidence with you. He thinks you're innocent. That, in and of itself, doesn't carry much weight but his speculations do."

"I been telling y'all I'm innocent. I didn't stab anybody."

"You have also been telling us you weren't near the carjacking, the BMW or anything else. Isn't that right?"

"Are we on the record here, Ms. Brill?" Johnson asked.

"No tape recorder, no note-taking. Very off the record. We just want to be sure we have the right man. At this moment, your client is the right man."

"Okay, my client might have been mistaken about when he was at that convenience store. He gets dates confused. So now what?"

"We want to show you the two surveillance tapes from the convenience store on the night of the carjacking that are part of your discovery request. He doesn't need to say anything. We want him to know how serious the evidence is against him. Lieutenant Bisse, will you run the tape."

Ray turned on the TV and cued up the black and white tape. It showed the date and time. "This is the first tape, made inside the store," Bisse said.

The room remained quiet as Robert Carter in sharp focus came to the counter and paid for a six-pack of Coors Light. He even had to show his driver's license. Bisse ejected the tape and inserted another.

"This is from the outside camera on the left side," he said. The tape showed Robert Carter leave the convenience store carrying a bag. He touched the top of the BMW as he strolled by, then he walked past the camera angle into the night. Bisse stopped the tape.

"See I told you. I didn't do nothing. Bought some beer and left," Carter said. He'd finished the donut and was eyeing the box.

"Why that convenience store, Mr. Carter? There are several much closer to your home."

"Just cause. I was out driving. I bought the beer, got in my car and drove off. I'm not crazy enough to do anything in that parking lot. Everyone knows about those cameras."

"Were you there to buy crystal meth?" she asked.

"My client's not charged with any drug charges."

"Nor will he be. But we'd like to hear the truth, not this crap."

"No crap. I got in my car and drove off."

"Who was with you?"

"No one."

"Then who is this?" She nodded at Bisse and punched play on the player. A woman left the convenience store and turned right. Then a man who looked like Robert Carter came running back into the scene. He went straight to the BMW, opened the door, and climbed in. The car reversed and was gone into the dark. The tape stopped.

"So Robert, perhaps you can see why we think you are the right guy."

Robert sat looking at the TV. No one spoke. They all looked at Robert.

"Play the whole tape from the outside camera again, please, " Bubba said.

Bisse cued it up and the tape rolled. When the man came running back into the scene, Bubba said, "That's it. Stop the tape. Look at the shoes." The man was wearing black running shoes. The others looked at Bubba.

"Run the tape back to Robert leaving the store," he said and waited. "Stop. There. What color are the shoes?"

The shoes were clearly white. Everyone looked at each other, except Robert. He continued to look at the TV screen. Bisse punched out the tape and slapped it on the table. "So Robert had an accomplice. Still makes it murder one. Still sends him to the chair. He killed her, his partner killed her, makes no difference does it, Ms. Brill?"

"Not much. Who drove off in the BMW? You had to see him go by."

"I didn't kill anyone." Carter's voice was barely audible.

Lieutenant Bisse kicked the leg of the table. "I told y'all before this meeting started that this mope killed Marlene Bridges. Now we know he has an accomplice. The tape shows him indicating the car for his partner. Then he slips off the scene and his partner does the deed. It's cold Murder One. Let me take him back to his cell. We caught ol' white shoes. We'll find Mr. Black Shoes."

Ms. Brill shook her head. "He says he didn't do it, but I think he knows who did. Mr. Simms, we appreciate your noticing the discrepancy with the shoes. So tell us again what do you think happened?"

Bubba finished chewing his last bite of donut and pushed the box toward Robert, who took another without changing the blank expression on his face. Bubba sipped his coffee before he spoke.

"I think that Robert is being set up. I think that Mrs. Bridges was killed deliberately. Anybody think about why a guy like Bridges in that 7-series BMW was in that neighborhood on a Friday night? Why he would leave the car unlocked with the engine running? Why were there two skinny, mullet-heads in a white T-shirts waiting in that parking lot?"

"Robert, as your attorney I must tell you that withholding any information at this time is a bad idea. You didn't kill Mrs. Bridges, but someone did and you don't need to go to jail for their crime."

Robert didn't speak, just held the donut unbitten in his hand. The assistant state's attorney spoke in a quiet voice. "Between all of us in this room, the tox screen from Marlene Bridges's autopsy came back this morning. She had enough Valium in her system to render her unconscious at the time of her death. Her life was heavily insured. We think this was a murder for hire. Now, Robert is either an innocent participant or he was a hired killer. Not much in between," Ms. Brill said.

Lieutenant Bisse kicked the table again, everyone startled. He glared at Robert and said, "By the way, Taylor, your brother, deposited four thousand dollars in new crisp hundred-dollar bills the day we arrested you. How much money do you have in the bank?"

Robert leaned toward his attorney and whispered to him. Johnson nodded. "Could I have a moment alone with my client?" Carter whispered again. "And could he have a Pepsi?"

Linda grinned at Bubba as they stood up. He smiled back into her brown eyes. Ray slapped him on the back as they filed out of the room.

Bubba parked under the shade tree at the Carter trailer. It was almost three in the afternoon. Jennifer met him halfway cross the yard. She was wearing cutoffs and a striped tube top. Her hair was pulled back.

"What's happening? We heard that they arrested Taylor."

Bubba told her about the morning's meeting, about how Robert told them that he and Taylor had gone to score some crank that night. That Taylor had told him he could make some money muling for a guy. That Robert had driven off after buying the beer and met Taylor an hour later over near the Mall. Taylor had given him fifty dollars for driving him around. The detectives were questioning Taylor and Mr. Bridges at the moment. Robert would have to testify, but that the murder charges were going to be dropped.

"Gilroy will probably go the bond for the grand theft auto again," Bubba said.

Jennifer threw her arms around him. He held her shoulders, feeling the roped muscles of her deltoids as she spoke into his chest, "He can beat the auto charge. That's not a problem. Stevie will have his dad back. That's what matters. How can I ever thank you. Bubba?"

Bubba stepped away from her. He pulled an envelope from his pocket and handed it to her. She took it and looked sideways at him. "What's this?"

"Your retainer. I negotiated a fee from the insurance company that had Mrs. Bridges's policy."

"But you earned this."

"I tried to call you last night at the Peacock Club to let you know what was happening. They said you hadn't worked there since they fired you for dating customers."

Jennifer flapped the envelope against her leg, folded it, and stuck it in her hip pocket. Her eyes were cold when she looked up at Bubba.

"Somebody had to pay the bondsman. Somebody had to get Stevie's father home. But I guess you're too good to take my money."

"No, but I figure you need it more than I do, that you worked a lot harder for it than I did."

"You can't imagine. You have no idea. But Stevie's father is coming home, so I have to thank you for that." She turned and walked toward the trailer. Myrtle opened the door and laughed. Jennifer pushed past her.

Bubba climbed into the Bronco and drove away. Afternoon traffic was building on Combee Road and the flow was frantic. Bubba thought it was time to get Elvis and head for the woods. A long walk and the scent of a raccoon might make the evening bearable.

Second Story Sunlight

by John Lutz

NUDGER DIDN'T SO MUCH MIND that he always found himself in the longest line, but he wondered why there was never anyone behind him. That was how it was now, while he waited to deposit the check he'd received for recovering a lost deer. The animal had been one of many removed from a wooded area in one of St. Louis's wealthier suburbs. The residents there resisted any effort to trap or shoot the animals, though they were problematic and a traffic hazard. So with the best of intentions and at great expense, they'd had scores of the deer tranquilized and transferred to various wilderness areas, where most of them died from the shock of relocation or were killed by hunters.

A problem arose when one of the community's leading families had looked on one of the transported deer as a family pet. They had fed it, named it Beamer, set out a salt lick, and the animal had begun hanging around and the children had become fond of it. The family missed the deer and had hired Nudger to get it back. Armed with a photograph of Beamer wearing a frivolous hat at an outdoor birthday party, Nudger had flown to Fargo, North Dakota, paid most of his promised fee to a scout and trapper, and had actually located the animal and had it transported back to St. Louis County, where it was struck by a car.

Now here was Nudger standing in line before a teller's cage in Maplewood Bank. He had to get the Beamer check deposited so it would clear and he could mail his alimony check to his horrendous former wife Eileen. She and her lover-lawyer Henry Mercato were threatening to take Nudger to court again in an attempt to raise his monthly payments. How they could do this, since Eileen, at the apex of one of those barely legal home product pyramid schemes, earned more money than he did, was beyond Nudger. But then, he was always last in line with no one behind him. He loathed the idea of going back into court to do battle with Eileen and Mercato. He was afraid of the whole business and wanted nothing to do with it.

Eileen had left another message on his answering machine referring to him as "the turnip that would bleed." She and Mercato were a bad influence on each other. Matchmakers say there is someone for everyone, but it was amazing that those two had found each other.

Ah! Nudger, was finally at the teller's window, As the man ahead of him moved to the side and left, the woman behind the marble counter moved the hands of a small mock clock to read 2:00. Beside the artificial clock was a sign declaring that deposits after that time wouldn't be posted until the next day's date. Nudger glanced at his wristwatch. Two o'clock.

"But I've been standing in line twenty minutes," he told the woman.

"I'm sorry, sir," she said with a sad shake of her head. "I can't make an exception. It's all done by computer now, you know."

Nudger knew. He made his deposit anyway. Eileen's check would be a day late and there would probably be another turnip message on his machine. There sure wasn't going to be much left of his Beamer fee, he thought, gazing at the deposit slip as he walked from the bank. Money wasn't going very far these days, especially since the area where his office was located was becoming gentrified.

Nudger still didn't know quite what to make of this gentrification, but it was undeniable and as insidious as floodwater. First it had been a trendy Creole restaurant opening down the street, then several antique shops had appeared. So it continued, along with an article in the newspaper about how Maplewood real estate was appreciating so rapidly. Then along came a coffee shop, a café, a music shop, a health food store. The B&L Diner, where Nudger sometimes used to have lunch or breakfast, he noticed was now called Tiffany's. Probably the food had improved, like a lot of other things in the area, but Nudger missed his old, down-at-the-heels neighborhood.

His office hadn't moved or improved, its old window air conditioner protruding from a second-floor window over Danny's Donuts. And at least Danny's was still there. Though Danny had made a concession to the march of progress by featuring a "donut de'jour" every week.

As Nudger entered the aromatic doughnut shop, he saw that this week's spotlighted confection was the same as last week's, something called the Plowman's Feast that had cheese and vegetable bits imbedded in the dough. Nudger had been appalled when he'd first seen one of the things, but Danny had assured him that the "artsy types" who'd moved into the neighborhood saw them as brunch food and were buying them as fast as they could be deep fried. Nudger wasn't sure Danny was being completely honest, as there seemed to be the usual dearth of customers whenever he was in the shop.

"Hey, Nudge!" said the basset-hound-featured Danny as he stood behind the counter wiping his hands on the gray towel always tucked in his belt. "You had lunch?"

"Just a while ago," Nudger said quickly. The thought of Danny's dark and turgid coffee, along with what he invariably offered Nudger, the always featured and unpopular Dunker Delite, made Nudger's delicate stomach kick and turn. Nudger swallowed and got up on a stool at the counter. "I'll take a glass of ice water, though."

Danny shoveled some crushed ice in a glass, then ran tap water. He set the glass on a square white paper napkin in front of Nudger. "You notice my mural, Nudge?" He motioned toward a side wall. "An artist fella just moved in a few blocks from here painted it for me in exchange for a gross of Plowman's Feasts last week."

Nudger hadn't noticed any mural. He turned on his stool to look. A mural, all right, covering most of the east wall, an undersea scene of whales swimming among smaller fish above exotic sea growth on the ocean floor. It wasn't half bad. "Beautiful," Nudger said. "And environmentally correct."

Danny was grinning. "You notice something?"

Nudger looked again. "Whales, mostly."

"You look close and you can see the other fish are just fish, but the whales ain't just whales. They're shaped like Dunker Delites."

"Um," Nudger said, turning away and sipping some water while his mind absorbed this. "Painter's a talented guy."

"Sure is. And generous, considering all the other work he's doing."

"He's got a job other than painting?" No surprise there.

"None as I know of, but he and his new bride are fixing up a house on Emler Avenue, one of them old Victrolians. That's what the Plowman's Feasts were for, their wedding. I went to it. They got married over in the park wearing clothes made completely out of leaves and stuff. Everything natural."

"Romantic," Nudger said, thinking maybe it was.

The door opened and Nudger and Danny were surprised to see the bulk of St. Louis Police Lieutenant Jack Hammersmith enter the doughnut shop. It was almost ninety degrees outside, but Hammersmith, as usual, appeared cool as a scoop of vanilla mint. He was wearing blue uniform pants and no cap. His sleek gray hair was unmussed by summer breezes, and his smooth pink chin and jowls bulged over a white shirt collar. Visible in his shirt pocket were two of the putrid greenish cigars that he loved to smoke when he wanted to be alone.

He said hello to Nudger and Danny, then stared at the new mural.

"What the hell are Dunker Delites doing with fins?"

"They're supposed to be whales," Danny said in an injured tone.

"Sort of a combination of each," Nudger said, trying to protect Danny's feelings.

"You're kinda out of your jurisdiction," Danny said, knowing Hammersmith was a city cop and this was the municipality of Maplewood.

"Got a Major Case Squad crime," Hammersmith said, easing his way up on a stool two over from Nudger so there'd be plenty of room. The Major Case Squad was made up of city and county cops and called into action whenever a serious crime was committed in the area. That way there would be less territorial squabbling, and the facilities of the largest departments were available.

"You want a Dunker Delite?" Danny asked.

Hammersmith looked at him suspiciously. "Yesterday's unsolds?"

Danny blushed. Odd in a man in his fifties.

"Just some water like Nudger's," Hammersmith said.

As he placed the glass of ice water on the counter before Hammersmith, Danny asked the question Nudger was considering. "So what kinda crime brought the Major Case Squad to Maplewood?"

"Homicide," Hammersmith said, sipping water, then using his paper napkin to dab at his lips with the peculiar delicacy of the obese and graceful. "Guy named Lichtenberg, over on Emler Avenue."

Danny released his grip on his gray towel, letting it flop back over his crotch. "Huh? That's the artist did my mural!"

"I know he is," Hammersmith said. "That's how come I knew those whales were Dunker Delites."

For Danny it was a slam dunk. After Hammersmith had gone back out into the summer heat, Danny had easily talked Nudger into trying to find out who killed Lou Lichtenberg. That it was an open homicide case didn't dissuade Danny; being Nudger's ersatz receptionist and sometimes helper, he knew Nudger's occasional disregard for rules. And of course Nudger was breaking one of his rules he least liked to disregard. He tried never to get involved in homicides. Already one person was dead, so was it all that unlikely another would wind up in that state? And with his luck . . .

"Just report to me whenever you want, Nudge," Danny was saying as Nudger waved a limp goodbye and pushed out through the grease-stained glass door into the heat.

Later that day in his hotbox office, Nudger phoned Hammersmith and got the basics: Lou Lichtenberg and his bride Linda had bought an old Victorian house on Emler a couple of months ago and had been living in it while they fixed it up. Like many rehabbers, they couldn't afford to stay in their own digs and be eaten up by rent money along with the funds they were pouring into the project house.

Last night, while they were stripping paint from an old wooden banister, Linda had taken a break and driven to Mr. Wizard to buy them a couple of chocolate strawberry concretes. She'd returned to find her husband sprawled at the base of the stairs. At first she assumed he'd accidentally fallen and was unconscious. The paramedics who responded to her 911 call saw immediately that he was dead. At St. Mary's Hospital emergency, it didn't take long for a nurse to notice the bullet hole behind his ear.

So, murder without a doubt.

"Any hint of motive?" Nudger asked.

Hammersmith chuckled on the other end of the connection. "Hear tell, everybody liked the dead guy. He was one of those free spirits, and a talented painter, according to his friends. Since he'd just turned forty, he decided to settle down, become a husband and home owner."

"What about the wife?"

"Linda. Skinny, pretty, distraught. She isn't faking it, Nudge; she really is grieving over hubby. Course, I could be fooled."

Nudger doubted it.

"She and the painter lived together the past five years, dated a couple of years before that. She's a photographer, but her stuff doesn't sell."

"Did her husband's paintings sell?"

"Yeah, but not for much."

"Should I ask if you found the murder weapon?"

"All we know about it," Hammersmith said, "is it was a twenty-two caliber."

"Could it have been a professional hit, Jack?"

"Crossed my mind—small caliber weapon, one shot behind the right ear, soft bullet that spread and tumbled inside the skull. I don't guess we can rule it out. Or maybe the killer's somebody who saw a movie about a professional hit man."

Nudger hoped the latter was the case. The idea of crossing paths with a pro made his sensitive stomach twitch. He didn't like playing in somebody else's backyard, especially if the somebody was the sort of person who might bury him there.

"Nudge," Hammersmith said, "tell me you aren't going to be mucking around in this case."

"Can't do that, Jack."

"Danny hire you?"

"He was fond of the dead guy," Nudger said. "Went to his wedding, supplied Plowman's Feasts in exchange for the guy painting those Dunker Delite whales. Dead guy was a regular customer of Danny's, and how many of those are there?"

Hammersmith knew the last was a rhetorical question. He didn't give Nudger the usual stern warning about overstepping the line in an active case. Merely hung up without saying goodbye. Nudger wasn't surprised by this abruptness. Hammersmith insisted on being the one to terminate phone conversations, and he often acted suddenly so as not to lose the opportunity. Had a thing about it. Nudger didn't mind. Almost everybody had a thing.

After replacing the receiver on his desk phone, he sat in his tiny, stifling office above the doughnut shop and gazed out the window at pigeons roosting on a ledge of the building across Manchester. The pigeons seemed to sense his attention and gazed back at him. He had never liked the way pigeons looked at him, as if they took for granted something about him that he maybe didn't even know himself.

He turned away from the window, wincing as his swivel chair squealed like an enraged soprano. Bile lay bitter beneath his tongue. Something square and on fire seemed to be lodged low in his throat. The cloying scent of baked sugar from the shop below was making him nauseated. His stomach hurt. Really hurt.

Wrong business, he told himself for the thousandth time, and reached for the roll of antacid tablets on his desk. I'm in the wrong business. Wrong world, maybe.

He barely chewed several antacid tablets and almost choked swallowing the jagged pieces.

Lou Lichtenberg's obituary in the paper the next morning said that he would be cremated, his ashes spread over the Mississippi that he loved to paint, and that there would be a memorial service at a later date.

Nudger put down the *Post-Dispatch* and used the number Danny had given him to phone the widow. When he mentioned Danny, she agreed to talk with him.

Linda Lichtenberg was twenty pounds too thin to be healthy and had a long, wan face out of a Renaissance painting. Telling her how considerate she was to agree to see him at such a time in her life, Nudger thought she looked born to grieve.

They were in the spacious living room of the old house on Ender. It was a mess, with an attached living and dining room, rough hardwood floors, yellowed enameled woodwork partly stripped to its original oak, and bare plaster walls too rough for paint or paper. Beyond where Linda sat on a threadbare sofa was the stairway with the long wooden banister she and her husband had been stripping. The upper part was paint-streaked bare wood, the lower the same yellowed white of the rest of the unstripped woodwork. A worn gray carpet ran up the stairs, the sort of thing easy to trip over.

"If Danny says you're okay, I want to talk to you," Linda said. Her pink-rimmed eyes were pale blue and bloodshot from crying. "I never thought I'd say this, but I'm beginning to believe in the death penalty. I gotta be honest—I want revenge. I want to see the bastard that killed Lou roasted alive!" Strong words from such a frail-looking woman.

With Nudger gently urging her along, she related the simple story told to and by Hammersmith. She and Lou had been stripping paint from the banister. She'd gone out to get ice cream. When she returned, she found Lou at the base of the stairs. She thought he'd fallen and was unconscious, so she called 911. It was the paramedics who discovered he was dead.

When she was finished talking, Nudger glanced around the partly rehabbed living and dining rooms.

"I know it doesn't look like much now," Linda said, "but Lou and I had plans."

"I don't see any of his paintings. I mean the kind you do on canvas."

"His temporary studio was going to be upstairs. Some of his work is up there, if you want to see it."

Nudger told her that he did, then followed her up the steep flight of steps and along a hall to a large second-floor room that was part of an addition to the house. There were skylights set in the slanted ceiling.

"It would have been a good place to work," Linda said sadly. "Lou didn't even have a chance to get properly set up."

Nudger walked over to where two canvases leaned against a wooden railing at the top of the steps. "Mind if I look?"

Linda shrugged. "It's why we came."

Nudger examined each painting. One was an unremarkable woodsy landscape. The other was of a slender nude woman standing near a window and bathed in golden sunlight. Her head was bowed and her long aims hung languidly at her sides.

"Lou's *Woman in the Light,*" Linda said. "His last painting. He did it here because of the skylights."

"You?"

She bit her lower lip. "Me."

"It's beautiful." Nudger meant it.

Linda turned away. "Lou was so talented. His death is such a damned shame."

"What made him paint the whale mural in Danny's?" Nudger asked, thinking it was a long way from the elegant, glowing woman on the canvas before him.

"Doughnuts. He did it in exchange for doughnuts for our wedding. It isn't that good, and he knows it."

"Danny likes it."

"Danny is sweet."

"From all those doughnuts," Nudger said. Got him a smile. "Can you think of anybody your husband might have angered lately, anyone who might have wanted to get even with him?"

"No. I told the police no, too. Lou was an artist; he didn't have any real enemies. Hell, he didn't even live in this world."

Nudger told her he understood, but he wasn't sure if he did.

He found his own way out, leaving her with her grief and the canvas image of herself in sunlight that no longer existed.

Nudger met a woman he knew named Roseanne. She was slim, attractive, and the director of a small, privately funded museum near Grand Avenue. She wasn't from New York, but she had been there and often dressed in black. He regarded her as his art expert.

"Lou Lichtenberg," he said, standing near a life-size bronze Apollo in the museum. It made him feel inadequate.

"Dead," Roseanne said. She was a woman who got to the point.

"Did he have talent?"

"Yes."

"Was he going to make it as an artist?"

"Who knows? He didn't understand or accept the marriage of art and commerce."

"Meaning?"

"Look around you, Nudger."

He did, and saw several ordinary objects—a clock, a chunk of concrete with steel rods protruding from it, a toaster, a suitcase, a small refrigerator. Next to each object was an X-ray view of its insides.

"The museum has an exhibit running this week of work done by the Anti-Christo."

"Isn't Christo the guy who wraps unlikely things in cloth—I mean, like coastlines or whole buildings?"

"The same. But the Anti-Christo displays solid objects, along with their fluoroscopic images or X-rays. The idea is he shows them unwrapped, bare of any surface or subterfuge. His work sells for a fortune."

"Is it art?"

"The market says it is. Is he as talented as Lou Lichtenberg was? Not on your life! Is he more successful as an artist? Yes."

"I don't like your business," Nudger said. "It's full of phonies."

Roseanne smiled. "Yours isn't?"

Hammersmith had told Nudger the Lichtenbergs bought their aged Victorian lady from Norton Anston, the last of a family that had lived in the house for almost a hundred years. Once wealthy from the timber business, they'd fallen on hard times during the Depression and never gotten up. Norton Anston had been reared in comparative poverty that he'd managed to raise only to bare sustenance through a struggling antiques shop. He'd jumped at the Lichtenbergs' offer for the old house. The closing brought him the most liquidity he'd ever experienced.

Anston now lived in an expensive condo in West County, where he agreed to talk with Nudger.

"To tell you the truth," he said, "it was a relief to get rid of the old family house. It had become a costly and troublesome relic. Better somebody young battle the termites and mold than a man my age."

That remark kind of bothered Nudger, because Anston seemed to be in his late forties, Nudger's age. Though he looked older, Nudger assured himself, assessing Anston's thin hair, double chin, thickened waist, crow's-feet. Nudger's hair wasn't all that thin. Except on top, bald spot the size of a half dollar—quarter or maybe nickel.

"I understand you sold the house yourself," he said to Anston, "rather than go through a realtor."

Anston smiled with a kind of toothy avarice, reminding Nudger of someone he couldn't quite place. "Sure. Why pay a commission?"

Why indeed? Nudger thought.

"In my business—buying and selling antiques—there's not much profit margin. I've learned to squeeze a dollar till it bleeds, and I don't apologize."

This guy talked disturbingly like Eileen. "Were the Lichtenbergs satisfied with the deal?"

"They wouldn't have made it if they weren't," Anston said. "Matter of fact, I'd say they were overjoyed. You know, young people, first-time home owners. Kind of touching."

Nudger remembered when he and Eileen, as man and wife, had bought a subdivision house, how for a while it had seemed like a castle. Then a dungeon.

"They had big plans for the place," Anston said. "Talked of turning it into a bed and breakfast."

"Really?" That was the first Nudger had heard of a B and B plan.

Anston glanced at his wristwatch. "I hate to rush this," he said, "but I'm supposed to meet someone at the Gypsy Caravan."

Nudger raised an eyebrow.

"Big antiques show comes to town every year. Dealers from all over the country. Nothing to do with real gypsies."

Nudger chuckled in a way that should let Anston know he wasn't that naïve, then thanked him for his time.

Nudger had parked in the shade, but as usual, starting his old Honda was a struggle in the heat. When he finally was able to get the balky little engine running, he saw Anston pull from the condo driveway in an even older car, a rusty Ford station wagon. It was the proceeds from the sale of the family home, Nudger decided, that had enabled Anston to afford such a nice condo, and maybe with cash left over. He probably hadn't gotten around to buying a new car yet.

Nudger's phone was ringing as he entered his apartment on Sutton, noticing how shabby it looked after Anston's condo. As he picked up the receiver, he reached out with his free hand and switched on the window air conditioner.

Hammersmith was on the phone. Nudger moved as far away from the humming, rattling window unit as the cord would allow so he could hear.

"What I hear," Hammersmith said, "is that you've been nosing around the Lichtenberg case like a pig digging for truffles." Hammersmith would know about truffles. Food. "What have you discovered, Nudge?"

"Facts or truffles?" Nudger asked. "I'll trade either or both."

"Make it both," Hammersmith said. "That way you might stay out of trouble."

"Facts: Lichtenberg was a genuinely talented painter. If he had any enemies, I haven't uncovered them. He and his wife were happy with their new home. And they were considering turning it into a B and B."

"Breaking and entering?"

"B and *B*. Bed and breakfast."

"Oh. And your truffles?"

"The house's previous owner, Norton Anston, needed the money when he sold the place. The wife, Linda, is genuinely grief-stricken, and my guess is she had nothing to do with her husband's death. And it seems to me that there aren't many Lichtenberg paintings lying around the place, considering what a dedicated artist he was. Of course, all truffles are subjective."

"Sometimes when a painter dies, his work suddenly is in demand and the price goes up," Hammersmith said.

"You thinking somebody with lots of Lichtenberg paintings might have killed him?"

"I admit it's only a truffle," Hammersmith said. "Here's another one: a real estate agent says Anston took advantage of the young, artistic, and naïve couple and sold the house for more than it was worth. Only opinion, of course."

"What about your facts?"

"Official cause of death was what you'd expect, Nudge—bullet to the brain, massive damage. No powder burns on the victim's hands, though he was shot from close range. So no chance of suicide. And whoever killed him was probably a smoker."

"Huh?"

"Fresh burn spot on the stairway carpet where the gunman must have stood, from a cigarette or cigar ember."

"Lou and Linda were stripping the banister. Maybe they burned off some of the old paint and singed the carpet," Nudger suggested.

"A possibility," Hammersmith said grudgingly. "I'll check with the wife, who incidentally ran into some friends while buying ice cream at Mr. Wizard's at the time hubby was being shot Not to mention the kid who waited on her. He lives across the street from the Lichtenberg house and remembered her being there. So her alibi checks out strong."

"Maybe she shot Lou before she left the house," Nudger said "Or right after returning."

"Not according to people who heard the shot. Though they didn't know at the time that was what they heard. Also there was no gunpowder residue on her hands."

"You still considering a hit man?" Nudger asked.

"Yeah, but one thing doesn't ring true. We got a misshapen twenty-two bullet like a pro might have left in a victim, only it's more misshapen than it oughta be, considering the soft tissue it went through once it entered the skull. There's no way we can ID the make of gun, or even match the bullet in ballistics tests."

"Did the killer leave a shell casing?"

"Nope. That sounds like a pro. Unless it was an amateur using a revolver and the casing stayed in the cylinder. The way the bullet doesn't provide a lead, or any potential court evidence through ballistics, it mighta been a pro with some new kind of gun that makes his job safer."

"Have you noticed how everything's become a battle with technology?" Nudger asked.

"Tell me about it, Nudge. I'm recording this conversation, gonna convert it into print, then scan it into my electronic murder file. Might write a book someday."

"Is that legal, Jack?"

But Hammersmith had hung up.

"I heard you and your husband were going to convert the house into a B and B," Nudger said, standing on the Victorian home's wide gallery porch and enjoying a glass of lemonade Linda Lichtenberg had just handed him.

"Not right away," Linda said. "But yes, that was the plan. Eventually, we were going to convert the garage to Lou's studio and put in another garage under the house at basement level. He could-work out there in peace and quiet while I was dealing with guests." She slumped down in an old wood glider hung on rusty chains, as if her energy had just left her in a rush, and was obviously trying not to cry. "It's awful, how everything can change in an instant. Now, without Lou's income, I won't even be able to afford to stay here."

"Will you sell the house?"

She shook her head no. "We owe so much it wouldn't make sense. I'm going to let the bank take it. People like me, like Lou, I think we just weren't born to be property owners, to live normal lives."

"What about your husband's paintings? Can't you sell some of them?"

"There aren't any left except the two upstairs. I won't part with *Woman in the Light,* and the landscape is old work and practically worthless. We sold Lou's backlog of work in order to make a down payment and pay closing costs on this place."

"Who bought Lou's paintings?"

"I couldn't tell you. You'd have to check with the Plato Gallery. That's who sold most of Lou's work. When it sold."

Standing on the porch and looking at the dejected figure in the glider, Nudger felt his eyes tear up. He turned away and swiped at them with a knuckle, then talked with Linda Lichtenberg about anything other than her dead husband until the lemonade glass was empty.

The Plato Gallery was in the wealthy suburb of Clayton and displayed antiques as well as artwork. A gaunt man with a white Vandyke beard approached Nudger just inside the door and asked if he could be of help. He was dressed in black except for a white handkerchief that flowered from his blazer pocket.

"Do you have any Lou Lichtenbergs?" Nudger asked.

The man smiled sadly and shook his head. "I wish we did. The artist died recently, you know, and the value of his work has risen. But we sold the last of his paintings over a month ago, cheaper than we should have even then because he needed the money."

"For his Victorian house," Nudger said.

The man's dark eyes brightened. "Oh, you knew Lou?"

"No," Nudger said, and explained.

The man in black turned out to be Plato Zorbak, the owner and manager of the gallery, and when Nudger was finished talking he said with surprising fervor, "I hope they catch the evil swine who shot Lou. He doesn't deserve any mercy."

"Who bought his paintings?" Nudger asked.

"Most of them sold to a dealer in New Orleans—he buys for a number of clients."

A well-dressed man and woman entered the gallery, and before Zorbak excused himself to wait on them, Nudger asked a final question: "About how much have Lou Lichtenberg paintings appreciated since his death?"

"As of now," Zorbak said, "about three hundred percent. And climbing, because Lou was a bona fide talent." He backed away, eager to greet his clientele and escape Nudger, who was obviously no art buyer. "Please feel free to look around before you leave," Zorbak said politely.

Nudger thanked him and did stay for a few minutes. Something had caught his eye.

When he returned to his office, he stopped in Danny's for a cup of coffee to go. After climbing the steps in the stifling stairwell to his office door, he went inside, walked to the tiny half bath, and poured the horrible brew down the washbasin drain slowly so Danny wouldn't hear pipes gurgling below.

Then Nudger switched on the air conditioner and sat down behind his desk. There was a message on his machine. Eileen's voice: "Nudger, if you call the bank you'll see that your measly checking account has been frozen. If you don't—"

Quickly he pressed DELETE.

He slid the desk phone over and called Maplewood Bank, but he didn't ask about his account. He talked to someone he knew in the loan department and asked what would happen when the bank repossessed Lou and Linda Lichtenberg's house.

"Banks don't really want to foreclose on anyone's house," he was assured. "We're not in the real estate business and don't want to be. The house will be sold on the courthouse steps to the highest bidder."

Nudger said thank you, depressed the phone's cradle button for a dial tone, then called Hammersmith at the Third District.

"Nudge," Hammersmith said, "I don't have time for you. Crime in our fair city demands my constant attention."

"If you promise not to hang up on me," Nudger said, "I'll tell you who killed Lou Lichtenberg." Now and then life provided a sweet moment outside the doughnut shop.

The next morning, Nudger sat at the counter in Danny's Donuts. Before him were two free Dunker Delites and a large foam cup of coffee. He was trying to figure a way not to consume any of it without bruising Danny's feelings. Next to Nudger sat Hammersmith. He'd devoured three Plowman's Feasts and was determinedly working on a fourth, drinking only ice water, pretending everything was delicious. Showing his human side, Nudger thought.

"So how'd you figure it out?" Danny asked Nudger.

"By putting together facts and truffles."

Hammersmith glared at him while chewing a mouthful of doughnut.

"Property values in Maplewood are skyrocketing. The Lichtenbergs were going to open a B and B and build a new garage at basement level. With Lou's death, the house will be foreclosed on and sold on the courthouse steps. A straw party from New Orleans bought up Lou's paintings at the Plato Gallery. Seeing the antique guns at the Plato Gallery was the final tip-off."

"Yeah?" Danny asked, looking at Nudger like a curious basset hound.

"Shnot nishe to toy with people, Nudge," Hammersmith said around a large bite of featured pastry.

"I asked myself questions," Nudger said. "Who might have been surprised by increasing property values and want to buy the Lichtenberg house at auction? Who would know enough to buy Lou's paintings through a straw party as an investment if they planned on murdering him? Who dealt in antiques and had access to an antique flintlock gun that might shoot a chunk of lead pried from a twenty-two cartridge, leave a burned spot on the carpet from powder dropping from the gun's flash pan, and leave a deliberately mutilated slug impossible to trace or match with modern weapons? Who might have left behind one of Lou's best and most valuable paintings because he'd know the subject was the painter's wife and having possession of it might draw suspicion to him? And who might have something to hide if the cellar in the old family home were dug up to accommodate a basement garage?"

"The answer's pretty simple when you stop to think about it," Danny said.

"And the proof came," Hammersmith said, "when we dug beneath the house and found the bones of antiques dealer Norton Anston's wife, who was supposed to have run away to Las Vegas twenty-five years ago."

"Poor woman didn't get any farther than the basement," Danny said.

"She's gotten even with Anston now. He's confessed to her murder, and to Lou Lichtenberg's. And he says he'd like to murder Nudger."

"Make sure he's locked up tight," Danny said. Nudger didn't feel he had to second that. He gathered his complimentary Dunker Delites and coffee, along with a paper napkin, and slid off his stool.

"Where you going, Nudge?" Danny asked.

"Gonna eat breakfast upstairs," Nudger said. "Lots of paperwork to do, and I'm expecting a phone call."

"Lemme know if you're still hungry later," Danny said.

Hammersmith was grinning at Nudger as he went out.

Nudger hadn't mentioned the real reason he'd begun to suspect Anston of Lou Lichtenberg's murder. One of the barracudas swimming among the Dunker Delite whales in the mural Lou had painted for Danny looked amazingly like Norton Anston.

To Nudger, anyway.

Aftermath

by Jeremiah Healy

I HAD JUST FINISHED a grueling, three-set match against Max Limbeck, a terrific singles player from Austria, on one of those hundred-ten humidity mid-October days that South Florida doesn't trumpet to potential tourists. Max and I were walking back to the Lauderdale Tennis Club's patio when a female voice from the tiki bar called out, "Rory?"

I turned, Max saying he had to go on the Internet for the book he was writing about his homeland's political history The female voice belonged to Kathy Rifflard, one of the tennis center's administrators. She perched on a stool next to another woman I'd never seen before.

"Kathy," I said, moving toward her while using a hand towel from my racquet bag to mop my face.

She turned to the other woman. "This is Greer Ballantine. She'd like to talk with you. Professionally."

As Kathy returned to the center, I smiled at Ballantine, then used the towel to sweep down my sweat-soaked shirt and gesture over my shoulder toward the condo unit I rented. "Maybe after I take a shower?"

Ballantine looked as though she hadn't smiled in a while. "Mr. Calhoun, I've flown all the way from New York. How about we talk now instead?"

I moved us to one of the umbrellaed patio tables, mostly for privacy, partly to keep Greer Ballantine out of the sun. Like most of our Northeast snowbirds, she didn't have any summer tan left. Some of them had already arrived, many shaken by the terrorist attacks on

September 11 the month before. They were people I knew, so I'd asked them, gently, if they and theirs had come through the tragedies safely. Given how somber Ballantine appeared, I didn't ask her the same question.

As we settled into the white resin chairs, I tried to gauge the woman. Pushing fifty, Ballantine was matronly, with even features, brown hair, and piercing green eyes. She wore a light, daisy-print dress and sensible heels, which tempered rather stumpy calves. I couldn't see her teeth, less because she still hadn't smiled and more because her whole face seemed set in a frown as permanent as stone.

Ballantine laid her handbag on the table. "Want to know how I picked you as a private investigator?"

"My name?"

"That's right." She showed neither surprise nor satisfaction. "When I was a kid, the actor Rory Calhoun was in this TV series called *The Texan.* I had a crush on him, so when I saw your name in the Yellow Pages down here, it seemed kind of an omen."

My mother'd had similar feelings toward Calhoun though at a later, more dangerous age, which led her not just to marry a guy with the same last name but also to give me that first one. However, I wasn't sure I got Ballantine's "omen" allusion, and said so.

She rolled her shoulders, some wisps of hair getting stuck to her forehead by the stultifying breeze. "Did you lose anyone to September eleventh?"

"I have some friends down here who lost friends, or former neighbors. Nobody I knew personally, though."

Ballantine nodded. "My husband, Ted, became an international insurance broker twelve years ago. He was attending a seminar in the World Trade Center that day."

From the tone of her voice, I didn't ask the next logical question. "Ms. Ballantine, I'm sorry."

"Would it be okay if . . . I've never done this kind of thing before. Do you have to call me 'Ms. Ballantine' because of some professional reason?"

A person who could think past her pain. "No. 'Rory' is fine with me if 'Greer' is fine for you." Not exactly a smile, but maybe a little sidestep from the frown. "Ted and I were married twenty-three years ago. Our daughter, Lisa, is a junior in college, and our son, Kevin, graduates high school in June." From her handbag, she drew a family candid showing her, two clean-cut kids, and a man with reddish, curly hair, all four smiling. "My own family—Mom and Dad, I mean—were well off, and I was an only child, so money's not the problem, especially with the group-life policy from Ted's company."

I didn't see where Ballantine was going, but I figured to let her take me there.

"Ted and I have been . . . " Now a sigh. "Jesus, for over a month, I tried to stop doing that—talking like he was still alive? But now I don't . . . "

Her hand snaked back into the handbag like it was the most natural act one could perform. She came out with a packet of tissues and used one to dab at her eyes, twice on each side. "Sorry."

"No need to apologize, Greer. You just lost your husband."

Ballantine seemed to freeze, the tissue now fluttering in the breeze. "That's why I'm here, Rory. I'm not sure I have."

I came back to the table from the bar with a coffee for Ballantine and a Diet Dr Pepper for me. "There's some reason to think your husband survived the attack?"

She nipped at the rim of the cup. "Ted hasn't been accounted for, which isn't conclusive, of course. However, several more people from his company are also missing, and we family members posted on the Web site the city set up as kind of an information-exchange bulletin board."

Not being into computers, I probably looked a little blank, because Ballantine added, "You know, 'This is my husband's name and description; have you seen him or talked to anyone who has?'"

"I understand."

A nod, and then more coffee. "Well, another broker, José Acosta, also attended the seminar. His wife, Carolina, contacted me, because her husband was among the missing, too. In fact, I'm staying at their place in Miami Beach." More coffee still. "Carolina says José called on his cellular after the plane . . . after the explosion to tell her he was going to try to go down the stairs and . . . and then some personal stuff." Ballantine used another tissue as efficiently as she had the first. "Carolina said José didn't mention Ted, though."

"And you thought that was odd?"

"No. No, given the . . . I'm not sure Ted would have mentioned José if the situation was reversed. I mean, they were friends, but given the distance between their offices, more from seeing each other at business things like the seminar." Another dab at her eyes. "It's just that I had no information about Ted, whether he got out or not." Her hand went again into the bag, this time withdrawing a folded paper. "Until this arrived."

Ballantine handed it to me. I opened what proved to be a credit-card statement. Lots of entries on it.

I glanced up at Ballantine, who without saying as much, implied that I should read the thing more carefully.

I did. Dozens of entries pre-September 11, but none on that date or thereafter. Except for the last one, "TASTE OF CHINA FT LAUDERDALE FL," with both a "transaction date" and a "posting date" of the twenty-ninth. Over two weeks after the terrorist attacks.

I stared up at Ballantine now.

She said, "See?"

"You didn't cancel the charge card?"

"No." A dismissive wave of her hand. "It just wasn't very high on my list of priorities. And besides, I never dreamed anyone could be such a . . . bastard as to take and use it."

I'd read about a "friend" of another victim actually stealing a charge card from the decedent's apartment in Brooklyn and running up a huge bill. "Have you contacted the police?"

Another sigh. "I figured they were pretty swamped, and even if I did, they'd still have to come down here to find anything out about this restaurant, assuming that's what Taste of China is. And no other money—ATM, checking, money markets—has been touched since the eleventh."

"Greer, you realize this could mean any one of several things."

A slight hardening of the features now. "I'm not stupid, Rory. In the week since that statement arrived, I haven't thought about much else. The restaurant could have made a mistake writing down somebody else's card number. Or that random bastard could have found Ted's card in the rubble somewhere, although I don't see a low-life traveling fifteen hundred miles not using it until he had a yen for Szechuan. Or . . . or Ted could be alive and staying down here."

"And you'd like me to find out which?"

Ballantine blinked a few times, but without tears now. "I've though a lot about that, too. I'm not sure I really want to know, but I owe it to Lisa and Kevin to find out what actually happened to Ted."

As Greer Ballantine wrote me both a retainer check and the address of the Acosta home in Miami Beach, I wondered why she hadn't included herself in the "owe" part of that last sentence.

After showering in the condo I rented next door to Court 13, I checked the telephone book under "Taste of China" and found an entry for it on a boulevard near the Hollywood line south of downtown Fort Lauderdale. Then I changed into a clean T-shirt and shorts before climbing into my Chrysler Sebring convertible.

No one born in South Florida would ever mistake me for a native son. For one thing, I have a year-round tan while most people brought up down here try to avoid the sun as much as possible. For a second, I don't just own a convertible: I drive with the top down during the day, even in the withering heat and humidity of June onward, though I do run the air conditioner full blast. But then the "real" Floridians have never been through the kind of winters I used to face, playing mostly satellite tournaments in European and smaller American cities when tennis meant indoor facilities and erstwhile spectators who kept asking each other which one of us second-tier pros was Becker or Agassi or Sampras.

Like many restaurants in the area, Taste of China turned out to be tucked into a strip mall between two budget motels. I found a parking space a few doors down, then walked past the place once, T-shirt already plastered to my shoulder blades. Kind of a hole-in-the-wall, with a counter for takeout and a few tables for eating, a big WE DELIVER sign in red letters on the window. The sort of place a cost-conscious tourist might patronize for something to bring back to the room.

Retracing my steps, I went in, a string of brass balls tied to the door making an incongruous "jingle-bells" sound as I both opened and closed it. The short, plump man behind the counter was Asian and middle-aged, with a front tooth missing as he smiled and said, "Help you?"

"I hope so." I showed the man my identification. He took a while to read it, and I noticed that the pale green order slips in front of him on the counter bore what I assumed were Chinese characters.

Then he said, "We have no troubles here."

"And I'm not trying to cause you any." I took out the charge-card statement Greer Ballantine had given me. "We think this last entry might be a fraudulent one, and I thought you could tell me why."

The man looked down .at the paper, but not for nearly as long as he had my license. "You wait."

He disappeared through the swinging door into the chatter and clatter of a busy kitchen. When he came back out, a young Asian woman with his build but a suspicious cast to her eyes trailed behind him.

She said, "What do you want from us?"

No accent on her words. "As I told this gentleman, I'm a private investigator. My client has reason to believe this entry from your restaurant may be fraudulent, and I'd like to find out what you know about the person you served."

The young woman glanced down at the statement for even a shorter period than the man had. "We serve a hundred people every day. How would my father or me remember that?"

I showed her the candid of the Ballantine family. "Could it have been this man?"

I caught a flicker of emotion as the father glanced toward his daughter, though she might have been a poker player betting the mortgage, saying only, "I don't recognize him."

"Well, would your records show whether the person who used the card ate here, ordered takeout, or"—I pointed to the window sign—"had something delivered?"

"We don't have to show you any records without an order from the courts."

I was running into the Great Stonewall of China. But why? "If there is a fraud problem here, wouldn't you like it resolved without having to *involve* the courts. Or the police?"

She had all her front teeth, and now they nibbled on her lower lip.

I said, "Or the newspapers, and the resultant bad publicity."

More nibbling.

I leaned forward now, my elbows on their counter. "Or the Immigration and Naturalization Service?"

Now she leaned into me, nose-to-nose since I was bent at the waist. "My father became a citizen five years ago, and I was born here. You can't scare us, and you can't make us talk to you. So leave, or I will call the police myself."

Technically, she was right. I couldn't make them cooperate, so I left with what remained of my bluff intact for possible later use. And by the time I reached the Sebring, I'd thought of a question I should have asked Greer Ballantine.

Carolina Acosta lived in a neighborhood of beautiful homes with pastel stucco walls and orange-tiled roof in Miami Beach about six blocks back from the ocean. When I pulled into the semicircular driveway, I saw a Mazda Miata convertible parked behind a Lexus sport ute. Ringing the doorbell brought a willowy, olive-skinned woman with long black hair and a stylish silk dress, yellow in a way that nearly matched her eyes. I pegged her as fortyish, careful about her appearance, a quiet resignation radiating from her face.

"Yes?"

"Ms. Acosta, my name's Rory Calhoun."

"Ah, Greer's private investigator."

"Yes. Is she here?"

"No. Greer said that after speaking with you, she just wanted to walk for a while along the beach, so I took her in the Miata and will pick her up again in a few hours. But please, come in."

I followed Acosta through a terra-cotta foyer, her sandals clicking off the fired clay like the shoes of a horse trotting along a paved street. We entered a living room decorated with oil paintings, the similar style and brush strokes depicting what I guessed to be Cuban street scenes.

"Do you paint?" I said, taking a seat on a plush chair as Acosta settled into her couch.

"No, but my husband's father did in Havana, before the Revolution. When the family ran from Castro, they couldn't bring his works with them. Everything you see on these walls he painted from memory. A way for him to deal with his . . . loss."

Acosta cleared her throat, no doubt reminded of her own.

I said, "Greer told me about your husband. I'm very sorry."

"Thank you. It's not been an easy time for any of us."

"I wonder if I could leave a message for her?"

"Certainly. Do you wish to tell me, or would you rather write one down for confidentiality purposes?"

Another woman who could think past her pain. I said, "Writing might be easier."

She reached over to a telephone on a small table, came back with a pad and pencil.

As I wrote my request for Ballantine to call her husband's credit-card company to see what signature the original receipt from Taste of China had on it, Acosta said, "In a way, I was luckier than most."

I looked up at her.

She drew in a breath. "José was able to call on his cellular before . . . before the tower he was in collapsed."

"Greer told me you'd had that chance to speak with him."

A sudden sniffle and a hard swallow, making me realize that the resignation covering Acosta's sadness was only a thin veneer. "Actually, no. I was out. A routine errand, nothing that couldn't have waited, but he therefore had to leave a message on our tape machine." She shook her head now "José was such a gregarious man, always introducing people he knew and liked to each other at parties, kind of a . . . one-man welcome wagon." The tears began. "We always communicated so well with each other, too. But now, I have his last thoughts and words only on a scratchy, ninety-nine-cent audio cassette."

As Carolina Acosta began to cry, I thought that, even then, she'd come out ahead of Greer Ballantine.

"So, Rory, perhaps we shall play again tomorrow, yah?"

I'd just parked my car in one of the dedicated spaces for residents of the Wingfield building, and Max Limbeck was corning off Court 13, a smile on his ruddy face, the short, blond hair on his skull looking almost like acrylic fuzz on a stuffed animal.

"I hope so. How's the book coming along?"

"Slowly, but it comes. I made contact with an important source today on the Internet. A magical system, don't you think?"

"For some." Then I had an idea. "Max, could we visit a Web site using your computer?"

"But of course." A slight, courtly bow. "Come by in one half hour, and I will be ready to assist you."

"Rory, this is the Web site you wished." Max bowed his head. "Tragic, tragic, but perhaps a way for those hurt to find closure, yah?"

I looked over his shoulder. The screen seemed impossibly complicated to me. "Can you tell how it's organized?"

"I believe so." Max did something to make the images jump back and forth. "Families or friends post the names of those missing, with contact addresses or telephones. Then those who believe they have information communicate to the survivors."

I gave him the names I'd come across so far. Greer Ballantine and Carolina Acosta had indeed listed their husbands.

"Max, is there any way you can find out if other people from South Florida posted as well?"

"Some moments, and we shall see."

It did take a while, but eventually he came up with many missing people posted with contact addresses in the area. Three names caught my eye, because each was connected to insurance as an industry.

"Do you wish anything further, Rory?"

"Maybe if you could print out the insurance ones we found?"

"The push of a button." Then a grim cast to Max Limbeck's eyes as he twisted his head my way. "If only it could be so easy to find them in real life, yah?"

Patrick Kelly worked at an Irish pub in Delray Beach. It didn't take very long to establish that the thirty-something with beefy forearms, receding hair, and seashell ears answered to that name.

Kelly had been using a wipe cloth like a squeegee on the mahogany bar. At two-thirty on a weekday afternoon, things were slow enough that he said he could talk with me over the Guinness I'd ordered. My guess was that, as soon as I mentioned my mission, Kelly would have found time to talk during happy hour on his saint's day.

"Have you any news at all about my Fiona?"

"I'm sorry, but none. You might be able to help me, though, with somebody else in the Towers that day."

Kelly's eyes had gone funny as soon as I'd replied in the negative, but he nodded his head abruptly. "I'm sure they'd as do the same for me."

"How did your wife come to be in New York on the eleventh?"

"She did insurance brokering for a big outfit down here. I'm not certain I ever understood what all it involved. But I do know Fiona had to travel several times over the summer toward arranging something for one of her firm's real estate clients."

"Did she mention her attending a seminar in the World Trade Center that day?"

"A seminar? Do you mean for insurance lessons and so forth?"

"Yes."

Kelly weighed that. "No. No, and Fiona did go to one of those over in Fort Myers on the Gulf Coast six or seven months past. I'm sure she would have told me if she'd been doing the same this time around."

I asked about the Taste of China restaurant in Hollywood.

"Man, that would be forty miles or more to the south of us. Bit of a hop just to take away some egg rolls, eh?"

"Did your wife ever mention another insurance broker named Ted Ballantine?"

"Like the ale, you mean?"

"Yes."

More weighing. "No. Was he from the Big Apple?" A grunt that I realized constituted a small laugh. "That's what Fiona always called it, you know. 'The Big Apple.' Loved to get out of Delray in the heat of summer, even for more of the same up north. In fact, we talked the night before by telephone, herself telling me from the hotel bed that it was to be a grand fall day dawning that next morning."

As someone clamored for a Harp draft, Patrick Kelly ran the wipe cloth under his nose before slapping it over his shoulder. "Couldn't have been more wrong now, could she?"

The second person posting on the Web site lived in one of Boca Raton's many gated communities. I didn't think I'd get beyond the sentry box until I mentioned September 11 to the guard, who spoke into a telephone before putting a three-hour, dated pass on the dashboard of my Sebring and giving me left-right-left directions to wind through the maze of town-housed blocks. I ended up in front of a generic cluster, a woman already outside her front door despite the humidity. From fifty feet away, I underestimated her age by twenty years, but up close, the shiny skin and slightly popped eyes betrayed one facelift too many.

"You're the private investigator?"

"Yes, ma'am. Doris Steinberg?"

"I don't want to seem suspicious, but could I see some identification?"

"You bet."

She read my license quickly, then said, "We'll be a lot cooler inside."

The interior of the house was furnished starkly, but despite the fact that the decor was mostly lost on me, it seemed very upscale, as though I'd stumbled into a museum of modern art. Steinberg gracefully settled on a chrome-and-leather chair while I took its mate across from her. Then a skittering sound, and I turned to see a moppy mongrel the size of a toy poodle jump up into my lap.

"Oh, I'm so sorry. Sabra, get down from there."

The little thing looked up mournfully at me. "It's okay, Mrs. Steinberg. I like dogs."

"She's been like that, ever since . . . ever since Sam didn't come home last month." A pause, maybe Stein-berg's way of holding it in as I scratched my new best friend between the ears. "'Sabra' means an Israeli-born girl. Sam saw her wandering a street in Jerusalem when we were visiting two years ago, and he resolved to bring her home. The paperwork? Don't ask. But Sabra imprinted on him as though she sensed he'd saved her."

"Mrs. Steinberg, I'm sorry to cause you to revisit September eleventh, only—"

"Mr. Calhoun, you're not the one 'causing me to revisit.' I've done it every day since, and right now I can't imagine not doing it every other day I'm on this earth." A second pause. "Do you . . . Is there anything about Sam I should know?"

Which is when it hit me. Doris Steinberg, and maybe Patrick Kelly as well, thought I might be the bearer of bad tidings, a definitive DNA match or something like that. "No, I'm afraid not. But you might have some information that could help me on another person caught in the Towers that day."

Steinberg's face indicated neither relief nor disappointment. "Go ahead."

"How did your husband come to be there on the eleventh?"

"Sam was trying to pave the way for his son-in-law."

I noted the "his" as opposed to "our," but when Steinberg didn't go on, I said, "Pave the way?"

"In the insurance brokerage business. Sam was seventy-two, and he'd retired six years ago to get out of the New York winters. We met down here thereafter. He'd lost his first wife to cancer nearly thirty-five years into their marriage, and I'm afraid their daughter didn't marry too . . . wisely. So Sam flew back up there from time to time, trying to get the boy a good job. They were both in the World Trade Center that morning, kind of the mentor tutoring his protégé through an interview with a friend in the business. Sam was like that, always trying to give back." Now a longer pause. "The son-in-law got out, by the way. Sam's friend was . . . He'd had polio as a child, and Sam lagged behind to help him. Giving back in a different way, I guess."

I was sorry I hadn't known him. "Did your husband ever mention a Ted Ballantine, also an insurance broker?"

Steinberg looked down at the floor. "No. No, I don't recall that name. But then, Sam finished in the business before he met me, and I think he believed that any reference by him to the 'old days up north' might make me suspect that he was really missing his old life with his dead wife."

I thought it safest just to nod rather than mention the Chinese restaurant.

Steinberg said, "Now I'm learning in my own way what Sam might really have felt."

When this time she closed her eyes and brought a hand to her face, I quietly set Sabra back onto the floor and let myself out of Doris Steinberg's now even more museumlike town house.

Stepping across the threshold of the small single-family on a postage-stamp lot in Dania, I felt as if I were in a chapel. Religious icons sprouted all over the place, the most prominent an indoor shrine to the Blessed Virgin Mary, a miniature fountain burbling beneath her feet.

Mercedes Delgado, maybe sixty and dressed in a black veil and kerchief, ushered me toward the only chair in the living room. The man of comparable age sitting on the couch had to use a cane to lever himself up and shake my hand. I didn't suggest he stay seated, as it felt somehow wrong to excuse him from being polite.

Eduardo Delgado said, "Wine, beer, coffee?"

There was none showing on their little tables. "No, thank you. And I hope I won't have to take up much of your time."

"Time we have," from Mr. Delgado, settling back down. "And much to be grateful for."

Since his wife appeared dressed for a funeral, I was taken aback a bit. "How so?"

She said, "Our Azura is return to us from the Gates of Hell."

"Your daughter?"

"Yes," said the father. "Azura always is trying to improve herself, so she attends a 'seminar' in New York City."

Bingo. Maybe.

He went on. "She wishes to become a partner in her firm of insurance."

The mother put in, "Even before she marry."

Mr. Delgado shrugged. "It is the way here. We bring Azura over from Cuba in the Boatlift, the time of the Marielitos. She is just seven years old, and she sleeps in my arms the whole way. But we are able to raise her in our religion, because Florida is the United States, and we find freedom here for everything. The Muslim terrorists, they do not understand this any more than Fidel's communist ones."

Delgado muttered something in Spanish that had the ring of a curse to it.

Fairly certain of where they stood on that issue, I said, "You mentioned 'seminar' before?"

"Yes," from the father. "Azura studies hard here, learns to speak English with no accent I can hear. But to advance, she must go to other places, like New York. Each month for almost one year."

"Did she ever mention a man named Ted Ballantine?"

The mother looked at the father, but he stayed on me, a little glassy-eyed now.

Mr. Delgado said, "Not that last name, but close. Teddy Ball, the man who saves our Azura from the Towers."

"God bless his soul," from his wife.

I turned to her. "He's . . . dead?"

The mother looked shocked. "Dead? *Muerto*? No. No!"

Some machine-gun Spanish from the husband, but in a soft voice. Then to me, "Mercedes does not understand English quite so good. She means Teddy should be blessed for all eternity, because he keeps our daughter from being kill when so many others are."

I tried to tread lightly. "Are they living up in New York City?"

The father said, "No. After the disaster, when Azura leaves the hospital there, they move into the house he buys for her in Hollywood."

"Before they marry," observed Mrs. Delgado, in English but using her curse tone.

I said, "Before . . . ?"

Her husband smiled in a worldly way. "Mercedes does not like that our daughter lives with a man before marriage. But they go to the church next month, more sooner than they plan for. And it is good, because Teddy can be with Azura more now."

The mother said, "A hero, is true. But he want no fame for it."

Somehow I wasn't surprised about that. "Since their names are so similar, maybe your Teddy might know the man I'm trying to help. Could you give me the Hollywood address?"

It turned out to be a nice starter home there, maybe ten blocks from the Taste of China's strip mall but set back into a residential neighborhood. Basketball hoops on the carports and bicycles in the drives, a perfect spot for prospective . . . newlyweds.

I parked the convertible on the street and walked up to the front door. Knocking, I heard an immediate "Coming" from a male voice, and moments later the man with reddish, curly hair in the Ballantine family candid opened the door.

"Can I help you?" he said.

I held up my license and the photo his wife had given me.

"Oh, no."

"If you let me in, this might be easier."

"Who is it?" called a female voice from the rear of the house.

Ballantine called back. "Just someone to see me about a . . . job reference."

I thought that was pretty cute.

Then he said, "Please, don't say anything to Azura."

"She's going to find out sooner or later."

"Maybe not," said Ballantine, though without even a hint of threat in the way he said it.

We went toward the other voice, now asking, "Teddy, maybe I should meet him?"

Ballantine ushered me into the Florida room, a glass-walled area that in cooler weather would give way to screens and a pleasant view of a gardened backyard.

A view that Azura Delgado couldn't appreciate.

The sunglasses were wraparounds, but just the way she stood from the swinging sofa and slightly misdirected her face told me the eyes behind them didn't know quite where I was. She extended a hand, also off-kilter. I stepped forward and took it, Delgado angling fifteen degrees to now face me squarely.

"Aren't you going to introduce yourself?" she said.

"My name's Rory, Rory . . . Calvert. Pleasure to meet you."

"Believe this: It's a pleasure for me to meet anyone." Then a bright, musical laugh, and I noticed a pair of Walkman headphones down around her collared blouse, almost like a necklace.

Ballantine said, "Mr. Calvert wants to talk with me alone."

"That's fine, Teddy. But, please, Mr. Calvert, stop by to say goodbye before you leave, okay?"

"I will."

Ballantine led me back into the living room. I let him sit first.

He waited, then said, "I'm pretty sure she'll have the headphones back on now."

I eased into a chair. "How bad is it?"

"The blindness? Permanent."

"Nothing the doctors can do?"

"Mr. Calhoun, it's not just her vision that's gone." Ballantine looked at his hands. "The dust storm took Azura's eyes themselves."

Jesus Christ.

He glanced over to me. "As an insurance broker, I used to be pretty good at making pitches. Let me try to make you understand."

"That might not be any of my business."

He began to wring his hands now "Indulge me. Please?"

After a moment, I leaned back in my chair.

Ballantine canted his head toward the Florida room. "I hooked up with Azura last year, through a friend of mine from the trade named José Acosta."

"I've met his wife."

"You have?"

"Through yours."

Ballantine blanched, but drove on. "I was nuts about Azura from the get-go. Well, José didn't know her that well—she'd just interned with his office down here for a few months. And he didn't mention to her that I was married."

"And, conveniently, neither did you."

"No. No, I . . . Azura'd told me about her family, how they'd escaped Cuba over freedom of religion. I knew she, and her parents, would never go for it. So I told her a . . . white lie."

Or a dark gray one. "That you were a widower?"

"No. Divorced. That was okay with Azura, but wouldn't have been with her family, so we agreed to use a different last name for me—just with them—to keep 'Ted Ballantine' in the background afterward."

"Meaning after you skipped out on your wife and kids."

Ballantine gave me a fighting look, then stood down. "There wasn't anything left of that marriage, Mr. Calhoun. I was staying in the house, and on the job, just to see our younger—Kevin—through high school. I set some money aside over time, enough for this house, a car. Once Kevin graduated, I planned to move out. Start divorce proceedings against Greer in New York, fly down here, the works."

"But then comes September eleventh, and you see your big chance."

He flinched. "Azura and I met at the seminar, as we always tried to do whenever she came up to New York on business. We were about to get on the elevators when the first plane hit. Thank God we headed directly for the stairs and got a good ways down before the second . . . I mean, I saw it later on the news, and I couldn't understand how even . . . "

Ballantine shook his head. "Anyway, we reached the plaza level, but it was chaos, and a lot of people were milling around, watching the flames pour out of both towers above us. Some people . . . some people trapped higher than the fire just jumped rather than be burned alive. It was horrible, like something out of Hieronymus Bosch, that medieval painter of hell?"

I sensed a deflection. "Sounds to me that you got a good enough start, you should have been clear of the danger zone."

"We would have been. But Azura insisted on staying behind to help people. She'd taken first-aid classes, and a lot of rescue-unit firefighters were blowing past the less injured to go up into the Towers after the ones more . . . Well, I stayed to help, too, and I'd just gotten an older man behind an ambulance when the first tower, the second to be hit, began coming down. It was . . . indescribable. Like a gray, swirling blizzard, but not just dust. Shards and chips and . . . When the air cleared a little, I could see the ambulance was riddled like it'd been through a war. And people were on the ground everywhere, coughing and choking, writhing and moaning. And I started screaming for Azura, and she didn't answer and didn't answer, and then I heard her voice, and I had to push through a horde of terrified people covered in ash like . . . zombies, trampling over her, trying to just breathe. Azura could talk, barely, but her . . . her eyes, she must have turned into the dust storm, I don't know. I managed to get her to another ambulance, then waited for somebody to help us. I didn't know how to contact Azura's parents right away, and then I . . . I admit it I started thinking."

"That you could just fade away with the thousands of others who didn't make it out."

Ballantine clasped his hands now. "Try to see it from my side, please? I'd have received something from a divorce, but basically Greer would have gotten the house, and the court would have ordered me to put both kids through college. Fine, I expected that. Only there'd always be the chance that somebody would say something, even José or his wife at our wedding, since Azura insisted on inviting them for his having introduced us. But then, with the terrorist attacks, I had a way out. Plenty of money for Greer, both from her parents' side and my life policy. More than enough to educate Lisa and Kevin, even for condos and cars of their own. And no pain of betrayal for Greer and our kids, or for Azura and her family."

"But then why use the charge card at Taste of China?"

"I didn't." A slow breath. "I'd established an account at another takeout place. But one day I was on a job interview in Miami, and when I called home, Azura said she'd order Chinese for us. Only our regular restaurant's delivery guy was out sick, and Azura didn't want to 'bother' me or have me drive out of my way to pick it up. So instead she called Directory Assistance, got the number of another nearby place that could deliver, and ordered from there instead."

"Taste of China."

A slump to his shoulders. "I'd kept one charge card from my 'old life,' just in case of some unmanageable emergency. The thing was in a dresser drawer here. Well, Azura somehow stumbled on it, maybe while learning to put clothes away. She had no cash on hand, so she used the card to pay for the delivery."

"And signed the receipt?"

"Yes, but I examined it that next morning, when she 'surprised' me by revealing what she'd done, and her signature was illegible."

Which meant that Greer Ballantine wouldn't find out anything by asking the charge-card company whose name was on their original.

"Azura was so . . . pleased." A note of pride crept into Ballantine's voice. "That she could accomplish even a simple task like that without her . . . her being able to see? But when I went to Taste of China—"

"—they'd already processed the transaction."

Just a nod. "I bribed them, saying that my wife was an illegal immigrant, and that I was afraid she'd be deported if the truth came out. The owner and his daughter seemed to. . . understand."

"All so neat and tidy."

Ballantine finally flared. "Look, Mr. Calhoun. I'm not blameless here, and I don't pretend to be. But I love Azura, and I owe her for what happened, especially since she really was at that seminar as a cover story toward seeing me. She needs a husband now more than my prior family does, and truly, Greer and the kids are better off both emotionally and financially with me 'dead.' How about sparing everybody any more heartache from the aftermath of this horror?"

I told Ted Ballantine I'd think about it, but by the time I'd stopped back in the Florida room and touched the bravely extended hand of the future Azura 'Ball,' I already knew I was going to be telling Greer Ballantine about the "random bastard" who must have fraudulently used her dead husband's credit card.

The Shamus Winners
Volume II (1996-2009)

1996

The Eye (Lifetime Achievement Award): No Award Given

Best P.I. Hardcover Novel: *Concourse* **by S.J. Rozan**. Other nominees: *The Vanishing Smile* by Earl Emerson. *Come to Grief* by Dick Francis. *Movie* by Parnell Hall. *The Neon Smile* by Dick Lochte.

Best Original P.I. Paperback: **Native Angels by William Jaspersohn**. Other nominees: *Zero Tolerance* by J.D. Knight. *Interview With Mattie* by Shelley Singer. *Charged With Guilt* by Gloria White. *Way Past Dead* by Steven Womack.

Best First P.I. Novel: **The Innocents by Richard Barre**. Other nominees: *Who in Hell Is Wanda Fuca?* by G.M. Ford. *If Looks Could Kill* by Ruthe Furie. *Penance* by David Housewright. *The Harry Chronicles* by Allan Pedrazas.

Best P.I. Short Story: **"And Pray Nobody Sees You" by Gar Anthony Haywood**. Other nominees: "Trial by Fire" by David Dean. "Plain and Honest Death" by Bill Pomidor. "Home Is the Place Where" by Bill Pronzini. "Enigma" by D.H. Reddall.

1997

The Eye (Lifetime Achievement Award): **Stephen Marlowe**

Best P.I. Hardcover Novel: **Damned in Paradise by Max Allan Collins** and ***Sunset Express* by Robert Crais**. Other nominees: *Flesh Wounds* by Stephen Greenleaf. *Invasion of Privacy* by Jeremiah Healy. *Sentinels* by Bill Pronzini. *When Wallflowers Die* by Sandra West Prowell.

Best Original P.I. Paperback: **Fade Away by Harlan Coben**. Other nominees: *Chain of Fools* by Steven Womack. *Natural Death* by Ruthe Fury.

Best First P.I. Novel: **This Dog for Hire by Carol Lea Benjamin**. Other nominees: *Keeper* by Greg Rucka. *The Low End of Nowhere* by Michael Stone. *This Far, No Further* by John Wessel.

Best P.I. Short Story: **"Dead Drunk" by Lia Matera**. Other nominees: "Eye of the Beholder" by Ed Gorman. "Turning the Witness" by Jeremiah Healy. "The One About the Green Detective" by John Lethan. "The Girl Who Talked To Horses" by Robert J. Randisi

St. Martin's Press/PWA Best First P.I. Novel Contest: *A Cold Day in Paradise* **by Steve Hamilton.**

1998

The Eye (Lifetime Achievement Award): No Award Given

Best P.I. Hardcover Novel: *Come Back Dead* **by Terence Faherty**. Other nominees: *Indigo Slam* by Robert Crais. *Deception Pass* by Earl Emerson. *Sacred* by Dennis Lehane. *Down for the Count* by Maxine O'Callaghan. *No Colder Place* by S.J. Rozan

Best Original P.I. Paperback: *Charm City* **by Laura Lippman**. Other nominees: *Back Spin* by Harlan Coben. *A Whisper of Rage* by Tim Hemlin. *Father Forgive Me* by Randye Lordon. *Sunset and Santiago* by Gloria White.

Best First P.I. Novel: *Big Red Tequila* **by Rick Riordan**. Other nominees: *Baltimore Blues* by Laura Lippman. *Legwork* by Katy Munger.

Best P.I. Short Story: **"Love Me For My Yellow Hair Alone" by Carolyn Wheat**. Other nominees: "Copperhead Run" by Doug Allyn. "Lord of Obstacles" by Greg Fallis. "A Front-Row Seat" by Jan Grape."Nightcrawlers" by John Lutz.

St. Martin's Press/PWA Best First P.I. Novel Contest: *The Losers' Club* **by Lise S. Baker.**

1999

The Eye (Lifetime Achievement Award): **Maxine O'Callaghan**

Best P.I. Hardcover Novel: *Boobytrap* by **Bill Pronzini**. Other nominees: *Gone Baby Gone* by Dennis Lehane. *No Badge, No Gun* by Harold Adams. *Flying Blind* by Max Allan Collins. *The Only Good Lawyer* by Jeremiah Healy.

Best Original P.I. Paperback: *Murder Manual* by **Steven Womack**. Other nominees: *Too Easy* by Philip Depoy. *Butcher's Hill* by Laura Lippman. *The Widower's Two-Step* by Rick Riordan. *Death in a City of Mystics* by Janice Steinberg

Best First P.I. Novel: *A Cold Day in Paradise* by **Steve Hamilton**. Other nominees: *Like a Hole in the Head* by Jen Banbury. *Dead Low Tide* by Jamie Katz. *Zen and the Art of Murder* by Elizabeth Cosin.

Best P.I. Short Story: **"Another Day, Another Dollar" by Warren Murphy**. Other nominees: "Sidewinder" by David Edgerley Gates. "No, Thank You, John" by Michelle Knowlden. "All About Heroes" by Dan A. Sproul. "More Light" by James Sallis.

St. Martin's Press/PWA Best First P.I. Novel Contest: *Street Legal* by **Robert Truluck**.

Friends of PWA (a new award): **Michael Seidman**, editor at Walker, former editor of *The Armchair Detective*. **Joe Pittman**, senior editor at Signet

2000

The Eye (Lifetime Achievement Award): **Edward D. Hoch**

Best P.I. Hardcover Novel: *California Fire and Life* by **Don Winslow**. Other nominees: *L.A. Requiem* by Robert Crais. *Monster* by Jonathan Kellerman. *Prayers for Rain* by Dennis Lehane. *Stone Quarry* by S.J. Rozan.

Best Original P.I. Paperback: *In Big Trouble* by **Laura Lippman**. Other nominees: *Deadbeat* by Leo Atkins. *Fulton County Blues* by Ruth Birmingham. *The Last Song Dogs* by Sinclair Browning. *Steel City Confessions* by Thomas Lipinski.

Best First P.I. Novel: *Every Dead Thing* by **John Connolly**. Other nominees: *East of A* by Russell Atwood. *The Immortal Game* by Mark Coggins. *Maximum Insecurity* by P.J. Grady. *The Answer Man* by Roy Johansen.

Best P.I. Short Story: **"Akitada's First Case" by I. J. Parker**. Other nominees: "Unchained Melody" by Doug Allyn. "Hodegetria" by Jeremiah Healy. "The Reluctant Op" by Barbara Paul. "Cro-magnon, P.I." by Mike Reiss.

St. Martin's Press/PWA Best First P.I. Novel Contest: *Catching Water in a Net* by **J.L. Abramo.**

2001

The Eye (Lifetime Achievement Award): No Award Given

Best P.I. Hardcover Novel: *Havana Heat* by **Carolina Garcia-Aguilera**. Other nominees: *A Smile on the Face of the Tiger* by Loren Estleman. *The Deader the Better* by G. M. Ford. *Ellipsis* by Stephen Greenleaf. *Listen to the Silence* by Marcia Muller.

Best Original P.I. Paperback: *Death in the Steel City* by **Thomas Lipinski**. Other nominees: *The Blazing Tree* by Mary Jo Adamson. *The Sporting Club* by Sinclair Browning. *The Hindenburg Murders* by Max Allan Collins. *Bad to the Bone* by Katy Munger. *Dirty Money* by Steven Womack.

Best First P.I. Novel: *Street Level* by **Bob Truluck**. Other nominees: *Brigham's Day* by John Gates. *The Heir Hunter* by Chris Larsgaard. *Resurrection Angel* by William Mize. *Lost Girls* by Andrew Pyper.

Best P.I. Short Story: **"The Road's End" by Brendan DuBois**. Other nominees: "What's in a Name?" by Jeremiah Healy. "The Sleeping Detective" by Gary Phillips. "The Big Bite" by Bill Pronzini. "The Good Daughter" by Mike Wiecek.

2002

The Eye (Lifetime Achievement Award): **Lawrence Block**

Best P.I. Hardcover Novel: *Reflecting the Sky* **by S.J. Rozan**. Other nominees: *Angel in Black* by Max Allan Collins. *Ashes of Aries* by Martha C. Lawrence. *The Devil Went Down to Austin* by Rick Riordan. *Cold Water Burning* by John Straley.

Best Original P.I. Paperback: *Archangel Protocol* **by Lyda Morehouse**. Other nominees: *Ancient Enemy* by Robert Westbrook. *Keepers* by Janet Lapierre.

Best First P.I. Novel: *Chasing the Devil's Tail* **by David Fulmer**. Other nominees: *Epitaph* by James Siegel. *Rat City* by Curt Colbert. *A Witness Above* by Andy Straka. *Pilikia Is My Business* by Mark Troy.

Best P.I. Short Story: **"Rough Justice" by Ceri Jordan**. Other nominees: "The Jungle" by John Lantigua. "Last Kiss" by Tom Sweeney. "Golden Retriever" by Barbara Paul. "The Cobalt Blues" by Clark Howard.

St. Martin's Press/PWA Best First P.I. Novel Contest: *The Sterling Inheritance* **by Michael Siverling.**

Friend of PWA: **Jan Grape**

2003

The Eye (Lifetime Achievement Award): **Sue Grafton**

Best P.I. Hardcover Novel: *Blackwater Sound* **by James W. Hall**. Other nominees: *North of Nowhere* by Steve Hamilton. *The Last Place* by Laura Lippman. *Hell to Pay* by George Pelecanos. *Winter and Night* by S.J. Rozan.

Best Original P.I. Paperback: *The Poisoned Rose* **by D. Daniel Judson**. Other nominees: *Cash Out* by Paul Boray. *Juicy Watusi* by Richard Helms. *The Lusitania Murders* by Max Allan Collins. *Paint It Black* by P.J. Parish.

Best First P.I. Novel: *The Distance* **by Eddie Muller**. Other nominees: *Westerfield's Chain* by Jack Clark. *The Bone Orchard* by D. Daniel Judson. *Open and Shut* by David Rosenfeld. *Private Heat* by Robert Bailey.

Best P.I. Short Story: **"The Second Coming" by Terence Faherty**. Other nominees: "Setting Up the Kill" by J. Michael Blue. "Aftermath" by Jeremiah Healy. "Second Story Sunlight" by John Lutz. "The Jewels of Atlantis" by James Powell.

St. Martin's Press/PWA Best First P.I. Novel Contest: *Tonight I Said Goodbye* **by Michael Koryta.**

2004

The Eye (Lifetime Achievement Award): **Donald Westlake**

Best P.I. Hardcover Novel: *The Guards* **by Ken Bruen**. Other nominees: *Scavenger Hunt* by Robert Ferrigno. *Blood Is the Sky* by Steve Hamilton. *Fatal Flaw* by William Lashner. *A Visible Darkness* by Jonathon King.

Best Original P.I. Paperback: *Cold Quarry* **by Andy Straka**. Other nominees: *Thicker Than Water* by PJ Parrish. *Wet Debt* by Richard Helms. *Dragonfly Bones* by David Cole.

Best First P.I. Novel: *Black Maps* **by Peter Spiegelman**. Other nominees: *Spiked* by Mark Arsenault. *Lovers Crossing* by James C. Mitchell.

Best P.I. Short Story: **"Lady on Ice" by Loren D. Estleman**. Other nominees: "Munchies" by Jack Bludis. "The Rock in the Orange Grove" by Mitch Alderman. "Slayer Statute" by Janet Dawson. "Valhalla" by Doug Allyn.

St. Martin's Press/PWA Best First P.I. Novel Contest: *First Kill* **by Michael Kronenwetter.**

2005

The Eye (Lifetime Achievement Award): **Sara Paretsky**

Best P.I. Hardcover Novel: *While I Disappear* **by Ed Wright**. Other nominees: *Fade to Clear* by Leonard Chang. *The Wakeup* by Robert Ferrigno. *After the Rain* by Chuck Logan. *Choke Point* by James Mitchell.

Best Original P.I. Paperback: *Fade To Blonde* by **Max Phillips**. Other nominees: *Call the Devil by His Oldest Name* by Sallie Bissell. *Shadow of the Dahlia* by Jack Bludis. *The London Blitz Murders* by Max Allan Collins. *Island of Bones* by P. J. Parrish.

Best First P.I. Novel: ***The Dead* by Ingrid Black**. Other nominees: *Little Girl Lost* by Richard Aleas. *The Last Goodbye* by Reed Arvin. *Aspen Pulp* by Patrick Hasburgh. *Some Danger Involved* by Will Thomas.

Best P.I. Short Story: **"Hasidic Noir" by Pearl Abraham**. Other nominees: "Burnt Wood" by Mitch Alderman. "Trumpeter Swan" by John F. Dobbyn. "Dog on Fire" by Gregory S. Fallis. "Tricks" by Steve Hockensmith.

2006

The Eye (Lifetime Achievement Award): **Max Allan Collins**

Best P.I. Hardcover Novel: ***The Lincoln Lawyer* by Michael Connelly**. Other nominees: *Oblivion* by Peter Abrahams. *The Forgotten Man* by Robert Crais. *In a Teapot* by Terence Faherty. *The Man with the Iron-On Badge* by Lee Goldberg. *Cinnamon Kiss* by Walter Mosley.

Best Original P.I. Paperback: ***The James Deans* by Reed Farrel Coleman**. Other nominees: *Falling Down* by David Cole. *Deadlocked* by Joel Goldman. *Cordite Wine* by Richard Helms. *A Killing Rain* by P. J Parrish.

Best First P.I. Novel: ***Forcing Amaryllis* by Louise Ure**. Other nominees: *Blood Ties* by Lori G. Armstrong. *Still River* by Harry Hunsicker. *The Devil's Right Hand* by J. D. Rhoades.

Best P.I. Short Story: **"A Death in Ueno" by Michael Wiecek**. Other nominees: "Oh, What a Tangled Lanyard We Weave" by Parnell Hall. "Two Birds with One Stone" by Jeremiah Healy. "The Big Road" by Steve Hockensmith. "The Breaks" by Timothy Williams.

2007

The Eye (Lifetime Achievement Award): **Stuart M. Kaminsky**

The Hammer (a new prize celebrating a memorable private eye character or a series, named after Mickey Spillane's Mike Hammer, of course): **Shell Scott by Richard S. Prather**

Best P.I. Hardcover Novel: ***The Dramatist* by Ken Bruen**. Other nominees: *The Darkest Place* by Daniel Judson. *The Do-Re-Mi* by Ken Kuhlken. *Vanishing Point* by Marcia Muller. *Days of Rage* by Kris Nelscott.

Best Original P.I. Paperback: ***An Unquiet Grave* by P.J. Parrish**. Other nominees: *Hallowed Ground* by Lori G. Armstrong. *The Prop* by Pete Hautman. *The Uncomfortable Dead* by Paco Ignacio Taibo II and Subcomandante Marcos. *Crooked* by Brian M. Wiprud.

Best First P.I. Novel: ***The Wrong Kind of Blood* by Declan Hughes**. Other nominees: *Lost Angel* by Mike Doogan. *A Safe Place for Dying* by Jack Fredrickson. *Holmes on the Range* by Steve Hockensmith. *18 Seconds* by George D. Shuman.

Best P.I. Short Story: **"The Heart Has Reasons" by O'Neil De Noux**. Other nominees: "Sudden Stop" by Mitch Alderman. "Square One" by Loren D. Estleman. "Devil's Brew" by Bill Pronzini. "Smoke Got in My Eyes" by Bruce Rubenstein.

2008

The Eye (Lifetime Achievement Award): No Award Given

Best P.I. Hardcover Novel: ***Soul Patch* by Reed Farrel Coleman**. Other nominees: *Head Games* by Thomas B. Cavanagh. *The Color of Blood* by Declan Hughes. *A Welcome Grave* by Michael Koryta. *A Killer's Kiss* by William Lashner.

Best Original P.I. Paperback: ***Songs of Innocence* by Richard Aleas**. Other nominees: *Exit Strategy* by Kelley Armstrong. *Stone Rain* by Linwood Barclay. *Deadly Beloved* by Max Allan Collins. *Blood of Paradise* by David Corbett.

Best First P.I. Novel: **Big City, Bad Blood** by **Sean Chercover**. Other nominees: *The Cleaner* by Brett Battles. *Keep It Real* by Bill Bryan. *When One Man Dies* by Dave White. *The Last Striptease* by Michael Wiley.

Best P.I. Short Story: **"Hungry Enough" by Cornelia Read**. Other nominees: "Kill the Cat" by Loren D. Estleman. "Trust Me" by Loren D. Estleman. "Open Mike" by James Nolan. "Room for Improvement" by Marilyn Todd.

2009

The Eye (Lifetime Achievement Award): **Robert J. Randisi**

The Hammer: **Matt Scudder by Lawrence Block**

Best P.I. Hardcover Novel: **Empty Ever After** by **Reed Farrel Coleman**. Other nominees: *Salvation Boulevard* by Larry Beinhart. *The Blue Door* by David Fulmer. *The Price of Blood* by Declan Hughes. *The Ancient Rain* by Domenic Stansberry.

Best Original P.I. Paperback: **Snow Blind** by **Lori Armstrong**. Other nominees: *Shot Girl* by Karen Olson. *The Stolen* by Jason Pinter. *The Black Hand* by Will Thomas. *The Evil That Men Do* by Dave White.

Best First P.I. Novel: **In the Heat** by **Ian Vasquez**. Other nominees: *Stalking Susan* by Julie Kramer. *Swann's Last Song* by Charles Salzberg. *The Eye of Jade* by Diane Wei Liang. *Veil of Lies* by Jeri Westerson.

Best P.I. Short Story: **"Family Values" by Mitch Alderman**. Other nominees: "Last Island South" by John C. Boland. "The Blonde Tigress" by Max Allan Collins. "Discovery" by Kristine Kathryn Rusch. "Panic on Portage Path" by Dick Stodghill.

CPSIA information can be obtained at www.ICGtesting.com
Printed in the USA
LVOW042110041111

253635LV00003B/146/P